PRAISE FOR WALKING WOLF ROAD:

"[*Walking Wolf Road*] has everything. Ghosts, werewolves, romance, and some beautifully arranged prose. I hope to see more work from author Brandon M. Herbert on our platform soon!"

Heather Weid, Kbuuk "*Halloween Weekend Reads*"

"Brandon M. Herbert has written an exciting urban fantasy that kept me highly entertained. I highly recommend this book if you love paranormal, shifter or urban fantasy genres!"

Lynn Worton, *Book Reviews by Lynn* blog.

"I loved it! This is a great, fast-paced read you can really sink your teeth into, no pun intended!"

Janell Rhiannon, author *Invisible Wings* and *Uncross the Stars*.

"[Herbert] kept the tension high right up to the end, and provided a great finale using all of the elements he began building from the start. Needless to say I was satisfied… and I am (not so) patiently awaiting a sequel!"

J.D. Wiley, award-winning author of *The Bitter Bullet* & *Sky Gala*

"*Walking Wolf Road* was filled with the mythology of werewolves, shamanism, and philosophy. All of this hit exactly the right spot for me. I thoroughly enjoyed this book!"

K.C. Faelan, author of *If At First You Don't Succeed*.

WALKING WOLF ROAD

THE WOLF ROAD CHRONICLES: BOOK 1

BRANDON M. HERBERT

WOLFGATE
PRODUCTIONS
DESIGN & PUBLISHING

ISBN-13: 978-0-692-26517-7
ISBN-10: 0692265147

WALKING WOLF ROAD

Printed in the United States of America

The text was set in Adobe Garamond Pro and Donatello LP.
Book cover design and typography by Wolfgate Productions, LLC.

DEDICATION & ACKNOWLEDGMENTS:

It is said, that behind every great man, stands an even greater woman. I'm far from a great man, but I have a beautiful woman who loves me, believes in me, supports me, and puts up with my crap. That's gotta mean I'm worth something, right?

I love you so much Julie, without you, I would be nothing!

Thank you Julie and Nick, Mom and Dad, Paige and Jay; for all the love, help, and encouragement you've given me as I've fought my way down this long difficult road. Thank you to my editor Debra Ginsberg who gave me the hard truths when I needed to hear them.

Special thanks to those of you who have stood with me since the very beginning. In particular I would like to thank my family, Justin & Nic Wiley, Lance & Kat Hartzman, Melissa Sauer-Locy, Jaclyn Hebb & Victoria Fair, for their support and encouragement over the years. Joel Deaton, Jordan Dail, and Jacob Atteberry; who know why. Shout outs to my old MySpace friends Jet, Fel, and Haley who remember the original 51 chapters, The Pack forum members, and therianthropes everywhere: we are not alone.

This book is dedicated to every young person, therianthrope or otherwise, who has felt like they don't belong; alone, hopeless, powerless, or bullied.

Transformation happens when you choose to let it.

Howls.

~B

CHAPTER 1 — BITTEN

It chased me.

The thing had no face or body, but it pursued me like a wall of darkness, malice, and hunger. I ran with all my might down the forest path, surrounded by dark forbidding trees and hateful eyes.

My vision narrowed as I ran until all I could see was the gravel of the road right in front of me. My lungs burned from fear and exhaustion, and the scar on my calf burned like a hot coal. I felt the thing at my heels as I slammed into a pair of fog-wreathed wrought iron gates.

I strained at the bars but the gates were locked. I screamed as the dark void reached to devour me…

"Jimmy! Are you even listening?" My stepfather, John, barked at me, snapping me back to reality. John, Mom, and I sat in the office at my new high school, a worn gray desk between us and the spider-like student counselor.

"Sorry, sorry, I'm just tired…" I rubbed my burning eyes and bit back the comments on my tongue; I'd barely slept for weeks.

1

Partly because that damned dream had haunted almost every night since John announced that we were moving to Colorado. The rest was thanks to John packing our lives into a moving truck last week and dragging us almost halfway across the freaking country.

Thanks John.

Isn't it funny how the moments that define our lives the most are almost always the smallest? A scattering of almost inconsequential seconds steers our course; the proverbial flap of butterfly wings producing the hurricanes of our lives. Single sentences, concepts, and choices—especially choices—make or break who you are and who you will become.

What makes it worse is when the choices aren't yours.

"This is important, now pay attention and quit daydreaming," John hissed in my ear, while Mom stared straight ahead and refused to look at me. The counselor's dark beady eyes scrutinized me through black-rimmed glasses, his gaunt face etched with a scowl. I couldn't help but wonder what he saw when he looked at me; a dullard or a miscreant? I knew better than to expect anything else as I watched the judgments form in his head.

"Where were we," the counselor said, his voice reminded me of two rocks grinding against each other through a layer of oil. He pursed his lips and deep creases folded like fault-lines around his mouth. "Ah, yes, Jimmy should still be allowed to graduate this year as long as his grades stay high enough, though the academic probation means he'll be suspended if they fall below the minimum."

"We understand, don't we?" John looked pointedly at me, and I muttered my consent while they slid what little pride I had left across a cheese grater.

"I sincerely hope you do. You can't afford to fail a single class, and if you receive more than three Cs you won't make the cutoff either. So Jimmy, *do* you understand?"

"Yes."

"Good. Now, about this discipline record." I flinched. "You're in Colorado now, not Chicago, and *any* signs of aggressive behavior, vandalism, gang paraphernalia, or drugs will be dealt with swiftly and severely, am I understood?"

"Mr. Spritari, Jimmy's never had a problem with drugs, and he was the victim in every incident on that report." Mom finally spoke up, but the counselor looked at her like she'd just told him that Santa Claus vacationed with Bigfoot in the Bermuda Triangle.

"I'm sure that's the case, Mrs. Walker—"

"Mrs. Mason, if you please," she corrected him, irritated.

"My apologies Mrs. Mason," he said, sounding anything but apologetic, "but we have a commitment to keeping our student body safe, a commitment I take *very* seriously, and his record indicates a history of altercations. I want to stress that we're taking a risk even admitting Jimmy to this school, and he will be watched very closely."

John grabbed Mom's hand to stop her from saying anything else and nodded, his jaw muscles clenching.

Mom and John signed the stack of papers while the counselor built my schedule. The office receptionist let us out through a side door, and I walked behind John. He loomed like a middle-aged linebacker, and I could tell from the way the muscles bunched on his shoulders that a storm was brewing...

This was gonna suck.

John slammed his hands down on the kitchen counter. I flinched and looked away while Mom stared at a stack of unpacked boxes, silent, refusing yet again to stand up for me. My six-year-

3

old half-brother Jacob watched wide-eyed and silent from the stairs in the hallway, trying not to be noticed. Jake didn't have to worry, though. John never got this mad at his own son.

"This is unacceptable!" John brandished the papers from the counselor's office at me like a weapon, crumpled in his clenched fist. His sandy blond goatee made his livid face look even redder.

"You heard the guy; they'll still let me graduate this year if my grades stay high enough."

John's blue eyes hardened as he scowled. "What are you going to do about this?" His voice was quiet. Dangerous.

"Do my homework, ask for extra credit, kiss the teacher's ass," I looked down at the floor as I pushed my glasses back up my nose, "Listen, *Dad*, I've tried really hard—"

"Do you think this is some sort of game?" he shouted in my face. "This isn't playtime anymore, Jimmy! You need to sort your shit out, pull your nose out of those stupid fantasy books, and grow up! Your grades *now* are going to decide how you live the rest of your life, not to mention whether or not you get into college!"

I flinched at the cursed 'C'-word and clenched my shaking hands into fists. "Yeah John, and hauling us through a five-day gauntlet of McKentucky Fried Taco Kings and carryout Chinese, to some town in Colorado I've never heard of, and doubt *anybody* else has either, *days* before Jake and I start school is bound to do marvelous things for my GPA! I guess you've conveniently forgotten what happened when we moved to Chicago. And Miami. Oh, and amazingly enough, even Corona! Of course, that couldn't *possibly* have anything to do with my grades dive-bombing, oh no!" I gestured sarcastically while I ranted.

My rage was getting harder to control, almost sentient, as if a dark dragon had coalesced inside me from the torn and broken fragments I tried to lock away and hide. So real, I felt it move inside me...

"Excuses never hold water in the real world son, so stop making them and start doing the damn work."

Something snapped inside me at the word 'son' and I laughed.

"You know what, John, I'm sorry." My voice reflected the cold rage that sliced through my blood as the dragon stirred inside, "I'm sorry I'm stupid. I'm sorry I'm a disappointment. I'm sorry I'm not good enough to have your goddamn genes. Maybe—just maybe—someday you'll call me 'son' because you're proud of me. Not because you married my mom and think you fucking *have* to!"

I moved toward the back door, but John grabbed my jacket as I pushed past him. I pulled myself free and then turned around and shoved him over an unpacked box. He tripped and fell, while Mom finally remembered how to move.

She went to John, not me.

"Don't you fucking touch me John; you're not my father, so stop pretending you care!" He yelled something incoherent behind me as the back door banged against the wall behind me. I shoved the gate open and ran down the alley.

A dark angry haze clouded out everything as I tripped over sidewalks and curbs, until the burning pain brought me to my knees panting. My heart thundered in my ears as I sucked at the thin mountain air and pressed a hand to the aching scar on my left calf. I was in poor shape to begin with, soft and round, far from the football Adonis John wanted. At least a heart attack would bring a welcome departure from my usual shit.

My glasses slid down my nose on the sheen of sweat and tears, and I shoved them back into place as I looked up and realized I'd stumbled into a park. The grass was dry and browned in spots where the trees couldn't keep out the sun's heat, and a couple shabby picnic tables sat near a dense copse of massive elm trees.

Behind me, I heard John's voice yelling my name. I glanced over my shoulder, and then limped deep into the shadow of the trees. I hid behind the thickest trunk I could find and watched John drive by in the suv. He stuck his head out the open window, and slowed down as he called my name. I shoved the tears out of my eyes and let my head fall against the trunk with a dull thud as he drove away.

Dammit...

Damn *him*...

No matter how hard I tried, no matter what I did right, there would always be something; some minutia or monstrosity somewhere, somehow, that was utterly insufficient. Nothing was ever good enough for that bastard. Sometimes the temptation to set it all on fire just to show him how fucking awful it *could* be was almost irresistible.

I looked back at my quests for his approval with shame. How stupid could I be? How could I have honestly expected a father's love and pride from a man who only took the job because marrying Mom came with a package deal?

John's not your father; that guy didn't want you either...

I dug my nails into my palms. Only pain lay down that road, and witlessly as I often stumbled upon it, I would not tread its familiar path again this time. I'd walked it enough to memorize every last twist and turn of the tragic tale.

As my rage drained away into the dragon's hole, I went cold and numb inside. I took a shaky breath and slowly forced my blurry eyes open. They cleared as I focused on the sunset blazing through the mountains. The world fell silent apart from the drone of cicadas and a dog barking blocks away.

Why couldn't I pull myself out of the past, even as my future shredded because of it?

Why couldn't I?

The last of the sun's rays caught on the edge of the world, and on that shard of light I prayed for the first time since I was a small boy.

"It's gotta change. My life, my grades—my world—*everything* needs to change." Exhausted, I closed my eyes again as the clouds burst into flame and the sun vanished, but the glowing blobs lingered on my retinas like eyes in the darkness. Exhaustion overcame me and I slipped back into a familiar nightmare…

It chased me.

The dark being had no face or body, but it was real and inescapable nonetheless; a tsunami of hunger and rage. I ran with all my might down the forest path, the dark trees that surrounded me full of hateful eyes. Rows of people stood beside the trail but I didn't know who they were. As I ran, I grabbed and shook them. I begged for help, warned them to run, but they just stared off into the night with vacant eyes until they fell into the pursuing darkness one by one. A feeling of horrendous loss and sorrow weighed on my chest, and I didn't understand why.

My vision narrowed as I ran until all I could see was the gravel of the road right in front of me while my lungs and legs burned from fear and exhaustion. I felt the thing at my heels as my feet skidded on the rocks and I looked up at the tall wrought iron gates looming in front of me. Tendrils of fog caressed the cold metal as the moon loomed full overhead, framed by their skyward reaching bars.

Just as the darkness was about to claim me, I tore open the gates and surged through them, only to stumble and fall face first onto a cold tiled floor. I picked myself up and looked around the unfamiliar classroom I'd fallen into. Windows lined one wall, and bookcases lined the other, separated by rows of blank staring students.

"Jimmy Walker…" A foreign but somehow familiar voice whispered my name behind my back, and a chill ran down my spine as I turned.

The figure stood right behind me, its head bowed. A figure of shadow, not the faceless demon that pursued me, but a silhouette cut from the fabric of reality, like a vessel waiting to be filled. I felt the hungry darkness clawing at the door, and almost against my will, I reached out toward the figure until eyes snapped open in the shadow's face…

Feral amber eyes stared through me.

I jolted awake and shivered. Disoriented, I looked around as I slowly remembered where I was. I stood and stretched the knot in my neck. Night had devoured the sky and moonlight sliced between the branches, illuminating the mist that filled the air, cold with the promise of autumn.

My breath steamed as I stood up and looked around. Which way had I come in? I turned around a few times, but nothing looked like it had when the sun was out. Frustrated, I picked a random direction and started walking. This place couldn't be that big.

My skin crawled as I crept through the midnight trees. I felt like I was being watched. The sound of a distant crow wore away at my nerves. I strained to see in the dark as my imagination conjured all sorts of phantoms to fill the darkness.

I heard a twig snap. I swallowed and looked over my shoulder as my pulse jumped. I knew there were bears in Colorado, and I very much wanted *not* to meet one. I moved away from the sound, deeper into the fog. As I wandered further and further, I realized just how lost I'd gotten in the maze of trees. Through the panic, I felt a tug in my chest, insistent, pulling to my left.

I pushed down the anxiety that tempted me and trusted my intuition as I ran. I must have picked the right path, because more light filtered through the darkness as the fog thinned.

I slowed and stopped for air in a pool of moonlight, like a spotlight between the trees. I felt that tug in my chest again as the dream stirred in the back of my mind. *The cold blue moon framed between the claws of the iron gates.* I panted for air as the night went dead silent around me.

Something's not right…

A branch snapped to my right and I glanced into the darkness beneath the trees. I couldn't see anything, but that just made the feeling worse.

"What the fu—"

Something slammed into me, and I raised my arms to defend myself. Everything moved in a blur. Only one thing stood clear as time froze and my heart flooded with fear.

Two eyes blazed with feral amber fire, intense and alien in a human face. An image of white fur flashed in my mind as teeth broke through my skin and touched blood.

I might have screamed, but couldn't hear anything past the rush of blood in my ears as the world narrowed down to those blazing eyes.

That moment stretched into an eternity. The next thing I knew, my attacker disappeared into the shadows of the trees, and I looked up into the bright sky and the full moon that loomed overhead.

My skin buzzed with electric heat as I cradled my hand to my chest and staggered to my feet. My blood felt cold as it soaked into my shirt, and I stumbled toward the edge of the trees. My vision cycled from vivid shades of gray to a looming tunnel of darkness and back again and I fell out of the tree line. I shivered as the heat faded away into tooth-rattling cold, and the darkness claimed me.

CHAPTER 2 — FEVER

"Hey, are you okay?" A girl's voice pierced the darkness as someone shook my shoulder. I groaned and lifted my throbbing head from the grass while my mind tried to piece together fractured memories. I moved to sit up and hissed as searing pain lanced through my left hand when my blood-soaked shirt peeled away from it.

"Fuck…" the girl muttered when she saw my hand. I couldn't help but agree. Blood covered most of my hand and the punctures, swollen and puffy, glistened red where the meat was exposed. "Can you stand?"

"I think so…" I muttered. I sat up and tried to bring her face into focus, "I can't see though, shit, where are my glasses?" I glanced around too quickly and was rewarded with a wash of vertigo. She retrieved my frames from the base of a nearby tree and held them out to me.

I reached out to take them and something sparked between us when my fingers brushed her skin. Grey and chestnut mottled fur flashed in my mind, and she jerked her hand back. I pushed my glasses back into place with my good hand just in time to catch the look of surprised recognition in her green eyes.

A sick feeling of déjà vu slithered through the pit of my stomach. She seemed familiar, thought I couldn't quite place her. She wore a baggy black hoody, and the chains on her pants jingled when she stood. Black hair flowed around her pale face, and dark liner outlined her eyes.

I stood and tried to walk, but I only made it a few steps before my knees buckled and I crashed to the ground, panting. "I guess I can't walk after all…" I slurred.

"Not a problem. Geri, can you give me a hand?" she called into the dark trees, and I winced at the too-loud sound of her voice. Footsteps crunched on the grass—also way-too-loud—as a stocky form emerged from the shadows of the trees.

The boy was about a solid foot shorter than me, but built like a tank. His mouse brown hair was cropped short and spiked over his forehead, and his eyes darted around nervously, searching for something.

"Loki, where is—" he started to ask, but the girl cut him off with a sharp gesture.

"C'mon, upsy-daisy." The girl, Loki, lifted me onto my feet with surprising strength. Geri took my other arm and they carried me on their shoulders. "Do you need us to take you to the hospital?"

"No," something inside me reacted violently to the thought of visiting the ER, "My mom used to be a nurse, could you take me home?"

"Yeah, that's no problem, where do you live?" Geri asked.

My stomach twisted and I clenched my eyes shut against the sudden nausea, "Wolf Road… near Seventh…"

"Of course you do," Loki muttered in a deadpan tone as they carried me between them. They radiated so much heat, my body tried to soak it up as I shivered. They seemed to know exactly where I lived because they drove me home and parked right in front of my house.

I got out of the car and a wave of vertigo swept over me. The streetlight overhead flared to painful intensity before it flickered and went out. I leaned against the trunk for a moment as I breathed and waited it out.

I heard the car door open behind me, and Loki took my arm to help me to the door. Thankfully my knees decided to hold me up again. I shuffled carefully up to the porch, and heard the front door open.

"Where the hell have you—Jesus Christ Jimmy, what happened?" John crossed the porch in two strides and grabbed me under my other arm.

"I didn't see it happen; I think it was a dog…" Loki said for me as a whisper slithered through the back of my mind.

Tell no one…

"You got it okay?" Loki watched me, concerned.

"I should be fine, thank you again." I forced a smile for her and let John help me up the porch steps as he thanked her for bringing me home.

"Not a problem, get some rest. I've got a feeling we'll be seeing you soon." she said and hopped back to the car. The boy pulled away from the curb and they disappeared down the road.

I stared after them for a moment until John pulled on my arm, "Come inside; let's have your mother take a look at you."

I woke up the next day, and immediately wished I hadn't. My head pounded, and all the lights seemed too bright as I walked

Jacob to school. The argument over whether or not to take me to the emergency room had lasted half an hour, but eventually I talked them out of it. Mom cleaned me up and dressed the wound, and John promised that we would discuss the repercussions of my "little escapade" later.

My new school loomed like a monster from across its front lawn. Kids streamed in through the doors like lines of ants, and I prayed my teachers wouldn't be sadistic and introduce the new transfer student in front of the class. Ceiling-high panes of glass walled in the front lobby, and I stopped in my tracks when there wasn't a metal detector waiting inside.

Definitely not in Chicago anymore Toto…

There was a cop though, who stood in the corner scanning faces as they passed. His eyes followed me as I walked by, and I read the name 'Jenson' off the patch on his chest; I assumed Mr. Spritari had set him on watch for me.

I checked in at the front office and showed them the signed papers and my class schedule. I slipped in to my first period math class just as the bell rang and handed the counselor's note to the math teacher, Mr. Heinen. I found a seat near the back of the room and tried to disappear as I picked at the tape on my bandaged hand. Any delusions of having a social life that I might have entertained years ago had died; all I wanted was painless invisibility. Please just let me finish my twelve-year sentence in peace…

Senior year. The year every high-schooler looked forward to with hope and anticipation; I just wanted out. I'd put in eleven years of this crap, and for the icing on this shit cake, I got to spend twelfth grade in some hicksville high school halfway across the continent from everything I knew. Not that I'd felt particularly attached to my old school in Chicago, I didn't have any friends to miss either, but being a senior and a freshman at the same time kinda screwed with my head.

When the bell rang, we were herded like cattle into the gymnasium for a dismal school assembly. The principal and a few of the school clubs and teams made a laughable attempt to foster team spirit under the piss-yellow glow of the buzzing gym lights. I spotted the counselor's dour face in a row of folding chairs with the other faculty. The entire school fit into the gym with a minimum of effort; the entire student body was smaller than my freshman class back in Chicago.

After the assembly, I carefully navigated the crowded cafeteria and escaped outside to eat on the front lawn. I watched the smokers across the street with little interest while I picked at my baked pepperoni… pizza… stick… things… and scratched absently at the bandage on my hand

A cool breeze blew across the field and a chill crawled down my spine as I felt someone watching me. I turned and looked over my shoulder but there was no one there. A crow cawed nearby and I frowned, remembering last night, but I pulled a paperback out of my book bag. The harder I tried to distract myself, the more memories flitted around as a stubborn part of my brain strained to remember something, anything, about whatever bit me. The only thing I knew for sure was that it was *not* a dog…

I jumped when the bell rang and jolted me out of my reverie. The clanging metallic sound cut across the field, and I joined the rest of the students who filed back inside like they were headed for the gallows. I was no exception.

Some jackass junior gave me bad directions, but I found the art room halfway down Sophomore Hall. The teacher breezed through the door as the bell rang, and pulled it closed behind her.

"Hello class, for those of you who don't already know, I am Mrs. Ashcroft," she said as she pulled her long straw-colored hair back into a ponytail and then wrote her name on the board, "I recognize most of you, but to those new faces, welcome! Now, I don't know what kind of art teachers you've had before; but I can assure you my class is different. I'm not just some hippie teaching to make ends meet. You will have expectations in this class, and if you do not meet them; I will fail you. Understood?"

Someone knocked on the door as she passed out the syllabus. She pushed the door open and a blond boy stepped into the room with a note in his hand. "Sorry I'm late Mrs. Ashcroft, there was a mix-up with my schedule..." His sentence drifted off and his back stiffened. He frowned, and it almost looked like he sniffed the air.

She looked over the note and nodded, "Not a problem Fen, just take a seat."

He glanced over the room, and then stopped and stared directly at me as his golden amber eyes widened with recognition. I glanced away as my stomach tightened and a cold sweat broke out on my forehead.

Just like the dream...

He headed for the open seat across the table from me as Mrs. Ashcroft resumed the obligatory orientation routine. I heard a couple kids mutter to each other as he shuffled between the desks and threw dark glances at him. If he heard anything they said it never showed, and he dropped his bag next to the chair and sat down.

My pulse throbbed in my temples and I winced and rubbed them. Ringing filled my ears; I couldn't focus on anything Mrs. Ashcroft said.

"What happened to your hand?" Fen asked when he saw the gauze. I glanced at him and noticed how exhausted he looked; his eyes bloodshot with dark circles underneath them, like he hadn't slept in days. Or he was coming down off a drug binge, both were possible.

"I was mauled by a rabid squirrel." I muttered.

Something felt wrong. My stomach twisted again, and I asked to be excused to the restroom. I only made it halfway to the door before my knees buckled and I crashed to the ground, panting. Everyone crowded around me as I rolled onto my back and willed the world to stop spinning.

"Are you okay?" Mrs. Ashcroft knelt over me, her face creased with concern.

"I don't feel so good." I mumbled as she felt my forehead.

"Geez, you're burning up. We need to get you to the nurse."

"I'll take him." Fen volunteered and reached down to help me up.

I took his hand, but as soon as I touched his skin I jerked my hand back. Something electric sparked from his hand to mine and an image flashed in the back of my mind of gray and black fur. It disappeared in a fraction of a moment, but my skin crawled like I'd just touched a live wire.

Fen's eyes met mine for a moment, and reflected that same look of recognition Loki's had last night. His eyes reminded me of something, but the connection slipped out of reach as he took my hand again and hoisted me to my feet like I didn't weigh twice as much as him. Fen took most of my weight and we shuffled out of the room. I took a breath to thank him, and a violent spasm wracked my body.

His scent, whispered through the back of my mind. Hair stood on end all over my body, and my muscles twitched. Sweat covered me and every part of me ached.

"Shh, it'll pass soon," Fen whispered as he pulled something over his head and slipped it into my pocket. "Put this on later, it should help. He recognizes me."

17

"Who?" I croaked, and winced at the coarse grind of my voice. My head was too foggy to understand his words though; I almost thought he said "your wolf" while splinters of dreams flashed through my mind.

Whatever he put in my pocket radiated a cool exhaustion. My eyes started to close as I struggled to say something intelligent. "Huh?"

Fen sighed, "Let's see if the change even sticks; sometimes the body rejects it. You should rest though, the first few days are the worst, and you're changing very fast. The silver should help…" He carried me as I phased in and out of waking dreams, while my body burned.

My journey home was patchy and hard to remember, as if I'd fallen asleep at impossible times—like walking to the car—but the important parts were A: I was home, and B: I felt like absolute shit…

Hallucinations ate at my sanity until I wasn't sure if what I saw was real or not as I faded in and out. I smelled a hospital, but saw myself locked in a cage instead, terrified of the sterile white room that surrounded me as I turned in tight circles and gnawed on the bars.

I remembered people inspecting the wound on my hand, but my memory after that was blank until I snapped awake and ran up the stairs. I barely made it into the bathroom before the bile rushed up my throat. I slumped by the toilet after the retches subsided, and the fever raged like a caged beast.

Could I be done with the puking now? Please?

The last dying rays of the sun squeezed through the bathroom's tiny window to punish my eyes. Why did it always feel *so much worse* at night? I felt clammy and undead, so I ran some hot water for a bath and heard a knock. "Jimmy? Are you alright in there?" The door muffled Mom's voice.

"Dead." And my voice sounded like it, yikes…

"Well, if you feel like eating, there are some leftovers in the fridge." I listened to her footsteps as she walked away.

I undressed and it felt like I peeled off my first layer of skin, then I eased my aching body into the steaming water and laid my head down on the cool surround. The rational part of my brain insisted the nausea, irrational fever dreams, aches, and hyper-sensitive skin felt like the flu. Pieces of half-forgotten conversations drifted through my head. John asking a doctor what was wrong. Mom telling me the shot wouldn't hurt.

The shot. A rabies shot.

I looked at my hand, wrapped up with stained gauze and surgical tape. They thought I was bitten by a dog. I remembered that girl, Loki, saying that when John helped me inside. The girl's face lingered above my other thoughts for a moment as I idly pulled at the tape on my bandage. The tape plucked hairs out as I peeled it away from my hand and lifted the gauze to inspect the wound.

The puckered pink troughs were barely recognizable, and the worst gouges had already healed. How many days had it been? I thought I was just missing a few hours…

Another dizzy spell swept over me and I sank into the agonizingly hot water. As my body adjusted the pain faded to a dull numb. My foggy mind drifted and my senses twitched out. My stomach ached for meat—preferably red—and tiny things like the smell of mold, or the sound of the TV in the living room, leapt to painful clarity.

I felt loose in my skin, and the feeling triggered a cold but subtle terror that slithered out of reach whenever I tried to pinpoint it. The ugly patch of scar tissue on my calf burned and I closed my eyes—

I ran. Bushes and trees rushed by as I flew over the ground, free and powerful.

I jerked out of the bath, splashing water all over the room. It felt like more than just my imagination—more like I'd left my body for a moment and entered something else's—and it felt so real! I could still feel the give of the soil under my paws and the tannic smell of the forest floor, before the scent of wet denim flooded it out.

Wait... paws?

My head swam and I pulled on my neck to ease the knots that clenched at the base of my skull. A strange sensation crawled up my spine and I shivered again, even as the water steamed around me. Light flickered brightly through the small square window as a breeze tousled the trees outside.

Claws scrabbled over polished rocks as I raced along the shore of an obsidian lake. The moon flickered as it played hide and seek behind the treetops.

I tried to stand, but my legs wouldn't support me and I crashed back into the tub.

What the hell's wrong with me?

I crawled out of the bathtub on my hands and knees and dripped water all over the bathroom rug. My skin felt like it was splitting, and a balloon was inflating inside my skull. My body shook harder as I lifted my feverish face and looked out the small bathroom window.

The light of the full moon spilled over me and I flashed back to that wooded path again as my senses overwhelmed me. The sound of water dripping off my body, Mom's voice from across the house—so clear it was like she was in the room with me—and the smell of wet cloth. The bathroom light flickered erratically, too bright for my aching eyes. Disembodied voices yammered gibberish in an unfocused cloud of noise, and I thought I heard a bird cawing in the background. My thoughts forgot words, and processed in raw images and remembered sensations.

I pulled a towel around myself and dragged my corpse downstairs to my bedroom. I'd claimed the basement's blank concrete walls and high windows for my bedroom as soon as I saw it. Mom jokingly called it my 'Dungeon', and the title seemed rather appropriate. My dirty clothes sprawled all over the cold concrete floor while my bookcase loomed against the wall, loaded close to critical mass.

I moaned and collapsed into my bed, then I buried my head in the soft flesh of my arm and whimpered, panting for air. The fever pounded in my face as blood roared in my ears and temples. I slipped in and out of abstract dreams with my sheets tangled around me, like I'd been running in my sleep. Aching, I curled up in my sweat-soaked covers and held my head.

I've completely lost my mind, or at least what pathetic little was left of it.

As I lay there I felt muscles in my back relax and I felt... disconnected. I slipped out of my skin—out of the world.

I opened my eyes and stared at the full moon, looming within a silhouetted circle of towering pines. I sat across from a Native American woman with long white hair, a blazing bonfire between us. Her image swam in the heat from the dancing flames; her face was painted with three thin red triangles drawn down below each eye. Despite her alabaster white hair, she looked young.

She watched me with hooded amber eyes as she hummed a tune in a haunting minor key.

"Who are you?" I asked.

"A part of you," she answered slowly and smiled, revealing small fangs. "A part of what you're destined to become." She hummed her song in between sentences.

Helpful.

"Okay then, what's your name?"

She grinned, showing her sharp white teeth, and looked up into the sky as she thought. "Oh, there have been so many over the years, so many... But I think my favorite has always been Lupa."

"And...just what are you supposed to be?"

"Don't you remember?" she asked, and I answered her with an empty stare. "I one of the First Peoples, the spirit of all wolves, the memory and essence of our species. Our totem, you could say."

Black birds appeared out of the darkness of the trees and circled down around us. Crows and ravens whirled around the fire like a curtain of iridescent wings, and yet the only sound they made was the dry rustling of their feathers. Some of them landed and stared at me, switching their heads side to side to look.

The wind from their wings fanned the fire and it rose higher as bright yellow sparks reached for the moon. Overhead, the shadow of a huge raven blocked out the moon for a moment as it circled over us all.

Something was very wrong, this didn't feel like a dream. I felt the wind and the heat from the fire around my face. I smelled the smoke and the tang of pine-sap. I felt... here...

"You will change, and so will your mind..." The woman—spirit—whatever; stood and walked around the fire. "When you accept me into your life, you will fulfill your dreams." The fire flared up and blocked her from view, and when the flames receded the woman was gone. A porcelain white wolf walked where the woman had been and

continued around the fire. My heart sped up, and it spoke in my mind with the woman's voice.

"I am a part of you, a part of your destiny. You were marked by Brother Raven; you don't have a choice anymore." Even though I wanted to ignore the creepy words, I felt a strange feeling of longing curl inside me. I reached out and touched the wolf's coat, which flickered red and gold in the firelight. It was coarse, but soft, and I buried my fingers in the thickness of it. She pushed her ear into my hand and looked into my eyes. The ethereal dreamscape blurred and grew foggy as I focused on her eyes, so familiar…

"Go to him, he will teach you…" She said, and then she sank her teeth into my hand.

I dozed in delirium, and the pounding in my head seemed almost audible as voices echoed in the darkness. I floated though the abyss until something cool wrapped itself around me. Slowly, the fog cleared and I felt the oppressive weight of my body again.

I cracked my eyes open and realized that I was curled up on the pile of dirty clothes on the floor with my hand buried in the pocket of my jeans. I pulled my hand out and a silver necklace slipped through my fingers, a five pointed star dangling from the chain. The cool soothing sensation evaporated as soon as the necklace left my grasp, and I quickly retrieved it as the fever tried to ramp back up.

"What the hell?" I remembered that boy from art class, Fen, slipped something into my pocket while he was carrying me to the nurse's office. He'd said, 'The silver should help'. I struggled to remember what else he'd said. I remembered those creepy amber eyes, just like the woman in my dream. Fen had said something about changing very fast and… somebody recognizing him?

Then it clicked.

'He recognizes me'—Fen's eyes—'Who?'—the silhouette from my dream in the park—'Your wolf'— two eyes blazed with feral amber fire, intense and alien in a human face.

"You've got to be kidding me…" I muttered. Now I knew who bit me, even though I had no idea why. This was starting to sound like some B-rate monster movie.

I felt a tug inside my chest again, like I had that night in the woods. I staggered to my feet, dizzy, and gripped my bookcase to hold myself up as I looked out the small window high on my wall. Outside, the moon crawled into the sky beyond the jagged mountain skyline.

"You've got to be kidding me." I said again as war broke out inside my head. I looked down at the silver pentagram necklace in the dim twilight of my dungeon and laughed. "Impossible." I glanced at the moon outside the window, and finally crawled back into bed as I slipped the necklace over my head.

I couldn't think. Or maybe I just didn't want to…

CHAPTER 3 — DENIAL

In the morning, sanity returned. I threw my sheets back and sat on the edge of the bed while I held my head. I still didn't feel one-hundred percent, but I felt leagues better. I also felt claustrophobic and restless.

While I sat there, I thought about the night before while shame and anger rotted inside me. I couldn't believe I'd actually believed that shit, even for a moment.

Werewolves? Really? That's pathetic, even for you.

Guess I'd have to lay off the late-night novels for a while to remind myself what reality was. I knew had to go back to school and deal with the asshole that bit me, but at least I'd be out of the house. I seriously pissed about having to play catch-up right off the bat too, but I didn't have a hell of a lot of control over that.

I really wanted school to work out. Just once in my life, I wanted to actually do something right.

I went upstairs, showered, and brushed my teeth. I inspected my hand where the wolf in the dream bit me. The wounds had already closed over with scar tissue, not even a scab remained.

The flesh around the wounds looked a little puffy and flushed but otherwise fine.

On a masochistic whim, I pulled out the scale stashed beneath the sink and stepped on it. My mood darkened even more when I realized that I'd gained weight since the last time I measured. Skippy.

I threw the scale back in the cabinet and Fen's necklace bumped against my chest. I grabbed it in my fist to tear it off, and some whispered thought I couldn't quite grasp stayed my hand. Grumbling, I grabbed my backpack and headed out with Jake into the painful morning sunshine, the necklace hidden under my shirt.

If my brain had been working right it would have clicked sooner, but now it all made perfect sense. It was a new town, at an obscenely new altitude, with new bugs. I'd probably already had the damn flu brewing, and then passing out after that delusional freak attacked me in the middle of the night just gave it a foothold. The fact that he happened to be nuts—and decided to *gnaw* on me—was nothing more than coincidence.

I sat as far from him as I could in the art room and refused to look at him even though I could feel his stare. The bell rang and I felt his hand touch my shoulder as I stood to leave. I ground my teeth and turned to face him. "What do you want?"

"Your wolf is waking up. I want to help you—"

"Help me what? Become a 'wolf'? Really? Wow. So, what, we're going to transform under the full moon and run around howling and eating babies?" I snapped.

Fen blinked at me, confused. Apparently the thought that I wouldn't buy into his game hadn't even crossed his mind. The guy just didn't take a hint did he?

"I can't believe this shit. First, you chowed down on my hand in the middle of the night. Then, you stuffed a pentagram into my pocket—which was creepy enough on its own—and now you're spouting this crap? Werewolves are just a Dark Age superstition from when the world was flat and tomatoes were poisonous. They're. Not. *Real.* So maybe you should grow up, pull your head out of your little fantasy world, and join the rest of the twenty-first century." I blinked as I realized just how much I sounded like John. "Just leave me the fuck alone Fen. I'm not as dumb as I look…" I turned and left him, rubbing the back of my hand. Better to just leave him to his little werewolf fantasies.

Let him chew on somebody else next time…

As I walked away, I remembered I was wearing his necklace. I thought of giving it back to him for half a second, but decided to keep it instead to spite him.

The doorway to the locker room loomed like the gaping maw of my own personal hell. Instead of sulfur, the damp stench of mildew and body odor matched the jaundiced yellow lights and tiles. I followed some other students into the classroom beside it and took my customary chair in the back corner. I warily observed the other kids as they took seats around the room, and sure enough, my class hosted a parasitic infection of neckless meat-heads. It looked like I was going to share the class with about fifteen teenage Johns… Why, God; *why* did we have to take gym classes?

Mr. Parkman took roll while his assistant Jeremy wheeled in a TV cart. Nutrition and hydration was the topic of the week. While they were preoccupied, a muscular guy a couple inches taller than me with short peroxide-blond hair, and a stocky redhead with severely freckled skin, leaned in toward each other conspiratorially, whispering and pointing at some of the other students in the class.

I recognized the tall one from the assembly; he seemed to love being the center of attention. He noticed me watching them and I looked away. I swallowed against the sick feeling in my stomach, and when I glanced back, they were both looking at me. They looked away and chuckled at some inside joke I had a horrible feeling that I'd find out about someday.

I hunkered down lower in my seat and wished I could make myself invisible while the teachers got the program rolling. I thought torture was illegal, but the film that wasted the next forty-five minutes of my life proved me wrong. The animated food pyramid that hopped around with a pointing stick through most of the vintage seventies program made me want to crawl into my backpack and die. Where art class virtually flew by, the hour and fifteen minutes of PE hell crawled like a legless zombie. Near the end of class, Mr. Parkman assigned me a padlock and funneled the class into the locker room until the bell.

I kept my eyes glued to the floor as I walked past the other guys changing out of their gym clothes. I felt my face heat and hoped nobody saw it. I found a locker in the corner at the far end of the room in the most private location I could find. Something sticky on the latch smeared on my hand, and I went to the sink to wash it off while I tried not to think about what it could've been.

I deftly avoided my reflection in the mirror. I knew what I'd see; an overweight loser with spiky black hair and dusky skin. Flabby, ugly, and stained by the genetics of a deadbeat father; I looked like a train wreck of German and First Nations genetics. The only things I'd obviously inherited from my mom were her dark blue eyes, which looked weird with my genetically tan skin. Mom, John, and Jake all shared Nordic blonde hair and blue eyes; leaving me the literal black sheep.

I ground my teeth together while I scrubbed my hands and struggled to shove my dark emotions deep inside where nobody could see. Even then, as I looked at the pigment in the creases and lines of my hands, all I wanted to do was smash them into the mirror and cut off all that hideous skin and fat with the shards.

Movement drew my attention to the reflection over my shoulder. Some of the guys from class prowled down the locker block, poking jokes and mocking as they went, the tall blonde at the lead.

They were just like the kids who'd cornered me on the playground in grade school. The ones who'd sent me home from middle school bruised and black-eyed in Miami. Same model, just different colors.

Fortunately—at least for me—one of the kids in the locker block before mine caught their attention. The blonde and the stocky redhead crowded a slim boy with mouse-brown hair over his eyes. The familiar display made my heart thud in my chest. I glanced up toward the front of the room to see Mr. Parkman talking to another student, oblivious.

My hand gripped the strap of my backpack as I watched them out of the corner of my eye. They laughed at the poor guy's stuttered protests when they messed up his hair and took his backpack. They played keep-away with it until one of the guys toward the back stepped up and pulled the bag out of the blonde's hand.

"That's enough Jack, give him his bag back," he muttered as the blond, Jack, turned and gave him an annoyed look.

"What's'a matter Bo, we're just having some fun with our little friend Doug-y-pooh here," Jack replied as he smiled and put an arm around the kid's shoulders while the others snickered.

"It doesn't look like 'Doug-y-pooh' is having much fun to me," Bo replied in a surprisingly deep voice, and handed the bag back to the relieved looking kid who squirmed past them to wait at the front of the room near Mr. Parkman.

"What the fuck is your problem man?" Jack demanded as he got in the taller guy's face.

To his credit, Bo didn't back down. "Just trying to keep your ass out of trouble Jack. You know your dad; you don't have many chances left…"

Jack snarled and shoved Bo into one of his buddies. "Mind your own fucking business bro…" Jack spat and stormed away as the bell rang. "Malcolm, c'mon!" Jack snapped and the redhead hustled to catch up. The guy who caught Bo pushed him upright again, but then joined Jack and Malcolm with a venomous glance behind him at Bo.

"Whatever you say, *bro*…" Bo muttered as he collected his own backpack and headed out, alone. I kept a safe distance as we filed out of that foul room and plunged into the hallway's human current. I passed the elaborate woodwork of the auditorium doors, and got mired down in the mass of students that clogged senior hall like a blocked artery.

My final class was right down the hall from my locker. The English teacher, Mr. Decker, looked like a skinny, bookwormish, Arnold Schwarzenegger. Windows lined one wall of the cramped classroom and tormented me with a bright blue sky, warm sun, and flying birds just outside the windows of my cage. I took a seat toward the back corner of the room and yawned as Mr. Decker droned on about poetry, and then laid my head down on my arms until the bell rang.

After the bell, I stopped by my locker to pick up my algebra textbook. I noticed Fen watching me down senior hall and I turned to leave as a wall of flesh slammed into me like a wrecking ball. I tried to backpedal but my feet tangled and I fell while my papers and books spilled all over the hall.

"Watch where you're going, fatass," Jack snapped and kicked my textbook. Kids laughed all the way down the hall as his posse walked past. I kept my face down as I turned beet red and tried to pick up my papers before they got scattered and trampled. My dragon rolled inside me as destructive images flitted through my head, I knew I'd just made it onto Jack's radar. Someone walked up behind me and I gritted my teeth, waiting to hear Fen's voice.

"Hey, you hurt?" Bo had picked up my book, and his concern took me off guard.

"Um, mostly just my pride." I muttered as I glanced around to make sure there wasn't anyone else with him. When you're overweight and antisocial, High School is a war zone. If you're not constantly on guard, you're upside down in a trash can.

"My name's Bo," He said as he offered a hand to help me up. "Are you all right?"

No, I'm not... I slid my fingertips under my glasses and pressed them into my eyes as I sighed. "I'm sorry, I don't mean to be rude. I'm just—" Embarrassed, insecure, socially incompetent, afraid to trust anyone, pissed off at the world in general? "—tired. It's been a shitty day."

"Yeah, I totally hear ya there. You just moved here didn't you?" The way he said it sounded more like a statement than a question.

"Uh, yeah about a week ago."

"Ouch," he winced, "talk about short notice." He handed me my textbook and I loaded it into my backpack. "Well, I'll see you around man."

Bo turned and trotted after Jack, and my eyes found Fen. He noticed me looking at him, and he knit his eyebrows and tilted his head to the side. It was an odd gesture; like something a dog would do.

I frowned and scratched the itch in my hand as I turned and left to pick Jake up from school.

The next day I ignored Fen completely, though it seemed he couldn't ignore me. I caught him watching me in the lunch line, and then he said something to that girl Loki, who glanced at me.

Of *course* they knew each other. Why else would she be out in the woods in the middle of the night? The other students gave them a wide berth; and now I understood why.

There'd been kids in my old school who thought they were vampires, they smoked clove cigarettes across the street and read Anne Rice novels in class. We'd nurtured a successful relationship by mutually ignoring each other.

Werewolf wannabes were a new one though.

Weeks passed in much the same way. Fen watched me from a distance as though waiting for something. I felt desperately lonely, especially when the flyers for Homecoming popped up all over the halls. What was one more dance voided by social isolation anyway?

I ached, but still wasn't quite desperate enough to seek acceptance from Fen—or maybe just too stubborn—to willingly spend time with a delusional freak. Plus, I also had the added bonus of football season to deal with. The hallways oozed team colors and 'Go Tigers' slogans, not the mention the propaganda featuring Jack and some of the other players in their full black and gold spandexed glory.

Jack and the other 'dude-bro's in gym became unbearable as we got closer to game day. Doug and I were definitely on their shit list. Whenever I ended up with the ball I got rid of it as fast as possible. My tactic *mostly* worked despite the near-constant ache in my scarred calf. Doug had several "accidents," but I avoided most of their attempts to trip me.

I barely slept for weeks after the sickness though, and a ravenous hunger set in. It wasn't the first time depression had triggered a shift in appetite, but my clothes didn't feel tighter. And every night after dark, chaotic and unfamiliar images flooded my brain and made what little sleep I got worthless.

As an extra special bonus, a low migraine crept into the background almost twenty-four-seven. No matter how many times

I cleaned my glasses, things just wouldn't focus, and the world looked blurred, like staring through a greasy window.

I thought my eyes were getting worse until one day in math when I strained to make out the formulas Mr. Heinen had written on the board. My eyes throbbed from the effort and I took off my glasses to clean them again and just happened to glance up. The board still looked blurry, but it was clearer than with my glasses on. Weird.

I left my glasses off for the rest of the day and a little of the pressure released from my neck as the headache eased. I didn't want to deal with Mom's questions, so I put them back on when I went to get Jake. By the time I got home and went downstairs to do my homework, the headache was back in full swing.

Before dinner, I stepped into the bathroom to take some medicine for my headache, and pulled out the scale. I stepped on, then stepped off and then on again. Then I kicked it.

"Mom," I yelled, "is the scale broken?"

"Not as far as I know." she yelled back, then walked in and slung her dishtowel over her arm. She pushed me off the scale and checked the calibration, then stepped on herself and clicked her tongue. Then she stepped off and pulled me back on it.

"Nope, looks like you've lost a couple pounds honey. And I think I may have picked them up for you." She muttered and poked her stomach.

The last time I'd told her my weight was in Chicago a couple months before we moved. She had no idea that I'd gained six pounds... and then dropped ten in the space of a few weeks, while eating *more*. It just made no sense.

Over the years, I'd tried dieting, exercise, nothing worked so eventually I'd given up. The doctor Mom took me to couldn't figure it out either; they gave up and diagnosed me with an 'unspecified eating disorder'.

By the end of the week I started using belt holes I hadn't touched since middle school. I didn't tell Mom, but I started to lose almost a pound a day, sometimes more. When it got noticeable, even the ever-scorning-never-rewarding eye of John caught on.

One day in PE I blocked Jack's pass and my team scored. I realized my mistake as soon as I saw his face. To make sure I knew my place, Malcolm body-slammed me later and I went down hard. I tore most the skin off my elbow, but by the end of the period, it was just raw and pink.

I came home from school with my stomach growling, like usual. I closed the heavy wood door behind me and leaned my head against it as I sighed. Mom sat next to the big living room window, elbow deep in cardboard. "Hey Jimmy, how was your day?"

Would you like the truth, or do you just want to hear what'll make you feel better? "Not bad, yours?"

"Okay, it was… okay… Um, would you come into the living room please? We need to talk…"

Every teenager dreads that sentence. Adrenaline dumped into my bloodstream while questions blurred through my mind a mile a minute. I remembered every bad thing I'd ever done or even thought about, plus a multitude of 'what ifs' 'is it becauses' and 'did they find out abouts'.

Mom summoned John from his office and they sat down across from me. All I needed was a bare light bulb hanging in my eyes.

"Jimmy, we've been talking about it and both of us have noticed." John took the lead. Mom looked on the verge of tears and I felt utterly confused. "And… well… is there anything you need to tell us about?"

"Um…" My brain raced as I tried to predict which of my multitude of lies was about to be exposed. "Nothing comes to me; it sounds like you have something on your mind though?"

"Well, we're concerned about your weight. It almost looks like you're shrinking every time we look at you."

"And… this is bad? Aside from needing some smaller clothes, I don't see how losing weight could be a bad thing." When in doubt, be sarcastic, I thought.

"Have you… um…" John leaned forward and gestured with his hands as he chose his words. "Jimmy, no matter how desperate you are, there's a right way and a wrong way to do things. We didn't want to say anything prematurely, but we can't just write it off to our imaginations anymore. After you eat, do you—um… Jimmy, do you know what bulimia is?"

"Yeah, it's where someone, oh… *oh!*" I think I scared them when I threw my head back and howled with laughter. After all my dread, it was just a *massive* false alarm.

"Guys… I can assure you, that of all the things wrong with me; Bulimia is not on the list."

"Oh, thank goodness…" Mom sighed with relief.

"C'mere." John almost never hugged me; it felt like hugging a stranger. He squeezed me once, then set a hand on my shoulder and looked at me. Standing so close, I realized I was almost as tall as him now. "It'll take a little getting used to, but I sort of like having less of you to hug."

"Careful, you're about to overdraw your fatherly love account." I frowned. Please, spare me… "Besides, you seem to have more of a keg than a six pack yourself."

"Just go clean up and get your brother, we're going out for supper tonight." John scowled and walked away.

I picked up my backpack from where I dropped it near the door, and headed down the dungeon stairs when Mom came up behind me.

"Jimmy? I'm sorry but I have to ask… how *are* you losing weight? Is it…*drugs?*" She whispered the last word like it was dirty.

I looked into her eyes and did something unusual. I told the truth. "I have no idea. It might be the new elevation, but... I just... I really don't know." I shrugged.

"Well alright... Oh!" She turned back as she remembered something "Is something wrong with your glasses?" I realized I'd gotten lazy and left them off.

"Yeah, I was gonna tell you about that. I, uh—my eyes seem to be getting better."

She quirked her eyebrow, "Well, that's good. Strange, but good. Do you want to see an optometrist and get your prescription fixed?"

"Maybe, I'll let you know." Wow, that went easier than I'd expected. I turned and walked down the stairs while something stirred in the back of my mind. A whisper I fought to forget and a fractured memory of a dream. I brushed it off, but that night, the truth that had been lying in wait within me uncoiled and pounced.

The first dream I didn't realize was a dream until I woke up from it; something about a girl with brown hair. She seemed so familiar for some reason... meh... the harder I tried to remember, the faster it slipped from me. All I could really remember was the girl herself, not her exact face, but the feel of her soft brown hair and deep contentment.

I surfaced from the dream and clutched at a sharp burning pain from the scar on my leg. Exhaustion pulled me down despite the pain and I slipped out of my skin...

I opened my eyes on top of a tall spire of rock, overlooking a circular sapphire pool. Maple and aspen trees ringed the shore. I lifted my arms and dove in. I swam toward the bottom amidst dancing spears of sunlight and saw the dark mouth of a cave.

Brightly colored fish darted away and disappeared as shadows dimmed the light. I looked up toward the surface and bit down on a scream.

Snakes. Snakes everywhere, their undulating silhouettes darkened the light as they converged in the water above me. Searing pain lanced through my calf, but I fought it as I turned and desperately swam inside the cave to escape them. The darkness swallowed me until I came up into an air pocket.

I froze. A pair of amber eyes stared back inches from my face.

The wolf looked starved, emaciated and neglected, but he held himself proud. His coat gleamed iridescent in the darkness of the cave, and his eyes burned with life and intelligence. Slowly, I lifted my hands and touched him, sliding my fingers into the dense fur on either side of his ears. His eyes hooded and he made a happy rumbling sound as he stepped forward and touched his forehead to mine. Warmth filled me at the familiarity of the sensation.

I knew I had to get him out of there. I led him into the water and clutched him to my chest as we swam out of the cave. As we rose through the water, his fur waved against my arm and I felt his heartbeat against my chest, racing in sync with my own. The snakes rushed toward us as the wolf and I started to merge, like they were trying to stop us. I saw through his eyes, felt his fur over my skin and our heartbeats became one. We defied the suffocating terror as we raced to the sunlight and the snakes closed in.

I kicked one last time and broke the surface, drawing in a deep breath. Before the snakes reached me, I felt everything shift around us as the light dimmed past my closed eyelids.

I opened them and found the moon in place of the sun. The sky was depthless obsidian, without a single star to break the curtain. Only the moon hung there, eternally full.

"My son; I'd feared you lost again…" I recognized that voice instantly and it sent a chill down my back.

I tore my eyes from the moon and saw Lupa standing there. Her white fur gleamed in the moonlight, perched on rocks almost as black as the sky. She climbed down like a pool of platinum liquid spilling from ledge to rock. Everything was black as onyx despite the full lunar light, even the towering trees that surrounded us. The only thing that reflected light was her coat.

"You rejected us. You forced me out and tried to hide from me again, just when we'd finally recovered you." I felt her pain and her rejection inside me as though it was my own, *"Why, my son?"*

As she approached I felt fear and uncertainty; but also a strange giddiness, almost… joy.

"Because… because I was afraid…" What was I saying? I meant to say *'because this isn't real'*, but as soon as I said it, everything clicked into place. This was the answer; the weight loss, the bizarre dreams, my eyesight; all of it. Fen wasn't completely deranged; I was changing…

It was all real, this place, Fen, Lupa; all of it, and I felt… right. Acceptance seeped into my bones, and I felt it inside me; a restless energy behind my breastbone with yellow eyes and ink-black fur. I took a deep breath and set my jaw.

"But… I'm sick of being afraid."

Lupa smiled again and joy lit her face, and then she turned and looked over her shoulder at me. *"Then run with me…"*

I moved after her and my body spilled from one form to another like water; my hands were paws by the time they touched the rocks. I didn't even pause, that would have given her a bigger head start, but I was surprised that I didn't feel any different.

I was still me, my soul, just a different shell.

The world flushed to life like never before, and we left the river-bed and charged into the trees. The woods lost their ominous darkness *and stars emerged from the velvet sky overhead, netted in the faint glow of the Milky Way. Trees and shrubs flew past, every detail clear in vivid sepia, dead pine needles the color of rust crunched underfoot as I flew after the spirit with my tail trailing like a banner.*

We played and raced around tree trunks and massive boulders. I doubled back under a fallen log, and thought I'd lost her until she barreled out of the underbrush and broadsided me; we rolled a couple times then jumped back onto our feet and took off again. We panted and laughed, grinning with our cheeks pulled back and our ears down.

For the first time that I could remember, I felt whole.

We broke free of the forest and raced along the shore of a huge lake. The moon reflected in the perfect mirror of the water was as crisp and clear as the original, along with the green ribbons of light that danced over the trees on the northern shore. We kicked up sand and pebbles behind us as we flew and the soft silt squished between my toes. We reached a tall spire of rocks and leapt our way up to the very top and looked out over the lake and the forest.

I knew this place, knew it with a deeper memory inside me. It was like this world had been lost in time, but my soul remembered it.

"What is this place?" I asked her while we looked out over the vast black wilderness.

"Some humans call it the Lowerworld," she said while we curled up against each other, our white and black coats like the halves of a yin-yang, "This is the realm of souls and spirits, but it's shaped by memory and belief. This lake," she looked out over the rippling water, "is a reflection of your memories, Jimmy. Long ago, this was your home."

Memory stirred, and I realized that we had run like this before, years ago. Time meant nothing, a strange human concept that had no place here. My memories were shattered, half remembered and buried in the depths of my mind behind a shroud of terror, but still very much real.

"*How many times have we run like this?*"

"*Too many to bother counting. Do you finally remember now?*"
She rumbled against my side, that same contented sound my wolf had
made in the cave.

"*Sort of… Have I been like this all along?*"

"*You pushed it down, buried it deep and tried to forget it.*"

I felt uneasy, and a twinge of pain rippled through my hind leg,
"*What happened to me?*"

She was quiet a moment, "*You'll remember when the time comes.
For now, I'm just glad you are home; I've missed you so much. You
needed someone to remind you who you really are. Someone like you.*"

"*Fen.*"

"*Yes.*"

*This calm, this peace—it almost hurt. I felt like I was home
for the first time. Lupa lifted her head to the moon and let out a
great soaring howl, and I joined in. Somewhere in the distance I
thought I heard an answer rise from the trees across the lake as my
eyes drifted closed.*

The next day, Fen waited for me, leaning on the wall outside
the art room door. Neither of us spoke for a minute, I was still
too stubborn to admit my mistake.

"I heard your call."

I frowned. I didn't remember calling him.

"Last night, from the lake?" he prompted and raised an
eyebrow. "I tried to answer but I was too far away, you were gone
by the time I got there." I swallowed and lowered my eyes.

Well, if I was looking for proof that it wasn't all in my head;
that would probably suffice.

"So… that place was real then?" I scowled as I tried to fit it all into my reality. It *didn't* fit, but I was working on it.

"Eh, sort of… We'll get to that later though. Meet me in the cafeteria at lunch; we have a lot to go over. You've been asleep too long." He turned to walk into the classroom, and then paused, "Oh, and happy new moon by the way."

CHAPTER 4 – THE PACK

I met Fen near the lunch line but said nothing. Embarrassed by my behavior and the lingering rationality that 'there's no such thing as werewolves'. Fen looked me over and narrowed his eyes.

"It's obvious the change has stuck; but you're off balance. You've still got a long way to go, and a lot to learn."

I followed him out the cafeteria door, "Where are we going?"

He didn't reply, and I took my cue, "Look Fen, I'm sorry. I'm sorry I was such a jerk, but… put yourself in my shoes. This isn't exactly easy for me; it's kind of a mind-fuck." I said as we walked across the front lawn.

He paused and sighed, "Yeah, you're right. I'm sorry too, we were all able to sorta prepare ourselves; you were just dumped in it headfirst." *How many more were there?* "Lupa told me you were coming years ago. At first I didn't believe it, I thought I misunderstood her, but then there you were." He shook his head, "I wanted to wait, but apparently Lupa had other plans. She chose you Jimmy; it was decided long before you or I had any say in the matter."

Okay, creepy. He didn't exactly sound ecstatic about it either.

"First things first, look into my eyes." I resisted making a Bela Lugosi pun, and did as he asked. His gaze was intense and I could only hold it for a few seconds before my skin crawled and I glanced away. We both shuddered and he blinked hard.

I rubbed at the goosebumps on my arms and felt that cool wash again from his necklace as it bumped against my chest. I pulled it out and looked at it, "So... why did you give me a silver necklace? All the stories say werewolves are allergic to silver."

"All the movies say that, but it's not exactly true. Most of us react to it, but nothing as dramatic as fiction makes it. The moon has been associated with silver since the dawn of time. See, silver and gold are both charged with spiritual energy. And before you give me one of those looks, think about it; didn't you feel better after I gave you the necklace?" I froze in the middle of making the exact face he mentioned and frowned. Damnit, he was right.

"Yeah, I thought so. You're gunna need to open your mind a bit... okay, maybe a lot in your case." He smirked at me so I knew he was just teasing and I smiled back. "Silver carries lunar energy, and werewolves are linked to the moon. But even that part is only half true. We're connected, but we're not slaves. So silver either boosts or deadens our shifting energy. It all de—"

"Wait, pause, what the hell is 'shifting energy'?" I rubbed my temples; it felt like he was speaking another language that I only half understood. The words were familiar, but the way he used them was different. I was going to need to take notes to remember all this crap.

"Sorry; shifting energy is something particular to werewolves, or shifters since we're not all wolves. It's like to the Qi of oriental medicine; the energy of our bodies, our auras. Shifters' energy is different though; it fluctuates more, usually in sync with lunar and yearly cycles. It peaks and dips, and when it peaks, it makes 'shifting' possible."

"You mean like turning into a wolf?" I fought very hard to keep the skepticism out of my voice as we sat down on the grass in the middle of the field, no one around to hear us.

"Potentially," he said carefully, "though I've never done it, or seen it done, or seen any proof that it's even *possible*. But...I dream about being able to actually shapeshift someday." He grew quiet for a moment, lost in his own thoughts. "Anyway, there are different kinds of shifts. You've already experienced at least one, last night, you shifted into your wolf form in your dream right?"

I nodded. The sun was warm; but the breeze gave me goosebumps as leaves skittered across the lawn.

"Anyway, like I was saying, our reaction to silver is based almost entirely on the individual. This particular Pack reacts to both silver and the moon. So it was pretty much just a good guess that the necklace would affect you the same way and help buffer your shifting energy."

"Wow, it only took you half the lunch break to answer my question." I muttered as I stuffed the last bite of food in my mouth.

He smiled with embarrassment, "Yeah, sorry. I'm notorious for my tangents. Do you have time after school?"

I swallowed my mouthful, "I usually walk my little brother home, but I could call my mom to see if she can pick him up."

"See if she can. You have a lot to learn, and we can't waste much more time."

I called Mom and she agreed to pick Jacob up for me. After school, Fen followed me to my locker and then led me outside.

We crossed the athletic field and he led me through the trees on the far side. I followed him to a hidden little patch of land overgrown with tall grass and weeds. Elm trees formed a wall and Fen led me to a path that snaked through the brambles. I heard voices up ahead and I gripped my backpack tighter.

The path opened up into a small clearing in the center of the wooded patch. Geri, the stocky boy from the night Fen bit me, sat on a fallen tree along one side of the clearing. Of course.

Geri struggled to stifle a laugh, and Fen glanced around the clearing, "Where's Loki?"

"Oof!" The next thing I knew, I was on the ground with the wind knocked out of me and her grinning face hovered over mine.

"Ha! You just got owned, pup! Too easy…" She cackled while I struggled, but she pinned my arms down with her legs. All I could do was stutter and blush. "Aw, he's turning red! Look at him, he's sho coot!"

"Loki, go easy on him…" Fen muttered.

"Aww, c'mon he's only a little maimed! You can take a little rough handling, can'tcha?" Loki grinned and a ring of amber bled in around her emerald green irises, "I'm just asserting my dominance is all."

She loomed over me, and stared into my eyes. Deep inside, a part of me understood and answered. My skin tingled as my wolf woke up and heat poured through my veins.

I arched my back and pushed us off the ground. I flipped us over and pinned her wrists down without even realizing it, surprised by my own strength. Whatever she did, the animal inside me didn't like it one bit, and, I felt him look out my eyes.

"Uh, Fen?" Loki stammered, her wide eyes unable to leave mine. "He's already manifesting!" With unexpected strength, she threw me off her and rolled out from under me. My body rolled on its own and came up on its hand and toes, disconnected from me.

"Look at his eyes," Loki muttered while she crouched, mirroring me.

"I know…" Fen looked at me intently, but not into my eyes, not threatening. He stared at my chest and frowned, "He's not wearing it…"

"Not wearing what?" Geri asked as he came up beside Fen.

"The silver I gave him."

What was going on? I took off the necklace so it wouldn't get caught on anything in gym, but couldn't remember putting it back on. The implication dawned on me; the silver dampened the presence of the wolf—and I'd removed it. My body backed up when Fen stood and walked toward me, messing with something around his neck while Loki and Geri fanned out around me.

A thought that wasn't my own whispered through the back of my mind; *it's a trap…*

I willed myself to stand up and realized I couldn't control my own body. Worse, I didn't know how to get it back. I panicked and fought for control through the numbness, but my lips still twitched and bared my teeth.

The next moment, all three of them pounced in a blur.

Loki attacked from my left, Geri from the right, and they wrestled me to the ground. The wolf raged when they forced me onto my back and his power ripped through me I lost control.

Loki braced an arm under my chin to keep my teeth away, while my arm smashed Geri across the chest. He barely held on to it as he crashed into the bushes, but it was enough.

In that moment, with my arms spread wide, Fen pounced. In a single swift motion he pushed my shirt up and pressed something cold against the hollow of my sternum. Lead weight bloomed inside me; a liquid exhaustion that flowed into my limbs and sapped all the strength from me. The wolf inside yelped in pain, closed his eyes and curled up in the darkness, drained and weary, while I seeped back into my body.

Everyone but Fen panted for breath, and Geri released my arm to inspect the violet bruise that was blossoming across his chest. I struggled to move, but my limbs just flopped weakly. I tried to ask what happened, but all that came out was a drawled slur.

"Don't worry, it's over now... Just make sure to keep that necklace on, okay?" Fen said, careful not to meet my eyes.

"Jeezus pup... don't ever do that again." Loki let go of my arm and it fell to the ground. She picked off bits of leaves and grass that stuck to her.

"Ease off him Loki, nothing would've happened if you hadn't challenged him," Geri growled at her as he gingerly prodded the red streak across his torso. She glowered at him, but didn't argue.

"I don't... I'm... sorry..." I felt exhausted, like my body had been frozen. *What the fuck just happened?*

"Didn't you tell him what would happen if he took off the silver?" Loki shot Fen a furious glare.

"No, I got distracted."

"Damnit Fen, you can't be so careless," she snapped and Fen winced like she'd slapped him.

"Yeah... you and your damn... tangents..." I panted. The mood broke, and everyone chuckled at Fen's expense.

"Sorry, I don't exactly have a syllabus..." Fen sighed and ran his fingers through his hair.

"I doesn't matter, can you put that thing away now?" Loki asked him, looking a little green. Geri didn't look so hot either.

"Yeah, I think so..." He pulled away whatever he'd pressed against my chest and I caught a flash of blue-green as he tucked it away. As soon as he did, I took a deep breath and felt sensation rush back into my limbs. Loki sighed with relief, and some color returned to her cheeks.

"What the hell was that?" I asked, "It almost looked like—"

"Turquoise? It was," Fen replied.

"Turquoise? Why not silver?" I asked and flexed my hands through the pins and needles.

"Silver's too dynamic," Loki answered as she stood up. "Sometimes it boosts shifting energy, so not always a good idea in an emergency. Turquoise on the other hand," she said, making a face, "nasty stuff… just seems to suck the energy right out of us.

"By the way, I'm Loki. My real name's Jessica, but only people who share genes with me call me that." She smiled at me as some thought passed behind her eyes and I was struck again by how familiar she looked. Her emerald green eyes sparkled when she smiled, a mischievous light within them. Freckles dusted her nose and cheeks and her only makeup was the eyeliner that made her eyes even more striking. "And the guy you just about threw across the clearing is Geri. See, I told you you'd see us again soon."

Geri gave a wry smile. "Hey."

"I'm… sorry…" I muttered, but he just shrugged.

"Don't worry about it, wasn't your fault." Geri shot a look at Loki, who glared at Fen, who pretended not to notice. At fault or not, I felt my cheeks flood crimson. I'd made some craptacular impressions in my life, but this was in a league of its own.

Fen ignored Loki's ridicule and checked his watch, "Crap, I need to go pick my mom up from work, I have the car today. You guys should hang out though, get to know each other. I'll see ya tomorrow." He grabbed his backpack and hurried away, leaving me alone with two almost total strangers.

Looking for an escape, I glanced at my watch. "Actually, I need to get home too, it'll be dinnertime soon."

Geri seemed to have an idea, "Hey Loki, wanna take him home?"

"Sure. Do you mind?" she asked me as she stood and picked

up her bag.

Truthfully, I wanted some time alone so I could get a get a grip on things. My mind struggled to categorize my reality, and force order on the impossible. It still just didn't seem real. Only a couple weeks ago turquoise was pretty jewelry, supernatural forms of energy were an X-File, and werewolves were Halloween costumes. Today, a teenage girl had lifted and thrown me like a sack of potatoes, and an animal spirit inside me had taken over my body. Even weirder; people actually wanted to be friends with me.

Just go with it, like it or not, you're one of these people now.

"Um, sure, I guess. Just… bear with me if I seem a little out of it." I looked down at the fallen leaves that crunched underfoot while they laughed and Geri and I collected our things. I dug the necklace out of my backpack and slipped the chain over my head. My head felt clearer right away, as the chaos ebbed, and I took a deep breath.

We left the little wooded sanctuary and Loki asked, "So, uh… how do you like it here so far?"

"Well, other than getting mauled by a werewolf within a week, it's just like any other place I guess except there's no air here." I smiled when they laughed. "People are the same dipshits no matter where you go… Oh, and this place is crawling with evil beasts of the night."

"Hey!" Loki looked insulted. She tried to make herself look cute and innocent—which was pretty fucking adorable—and my stomach fluttered. "Do I look like an evil beast of the night to you?"

"You're the worst of them all!" Geri cried and we laughed.

"Yeah, I guess I can't argue that." Loki conceded as we walked up to the last car in the parking lot, Geri's red Civic, and he unlocked the doors. While we drove, I disappeared into my head, thinking about her question.

The truth was, I hated this place.

And I fucking despised moving; the pointless 'fresh start', the ceaseless cycle of upheaval. Even the toughest goddamned house-plant would have croaked after being uprooted as often as I had. At least this town was the polar opposite of the homogeneous mass-produced suburbs in Chicago and Miami. Here, huge elm and maple trees dominated the sky and uprooted the sidewalk, and none of the houses matched.

I shook myself out of it and broke the silence. "So, Fen said you're a pack right? I remember reading something about wolf packs having different ranks, do you?"

"Yeah, Fen's the alpha male, our leader," Geri replied. "I'm the omega, lowest on the pecking order, but that might change now that you've come into the picture." He winked and grinned in the rear view mirror.

I grinned back, but it was more a bearing of teeth than an actual smile. "After what just happened, I wouldn't hold my breath."

"He's probably right Geri-boy; I think you're gonna be our scapegoat for a while yet." Loki patted him on the shoulder.

"Can't blame a guy for dreaming…"

"You're our omega, we can blame you for whatever we want!" She ruffled his short-cropped hair and they laughed, though Geri seemed genuinely sad.

"So, you're the alpha female?" I glanced at Loki and she seemed to choke.

"Noooo-ho-ho! I'm beta, second in command but usually first in trouble."

"So, Fen's at the top, Geri's at the bottom… where do I fall?"

"We'll find out soon enough. Pretty much everything else is just called 'mid-ranking'. In the wild, mid-ranking wolves usually have some sort of special job, but with so few of us, we don't have much use for that," Loki replied. "So, my fuzzy new wolf, tell us about yourself."

"There's nothing interesting about me," I muttered and looked out the window as the dappled sunlight flickered over us.

"Bullshit, we've got you outnumbered and surrounded, so start yappin' pup!"

"About what?" I asked, irritated.

"I don't care, grades?" She shrugged.

"Piss poor, thanks for reminding me." I grumbled.

"Sorry, but if you don't contribute anything, I'm just gunna dig for it."

When I remained quiet, she resumed her interrogation. Car? Nope. Driver's License? Yep. Grade? Senior. Girlfriend? Don't even go there. Favorite band? You want a freakin' list?

Loki had such an easy character; I never would've guessed it from the way she dressed. Her cheer was infectious and irresistible, I'd never been so open with complete strangers before in my life, but something about her just felt… comfortable. I wished I could put my finger on why.

Geri parked at the curb, and I led them up the porch that stretched the width of the old Craftsman house. The sage green siding contrasted with the dark red and black bricks of the porch's columns and the chimney that jutted from the side. It was cute enough to be annoying.

"Mom? We have visitors!" I called as we walked inside.

"What's that, Jimmy?" She came around the corner from the kitchen and wiped her hands on her apron. "Oh! Hello, come in, come in!" She waved Loki and Geri into the house "Welcome back! I wanted to thank you for helping Jimmy out that night. Would you like to stay for dinner? I could call out for pizza?"

I groaned inside and felt myself turn red. This was probably the first time I'd ever brought friends over from school—first time I *had* friends to bring—and Mom was making *way* too big a deal out of it.

"Well… sure, if it's okay with you; I'll just need to call my folks. What do you think Geri?" Loki glanced at her cohort.

"If there's pizza involved, I'm in!" he grinned.

"Great, what do you want on yours? I'll call them in right now." Mom wrote down our toppings and ordered a pizza for each of us. Loki looked at the family pictures on the wall while she and Geri called their parents.

I stepped close to Mom and muttered in a low voice. "Seriously, Mom, can you cool the overeager parent thing a bit? It's freaking us out."

"They don't seem to mind." she said.

"Okay, it's freaking *me* out. Can you please just ease down a bit?" Too late, I realized I'd hurt her feelings.

"Okay, fine, whatever you want Jimmy," Mom pursed her lips and rubbed her temple, "I'll stay out of your way." To avoid any more awkwardness, I led Loki and Geri through the kitchen to the back yard to enjoy the last rays of the sun.

Loki leaned in and whispered a question to me, "Sorry if this is awkward, but, were you adopted? Your mom looks *way* too young to be your—uh—*mom*…"

"And I look nothing like her or the guy in the pictures." I added. "Mom had me when she was seventeen. She married John when I was six; he's my brother's dad, not mine." Very little bitterness slipped through into my voice, and I felt proud of my accomplishment. Loki and Geri didn't seem to know how to respond, so we chatted about school for a while.

The pizzas arrived and Mom called us in just as the sun neared the mountains. We collected our pizzas and I led them down into the Dungeon.

"Sorry about the mess," I muttered. I glanced at the stuff

scattered around the room and the stack of still-unpacked boxes. Band posters and guitar chord diagrams hung from the sterile concrete walls in a pathetic attempt to make it my home. It had never struck me as slovenly before—Mom was a different matter—but I felt a burning shame as they entered.

"Ha! You call this a mess? You'd have an stroke if you saw my room…" Loki scoffed and I felt a little better as I kicked a spot clear of clothes and we sat down. I hadn't realized how hungry I was until the molten cheese touched my tongue and kicked my salivary glands into overdrive. I turned on some music and poured soda for everyone.

With a cheek full of food, Loki said, "Hey, is that a guitar amp over there?" She pointed with her pizza crust.

"Yeah," I muttered.

"Really? Play something for us!"

"I'd rather not, I'm not that good…" I muttered and felt my neck tingle with embarrassment.

"Whatever!" Loki jumped up and marched across my room. She grabbed my guitar off its stand and shoved it into my hands, "I hate excuses, so, rock my socks off!"

I shook my head as I plugged it in and powered on my amplifier. I tuned and started to play. Just one month without practice had made my hands clumsy and slow and I turned a darker shade of red with every mistake until my hands remembered what they were supposed to do.

My eyelids hooded as I lost myself in the music. When I couldn't think of anything else to play, I stopped and looked up at them with beads of sweat rolling down my face.

"That was the shit!" Geri laughed, wide-eyed and grinning.

"Sorry it sounded so rough, I haven't played since before we moved." I said and wiped my face with my sleeve.

"Really? Coulda fooled me!" Loki nodded her agreement.

Warmth, foreign and treacherous, leached into my heart. That was the first time anyone ever complimented my playing. Mom and John pretended I'd never touched the damn thing.

"That cinches it!" Loki yelled and jumped to her feet. "You're gonna teach me guitar. I've wanted to learn for years, but no one here teaches metal." She bounded across the room and hugged me so hard we both almost toppled over.

As soon as she touched me, gray and chestnut mottled fur flashed in my mind again, but now I understood what it meant; those were the colors of her wolf. "Have you ever played in a band?"

"Uh, no... I taught myself how to play a couple years ago."

"Hey, once you teach me how to play, we should start our own band! Ooh! A werewolf band! Fen can learn the bass and Geri; you can play the pots and pans." Loki almost vibrated with excitement.

"The what?" Geri and I said in unison.

"You know, 'pots and pans'? Drums? Oh never mind. It was *supposed* to be a joke, but y'all suck."

"Actually, that would be kinda cool. I can't think of any other bands with an all-out werewolf theme, and certainly not with real werewolves. Do you have good rhythm?" I glanced at Geri. He was so quiet; it was easy to forget him in the intensity of Loki's personality.

"I can't even play Guitar Hero."

Ouch...

When they left, I felt reluctant to see them off, like a starved slave who'd tasted chocolate for the first time. They opened the door and a cool breeze drifted inside. Loki closed her jacket and winked at me as she pulled the door shut. "Full Moon's the Saturday after next, so remember to keep that night free. As of now,

CHAPTER 5 — MOONRISE

The moon grew full like a looming presence in the back of my mind. As the weeks passed, an impatient itch festered deep inside me where nothing could ease it.

I ate lunch with the Pack every day out in their little wooded sanctuary. Fen and Loki took turns teaching me how to control my shifting energy, that heat that flooded me whenever my wolf stirred, and how to integrate myself with the animal spirit growing inside me. I practiced whenever I could, it eased the itch just a little bit when I burned off a little of that heat. I even figured out how to increase my night vision when I practiced at night.

I sure as hell couldn't sleep.

Whenever Fen came over to my house after school John just adored him. Fen was confidant, smart, in shape—*blond*—basically everything I was not. Fen relished John's attention too, and asked endless questions about him at school. I stowed the bitter jealousy out of sight, stuffing it down into the dragon's pit like everything else that hurt, while finding any excuse I could to keep the two of them separate.

Trees turned gold as the nights chilled, and Full Moon night descended at last. I thought I would explode if I stopped moving, until I heard a knock on the door.

Finally…

I beat John to the door and yanked it open. The tension in Fen's eyes mirrored my own.

"Ready?"

"As I'll ever be," I muttered and then shouted at my parents in the living room, "Fen's here, I'll see you guys tomorrow!"

"Don't forget your coat, it's supposed to snow tonight! Do we have Geri's number?" Mom yelled back.

"It's on the fridge!" I shrugged my coat on.

"Okay, have fun!" she called as I pulled the door closed, anxious to get Fen away. As he led us to the High School, the air around him almost seemed to shimmer; my own skin felt hot and just a little too tight.

The light breeze promised a cold night as the last light of sunset faded from the clouds and we waited for Loki and Geri in the parking lot near the football field. A chill ran down my spine and Fen's back stiffened. I glanced over my shoulder as the edge of the moon broke the horizon, wide and orange.

I stared, transfixed, until Loki's voice snapped me out of it, and I turned to see Geri's car pull up with her hanging out the window. "Hey you bums!" She grinned; a ring of topaz lined her irises.

I felt excited to see them, but terrified at the same time. I wanted to shut down and hide so I wouldn't risk ruining this precious, tenuous hope. I wanted to save it in a box and cherish it before I could destroy it. But the rest of me craved their company, the sound of their voices, and most of all that rare and dangerous feeling of belonging that had crept into my life. And for that fix, I knew I'd risk almost anything.

Fen walked toward the athletics field, Loki and Geri followed, roughhousing, and I tagged behind.

My senses came to life as heat curled through me and my wolf's awareness bloomed within my mind. Where the night was supposed to be dark, every detail was lined with silver, almost brighter than the day. Every bird, every creaking tree called out clear as a bell. My skin tingled and my nostrils flared to siphon in all the scents I could gather; cut grass, sprinklers, and cow manure wafting through the air.

Loki and Geri veered left and split off along the perimeter of the field, while Fen led me toward the football field. "Tonight, this is our territory," Fen said, "We patrol it, mark it, everything in it belongs to us. Just for tonight, this place is ours…"

"By 'mark', you don't mean—"

"You don't honestly think the restrooms are still open do you?" He smirked and patted my shoulder. "We just kill two birds with one kidney stone, so to speak." *Ugh!* "We just need to make sure there are no interlopers before the real fun begins. Since this is your first time, just stick with me." He led me into the shadow of the football bleachers and along the edge of a dry irrigation ditch toward the trees near our thicket. Everything around us shimmered. I glanced at the moon and my chest tightened from its power.

We followed the line of the ditch through the trees and then headed back through them toward the field. As we neared the end of the tree line, we both froze.

My heart sped up as adrenaline dumped into my bloodstream. My nostrils twitched as I backed up and crouched in the shadow of a large pine where my dark clothes blended in. Fen advanced slowly as his eyes swept back and forth.

A twig snapped to our right and I saw the shadow hurl itself at Fen out of the corner of my eye. Fen snarled as Geri tackled him from behind and sent them both grappling across the ground. Loki emerged from her hiding place and ran to help Geri, but I tackled her to the ground. Though startled for an instant, she jumped up as soon as I backed off and growled as she bared her teeth, her eyes yellow and vivid behind her eyeshadow.

The thought streaked through my mind that it wasn't right for people to act like this at our age, but I tuned it out.

Not all the rules of my old world held true anymore.

I jumped back and crouched with my hands touching the ground. She leapt at me and I tripped her over my foot. This time I pinned her and held her down despite her snarls of protest. The silver necklace weighed heavy around my neck like a ball and chain; but the eyes of the wolf in my mind's eye opened regardless, and he told me what to do in his strange language of image and sensation.

I bared my teeth as the wolf's eyes blazed through mine and when I looked at Loki I didn't just see a girl; I saw a feminine wolf overlying her, fair brown and gray in color. She struggled, but I refused to relent and eventually she gave up.

Satisfied, I looked over toward Geri and Fen. Geri was well built with a strong frame, but the lanky alpha had him subdued already. Fen watched us with deathly stillness. His face was in silhouette, so I couldn't make out his expression, but Geri seized Fen's distraction and rolled out from under him to counterattack.

I jumped up from Loki and rushed Geri as he disengaged from Fen. I reached for him, but my fingers slipped on his slick coat, and he took off running along the tree line.

Fen and I jumped up after him, but they quickly drew ahead of me. Even though he was shorter than me, Geri was somehow a lot faster. Behind me, I heard the patter of Loki's feet gaining as we dashed through the thickening snow. The scar on my leg burned from the strain, and I tried not to limp.

The wolf within me reveled in the chase, and as he filled me the distance between us stopped growing. I felt disconnected from the ground; the balls of my feet barely touching down as the wind washed around me.

Before I knew it, we'd reached the line of the ditch, and Geri turned to face us. Fen barely slowed before he slammed into Geri like a ton of bricks.

I slipped on the wet grass and slid a few feet on my ass until Loki pounced me from behind. I rolled and threw her off me. We came up on all fours and faced each other. A grin slowly spread across our faces and we relaxed a little.

"Not bad pup." I blushed from her comment. Her eyes had turned pure gold, and I assumed mine where the same.

"Good enough to beat *you* anyway." Fen said. I had the odd feeling of my ear swiveling toward the sound of his voice. "He's barely been at this a month now, and you submitted to him." Fen sat on top of Geri, scuffed up and sprawled on the ground.

"So? I was stuck, he wouldn't let go." She sounded defensive and almost sullen.

"You've never submitted to me like that." Fen's voice was level, but something made Loki's expression go dark. Fen looked at me. "Normally you'd be the new Beta, but I won't allow it yet."

"Why not?" I asked.

"Yeah, care to explain?" Loki crossed her arms and Geri's nervous eyes flicked back and forth between us.

"He's too new." Fen stood and Geri got up and brushed what snow he could off. Loki didn't look like she believed him, and pursed her lips. "That's the *only* reason, Loki. I don't think he's strong enough to handle the position yet."

"Not that I particularly like it, but he *was* strong enough to beat me." Loki countered while they matched stares. I squirmed inside. I didn't want to start a fight, even though it felt too much like bureaucracy.

"Loki, it's okay, don't worry about it." I tried to calm her down, and winced as something inside me with sharp pointy teeth expressed his displeasure.

She closed her eyes and sighed, her breath a plume in the cold air. "Fine."

The snow thickened into fluffy white puffs that drifted down around us and built up on the grass and trees. Fen looked up and smiled at the diffused halo of light on the other side of the clouds. He sighed. "I'd hoped it would be nice and clear for your first Full Moon, Jimmy."

"No worries, I like the snow." I smiled and walked over toward them. The heat of my shifting energy surged when my wolf moved.

Geri seemed to sense my intent a moment before I leapt at him and he took off running. He wove between the thick pines that bordered the ditch, but with my wolf's speed, he couldn't outrun me. Geri's fate was sealed with one wrong turn and I tackled him. We rolled over each other in a snarling ball of werewolf until we crashed into a tree, which doused us with cold slushiness.

Geri gasped at the sudden cold, and we laughed. Loki and Fen caught up and joined us.

After a moment though, they fell silent and I looked around at their surprised stares. Fen quickly hid his surprise, but I joined them when I noticed the tendrils of steam that evaporated off me as my wolf's energy pulsed within me. It was awesome, but sort of spooky. I stood up, and stared at the mist that rose from my bare hands, warm and flushed in the cold night air.

Loki seized Geri's distraction and pounced on him. He howled with frustration as he grappled with her. I felt guilty; because of me, everyone had to reestablish their place, and Geri just kept getting worked over.

Fen moved past me to watch them, and I wondered if it made him uncomfortable to see what a freak I really was.

I dashed over and shoved Loki off Geri, and then danced around on my toes until all three of them jumped up after me. I turned and ran with three werewolves in hot pursuit. My wolf still pounded through my veins, his eyes in mine as I ran a cat's cradle through the trees until they either fell out of sight or gave up.

I hid inside the overhanging branches of a big pine while I stopped to catch my breath and give my aching leg a break. I thought I felt the shadows move around me, almost as if they swallowed me, but I wrote it off to my imagination. Fen and Geri ran past my tree and disappeared into the veiling wall of snow, but Loki dragged behind breathing hard.

She waited until they were out of sight, and then looked around. When she didn't see anyone, she closed her eyes and raised her hands to the cloudy sky and twirled in circles as the snow fell around her. My breath caught when I saw the smile on her face, stolen in a moment she thought no one else could see.

She sighed and collected herself, and then took off after Fen and Geri. I shuddered as I stepped out of the pine's shadowy boughs, like they didn't want to let me go. The scent of the sap lingered on my clothes as I followed their tracks and considered ambushing Geri again.

I rounded a tree, and noticed marks in the snow. I crept over to inspect them; hiking boots like Fen's walked up, then sort of milled for a while before backtracking the way they came. I followed their line and saw the swirls in the snow where Loki had danced, like someone had watched.

My puzzlement lasted only a second before something hard rammed me in the side. I cried out and rolled through the slush, and then came up facing Fen's feral grin.

"C'mon pup, show me what you've got."

My muscles vibrated with tension, but when the attack came, it was faster than I could have imagined. I lurched back, but slipped on the wet lawn, and Fen's swipe glanced off my shoulder with a bruising thud, barely buffered by my coat. His speed overwhelmed me, and I ducked under his arm only to be tackled into the snow. I took Loki and Geri, but Fen was in a class of his own.

"C'mon Jimmy, I know you can do better than that…" Fen goaded while he circled me, and knocked me over again when I tried to get up.

The wolf inside me wanted to stand and fight, wanted to meet him head-on, but something in his posture triggered memories of every bully in my past. The wolf made me faster, made me stronger, but he couldn't make me forget my childhood. When Fen attacked again I faked right, and pushed off the ground with my hands in the opposite direction. Fen missed me, and it was the opening I needed to slip past him and run.

I heard his steps right behind me and somewhere behind, Loki and Geri called after us. Wolf shredded my guts, his disgust and frustration palpable in the thick metallic taste in the back of my throat, but I just wasn't strong enough to face him. Them. In my mind Fen had become every demon I'd ever had, he was John's every scorn, every black eye I'd carried home, every bruise and shame I'd endured. Every threat I'd ever run away from; my weakness, my fear, my uncertainty, pursued me in Fen's shadow, and the gate opened.

Blood scalded my veins, so much hotter than shifting energy it bordered on frigid. It spilled out from the dragon's pit like a black ichor, and rage consumed me.

Fuck running.

I stopped suddenly and turned to face Fen, my eyes burning with fury. I dropped low at the last minute and tripped Fen with his own momentum. My wolf seized the moment, and cast me aside reeling as he pounced on Fen with my body. My human mind couldn't even process the melee of biting, snapping, and clawing as I fought to regain control, until something broke.

My rage spilled into the wolf, and it ignited into a bloodlust frenzy that surged in a billowing cloud of power. It blinded me to pain and poured steel strength into my muscles, as the snow around us evaporated into steam.

Somehow, Fen managed to roll on top of me and tried to pin me again, all amusement gone from his face. He looked afraid. I defied his dominance and opened his cheek when I lashed out with my teeth.

The taste of blood sparked on my tongue, and the beast I'd become fought even harder. Darkness descended over me, and I knew only brief flashes of image and sensation, all connection to my body lost.

Fen…

Images of red gore, streaming blood…

No…

"No! Jimmy! Jimmy, wake up!"

Cold lifeless gray eyes, a mist of red… NO!

"Jimmy! Calm down; it's over! It's over now—LOOK AT ME!"

Something shook me, and my unseeing eyes locked onto Fen's face. He straddled me and pinned my arms to my sides while his eyes bored into mine with sadness and—fear?

Something hot and wet dripped onto my face, and my gaze drifted from his worried eyes to the angry red slash on his face that bled down his jaw and dripped onto my face, the dark scent of copper lush in the air. I stared at the wound as madness gnawed at me.

I made that… I made that out of a hate he didn't deserve; what have I done?

That wasn't the wolf; it was… it was *me!*

The images and desires that had only moments ago consumed me flashed through my mind again and the world swam. I twisted out of Fen's grasp and rolled over as I dry-heaved a few times on the snowy grass. I heard the others run toward us as Fen spoke softly.

"You've bottled so much rage inside you… When the wolf moves from the deep, sometimes the doors to other things are opened as well. Monsters we couldn't destroy, so we captured and buried them in the darkness."

"It wasn't the wolf. It was me…" my voice was thick and raw, "It was all me… I'm so sorry Fen… So sorry…"

You don't belong here.

I crawled over to one of the huge pine trees and curled up under the sheltering boughs while I cried and choked on shame in the spiny bed of fallen needles and cones. The others caught up with Fen, and their blurry shapes moved in the veil of snow until my eyes closed

I felt so weary, tired and weary of trying to force myself to live a life I could find no worth in.

Your father didn't want you, why should anyone else?

I drew back from the world, until I heard snow crunch underfoot and familiar scents filled the space under the tree.

"Are you done sulking?" Loki's voice was soft, but there was an edge to it. I opened my eyes, and their blurry shapes came into focus silhouetted against the moonlit gray of the sky. "Get out of there, the night's still young, and I'm in no mood for a pity party."

Fen and Geri grabbed me and pulled me up partway onto my feet as they dragged me out; but when they touched me, their energy poured into me and stirred the wolf. I held onto Geri's arm and gasped as a sharp pain blossomed in my leg. My back spasmed and arched as my knees gave out and I fell to the ground while my mouth gaped in a soundless scream.

My nerves caught fire and my body twisted and turned, like it was trying to split its seams and remake itself. The wolf inside me fought for freedom, but his frustration turned to anger as he hit an invisible wall.

Cool soft hands touched my feverish forehead and anchored me, and I looked up into Loki's eyes. "Shh, it'll fade in a moment; you just have too much shifting energy right now, we'll help you." She closed her eyes and breathed out; as she did a calm current settled beneath the chaos and pushed it out. Fen and Geri touched Loki's arms and the air around us vibrated.

Loki pulled her hands away and shook them like they were numb, while Geri bounced from foot to foot. "Holy shit, you're powerful," she said, "but you've got a lot of gunk you need to work out of your system. And we *all* have a lot to learn…" She shot Fen a dark look, and then shrugged, "So, I'm afraid you're stuck with us whether you like it or not."

"After everything I've done, you still want me?"

"More than ever," Fen replied, "You're Pack. Your wolf waking up had little to do with that ticking bomb inside you. As bad as you think this was, it could have been so much worse. We're fine, this'll heal in no time." He waved a hand past his bloody cheek and rolled his eyes. "You have the most healing to do, you didn't realize how deeply infected the wound was."

"Um," Geri started, as he pulled his sleeve back and looked at his watch. "I hate to be the bearer of bad news, but my mom wanted me home by two."

"You're not sleeping over? It's his first time!" Loki whined while I asked, "But I thought we were spending the night?"

"You are…" Fen said as he and Loki chuckled.

"…But not at Geri's." I finished for him.

"I'll take you over, but I can't stay, I'm already late," Geri muttered and looked at his watch again. "Besides, I have a raid in the morning too…"

"A raid?" I frowned.

"World of WarCrack." Loki volunteered, "Geri's addicted to video games"

"It looks like it's time for us to leave anyway," Fen muttered and pointed toward the parking lot, where red and blue lights flashed in the snow. Fen seemed to enjoy sneaking just a little too much, and none of the officers saw the four shadows that slipped past them and quietly drove away.

We sat in silence, each lost in our own thoughts while Geri's windshield wipers squeaked a gallant losing war against the snow.

"Um, Loki? What did you do back there?"

"Oh, I just used a little vampire trick I picked up. You had too much energy, we had too little; I just sorta—" she made a slurping sound "Drained it outta you and shared it around. Kinda like how Fen woke up your wolf actually…"

"It wasn't me…" Fen muttered.

"What do you mean?" Loki turned and looked at him over the back of her seat.

"I wasn't the one who bit him, it was Lupa. She—took over my body. I thought I was dreaming, I couldn't remember exactly what happened."

Loki stared at him for a moment, "Has she ever done that before?"

He shook his head, looking for a moment just as confused as the rest of us. "Never."

We fell silent; I didn't even know where to begin to process everything that just happened. The thoughts that I was important, that I was wanted, that I was powerful; they were so foreign to me. I'd been nothing my whole life; I didn't know how to be anything else.

Geri dropped Loki off at the mouth of a driveway that disappeared into the snow, the soft glow of her house lights beyond the curtain of snow. Then he drove us few blocks through a twisting maze of streets and let Fen and I out. His taillights disappeared into the white dark, and I followed Fen toward another irrigation ditch. Fen walked off the edge as though it wasn't even there.

What the hell do you think this is, Underworld?

He disappeared from sight until I reached the edge and looked down. Fen hadn't slowed at all and already faded from sight into the snow. I hurried down after him, and slipped on a patch of leaves, which dumped me on my ass in the snow. I followed his footprints as I trotted to catch up with him.

"Do you mind telling me where we're going?"

"It's a surprise." He smiled over his shoulder, and I blinked compulsively when snow landed on my eyelashes. I wiped my nose on the sleeve of my coat and watched clumps of snowflakes land in Fen's blonde hair until his body heat melted them. I caught myself staring, so I looked down at his footprints instead.

We came to a gap in the hedge along the ditch's rim, and without warning, Fen leapt up and disappeared through the hole. I stood and stared at it a moment in shock. The wall wasn't as high here, but it was still a good six feet up, and while Fen seemed to be capable of ridiculous feats, I had no such confidence. I took a few steps back and then leapt up as high as I could toward the gap.

I performed an ugly parody of a swan dive and belly-flopped hard onto the cold ground. I coughed and fought to catch my breath again as I pulled my knees beneath me and crawled the rest of the way through the thick hedge into a scrubby little patch of brush and trees. The foliage overhead blocked most of the snow, but my hands chilled as they shuffled through the fallen leaves. My nose told me that cows were nearby, and—something else— something familiar…

"Hey pup." Loki's voice surprised me, and I followed the sound to where Fen stood next to a dark blob on the ground with her grinning face. She rested her head on her arms while the rest of her seemed to disappear into the ground. "Took you long enough."

"But—" I stuttered, "I thought Geri took you home?"

"He did, I have to keep up appearances."

"She just sneaks out her window whenever she wants to," Fen muttered as he pulled off his coat.

"Yeah, my parents totally didn't know what they were getting themselves into when they gave me a room on the first floor," she laughed.

"But, where are we?"

"The Pack's den," Loki replied from her hole.

Hm, I didn't know we had a den. "That's useful, but where are we?" I repeated.

"My back yard." Loki crawled out and stretched her arms over her head.

I crouched and looked around. "You live here? Won't your parents see us?" I hissed.

She turned and pointed out over the pasture that spilled up to the edge of the thicket. "Do you see the house over there?"

"No…" I muttered, puzzled.

"Exactly. Even if they were still awake and looked right over here, they couldn't see us. We have privacy fence to keep the neighbors at bay, and the only other way in is the way you came," she explained while Fen rolled up his jacket and pushed it ahead of him as he crawled down the hole, head first.

"Down the hole with you." Loki nodded her head toward it. "You might want to take off your coat if you don't want to get stuck halfway."

"Oh, um, okay." I unzipped my coat and the greedy air sucked all my body heat out within seconds. I wadded my coat up like Fen did, and yipped when a sharp pain stung my butt. I turned and Loki smiled at me, feigned innocence written on her face.

"What happened?" She smiled, and her emerald eyes shone in the night. I remembered the way she looked twirling in the snow, and any sharp words or acts of retribution I'd planned fell from my head. I had to look away before my blush betrayed me, and could only shake my head as I turned back toward the den.

Bracken and twigs formed an arch just barely large enough to crawl through, the snow had settled into a thick frosting on top. I pushed my coat ahead of me, and found that the tunnel floor just a few feet in was dry. When I looked up, a framework of branches arched over the earthen part of the tunnel, and I saw patches of blue behind them, probably a tarp to keep the den dry. From the outside, it'd just looked like a mound of sticks and field discards. The tunnel curved before it opened up into a larger chamber.

I smelled Fen and heard him move, but light was pretty much nonexistent. Even the efficiency of my wolf's sight was powerless when there simply *was no light to see with*. Helplessly disoriented, I groped my way along one of the walls of the chamber. About halfway around, my fingers encountered warm flesh; some part of Fen obviously. Which part I had *no* idea.

Too late, my mind whirled down dangerous paths. I apologized, and Fen grunted an acceptance as I scuttled away from him as quickly as the cramped space would allow until I hit the cold earth wall on the other side of the chamber.

"Okay, so, new guy here. What do we do in here? What do we sleep on?" I asked.

"Each other," Loki's deadpan came from the darkness as she crawled in, and it took a moment for it to sink in.

"What!" I yelped and my eyes bulged in the dark.

"It's part of the exercise," Fen answered this time, annoyed.

"Relax pup, nothing kinky happens. We depend on each other for warmth and reinforce our bonds through touch." Loki's tone was subdued, "You might be uncomfortable at first, but you'll get used to it. Just try to trust your wolf, okay?"

Trust something with no real form, that shouldn't exist, while dogpiling with two other people. Okay, sure, no problem.

I kept my mental grumblings to myself, and gathered my coat under my head like a pillow. Exhaustion caught up to me with a vengeance, and I almost nodded off; but woke up shivering with the frigid dirt floor dug into my skin and drank away my body heat. My sweater was a pathetic barrier against the cold. I shifted and wriggled for what seemed like hours, struggling to find a spot that was—if not comfortable—at least *less* uncomfortable.

"Jus' settle down and go to sleep," Fen grumbled out of the darkness and I lifted my head to look toward the sound, not that it did any good.

"I can't, I'm freezing my ass off here," I muttered between chattering teeth and let my head thud on the dirt floor.

Loki giggled, "I think I just heard his butt cheek fall off."

"You're a wolf right?" Fen sighed, obviously sleepy, like the cold night had no effect on him.

I growled with irritation, "Workin' on it; of course that's if I don't die of hypothermia first."

"Are wolves cold in the snow?" he prompted.

"Of course not, they have fur – *I don't!*"

"Then grow fur." He said, matter-of-factly. I rolled my eyes in the darkness, even though he couldn't see it.

"Oh! Piece of cake; one furry motherfucker comin' right up! Dude, not even *you* can shapeshift."

"Obviously I don't mean literal fur, use your spirit wolf's fur to keep you warm. If you're really as powerful at Loki thinks you are, you should be able to bring enough of your wolf into the physical world to keep you warm. It's no different than if you feel claws or ears you shouldn't have. She and I can do it, let's see if you can…"

As soon as he mentioned the ears, I felt them twitch, as if responding to him. I closed my eyes and focused on my ears.

"Remember," Fen murmured, "Wolves have two coats. Their inner coat is downy, warm, and gray. The outer guard hairs are longer and coarser, their oils act like a raincoat and they're what give you your colors."

I imagined fur flowing over me from the tips of my ears. First a thick beige-gray undercoat and then longer black hairs sprouted up along my spine and washed out to the tip of my tail. I felt my wolf's shifting energy push through my body and fill me up like a hand filling a glove. I shuddered as my skin prickled, and heat crawled over my body in the wake of the prickling fur. My ears and face had been almost numb, but now they flushed with heat. I could feel *it*, my wolf, just beneath the surface like it was finally growing comfortable inside me. And it wasn't trying to take over this time.

Every time I almost fell asleep I lost it and woke up shivering. I heard somebody move behind me. Warm hands startled me when they touched my back and wrapped around my waist.

Loki's smell grew stronger and the small soft hands didn't feel at all like Fen's.

"Get over here, pup," she mumbled and pulled me closer. Fen's warm scent grew and I heard him breathing, already deep asleep despite the cold. Loki coaxed me to squirm up closer, and wrapped her arms around my waist and her body touched along the length of my back.

"Just relax and go to sleep," she whispered, her breath a wash of heat that bloomed where her cheek pressed against my shoulder. I closed my eyes, but still couldn't sleep.

Too much had happened tonight, too fast; my mind refused to settle down and my muscles locked up from trying not to disturb them or touch anything I wasn't supposed to, despite how much I wanted to.

I sighed with frustration and inhaled a nose-full of their scent. Their smell stirred the wolf, and his fur flowed back over me like flames over a log—I even felt a tail lying on the ground behind me. As the wolf ascended in my mind, it pulled my mind from unfamiliar bodies, to friendly smells.

These were my friends now, this was my Pack.

I felt Loki's face move into a smile, "Thaz more like't," she muttered groggily, and then sighed and fell back asleep. This time, I went with her.

CHAPTER 6 — FORBIDDEN

The sounds and smells of the nighttime forest surrounded me as I slipped along dark forest paths. The rich scents of alder and pine wove a tapestry in the moist air, while the layer of cedar needles under my paws padded my journey. The place reminded me of the forests my mother took me to near Coeur D'Alene, in a different life, in a different body...

I came into a field and saw a man playing a flute while wolves sang with him. He looked so much like me, but much older; with silvering hair and deep creases around strong dark eyes that seemed to look into my soul.

When I approached him, he stopped playing and turned toward me. He spoke to me in a strange language I'd never heard before.

"Chitskhuy hnt'lane', ɫe e hntsetkhw, kuchnek'we'et, kwn-qheminch."

As he spoke, ravens flooded the sky, blotting out the moonlight until the world went as black as their feathers...

The crow's cawing seeped into my brain and stirred it from warm soft oblivion. Something sighed near me and I cracked one dry eye open. In a rush, the prior night returned to me.

I opened my other eye and struggled to focus as I blinked the bleariness out. Fen, Loki, and I were curled up in a hodgepodge tangle of limbs. Fen used my calf as a pillow while my face rested on Loki's back. The den glowed a thin blue as the sun filtered through the tarp overhead.

Holy shit, I'd just slept with and girl and a guy, I thought, and immediately winced at the duel meaning. We were all clothed, nothing happened; we were fine.

Still, oddly fitting for a freak like you…

I told the spiteful voice in my head to shut up, and the moment faded. I closed my eyes and relished the soft warmth of Loki's body on my cheek; I'd never felt anything like it. Their familiar smell was almost intoxicating. I felt my wolf inside, content and comfortable inside my skin, a slight smile on his muzzle.

Cark, cark, cark!

I winced as the cawing continued relentlessly, and moment later Fen's face shifted against my leg as he mumbled, "I wish he'd shut up…" Loki hummed in agreement, and we unraveled ourselves. The den felt warm, and we all stretched and popped various joints. Everyone's hair stuck up at odd angles, and we looked more like a trio of anime characters than a pack of werewolves. Loki yawned, long and deep, and Fen and I joined her almost like a howl.

"Oh hey, I forgot to tell you. My folks are going to Colorado Springs this morning. If they're already gone, do you guys wanna come in?"

"Sure." I moaned as I stretched, Fen just nodded as he yawned so deeply his tongue curled.

"'Kay, I'll go check." She grabbed her coat and grunted as she worked her way out of the den.

Fen and I sat in silence while we dozed and tried to clear away the funk of sleep, until I muttered, "She really is beautiful isn't she?" more to myself than to him.

I heard Fen shift behind me, "Yeah, she is… But dating within the Pack is forbidden."

"Huh? Why?"

"The same reason you don't date coworkers. We're bound to these people; and if a relationship goes sour, it can hurt the entire Pack… I know what you're going through though, that girl flirts easier than most folks breathe."

"Oh… oh well. She's way out of my league anyway." It hurt, but it made sense. I couldn't control my body, or my heart, but at least I knew my limits. I snuck a glance over my shoulder at Fen, stretched out across the ground, facing away from me.

He's not exactly hard on the eyes either…

I flinched away from the unwelcome thought. Footsteps crunched at the entrance, and Loki called down to us, "Yeah, they already left. Come on inside, I'll make you breakfast." I shoved my insecurity and self-loathing down into the dragon's hole and caught myself on every damn stick as I followed Fen up the tunnel.

I squinted into the blinding light as I emerged into a dazzling world of white. Everywhere, crystals of ice flashed like a sea of white diamonds, unmarred across the entire field to Loki's house. The sky was bright blue, and the warm autumn sun had already melted through the snow where it was thin. That first breath of air felt so clean, as if the snow had scrubbed everything foul from it. Fen zipped his jacket up and we followed Loki around the glittering expanse, the big ridge of mountain along the edge of town loomed close by, frosted and bright.

Her house looked like a big ranch, with a tall peaked front that seemed entirely made of windows. We kicked the snow off our shoes as we stepped through the back door, then pulled them off altogether and set them on the tiles by the door. The sun poured in through a huge window over the sink and warmed the tile floor. Loki scratched her mussed hair while she opened the fridge and looked inside. "What do you guys want to eat?"

"Whatever's easy," Fen shrugged.

"I'm fine with cereal; I don't want to be a bother."

Loki threw her hands up, "What's the world coming to? A girl offers to make breakfast, and they want to eat cereal…"

Fen laughed. "If cereal's too hard, we could pick something else," he teased.

"How about we start with some coffee and work from there?" I mumbled around a yawn.

"Oh damn, I *must* be out of it if I forgot coffee." She stretched her back while she padded across the room in multi-colored socks and set up the coffeemaker.

We rifled through the fridge until we came up with ingredients for biscuits and gravy. I put the biscuits into the oven and sipped coffee while I poked the sausage around a skillet, half awake and yawning, until Loki snatched the spatula out of my hand. "Hey!"

"Don't make me maul you," she growled and took over the skillet, "this is my kitchen damnit."

We dished up our plates and took them with us into the cavernous living room. Raw log rafters met at the peak of the two story vaulted ceiling, while windows covered the entire front wall and flooded the room with sunlight. A blackened fireplace dominated the back wall and the room was decorated with western ranch décor; it even had a chandelier made out of an old wagon wheel.

We settled into armchairs and dug into our food. I felt like I hadn't eaten in days, probably from all the energy we'd burned last night. Fen sighed with contentment, "Damn, I wish *every* full moon had a breakfast like that…"

"Hell yeah, that was delicious," Loki moaned as she stretched over the arm of her chair. "Geri has no idea what he missed."

"I like the decorations, but it's weird, they just don't suit you; it's like we walked into a stranger's house." I said to Loki.

She snorted, "You can thank my mom for that. I try to spend as little time in here as possible. It's not as stifling as Geri's house, only a museum could be that cold; you'll understand when we visit him sometime. This living room isn't supposed to be *lived* in. It's to keep my mom busy and keep her mind off the ranch."

"What ranch?" I asked.

"We used to raise livestock out in Montana, but the market shriveled and we had to sell. My dad got a psychology degree; he does marriage counseling and stuff like that. They still like to pretend this is the old west though; he'll never give up his rattle-snake boots or his cowboy hats; and mom... well she *decorates*." She swept a hand across the room. I looked around and noticed the predictability of the decorations; every piece was tilted and tweaked until it was perfect. An image popped into my head, and a grin slowly crawled across my face. When Loki asked what was so funny, I just smiled wider.

"I just can't get the image of you as a cowgirl out of my head; black eyeliner, combat boots, chaps, and a cowboy hat..." I tried not to laugh, but Fen snorted into his hand and we came undone.

"That mental image is priceless!" Fen howled as he rolled with laughter.

"Y'all suck!" she cried and stomped her foot, then marched over to a door under the stairs and wrenched it open to expose a Cradle of Filth poster tacked up inside. "*Here!* Is *this* better?"

"Yes! Much!" I said, still laughing, "But did you have to say 'y'all'?"

"You jackass!" She yelled as she charged and tackled me onto the couch. I pinned her arms down and tickled her while she struggled to bite me. Fen jumped out of his seat and pulled me off her a little rougher than necessary.

"Consider that payback for slapping my ass last night," I panted.

Loki glanced at Fen and paused for a moment, then laughed; "Fine… Truce…!" We helped her up off the floor and she inspected her arm, "Ow, you bruised my elbow you asshole."

"You totally started it." I laughed and shook my head.

"Sorry Jimmy, but I think it's time for us to go…" Fen said as he walked back into the kitchen for his shoes. I glanced at my watch and saw that it was already almost noon. Shit, my parents would be worried, and I didn't want them calling around. Plus I still had homework to finish for both Mr. Heinen and Mr. Decker. I hadn't told my parents so I could go out last night.

Fen and I pulled our shoes back on and Loki walked us out. I hugged her goodbye, and while she hugged Fen, I grabbed a handful of snow and nailed her with it, accidentally catching Fen too. That sparked a brief—but intense—battle, until Loki and I tackled Fen to the ground and stuffed snow down the back of his shirt. While he danced around and tried to shake it all out, Loki shoved a snowball down the back of his pants. He howled and tried to evict it down a pant leg, while still trying to get the snow out of his shirt, and Loki and I almost hurt ourselves laughing.

He finally gave up and glared at us as a dark wet spot spread out from the inside of his crotch. We were all damp, flushed, and out of breath; but Fen and I waved and trudged through the snow to the street, while in the back acre that damn bird still cawed its freaking head off.

I *really* didn't want to go home, but I couldn't afford to miss a single assignment; my grades were finally coming up a little. I fabricated a story for my parents, and waved goodbye to Fen as I walked up the steps.

He called my name, and I turned around just in time to catch a snowball with my face.

My parents were, of course, *quite* curious as to how I got all banged up. I just told them I'd tripped into a bush while we were walking to Geri's. I'd done it before…

I rubbed at one of the numerous knots in my back as I sat in the art room and pushed my piece of charcoal over the paper with blackened fingers. Overall I felt like I'd been shoved through a meat grinder, but Fen seemed fine, except for the scab on one cheek that didn't look quite so huge in the daylight. I winced whenever one of the cuts on my hands reopened and the charcoal dust worked its way inside.

Mrs. Ashcroft made her rounds through the room while Hendrix played on a tiny boom box in the corner. She stopped and peeked over my shoulder, the scent of lavender gave her away before her voice did.

"Your composition is really good Jimmy, but you're so far behind. Are you sure you can finish this by the due date?" she muttered by my ear. "You know I can't give you points for what you *wanted* to do, only what you *have* completed."

"I know, I just…" Exasperated, I rubbed my face. "I guess I underestimated how long this would take, and there's not enough time left." I looked down at my desk and felt foolish and deflated as she brought up the very issue that'd been bothering me. "And there's not enough time to start over now."

"You know… I don't usually do this, but if you need to, we can arrange for extra work-time after school. Would that help?" Her voice dropped low, and she sounded hesitant.

My hopes blossomed. "Yeah, that'd be perfect! I'll have to okay it with my parents, but I'm sure they won't mind." A grin spread across my face as I looked up at her, and she snorted with laughter.

"Great! Fen, you're welcome too of course." Fen looked up briefly to nod his thanks, and then he snorted too when he looked at me. "Jimmy, you might want to wash your face…"

"Huh? Oh crap!" I looked down at the blackened hands that I'd just rubbed my face with. She followed me over to the sink as I washed up.

"You know Jimmy, I've been pleasantly surprised by your work since you arrived here. What are your plans for college?"

My balloon of hope deflated as soon as her words were out. "I don't have any. My GPA isn't high enough, and besides…" I sighed, and admitted something I hadn't even told my parents, "I have no idea what I want to do. My only natural skills are art and music, so I'm pretty much doomed to a lifetime of 'would you like fries with that?'"

She laughed, "Well, may I suggest something?" she asked and I braced for the inevitable college sales pitch. "Before you resign yourself to a rewarding career in fast food, maybe take a year or two off to figure it out?

"It's not like the world will end if you don't go straight to college after graduation. If you're not ready, I think it'd be more mature to take time and figure out what you want to do. Don't bulldoze in with no path or plan; only to drop out and become so mired in debt that you'd be unable to return for years, if ever."

"Why do I get the feeling there's a really big story behind all this?" I asked and she laughed.

"Just the story of my life." She rolled her eyes, "I'll spare you, but the abridged version is that I went to school because my father expected me to, regardless of what I wanted. When he saw my grades at midterm he blew his top. Dad cut my funding, kicked me out of the house. All of a sudden I was eighteen years old, homeless, schoolless, and desperately looking for a job with almost no experience.

"It took me nearly a decade to pull myself together. I slipped in and out of drugs and alcohol, jobs came and went, but eventually I found my husband and we cleaned each other up. We fought tooth and nail, worked two jobs and barely ate for six years so I could become a teacher."

Her confession made me a little uncomfortable, but wheels began to turn inside my head.

"I tell you what Jimmy, this high school culture is a lie. Prom queen? Team captain? The real world doesn't care." she muttered conspiratorially, and then winked. "Don't think about the paycheck. You have talent, and if you're smart, you can make it work. You're not meant for a cage. Just... think about it, okay?" She smiled and moved from the wall.

"Okay..." This woman had just contradicted almost everything my parents and counselors had pounded into my head; and I couldn't help thinking that maybe it was just crazy enough to work...

I called Mom during lunch, and she cleared me to stay. I met up with the Pack at Fen's locker after the bell, but Geri and I left Fen and Loki chatting at his locker.

We threaded our way through the hallway and a strange look came over Geri's face. I asked him what was wrong, but he just waved me off and said it was nothing. "I dunno, I just thought things would be different once you came," he muttered and left me at the Art room door. I felt sad he didn't think he could talk to me. I tried the door but it was locked, so I knocked and a few seconds later Mrs. Ashcroft peeked around the door.

"I'm glad you could come, you got permission then?" She stepped aside to let me in.

I nodded, "Yeah, I knew I would. Mr. Spritari put the fear of suspension into my mom, so the grade card works both ways."

"Well, I'm sure your parents appreciate it regardless." *Mom, maybe, John... fat chance.*

"Hey, I um. I wanted to thank you; for giving me extra time and... for what you said earlier."

She smiled, showing the lines in her tan cheeks. "No problem, some of us just need a little more time."

"Um, I meant about the college thing," I tried to clarify.

"I know. So, what do you think would happen if someone *didn't* go to college right away?"

"Their parents would be disappointed, their friends would mock them, and they'd go nowhere in life." I smiled without humor and she closed her eyes as she shook her head.

"That's what they want you to think; those schools, this entire culture," she said, weary, and then looked at me again. "The colleges want your money as soon and as much as possible, and they don't care if you waste it as long as they get it. So they encourage this..." She twirled her hand as she searched for the right words "'False Destiny' that leads so many young minds to ruin."

Her less-than-shining endorsement of higher education shocked me. Every other teacher out there seemed completely committed to the cause, and now this woman had contradicted them all twice in a single day.

I think she'd just become my favorite teacher *ever*.

I sighed. "My parents have been tripping over themselves trying to get me to enroll or choose a career, *any* career. But I think they've finally realized the futility of it."

"Well, you have to ask them, and yourself; *who* are you going to school for? Are you going because *you* want to, or because your parents expect you to? Is it in *your* best interest to go right away, or should you wait and get a bit more experience under your belt? Do everyone a favor and put your parents on the spot; make sure both of you know that they can't live vicariously through you. If they're decent parents, they'll encourage your happiness over their own ambition."

She glanced at her watch, "Shoot, I need to leave; and there are some things I need to tell you. First of all; the halls are closed after three-thirty, and there shouldn't be any students wandering around. Second; the door opens from the inside, but it locks automatically; so once you leave the room, for the bathroom or whatever; you might as well just go home."

"Would I still get in trouble, even though you gave me permission to be here?" I asked puzzled.

"Nothing serious, but I'd recommend just avoiding the whole fuss. I'd be reprimanded, you would have a mark put on your record, your parents would be called, Mr. Spritari would be pissed; just a big unnecessary mess, so it's best if you just don't get caught." She winked, "I'll see you tomorrow Jimmy."

"See ya," I said as she walked out, her shoes clicked in the hall until the door closed behind her.

I pulled my drawing out and there was a knock at the door. Nervous, I walked over and pulled it open, expecting to see Officer Jenson there to arrest me or something. Instead, Fen shoved past me without a word.

"Jeezus Fen, what crawled up your ass and died?" I closed the door behind him and returned to my desk.

"Nothing, it's none of your business…" he snapped. I felt a coil of rage begin to unfurl and the hair rose on my neck.

"Well, you're snapping at *me* for it; so either it *is* my business, or stop taking it out on me!"

He paused a moment then muttered an apology as he touched his head to the wall. I picked up a dizzying mix of emotions from him, too many to identify any single one. I had no idea why I felt them, I had most my life, but they seemed to be getting clearer and stronger with my wolf. Mom called it empathy; I called it a pain in my ass. I sighed and tried to relax the muscles in my shoulders. I opened my supplies box and selected a fresh piece of charcoal, "So, do you want to tell me what has you so wound up?"

"No…" he said simply, but without malice.

"Okay." I didn't push him, I didn't need to. We worked in silence as the echoing footsteps and muffled voices that leaked through the door dwindled until all that could be heard was the *scritch scritch* and occasional squeak of charcoal on paper. I just wished I knew what had the Pack all riled up, it might just be coming down from the full moon high, but I didn't know for sure, this was all too new.

"You know how werewolves in the movies are usually 'cursed'?" Fen muttered out of the blue.

"Uh, yeah?"

"Well, the movies are mostly bullshit, but that's one part that's only half wrong. It's not the way they make it though. You know what it is to be truly cursed?"

I made an encouraging grunt as I shaded.

"Some shifters never fully integrate themselves, so they never learn how to control their shifts, or even remember them sometimes. For the fortunate, it just fades away, but for some… Shifting stops being a gift, and becomes a curse.

"Some get so wrapped up in the phenomena and forget about the spiritual aspect, and it dies inside them." Fen sighed and shook his head, "Or they train their inner animal like a pet, feeding them anger, rage, and violence. I suspect that's what caused a lot of the 'evil werewolf' mythology in Europe. If they truly believed they were possessed by the devil to consume human flesh, by golly that's what they did!"

Fen rambled, but he was calming down so I just listened as best I could while I worked, nodding and agreeing where appropriate. He grew quiet, and an expression washed over his face so quickly I couldn't quite catch it.

"There's another way though, it happens when you least expect it—" His eyes grew distant, like he was watching a memory inside his own head. "—and strikes where it hurts most. If a shifter progresses too fast, or pushes too hard, their energy spikes higher than they can handle and they break. We all push ourselves to become more powerful and integrated with our animal selves, but there is a process, a natural evolution. Otherwise we might lose control and hurt someone; not knowing any better." Fen sighed and rubbed his temples. "The fear, the guilt… it'd drive you mad."

He looked at me, his face carefully guarded but something haunted in his eyes. "It's important to realize that you and your animal are the same; different aspects of the same soul. Not something to break and enslave, nor something to allow to dominate you."

His tangent didn't seem so random anymore. "So wait, do you mean *I* almost ended up 'cursed'? First, that day outside when I forgot the necklace, and then again the other night?"

He stared at his paper, "Your wolf was already too strong, and he almost seized control from you twice now. Thankfully, you're made of tougher stuff than any of us expected." He laughed without humor. "And boy did Loki light up my hide for pushing you so hard. I got carried away, and I'm sorry."

Ah, well that explained his pleasant mood earlier.

"There's so much I need to teach you," he muttered, "I promise Jimmy, I won't let you become cursed." The intensity in his eyes left me speechless, so I just nodded and went back to work.

"Jimmy."

"What?" I looked back at Fen, but he looked confused.

"I didn't say anything."

"No, you just said my name."

Fen looked at me like I had lobsters crawling out my ears, "Um, no, I didn't…"

"Oh…" Great, now I was hearing shit too, maybe it was already too late and I was losing it.

Sounded likely.

We stayed in the art room almost every day after school. I used the extra freedom to my full advantage. On days we didn't have any extra work to do, we snuck down the alley to Fen's house to study.

His place was tiny, a little two bedroom home with cracked stucco and a splinter-prone porch that eerily reminded me of the house in Coeur D'Alene I grew up in, and it was just a couple blocks down Wolf Road from mine. I could count on one hand the number of times I saw his mother; usually it was just a quick 'hello' and an exhausted smile as she shuffled through the living room in her scrubs to try and get some rest before her next double shift.

It reminded me of the way things were with my mom back in Idaho when I was young. Fen kept the house operating; he took care of the chores, and tried to make dinner for his mom before she got home. I helped him whenever he would let me; the guy had a stubborn streak a mile wide.

"I was raised by a nurse too, I know how it is," would usually shut him up though.

In truth, the similarity between us kinda creeped me out. Similar houses, raised by single mothers who put themselves through nursing school to provide for us. Both trained to shop on a slim budget and pinch pennies into plates before the age of ten. Neither of us had a dad. I couldn't begrudge him being enamored with John, but I couldn't quite stamp out the jealousy either.

It was a good thing I had the extra time available; Fen didn't just help me study for school, he was also bent on educating me in Werewolfery 101. Sometimes Fen would try to stuff so much into my brain that I would be reeling half an hour in. What made it harder was that this... *noise* kept fading in and out of the background, distracting me, like a fuzzy cloud of voices. I frustrated myself when I couldn't quite understand something, but the amused look in Fen's eyes made it worthwhile when I got it.

He explained the types of shifts that were—potentially—possible, and I felt like I needed a notepad to jot down everything as he spouted it off. My brain just about liquefied trying to keep up with all the jargon about possession shifting and bilocation shifting, one of them was where your animal form went out on its own like a ghost—but which one?

A notepad probably *wouldn't* be a bad idea...

When he started rambling about the 'Therian's role', I had no clue what he meant, so I asked.

"We're technically therianthropes, not lycanthropes," he replied, his charcoal never ceasing movement. "This isn't a mental illness; we just... seem to have animal souls. There are a lot of fakes on the Internet looking for attention, but there are real Therians like us out there too. The question we all ask is why are we here? Why are we the way we are?

"It's part of the reason why I want to study ecology and wildlife biology. Being human in appearance gives me an advantage to help protect the wild from humanity. But inside I am a wolf, and think like a wolf; so I see things differently. Like an inside agent; a wolf in man's clothing." He smiled, but it wilted a little at the edges.

"I have to find a way to use what I am. We're made this way for a purpose, we just have to figure out *why* we walk between worlds; but can never belong in any of them. A freak even among freaks… Only in other shifters like ourselves can we find even a moment's brief reprieve from the isolation, and yet even that is so often denied us…" His tone grew sour; but he quickly masked his expression.

"The shamans of the world… they know better than anyone else what it is like… They also walk between worlds, between the spirit and the flesh. They journey into the Lowerworld and bring back spirits to heal and make the world whole again."

"The Lowerworld? That place where I saw Lupa?"

"Yeah, though what you saw is just a fragment of the entire plane. The place is—literally—infinite. It's funny how much the Therian and shamanic worlds intersect, a lot of us develop shamanic skills. It's not very surprising though when you realize that most shifters have Native American heritage. It's like there's something in the blood that hasn't had the connection beaten out of it yet."

I bit my tongue. I couldn't stop myself from thinking about the man who'd knocked up my teenage mother and then disappeared into the Idaho woods. Was he like me? Did a fire-eyed wolf dwell within him as well? I shuddered and fought to suppress the wave of rage that surged through me.

It didn't matter, I would never know anyway.

He didn't want me, he didn't know anything about me. He disappeared and I would never find him. Never meet him. Never punch him in the fucking face for what he put us through—

My charcoal squeaked against the paper just before it snapped and shot across the room. Fen paused and looked at me as I reached into the box with grubby fingers for another piece, but my expression never slipped for a moment. He took a second to collect his thoughts before he continued, but I couldn't focus on his words as my mind spun off onto its own tangent.

Unexpected possibilities had stirred and now my mind flew over deep evergreen woods, over the rolling hills of the Idaho in my mind's eye, untouched and pristine. The land looked... familiar for some reason. Especially that huge greenish blue lake, with the tall spires of rock on the shore...

"Jimmy?"

Fen pulled me out of my head just as I felt I was about to connect something important. "What?" I asked.

"I asked where you want to go for college."

"I... don't know," I muttered as Mrs. Ashcroft's words cycled through my head again. "I don't know what I want to do yet. John's willing to pay for me to go, but I just... I don't think I'm good enough to actually *do* anything. I'm not smart like you; my only talents are next to worthless." I held up my charcoal, and sighed. Once I'd said it to Mrs. Ashcroft it was easier to admit, but I hadn't tried it on my parents yet.

Fen's expression grew dark, and he was silent for a moment. His voice was soft when he spoke, and I almost didn't hear him. "I'd give anything to have your problem. I know exactly what I want to do, but I can't afford it. You have a free ride, and you don't know what to do with it."

"I'd trade you if I could." More than he knew.

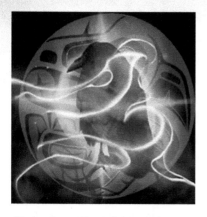

Chapter 7 – Haunted

I'd noticed it before, but after we celebrated the Blood Moon in October, the noise grew worse.

Noise. That was the only description that even came close to fitting. Just this... static inside my head. It was usually formless, but whenever I started to fall asleep random words emerged from the din; and on particularly bad nights, screams and crying. Every once in a while I heard someone speak my name and I jolted awake. Before long, I developed a state of lethargic insomnia, and I couldn't even think around the noise and the weariness. The exhaustion made me crabby, and it expressed itself in the most inopportune places.

I got a D on a math quiz, and John and I fought over it for a week. The academic probation loomed over everything in the back of my mind, and gnawed at me until I broke down and literally begged Mr. Parkman to let me do something, *anything*, for extra credit.

It was impossible not to hear how well the football team was doing on a daily—if not hourly—basis. They'd made it to the State finals, plus, the entire school was buzzing with cruel gossip about why Bo had quit the football team out of the blue a week before the big game. Mr. Parkman finally relented to my pestering, and agreed to give me some extra points for helping him and Jeremy swap out equipment from a storage shed out by the football field. I met him after school and dropped my bag off in his office. He propped the gym and hallway doors open and we loaded up all the summer gear into big carts and mesh bags.

Mr. Parkman undid the padlock on the storage shed and we started a chain-gang hauling stuff in and out through the cold autumn air while the football team ran through drills next to us on the field. Some other students sat on the bleachers and watched, mostly the team's girlfriends. Mr. Parkman stayed behind to help Jeremy wrestle with a big stack almost to the storeroom ceiling which threatened to avalanche hockey gear, so I went outside for another cart of basketballs while the team dispersed.

I heard voices approach the shed as I wheeled out my new load, but instead of Mr. Parkman, it was Jack and Malcolm walking down the track ring to where Jack's girlfriend Tabby waited on the first row of bleachers. A nasty spurt of surprise made me pause a moment, but I put my eyes on the ground and pushed past them as they sat down and watched me.

"Dude, check out the brownnoser." Malcolm sneered, and my ear swiveled toward them.

"Yeah. Hey, why aren't you out banging your Goth bitch girlfriend?" I ignored Jack as best I could and kept going. "I bet she's a real freak in the sack."

"Well, you got the freak part right…" Tabby joked, and they laughed while my face grew hot. A sick feeling welled up in my stomach as the dragon shifted inside me and I ground my teeth.

"Or—" Jack started like he'd been struck by divine genius, "Maybe he's more interested in that twink with the creepy eyes."

I walked faster and hoped they didn't see how red my face was. They chortled at each other, "Oh, I think we hit a nerve there. Hey, come over here, let's have a little chat." I heard them stand up and follow me.

My wolf growled low in my throat, but even he knew that we didn't stand much of a chance against the two of them together.

Just a little further and you can make it to the gate, maybe Mr. Parkman is coming out right now and they'll leave you alone.

"Hey, I told you to come here." I walked a little faster and heard their footsteps patter as they ran after me. I glanced over my shoulder, and panic spilled through me in an icy wave. The promise of violence was only too clear in their eyes, so I ditched the cart and bolted. I rounded the corner of the bleachers but the wind had blown the gate closed. "Fuck!"

I only slowed down for a moment, and then I drew on every bit of strength the wolf could lend me and leapt. I made it halfway and started to climb over, but a strong hand grabbed my ankle and pulled my foot out from underneath me. I biffed it hard on top of the chain-links and cried out as pain flashed through my chest and hand. Two pairs of hands pried me off the fence and threw me down on the ground. I glimpsed a white sneaker a moment before it collided with my head and I curled up to protect myself. Another kick wrenched my shoulder as a blow to my kidneys knocked the wind out of me.

Tabby screamed at them to stop just before Mr. Parkman's whistle cut through the air, shrill and painful, but welcome. Jack swore, and I heard their shoes patter as they ran away, and then the smell of rubber and sweat that defined Mr. Parkman came close.

"Jimmy, are you okay?" I looked at him, my chest cold, fighting to keep the frustrated tears inside. He hissed when he looked at me, and I finally noticed the huge crimson stain that saturated my shirt. "Can you stand?" I nodded uncertainly, and my knees wobbled. I felt cold and sick to my stomach. My hands shook as Mr. Parkman lifted one of my arms over his shoulder, and I felt so lightheaded I would have faceplanted if he hadn't.

Jeremy caught up to us and they helped me inside and had me lift up my shirt. Two ragged gashes dashed across my sternum where the top of the fence links had punctured my shirt, and a red hole pooled blood in the middle of my hand like stigmata. Jeremy called my house, and then helped clean me up with his first aid kit. The alcohol burned like hell, but I was just glad it wasn't worse.

"What happened?" Mr. Parkman asked as Jeremy scrubbed with a cotton swab and I gritted my teeth. I explained as best I could between hisses of pain. "I'll talk to the principal tomorrow, just let me take care of it…" I hoped it was Mom coming to get me, so of course it was John who walked through the door a few minutes later.

I slouched in sullen silence as he drove us home and ranted at me, but I couldn't even generate enough energy to give a damn. "These antics have got to stop Jimmy. Your mother and I can't keep dropping everything to come running every time you have a crisis. I'm supposed to meet the pastor to bid for that new church design in twenty minutes, and now I don't know if I'm going to make it in time. Money doesn't grow on trees, we *need* this contract."

"You didn't have to come get me, I would've walked home." I glowered at my distorted reflection in the window, and John's tone softened a little. My dragon moved again, like John called it by name and dangled a treat for it.

"Don't be ridiculous, I won't let you walk home looking like you were shot."

"Talk about ridiculous, you nag me about ruining your plans, but don't even give me a choice in the matter. I'll get out right now if it'd help." *And get me away from you.*

John was silent a moment, and when he spoke his voice was just a little softer. "That's not the point…"

I didn't know what the point was, and I didn't care.

I went to the school the next day with, if possible, an even worse mood than before. Mom had wrapped my hand up like a mummy, again, and the bandage she'd taped to my chest plucked hair out every time I moved.

Mr. Spritari pulled me out of Art before lunch and dragged me down to the counselor's office. Fen watched me leave with a puzzled look on his face. Mr. Spritari closed the door behind us, and walked around his cluttered desk where he steepled his fingers and stared at me.

"So Jimmy, why don't you tell me what happened after school last night?"

I swallowed nervously, and recounted events as best I could. His face remained cold and unreadable the entire time. When I finished, he looked down at his desk and took a deep breath. "Jimmy, do you remember last month when we discussed your academic probation, and I warned you that violent actions of any kind would not be tolerated?"

I swallowed again, feeling sick to my stomach, "But it wasn't my fault!"

"Look at it from my perspective Jimmy; you have a record of altercations that followed you from your previous schools. I don't know you. I know the other students involved though, who are some of our top athletes, and Jack Reinhart's father is a pillar of the community. Jack's statement indicates that you provoked him, contrary to your claims, and that you threw the first punch. His face had clearly been struck when we spoke this morning."

"But, I never touched him!" My jaw dropped open, and I sputtered with incredulous rage. Fucking small town bureaucracy. How could this be happening? I felt trapped, while the injustice of it burned inside me. "What about Mr. Parkman? He's the one that chased them off!"

"Well, yes, there is that. Coach Parkman's statement aligned with yours very closely, but he didn't see who started the fight. That's the only reason why you are not suspended yet. This is your last and only warning Jimmy. Should we need to, we will involve Officer Jenson and the police."

I gritted my teeth and nodded, my pulse throbbing in my temples as a thousand things I wanted to say raced through my mind.

"Fine, you are dismissed."

I stood up and turned to leave, but a thought struck me and I turned back to him. "By the way Mr. Spritari, before you default the blame to me, you should talk to a kid in my gym class named Doug. Ask him about Jack's character…"

I fought the urge to slam his door as I left, and as I walked back toward the art room when the lunch bell rang. I tracked down Fen and the Pack, a felt some of the sick feeling ebb. Loki made the mistake of asking me what happened, and I ranted about it almost all the way through lunch until the bell rang and the sick feeling returned.

Nervous, I walked into PE, but Jack and Malcolm weren't there as Jeremy passed out the final. Though, judging from the dark looks a few of the students threw my way; I guessed the rumor mill was going full speed. I saw Doug smirking behind them; the hair over his eye couldn't hide his vindictive glee as he nodded at me.

As we all left the locker room, I heard yelling in Mr. Parkman's office near the locker room door, but the blinds were down so I couldn't see who was in there. I walked most of the way to English before I realized I'd left my textbook in the gym locker.

Swearing under my breath, I let Mr. Decker know what was going on before I doubled back through the emptying hallways. I slipped silently past Mr. Parkman's door, the voices inside had quieted to a murmur, and walked through the deserted locker room. Most of the overhead lights had been turned off, and dark slanted shadows stretched across the dim lockers. I undid the padlock and grabbed my textbook, and then I heard Mr. Parkman's door open and footsteps squeaked on the tiles as people walked in.

I glanced around the corner of the lockers just as Jack led Mr. Parkman and an older man over to his locker. "When you're done cleaning it out, leave the padlock on my desk." Mr. Parkman said, before he turned and left me stranded in the locker room with Jack and the other man, who I assumed was Jack's dad.

Aw shit…

Please, don't see me…

A cool clinging feeling crawled over me, like when I hid in the tree my first Full Moon, but much stronger. The fluorescent bulbs overhead flickered erratically, and I swallowed the lump in my throat. John would disembowel me and hang me with my own intestines if I got in trouble again so soon, and Mr. Spritari would probably watch with a bag of popcorn.

I fought the flicker of panic and braced myself to wait them out.

As soon as Mr. Parkman was out of earshot, the older man glanced around the locker room to see if they were alone. The silence felt loaded as his eyes swept past my hiding spot, but he didn't seem to notice me. I closed my eyes and let out a breath I hadn't realized I was holding, and then jumped as something slammed into the lockers. My eyes snapped open and I bit down on my tongue.

The man pinned Jack to the lockers by his throat. Jack's face turned red as he choked. "What were you thinking boy? You weren't thinking at all. Typical... Pathetic..."

I didn't know what to do. I froze, while Jack struggled to choke out the words, "Dad, please!"

Jack's father released him, and he sucked in a ragged breath. "Look at me boy. I said look at me!" He lifted Jack's chin with one hand and then backhanded him across the face. "Can't you do anything right?"

Jack pushed his father away, his face livid and puffy while he panted for air and held his neck.

"Oh, so now you're a tough guy, Jack? You're a big man? C'mon boy, give me your best shot." He goaded Jack, who finally snapped and threw a punch at his dad's face. He used Jack's outstretched arm to throw Jack across the locker room, where he slid to a stop ten feet away from me. Jack tried to stand, but his father grabbed him and slammed him into the lockers right next to me.

Shit, shit, shiiiit! Adrenaline dumped into my bloodstream, but unbelievably, Jack's dad looked right past me like I wasn't even there. He was close enough that I could see the beads of sweat that rolled off his shiny balding head and the bulging vein in his temple.

"Don't you ever take a swing at me again. Know your place, boy. You're *nothing* in my eyes, and you're *nothing* in the eyes of the Lord."

I could hardly believe what I was hearing. What kind of person spouts their own hate in God's name?

"Dad, please—stop!" Jack sputtered as his dad pressed his face into the lockers, turning Jack's wide panicked eyes toward me until I could clearly see the black eye Mr. Spritari had mentioned. Even just a few feet away, Jack didn't notice me.

They can't see me! How can they not see me?

"God only favors the strong, but you're not strong, Jack. Your weakness shames my name. You've failed me, and you've failed God." Jack's father continued his tirade in a low venomous voice, "How could you let some little queer like that get the upper hand?"

"I'm—sorry…" Jack squeezed out.

"Damn right you're sorry; a sorry sack of shit! That faggot is nothing! Nothing! Just like you! You're not strong enough to do what God wants you to do; you'll never be strong enough!" Jack's dad spit into his face, and then shoved him to the floor right in front of me. Jack lay there, still, as his father marched away with the parting comment, "You're not good enough to be my son."

Neither Jack nor I moved for several minutes, both of us shaking. My own cowardice and powerlessness sickened me almost as much as what I'd just witnessed. I debated inside my head whether to stay hidden or reveal myself and offer support. Jack was an asshole, but no one deserved that.

Jack finally stirred, and the look I saw on his runny face made it clear I did *not* want to be the next person he saw. Seething, he buried his fist in the locker next to me, as all the hurt and hate inside him contorted his bruised and puffy face. I jumped, but held my ground; apparently still invisible in the coolness of the shadow.

Jack walked past me to the sink to wash his face and his split knuckles, and then finished clearing out his locker and stormed out of the locker room. After he left, I eased out of my spot by the fountain and shuddered as I felt the spell or whatever it was break like suction when I pulled away.

I was still shaking by the time I finally got back to English. The encounter in the locker room replayed over and over again in my head while I stared out the window. The leaves outside Mr. Decker's window shivered a rich auburn in the breeze and I fought to focus past the static in my head. The kid behind me, Brett, moved his leg and I jumped.

As if today wasn't screwed up enough already, an invisible tail was hanging out the back of my chair.

I felt its weight as it swished back and forth and things brushed against the fur. My face felt weird too. I twitched my nose as whiskers tickled, and I ground my teeth to push back at the pressure on their roots. I ran my tongue along them to make sure they were still normal and almost bit it when Brett stepped on the tip of my imaginary tail.

Well Jimmy, you're officially losing your mind. Maybe Jack knocked something loose. On the bright side, maybe everyone will just assume you're on meth.

After class, Fen went on to the art room ahead of me as I stopped at my locker to grab my art supplies. I fought my way down the hallway toward Mrs. Ashcroft's room, and froze when I glanced up.

"Shit…"

Jack, Malcolm, Bo, and another guy from PE named Randy stood in a circle around the corner from sophomore hall. Panic washed over me, and I jumped out of sight behind the wall. I strained my ears past the sound of my pounding heart.

"—who'da thought—wimp could pack a punch—that?" Randy's voice faded in and out and I tried to focus through the hallway noise and feigned looking for something in my backpack.

"Yeah…" Jack's voice replied and then I didn't hear anything but the hallway for a long moment.

"—your Dad, wasn't it?" Bo's baritone was easy to identify.

"Don't te—body—pulled some strings—" Jack sounded irritated. I guess I'd entertained the spiteful hope that they'd been suspended, but should've known better. It didn't take a genius to figure that most of the school's income came from sports, so the cash cow athletes got away with murder, especially in the heat of their football season.

"Why?" Bo asked my question for me.

"Just fucking—I tell you to! C'mon—go."

Too late, I realized the way to the exit was down the hall behind me. I backed up along the wall and glanced around in desperation for an open locker, a dark cranny, a convenient boulder, *anywhere* I could hide. A sound behind me caught my attention, and I looked over my shoulder as the Auditorium door cracked open and concealing darkness called to me on the other side. The cool air turned frigid as I ducked inside and pressed the door closed behind me, afraid to breathe.

I heard Jack's muffled voice through the door, "Hey, where you been babe?"

Tabby's voice answered him; anger and irritation clear even through the wood, "Obviously, I've been avoiding *you*…"

"Hey! Don't you walk away from me!"

"Ow, Jack, stop it!" The hallway quieted as Tabby cried out in pain. "Jack!" Bo shouted at the same time Randy said "Dude, let go!"

"What the fuck is wrong with you?" Tabby sobbed, "Are you completely mental? I can't take this anymore! It's always the same with you; you hurt me, you're sorry, but then you just do it again—Fuck you Jack! We're over!"

"It isn't over until I fucking say it's over!"

"Go fuck yourself Jack…"

"Tabby!"

"Let her go, Jack, let her go!" Randy yelled and I jumped as something big slammed against door, while Bo's voice from the other side, "Dude, it's bad enough they cut you from the team, going after her is only gonna make it a whole lot worse! Just calm down!"

"Fuck you both," someone grunted like they were pushed, "and fuck that slut too. I can't believe this shit; I'm losing *everything* because of him…" Jack's rant faded as he moved away from the door. I relaxed and blew out the breath I realized I'd been holding, while a fluttering sound drew my eyes toward the stage.

It was cold in here, but the stage-lights illuminated a single figure on the edge of the platform. He looked young, like a freshman, with black hair like mine, but he was sorta scrawny and his Dragonball-Z t-shirt hung loose off his frame.

"Hey, were you the one who opened the door?" He looked up at me, startled, like he was surprised someone was talking to him.

"Um, I haven't left the stage for a while now, s-sorry." He tilted his head a little in a jerky motion, almost like a bird. "Y-you're Jimmy aren't you?"

"Yeah, do I… know you?" I asked, and scoured my memory to try and remember if I'd seen him in the hall or any of my classes.

He winced and shoved his hands in his pockets, like he was embarrassed. "Not really, but I used to be friends with Fen and Loki." His tone grew sour, and he glanced toward the back of the room, "They don't like to talk about me, I'm not really a part of their world anymore." He smiled awkwardly and glanced around the room, but never once met my eyes. "I've wanted to meet you for a while now," he muttered.

"I'm sorry, but I'm supposed to meet Fen in the art room. Did you want to come with me and say hi?" I offered.

"Thanks, but no, Fen and I had a bit of a falling out, and—
If they saw me with you, it'd probably upset them." He smiled
sadly but laughed as if it was some kind of private joke.

"Well, maybe I'll see you in the hall sometime?" I tried to be
polite.

"Not likely…" He said like he didn't really believe it.

"Well, at least tell me your name." I snapped, irritated.

"Um… Corwin, but d-don't tell the others that you met me,
don't even mention my name," he stuttered nervously. "I've been
trying to talk to Loki, but I can never seem to get through to her.
Promise me you won't tell them? Please?" He pleaded and met
my eyes for the first time; his were dark cold cobalt and somehow
unsettling.

His urgency took me off guard. "Okay, sure, I promise not
to tell them."

He sighed, "Thank you," he muttered as he turned and walked
toward the back of the stage, and I went back up the aisle to the
hallway door. A cool breeze ruffled my hair and I looked back
toward Corwin, but all I saw was a gently swaying crimson curtain
and I shivered.

I cracked the door open and peeked into the hallway. No one
was nearby, so I slipped out of the room and the door closed
behind me with a definitive click. When I pushed back against
it, it had locked and refused to budge. I frowned and adjusted my
backpack on my shoulder as I walked to Mrs. Ashcroft's room,
and knocked on the door for Fen to let me in.

I got my stuff out, and stared at the splotchy mess that was
supposed to be my assignment, while my brain thought about
everything except art. Bit by bit, I told Fen about all the weird
things happening to me. Except, of course, what happened in the
locker room and my brief chat with Corwin. I didn't say anything

about disappearing into the shadows either; I didn't quite know what to make of that yet anyway…

"It's almost like—" I hesitated, "Like the night after you bit me; I hear these whispering voices and my skin's hypersensitive."

Fen asked if I was still wearing the silver and I showed him, then he sat silent a moment as his brush glided over his paper. "You can feel the veil thinning…"

"What veil?" My forehead scrunched in confusion.

"The veil between the worlds, the… membrane that separates the spiritual from the physical." Fen stood and paced behind me. "Halloween is the modern celebration of All Hallows Eve and the Day of the Dead, and even further back, the ancient pagan holiday of Samhain and the Autumnal Equinox. One of the few times each year when angels, demons, and spirits can cross the veil and influence or even manifest in the physical plane."

"So, how come I've never noticed this veil thinning before now?"

Fen heaved a long-suffering sigh. "Because you weren't becoming a wolf before. What we are, what you're becoming, exists somewhere in between. We straddle both planes, embedded in the physical world while always tethered to the Lowerworld.

"Loki has trouble with voices and visions this time of year. You might too… When you were first bitten, you changed faster than any of us could have imagined, it might have just plunged you deep into the middle ground. Either that or maybe you have some latent natural talent that just woke up. Has anyone in your family mentioned experiences like this?"

I shook my head and quickly changed the subject. "What about the tail and stuff? That can't have anything to do with the moon; it's waning, almost new. How can that be related?"

"Our wolf bodies exist in the etheric plane simultaneously over our physical one, different, but there. It's really very simple; as the veil thins it's easier for your other body to manifest."

"Okay, 'it's really very simple', except I still don't understand what the hell this 'etheric plane' even is."

He frowned, and then he held his hands out, palms flat over each other. "Okay, so, think of reality as the layers of a cake, the bottom layers are denser and thicker than the top ones. That bottom layer would be the physical world, where matter and energy and everything are most densely mushed together. Our bodies generate huge amounts of energy, the electricity that controls our nerves, the calories our cells burn, et cetera.

"The next layer up would be the etheric plane, which is still pretty dense, but mostly energy." He shook his top hand for emphasis, "Everybody has a uh… duplicate form there, an exact shadow made of their body's energy. If something were removed from the physical realm," he curled one of the fingers on his bottom hand, "the etheric counterpart would still exist, which is why phantom limb syndrome occurs, because the nervous system is still picking up feedback from the etheric energy body.

"We experience something similar because shifters actually have two distinct etheric bodies, human and animal, and sometimes we feel phantom limbs for appendages we've never physically had, like ears or a tail. That's part of the reason why our metabolism is so ridiculous; we're literally eating for two etheric bodies.

"Part of how shifting is possible is that our physical bodies and their etheric counterparts are more deeply enmeshed than most, so we can pull some of our etheric form into the physical realm." He curled his fingers and laced them together, "When the veil thins, it's easier for your wolf to manifest in the physical world, so his senses run parallel to yours, and they're *much* better than our human senses will ever be."

"Is this, like, that astral plane I hear people talk about?"

"Not quite, the astral plane is the next higher, it's more like the realm of thought and emotion. The energy in that plane is more diffused, which is why some people can see auras or share each other's thoughts, and because it's more removed from the physical that's how some people can astral project.

"Then what's the next layer up from that?"

"The whipped cream," Fen joked, and smiled, "Sorry, no one's really sure exactly what's above that though, but I think it's the plane of the soul, of consciousness and identity. Hell, for all I know, the next layer up is the Lowerworld" Fen shrugged and crouched on his chair, thinking. "Hmm, you might be able to prove a theory of mine."

Excitement blazed in Fen's eyes as his brow creased and he chewed on the tip of his paintbrush. "Since we straddle the line between spirit and flesh; wouldn't that make it more visceral for us to encounter spiritual forces? Especially on a day like Halloween, or Samhain, when the planes are meshed enough for even the supernaturally inept to notice strange phenomena? Ghost hunters have been able to record the voices of the dead; maybe we can hear them with our phantom wolf's senses. That could explain the voices I suppose... Then again you *could* just be mentally disturbed..." Fen smiled and winked at me.

"*I hear dead people...*" I whispered and he laughed.

"If that's true, it might even be easier for us to see spiritual manifestations too. Maybe some of the people who experience spirit phenomena have therian blood in their lineage. It might not be potent enough for them to become shifters like us, but it might be just enough to allow them to perceive the supernatural. For whatever reason, supernatural things and events are drawn to each other, like some law of paranormal attraction. Ghosts, werewolves, and vampires always seem to be caught in a loop with each other."

"Okay, vampires I could understand, but what do ghosts have to do with us?"

"Ghosts are either an imprint of an event, or the restless spirit of someone who died; in either case they're actually in the etheric plane, not the physical. However, because they used to be physical themselves, they can sometimes 'haunt' the physical world. Out of all the creepy crawlies out there, ghosts and demons scare me the most." Fen hugged his legs to his chest with a distant look in his eyes.

"Demons I get; but why, pray tell, is the big bad wolf afraid of spooks?"

He refused the bait, but his gaze grew hollow. "What if a soul came to a point of no return? If a soul remained trapped without resolution, it might just… diffuse into oblivion. The only true death; a final destruction of the undying spark with no chance for reincarnation. Just… gone…" Fen finally met my eyes "Everything you ever were or could be, utterly erased from existence…"

The hair on the back of my neck stood on end, "Holy shit dude, are you saying you believe someone could completely… *end?*"

He nodded, "The single most frightening part of life that has haunted us since the dawn of time is death. An afterlife, reincarnation, nirvana, heaven… even hell is preferable to a complete annihilation of the self."

"Come on Fen, what are the odds that something like that could really happen?" I swallowed hard as shadows stirred in my subconscious.

"I hope I never find out," He looked at me and rubbed a pale line of scar tissue on his arm, "What if you, or someone you love, ended up trapped?"

Fen went silent, disturbed by his own train of thought. I felt his emotions inside me as though they were my own, almost like a taste on my tongue. Not just fear and sadness, but also a fathomless melancholy. A loss so deep and rending it oppressed his very soul, and beneath it all... guilt...

"Who died Fen?"

He grabbed his book bag and stormed out of the classroom, leaving his project on the table.

His mood lingered like smoke in the air even after he left. I put away his assignment for him, but I couldn't focus on my own work anymore either. It was a bleeding black mess of ink anyway.

All alone in the cold art room the silence was not only deafening, but unnerving as well. My imagination conjured shapes in the corner of my eye, and the sensation of eyes watching me raised the short hairs on my neck. It reminded me of running down the trail in those dreams I'd had. Finally, my nerve broke and I cleaned up and got ready to go home.

"Damnit Fen, why'd you have to start talking about ghosts?" I grumbled to myself to break the silence, and hopefully remind my ears what real sounds were so they'd stop creating things that weren't there. Whispers writhed in the periphery of my hearing. I looked around the room before I caught myself, and ground my teeth in frustration as I repacked my bag

Today was just *not* my day...

I turned the light off and stepped into the empty hallway, while my eyes adjusted to the eerie orange light that filled the halls with slanting beams through the glowing classroom windows. Cartoon cutouts of vampire bats and witches decorated the halls, with some fake spider web taped to the ceiling.

As I walked past the auditorium doors, Corwin popped into my head and a thought teased the edge of my mind just beyond reach.

I shoved the ancient brass lever on the door with my foot and it crashed open with an echoing clang. Strips of brilliant orange clouds faded into the dark blue of night as I walked outside into the shadowy twilight and a thought finally slipped past the noise in my head.

Corwin said he used to be friends with Fen and Loki…

Was he one of us?

I shook the thought away; there was no way Fen or Loki would ever abandon a member of the Pack. Still, I couldn't shake the uneasiness I'd felt when he'd met my eyes. My distraction drowned out everything else, so I'd walked a couple blocks before I realized I wasn't alone.

I glanced behind me and saw nothing but an empty street with gold and orange leaves trickling in the breeze. Still, the feeling would not relent. I imagined Jack watching me from the shadows, waiting to exact his revenge. My shoulders bunched and my phantom coat prickled. The streetlights along the block flickered and went off. I *felt* something out there, watching me…

A fluttering sound drew my gaze up. I couldn't see anything at first but gaunt tree limbs silhouetted against the deep navy sky, but then a shadow moved. The iridescent feathers made the immense bird look even more powerful as it tilted its head to the side and looked at me. A little relieved that there *had* actually been something real watching me, I nodded at it and turned back toward home. It cawed and then fluttered down to the ground ahead of me. My wolf stirred as the sight of the bird triggered some instinctual memory, but something didn't feel right…

I walked past it and it flew ahead of me again to watch, cocking its head in sharp twitches to keep track of me. I didn't hear the rustle of feathers again.

Just as I thought the bird had grown weary of me, a wash of air moved behind me, and a sudden weight landed on my shoulders. I stopped dead in my tracks and looked over my shoulder to see the huge bird perched atop my backpack, looking at me. It curled its talons around the handle to keep its balance and cawed, impossibly loud so close to my ears.

"Well, hello…" I said awkwardly. It cawed again, its voice low and husky, and it tilted its head to the other side to watch me. I fought down the urge to run around flailing my arms and squealing, though my eyes followed the pronounced curve of its bill and an unpleasant image of him eating my eyeball flashed in my head. I turned my face away and resumed walking with my new 'friend' in tow.

The temperature dropped fast after sunset, and I sniffed my runny nose. I smelled dry crushed leaves, compost, and somewhere nearby the tantalizing aroma of rotisserie chicken. But there was something very obvious I *didn't* smell. I risked my eye again to turn my head and sniff at the bird, but it was like there was nothing there. I felt the weight, I saw him, but I couldn't smell him.

My class had gone to a raptor center in fourth grade; the smell of predatory birds was not easy to miss… Goosebumps rose all over me as my intuition screamed at me that this was *very not right!*

Almost as if he sensed my unease, the bird croaked and fluttered off my pack. I glanced back but couldn't see him, though I still heard his cries overhead. I turned down the alley and his voice grew fainter, but I still felt his eyes on me.

I pulled the shadows around myself again like I had in the locker room. It was harder to do while walking, but I wanted it to leave me alone. It didn't seem to have any effect though. Even after I walked inside I still felt watched. Eyes and whispers lingered as dinner came and went, as I finished my homework down in the dungeon, and tried to fall asleep despite the chaos inside my head.

After an hour of lying in bed, frustrated and sleepless, I went upstairs and took some Nyquil. The vile goo eventually took effect and I forced myself to sleep; but that was when the *real* fun began…

Shadows and fog…

Shapes stirred and dispersed in the mist, a solid blackness beyond; I struggled through the nothingness adrift, lost… so lost… not even the moon graced me with her light any more… The abandoned one…

Cursed…

He… He'd abandoned me, though he stood right there, I knew he didn't consider me Pack, how could he? I wasn't what he wanted me to be. He was disappointed. He hated me. The humans ostracized me, and now the wall had grown tall and strong between me and… everything else… Everyone else… It was no way to live… Couldn't even call it 'life' really… The life that I had practically begged him to steal from me…

My human family didn't exist anymore, so I'd pushed harder. I'd fought so hard to impress him, make him proud of me, make him want me in the Pack, no matter what I was… But it was all useless…

As I stumbled blind through the fog, a room was revealed to me, a deep russet curtain, and a cluttered menagerie of things lying about in dusty piles, litter that looked like stage props. A strong melancholy, a smoldering anger… And a pit of darkness that completely consumed me inside… I wanted it over…

No… I needed it over.

A figure curled up in the shadows, weeping…

It's too hard… too damn hard for me… So much easier…

No one will miss me…

I lurched awake gasping as the darkness was broken with a blinding crack. My heart pounded like a caged beast until I finally recognized my own room and I wept quietly in the dark, rocking back and forth. The deluge of emotions that crashed over me swept everything away.

"That wasn't me, that's not me…" I muttered over and over to myself as my pulse slowed. "And that won't ever *be* me…" I sniffed and closed my eyes, pushing hot tears down over my cheeks.

Was it just a nightmare? It felt too real though… too damn real… Were they somebody else's memories, or… a glimpse of my own fate? God knows I'd considered it often enough, the easy way out, an end to the weary procession of pain called life.

The sedatives in my bloodstream pulled at me, but I fought them, I didn't ever want to return to that darkness again. While the dream held me, it felt like there was no escape, no reason for me to even keep breathing anymore.

That's what it'd be like if you let the dragon win…

The thought raised the hairs on my neck, and stilled the frenzy of my thoughts. I glanced at the glowing green digits of my clock with despair. I'd have to get up for school soon, but I curled up and felt the drugs gnaw at me regardless, dragging me back into the darkness. As I faded back into a drug-induced oblivion, fear and uncertainty bloomed inside me.

It'd been All Hallows Eve for four hours… plenty of time to dream of death…

CHAPTER 8 – DAY OF THE DEAD

My alarm roared to life at 6:30 in the morning, and I swatted at it. I forced myself from the warmth of my bed and fetched some coffee while blessing whoever thought to put an automatic timer on a coffee machine. I made lunches for Jake and myself, and shoved an extra sandwich into my mouth for breakfast as I shrugged my jacket on and forced myself out into the cold gray pre-dawn. A chill wind blew swirls of dead leaves down the street, and extinguished Jack-o-Lanterns watched me from their porches as I walked back to school.

I walked into the library just as they unlocked the doors. The familiar smell of old worn paper permeated the air as I walked down the aisles of tall bookshelves and then scanned through the Natural Science section with burning eyes. I stifled a yawn and a red book caught my attention. I pulled it out and flipped through it until the warning bell told me to head for class. I checked it out and stashed it in my bag, then resumed page-crawling in Art.

Fen's mood seemed better, but he still guarded himself from me. I didn't bring anything up about his tantrum yesterday, but I did tell him about the bird.

Mrs. Ashcroft walked by just then and asked me what the book was for, and I lied that it was for ideas for our India ink assignment. My first attempt had been... miserable to say the least.

I flipped through the pages, finally crossing the section on the black birds. I passed blackbirds, crows, magpies, and finally stopped. A large black bird with a thick curved beak perched in glossy color on the upper right hand of the page.

"That's it," I pointed at the page so Fen could see. I flipped to the guts of the book. "Common Raven, Corvis Corax." I turned the page, and continued reading. I finished the paragraph and then traced the little grayscale map of its range with my finger until it drifted through our area.

Fen slouched back and busied himself with his painting, his hand flecked black from rebellious droplets of ink. "A raven huh... why am I not surprised." He snorted as he mulled it over for a moment, "You don't usually see them in cities, but ravens and wolves have always had a special connection, both in mythology, and in nature. Would I be wrong to assume you saw some with Lupa?"

"We were surrounded by them in my second dream." I muttered as I remembered it.

"And yesterday, you felt excited?" he prodded.

"Yeah, but it creeped me out too. Why would it follow me like that?"

Fen smirked and shrugged, "Maybe it sensed your wolf, as much as your wolf obviously felt it. Wolves get excited when they see ravens, because they lead them to food and sometimes they play together. Ravens and crows are extremely intelligent and curious, and with as much energy as you're putting out right now, he probably just wanted to check you out."

"Hmm, my wolf *was* really active just then..." I didn't mention anything about Jack or the shadows; I wanted to figure out exactly what happened before I shared. "But why couldn't I smell it?" I thought out loud.

Fen stilled, "You couldn't smell it?"

I shook my head. "It made my skin crawl; I remember taking a school field trip to a zoo in Boise when I was a kid. We went through the raptor center, and I can still remember that smell; dust and feathers and rotting meat. But yesterday, nothing. The damn thing used me as a taxi and I couldn't smell a thing."

Fen's stillness broke, but he stayed silent and hunched over his desk, his hand moved faster and sharper than usual, his body told me something he didn't want to say.

"What it is?"

"Nothing, it's not important..." he replied, a little too sharply.

"C'mon Fen, spill it. This whole thing has me completely freaked out, and I don't like thinking that you might be keeping secrets from me..."

He shot me a look that was gone before I could quite catch what it said. Then he closed his eyes and sighed, and when he reopened them he wouldn't look at me. "A couple years ago when I got my driver's license, I borrowed Mom's car and took Loki on a drive. Back then, she knew about me, but I hadn't changed her yet. We were driving back from Denver on this little back highway in the mountains near Woodland Park. The full moon had just risen, and she was looking at the map to make sure we were going the right way. She saw a lake just off the road and suggested we check it out.

"We pulled off the highway and at first it was just like any other campground, with tents and RVs and stuff parked off the side of the road. But once we drove past that, the forest grew dark, and something was... very wrong there..." He shook his head and grimaced, "there was something *off* about this place, like something didn't want us there. The trees seemed to... loom over the car, and the air grew so cold. I felt the weight of the forest on me, like some throbbing pulse of energy.

"When we got to the lake we pulled right up to the shore and got out; and there was nothing within eighty feet of the car. The forest was dead silent and absolutely still aside from the water on the shore, and the moon reflected perfectly on the lake. So, I took a couple pictures and turned back to the car, and there's this cat sitting there in front of it, just staring at us..." Fen's hand stilled and the muscles in his jaw worked as he clenched his teeth.

"So, what's the big deal?" I asked as I sketched a few lines on a new sheet of paper, using the raven picture as a reference.

"You might have noticed by now that we have *very* good hearing. Even before she was bitten Loki's ears could almost rival mine; yet neither of us heard it, and it wasn't anywhere nearby when we pulled up. It would have had to run full tilt to get to us from that building, but it was just sitting there staring, so white it seemed to glow in the moonlight... Loki and I were both startled, but we walked over to it anyway and she picked it up and started petting it. It didn't purr or anything, it just sat there in her arms and stared right into my eyes. Cats don't do that, especially not with wolf shifters, and that was when I noticed..."

He looked at me, his eyes wider and darker than usual. "The cat had no scent... absolutely *nothing*... I could smell Loki, the car's engine, even a fish rotting down the shore, but this... cat had no dander, no fur, no dust... like it wasn't really there..."

The hair rose on my neck and I stopped drawing.

"We got in the car and backed up to turn around, I looked in my rearview to make sure I didn't back over it, and it was still sitting there, washed red in the taillights. I glanced down for a second to shift gears, and when I looked back up it was gone. Loki and I both looked for it, but it'd just... *poofed*..."

"So what do you think it was?"

"I have no idea. Maybe the cat was some kind of ghost or something, but most animal ghosts act like they did in life. That cat, like your raven, did not. Whatever it was, it scared the crap out of us. Hell, it *still* creeps me out just remembering it…"

Well, that might explain last night a little… "What do you think it means then?"

"I don't know… Maybe they're nature spirits or something?" Fen said, "Ravens are associated with the afterlife in European mythology; they're a lot like shifters in that they walk between worlds. In their case, it's the world of the living and the dead; they help guide souls to the beyond. A lot of the Indian tribes in the Pacific Northwest usually see Raven as a trickster spirit, so no matter how you dice it, they have kind of a dual nature, just like us.

"Anyway, I looked into it a while later and it happened within a few days of the spring equinox; the opposite end of the year." Fen muttered and refocused on his assignment.

"That's another time when the veil thins, isn't it?" I asked and Fen nodded.

Great, all this fun, two times a year…

Aside from the usual—disembodied voices and phantom eyes boring holes in my head—the rest of the day passed uneventfully. Jack and Malcolm weren't in gym again, and I resisted the urge to flip off the locker room when I left for the last time, only too glad to get rid of the first quarter, and gym with it. I managed a decent mood until my brain melted as I tried to focus on my English midterm.

After school, Loki met up with Fen and I in the hall as we went to pick up our assignments from Mrs. Ashcroft to work on over the weekend. All anybody around us could talk about was the upcoming football game, and our odds of winning without two of the teams' best players. Loki looked exhausted; her eyes red and baggy like mine. Fen mentioned she had trouble with voices and visions this time of year. *Visions... I wonder...*

"Hey Loki, can I ask you something?" I filled her in on my recent weirdness and asked her about what kinds of visions she'd had.

"Honestly, I think Fen exaggerated my 'visions'," she made quote marks in the air with her fingers, "I've seen a couple things that ended up happening later. Sometimes... I dunno, I just sorta snap out of my body for a second and share somebody else's." She snapped her fingers and blinked repeatedly, "I see what they see, hear what they hear, then I flash back into myself and have to try and remember where I am... It makes it a real pain to study sometimes." She chuckled and rubbed her temple. "Usually, the things I see just don't make any sense at all, like living in an abstract painting. Honestly, I think the weird dreams are because the noise keeps us from shutting down and resting."

"So, the things you see don't come true, right?"

"Almost never." She smiled at me and I smiled back. I already felt better just from talking to a kindred spirit. Fen glanced back at us with an unreadable expression as we turned the corner and I saw the auditorium doors ahead of us. "Why, did you have any sweet dreams of me?" she asked and batted her eyelashes at me.

"Unfortunately, no," I said, mirroring her sweet tone. "Just something about red curtains and dusty stage props."

We were just passing the auditorium doors, and Loki stopped dead. Fen and I stopped and looked back at her, a muscle in Fen's jaw twitched and he turned and stormed down the hall. Loki's eyes widened and the color drained from her face.

I stepped up and touched her. "Loki, what's wrong?" She didn't respond, she just stared out into nothing until I shook her. "Loki!"

She startled out of her trance and looked around, disoriented. Then she shook her head and smiled shakily at me as an embarrassed blush flooded her cheeks. She looked down and hid her face as she brushed past me, "Sorry, I... zoned out for a minute there..."

"Loki..." I began as I rushed to follow her.

"It's fine!" she snapped as she pulled a stray lock of hair behind her ear. "I just thought I heard... never mind. Just some bad memories, the kind your dreams make you relive when all you want to do is forget." My eyebrows creased with worry as we turned the corner. I wondered if her unease was connected to Corwin, whom she apparently knew, but I'd promised not to mention to her. "Can't seem to get through to her", he'd said...

I scowled as a thought crossed my mind. If he was harassing her, in any way, I'd maul his creepy little ass...

Just then, Loki grabbed my shirt and yanked me into the shadowed corner by a classroom door. Her hands tightened on my hoodie until her knuckles turned white and the fabric creaked in her hands as she buried her face in my shoulder.

A streak of fire crossed my heart and almost brought tears to my eyes. I felt her pain like it was my own; some torturous agony she carried inside. I wrapped my arms around her, guarding her from the hallway with my body, and wished I could drain all her pains and throw them away forever. Something I could never do for her.

I pulled the shadows around us without meaning to and she tensed against me. "What was that?" She whispered into my shirt.

"You felt that? Sorry, I didn't realize I was doing it."

"That was you?" She lifted her face to look at me, "What did you do?"

"I don't know, I just figured out how to do it yesterday. It sounds crazy but, I kind of... pulled the shadows around us so people can't see us." She stood on her tiptoes and looked over my shoulder. Even though we were in plain sight, nobody looked at us, not even when she waved a hand at them. My heart ached as I noticed the dark spots where her tears had soaked into my hoodie. She looked up at me, her eyes a little red and her makeup blurred. Surprise and wonder and something else I couldn't quite place filled her eyes as a couple last tears rolled over her freckles.

"Come on raccoon eyes," I said softly and smiled as I wiped her tears away with my thumb, "Fen's waiting…" She didn't move, except to lift her hand and rest it on my chest. At her touch, my heart thundered against my ribs like a rebellious beast. Time stilled for a moment as our eyes locked, until Fen's voice whispered through my mind; *Forbidden…*

I closed my eyes and exhaled as I released the shadows and Loki shuddered when they broke. Only a couple people looked surprised as we stepped back into the flow of students.

I shook my head in amazement. People were so good at not seeing things they didn't want to see. Of course, I'd been just like them a couple months ago.

For a blessed moment, the voices in the hall drowned out the ones in our heads and she and I both sighed, like a last breath sucked in before drowning.

It was going to be a long night…

We already planned on hanging out after school, but as we walked home Fen decided to call an "emergency sleepover" instead. An actual sleepover this time, no sleeping outside in a snowstorm required… at least not tonight. I parted ways with Fen in front of my house, and went inside to pack for the night. It was easy enough to talk Mom into letting me sleep over since she was taking Jacob out trick-or-treating anyway. I also conveniently "forgot" to mention that Loki would be there.

I dumped my backpack on my bed, and stuffed it with extra clothes, my toothbrush, and anything else I thought I'd need. I left the house and glanced around as I stepped down from the porch. No sign of my spectral raven, the street was mostly empty other than a few grade-schoolers already decked out in costumes crunching through the autumn leaves. The sky was clear and blue overhead with only a couple wispy clouds, but as the sun neared the horizon, a feeling of foreboding set in.

I hoofed it down the street to Fen's, and walked inside just as he finished calling Geri. I volunteered money for pizza and then Fen and I cleaned up his small bedroom, stuffing books into whatever nooks and crannies we could find in his cluttered bookshelf. His book addiction almost rivaled mine, though his were mostly worn and yellow, with price tags from the used book store downtown. He took out some candles of various colors and set them around the room, and then lit a stick of incense as Geri arrived bearing a box wrapped in fabric, a stack of pizzas, and Loki with a black makeup box with a cartoon skull and crossbones on it. The twilight blue descended behind them through the doorway.

We wolfed down the pizza, while Loki and I slouched against Fen's bed, too exhausted to do much else.

"So, why did you want me to bring 'it'." Geri asked and nodded toward the wrapped box.

"Well," Fen took a sip of his root beer, "Something has been haunting Jimmy and Loki, and tonight we're going to deal with it. And, since it's Halloween, we'll still to try squeeze a bit of fun out of it. After all…" he smirked and raised his glass in a toast, "this is the only night we get to take *off* our masks. Loki, would you do the honors?"

Loki retrieved her box and opened it, exposing a multitude of makeup; most of it colors I couldn't imagine her wearing.

"Loki, I never would have taken you as one for pastel?" I teased and held up some sort of coral colored stick.

"Nor I you…" She winked and then looked at Fen. "So, him first?" She smirked and held up an ominous black pencil.

Fen nodded, and no one seemed to notice the confused look on my face. Loki scooted up close to me, "Close your eyes and try not to move them too much."

"What're you doing?" I stammered, and blushed when she cupped my cheek. My stomach tightened at her touch, her hand warm and smooth on my cheek.

"Making you wolfy, now stop twitching." I tried to relax, but I couldn't prevent my eyelids from twitching as the pencil scraped over them.

She sighed; "I guess that's as good as its gonna get…" and I opened my eyes as she moved on to Geri while he gnawed on a pizza crust. I excused myself to the bathroom to gauge the damage to my nonexistent masculinity.

I glanced into the mirror, afraid to see some sort of slutty drag-gone-wrong motif, but smiled instead. Dark lines peaked down toward my nose, and tapered out from the corners, giving the shape and impression of a wolf's eyes. As I stared at the eyes in my reflection, my pupils contracted and my irises shifted to dark honey gold. My wolf reacted to my own reflection, and I felt his energy flow through me.

Dark fluttering movement in the mirror drew my eyes over my shoulder, but there was nothing there. Suddenly the noise swelled, like someone cranked up the volume on five different radio stations at once.

Understanding clicked. *The shift!* The mental shift pulled me deeper into the spirit world. My phantom limbs evanesced into ghostly existence one by one and my fur rose as the voices unsettled both my wolf and me.

"*Jimmy...*" A voice whispered through my mind and I flashed back to my dream, only this time I wasn't watching. *The taste of metal and grease in my mouth...*

The wolf snarled inside me, freeing me from the image. The walls pressed in on me like a cage, and I lurched out of the small bathroom. The anxious storm of energy boiling around me silenced them all in an instant.

"What happened?" Geri asked, his jade green eyes livid in their black surrounds.

I couldn't get my voice to work; all I could do was pant as I glanced at Fen and his one finished eye. That yellow orb stared back at me and I glanced away as my stomach tightened. *Must be the stress...*

The dragon shifted inside me, and I winced.

I found my voice and tried to explain, then reeled as an intense shout floored me, nonsensical and wordless. I dropped halfway onto Fen's bed, holding my head and whimpering. Fen told Loki to hurry, and she did so with stark precision.

"Geri?" Fen's voice was cold.

"Yeah?"

"Get the board ready."

Geri crossed the room and picked up the box he'd brought, and unwrapped the cloth. "Don't want my parents to see what it is." He smiled and shrugged, embarrassed. The fabric came clear and revealed an old board game.

"Is that a real Ouija board?" I'd heard urban legends about them, but I didn't think they were any more than gag gifts.

"Yup, this is the real deal. Picked it up at a comic book store in the Springs, only cost me, like, five bucks too." He grinned.

"Fen, what are you doing?" I asked nervously; with all the urban legends of accidental demonic possession, I really didn't want to think about what could happen with four werewolves noodling with it.

"We're going to try and get this damn spirit off your ass." Fen's voice bore an edge of steel.

"I need the mirror to do my own eyes…" Loki muttered, but didn't move toward the door.

It took a second for me to realize why, and I started to stand, "I'll go—"

"No." Fen cut me off, "Geri, you go with her. I'll finish setting up out here."

Jealousy and rejection surged through me, "Why? I don't mind."

Fen didn't meet my eyes, "Because I don't want my two most psychic packmates alone in a place where you already had an encounter. Geri's a psychic null, like me, so he can anchor her."

I didn't like it, and my gut told me he wasn't saying everything, but I sat back down anyway and fought down a growl. Geri and Loki both glanced at me as they slipped out.

Dammit, I just wanted to help, why'd Fen have to shoot me down like that?

I flopped backward onto Fen's bed and ground my teeth in sullen silence as I stared at the cutouts from numerous wolf calendars that wallpapered his room. Fen lit the candles one by one as I toyed with a pizza crust.

I noticed a picture of a smiling man holding a baby, unruly golden blonde hair spilled over his forehead as he grinned down at the bundle in his arms.

"Is this your dad?" I asked and Fen glanced to see what I was looking at.

123

"Yeah, that was the day I was born."

"Do you ever get to see him?"

"Yeah, a few times a year. You can come along next time if you'd like." He glanced at me with an uncertain smile and I realized how much favor he was showing me.

"Yeah, I'd like that." I smiled back at him as he turned off the lights, and the room was lit only by flickering orange light. Shadows danced on the walls until Geri and Loki returned a minute later.

"Any problems?" Fen asked.

"No, nothing," Loki replied as she shut the door and they sat down, each on a different side of the board. I allowed myself a brief smirk before I wiped my face and took my seat by the board.

"Okay; first try to clear your mind of unnecessary clutter. Don't think about school, homework, or chores; nothing." Fen said. I tried, but the noise wouldn't leave me, so of course I kept thinking about *the noise*. Whispers nagged and burned my mind like a slow smoldering rot.

"Now, put your fingers on the piece. Barely touch it, but don't push it, just let it move on its own." It felt cool under my fingers, and dense like ivory or bone. It drifted a little in no particular direction. "I'll ask the questions." He whispered. "We ready?"

He glanced at each of us in turn as we nodded, "Okay... Is there a spirit with us now?" The cursor hovered a moment and nothing happened. Fen asked again, more forcefully, and the candles flickered like a soft wind entered the room and it slid over to the 'Yes' graphic with a soft scratching sound.

"Okay, reset back to the center." He swallowed. "We have questions, will you answer them?" Again, the pieced drifted to the 'Yes' graphic, and we recentered it. "Will you answer them truthfully?" *Yes.* "Is the raven that landed on Jimmy's shoulder a spirit of some kind?" *Yes.* "Does it have malicious intent toward us?" *No.* "Is the spirit in the room with us?" *Yes.*

"Are we speaking with it now?" *Yes.* The hair on the back of my neck bristled and a low growl rumbled in my chest as my wolf showed his displeasure. Fen glanced at me before he continued.

"Are you a nature spirit?" *No.* "Are you a psychic vampire?" *No.*

"Were you ever alive?" It paused a moment. *Yes.* "Are you aware that you are... no longer living?" *Yes.*

"Why are you haunting us?" Letter by letter, the cursor spelled out '*Unfinished Business*'. "With us?" *Yes.*

Fen looked up at Loki and what little color was left in her face drained away. "What's your name?" He asked like he really didn't want to hear the answer.

The cursor moved under our fingers. *C.* A name popped into my head, and I dismissed it. *O.* Shit, please no... *R.* My mind raced as Loki's eyes grew wide; darkness fell over her candlelit face so thick I could smell her fear. Gently, as the cursor moved toward the end of the alphabet, I pushed it just a little further and held it over the *Y*, then forced it back to center. The whispers erupted to screams inside my head. I clenched my eyes shut as a wave of pain swept over me. Now, if I could just get past the nausea...

I wiped my face blank to keep anything from showing as Fen looked around at each of us, his eyebrows furrowed with confusion. He looked back at me, "Did you know someone named 'Cory'?"

"Um... Yeah; he was a kid I knew in Miami, he uh... used to pick on me in middle school." I totally winged it, "I think he got suspended. Don't know why he would be haunting me though; he was alive when we left a few years ago..." I scratched my head, how pathetic that *that* was the best I could come up with. "Maybe that's why I encountered him in the bathroom, but Loki didn't." I was grasping at straws, but better they assume it was some specter from my past instead of the suspect in my mind.

"When did you live in Florida?" Geri asked.

"About three years ago, we lived just north of Miami Beach."

Fen frowned, and then refocused on the board, "Are you trying to reach Jimmy?" *Yes.* "You say your intentions are not malicious, but the cost of your attention has hurt us all. Will you leave us alone?"

4 Now.

Wow, text message lingo on a Ouija board. As soon as we touched the 'W', the voices faded. Not all the way gone, but diminished into the background. Loki gasped and looked around.

"What is it?" Fen asked.

"The voices, they… faded!" She grinned at me, her eyes sparkling with relief. I couldn't help but smile back, and she launched across the board and tackled me with a hug.

Levity flowed back into the evening like sensation returning to a numb limb, until the early hours of the morning when Fen's mom came home. Her weary shadowed eyes told what kind of night she'd endured, and we moved back into Fen's room without a word.

Since space was limited, we piled on Fen's bed and watched *An American Werewolf in London* instead. We turned the lights off and passed around a bowl of popcorn. In the dark I mused without anyone noticing, and I zoned out through most of the movie.

I wanted to write off the Ouija board… Any of them could have influenced the cursor, hell I *did*, but the name bothered me. I saw where the cursor was headed, but that wasn't possible… was it? God, *nothing* was 'impossible' anymore…

CHAPTER 9 — SECRETS

I slept through most of the three-day weekend. With the close of the first quarter, I traded third period Gym for Myths and Legends.

Best. Trade. Ever.

Leaving gym behind meant that I was leaving Jack and Malcolm's territory as well, and their best opportunity at retribution.

It didn't come a moment too soon either; the football team got slaughtered at the state final and everyone who knew about my role in Jack's fall from grace wanted my head on a spike. I expected the figurative glaring daggers part to turn into a more literal Julius Caesar event at any moment.

So naturally, as I walked into to my new Mythology classroom, I spotted Bo near the windows. Apparently we shared an interest in Mythology... *dandy*... I looked around the room, and picked a chair in the corner as far from Bo as I could manage. I had just worked myself into a good glower when Loki dashed in just before the bell rang. We grinned when we saw each other, and I risked relocating closer to Bo so I could steal the seat next to her.

Of course, the irony of two werewolves attending a course on myths and legends was enough to keep a stupid grin on our faces all class period.

The injuries from my spat with Jack and Malcolm left only shiny pale lines of scar tissue behind. November broke over our little slice of the world, and the weather grew too miserable for us to spend lunch outside. We tried the cafeteria, but we had to constantly censor ourselves and yell just to be heard across the table. After about a week of that, I had an epiphany and asked Mrs. Ashcroft if we could eat lunch in the art room. She said she usually ate in the teacher's lounge anyway, so Fen or I just had to stay behind to let the others in.

Things went well until my report card arrived. My gut twisted when Mom handed me the gray carbon-paper envelope. As I folded the edges and opened it; Mom leaned closer to try and read past my shoulder, and then jumped when I screamed in her ear. Mrs. Ashcroft gave me an A, no surprise there, but I also managed to worm out an A- in English despite my distraction during the midterm.

The thing that killed me was the B in PE I grabbed Mom and crushed her with a hug as I laughed, and she congratulated me. I felt like I could dance, despite the ominous C in Math. John asked to see it at dinner, and then launched into another lecture that I tuned out with a practiced ear. It was like he didn't even see the A's and just fixated on the C.

"But this is good right?" I prodded. John sighed, and my smile wilted as I waited for him to shoot me down.

"Honey…" Mom muttered, and touched John's arm.

"Just watch those grades; if they drop again, you'll lose your guitar." He was quiet for a moment while he chewed a bite of spaghetti, "So, I finally got word on the bid for the Victory church contract today."

"And—?" Mom paused from eating.

"And, we got it!" He grinned, while Mom jumped up and hugged him.

I stared at my plate and kept eating.

Clouds rolled in the next day as Fen and I walked downtown to the library, a big masonry building just a few blocks off Main Street. Geri went hunting with his dad for the weekend, and Loki wasn't interested, so it was just the two bibliophiles. The roads were wet from the gently falling sleet, and reflected the glow of the streetlights as we sloshed across the cold asphalt and up the steps. The musty odor of aging patrons and even older paper greeted us as I pushed the dark wooden door open and shook off what water I could onto the soggy carpet.

Fen seemed to know the place like the back of his hand, and dragged me around everywhere while he rambled about his favorite books. After checking in at the library's card-catalog computer next to a middle-aged man who smelled like rotten fruit and patchouli, Fen made a beeline for a secluded section in the back corner of the library. He pulled a book off the shelf as if he'd memorized its location, and handed it to me. I read the cover, *The Book of Werewolves* by Reverend Sabine Baring-Gould. The spine had been fixed at least twice that I could tell; the corners tattered and rounded off by the years.

"Be careful with this one, it's seen more than its share."

"No shit... how old is it?" I flipped to the title page and looked for the print date.

"Well the good Reverend wrote it in the late nineteenth century, but this particular copy's about a decade old. This should help you understand where we come from better. A lot of our history, accurate or not, is in here. Most of the stories I've told you were from here. As well as some of the reasons why we don't advertise what we are; folks who do that don't tend to live very long."

"Yeah, I'd imagine…" I flipped through the yellowing pages, paragraphs of text broken only by a rare illustration or two, copies of old woodcuts. "So, is this where all the baby-eating stories come from?"

"What is it with you and eating babies?" He shot me a look. "Should I be worried?"

"I dunno…" I looked him over and licked my lips, "You're a little old and gangly, but a little A-1 should do the trick…" He laughed and I glanced at my watch.

"Crap, I've gotta take off or else I'll be late for dinner. Uh, thanks for the book Fen!" I turned to leave and his face fell as though I'd slapped him.

"Oh, um… I guess I'll see you at school then." He faked a smile and turned back to the books. I stood there a moment, confused, and then headed toward the checkout. As I walked home under the slate gray sky, his reaction bugged me.

Fen was lonely. His mom was always working, and he obviously spent a lot of time at the library, but he didn't really have any friends outside of the Pack. I was the only one who read anywhere near as much as him, the only one he could share that part of himself with, and I'd just brushed him off.

I'd make it up to him, I told myself; I couldn't be late.

No denying it, I was nervous as hell. I kept reminding myself that this wasn't a date or anything, but—still—this was the closest I'd ever been to one. When I got home, I spent nearly ten minutes deciding what clothes to wear, and barely picked at a single plate of food. *Gawd*, I was pathetic!

The doorbell rang and I froze like a hunted rabbit, my heart pounding, before I bolted up the stairs two at a time. John had already let Loki in as I gathered my guitar and amp, and tried to keep my nerves from showing. She'd had the forethought to bring a large umbrella to protect us from the frigid drizzle.

A big red crew-cab pickup idled at the curb; its headlights ignited the splotches of slush that fell though their beams. Loki opened the back door for me to load my stuff, and I climbed in after her.

"Hiya Jimmy, it's nice to finally meet you!" A big man in a cowboy hat twisted in his seat to extend his hand, his face was obscured by a shadow from the wide brim of his hat. I smiled and reached for his hand, hoping he wouldn't notice that I was shaking.

"Pleasure to meet you too, sir." His hand was warm and firm, rough bits of callous scraped my skin; working hands. His grip was confident and well-practiced with none of my uncertainty. I pressed back as hard as I dared, and he nodded and released me as Loki buckled in.

"So I hear you're gonna teach Jess' how to play that guitar she's been farming dust bunnies with?" It took me a second to remember that Jessica was Loki's real name; it didn't suit her any better now than it did the first time I heard it.

"That's the plan anyway. I've never taught anybody but myself, so I hope I don't just make her worse."

"I don't really think that's possible," Loki pitched in, "I think it'd be safer if you just assumed I'd never laid eyes on a guitar until tonight."

"Oh come on, you can't be that bad."

Her dad coughed into his hand. "Worse!"

Loki smacked his shoulder, "Dad! You're horrible!" she cried.

131

"Look who's horrible? He's just a poor guy clearing his throat; you're the teenage hoodlum assaulting him!" He and I laughed while Loki glared at me over the seat.

"You're awful, both of you."

"Oh c'mon Jess, we're just having a little fun!" I heard the smile in his voice.

"Yeah, at *my* expense!"

"Precisely." I said.

I caught sight of his bright blue eyes in the rearview mirror, framed by crow's feet in his smiling face. The three of us chatted until we pulled down the long driveway to Loki's house, and trudged through the slush to the back door. Loki removed her muddy shoes, so I followed suit.

Her dad walked past us, "Jimmy, we're not neat freaks, you don't have to take off your shoes if you don't want to."

"Ugh!" Loki whined, "I don't want him dripping crap all over my room!"

"You mean on the clothes all over your floor? I swear girl, I can't even remember what color the carpet is in there." He shook his head, "Anyway Jimmy; welcome to our home. If there's anything you need, just ask." He smiled at me and walked off. He didn't know that I'd already been here, and what he didn't know couldn't hurt me.

We carried my stuff to her room, and I looked inside for the first time. Every inch of wall space was plastered in band posters and pictures from old wolf calendars. A cornucopia of Goth accessories, makeup, and school supplies cluttered her dresser, intermingled with small wolf statues and busts. A black electric guitar sat in the corner on a stand, its dusty little amp next to it, and in another corner a two-foot high pile of laundry sprawled like a fungus. Belts and buckled boots littered most of the floor like booby-traps for the unwary. "Yeah, this suits you a *lot* better."

"I told you my room was messier than yours."

"Why don't you clean it?

"Cause it pisses my mom off." she said brightly.

We fumbled around for a power outlet for our amplifiers, and in the process my eyes fixed themselves on a bit of a crimson and black lace bra that stuck out of a pile of discarded clothes. I swallowed hard as I became *very* aware that we were a boy and a girl, alone, in said girl's bedroom.

I felt the blush creep up my face, and somehow wrenched my eyes away. My stomach tightened with awkward uncertainty, not just because I didn't know where to even *start* with her lesson, but also because she was an attractive girl in close proximity, and the walls suddenly seemed a lot closer.

I shook my head to try and clear it, and my voice almost broke when I said, "So, uh, shall we get started?"

"Yeah, what's first, sensei?" she chirped, her emerald eyes disastrously mesmerizing.

What the hell did come first?

Shit…

"Um, well, I basically taught myself by learning to play my favorite songs. What are some of your favorites, the ones you know by heart?"

"Hell if I know; let's just cheat." She pulled out her MP3 player, turned it on shuffle, and hit play. She skipped through a dizzying selection of music, everything from death-metal to pop. I kept a mental tally as she went, checking off the ones I knew or knew I could get. I stopped her when she hit "Of Wolf and Man" by Metallica.

We had a winner.

I showed her how to make a power chord, and blushed when I had to move her fingers into the right place on the strings. Then she strummed it and we both winced.

"I think we should tune the guitar first…" I apologized as she blushed as well. The hour passed too quickly after that. We turned off our amps and I set my guitar down, and then slid onto the floor by Loki's legs as doubts nagged me. Was I teaching her wrong? What if she quit because of me? She didn't seem upset though, and she sighed and inspected her sore fingers.

"Damn, I'll get it eventually," she muttered, and then pulled her legs up onto her bed. I heard her move, and then jumped when her arm draped over my shoulder and across my chest.

"Can I ask you something Jimmy?" Her mouth was right behind my ear, her voice like velvet as my heart raced.

"Sure…" I whispered, just waiting for my voice to crack like a freshman's. My mind whirred as I tried to anticipate her question.

"What do you think of Fen?"

"How do you mean?" What did she suspect?

"Like, as a person; do you like him?"

"Well, yeah. He's the best friend I've ever had, and he helped me find my wolf. He gave me a place where I could finally belong." I squeezed her arm as I said that. "Is that what you meant?"

She sighed, "Yeah, I guess."

"So no, not really. What's eating you?"

"It's just…" She sighed again, "I dunno, it's Fen. Sometimes it just feels like something's not right about him."

"You mean besides the lycanthropy?" I joked and she sighed.

"We're therianthropes, not lycanthropes. And… yeah, aside from that. He makes me uncomfortable when we're alone, and he *always* tries to be there whenever I hang out with anyone."

"What does he do? I've never seen him touch or speak to you inappropriately, but maybe that's just when I'm around."

"No, he doesn't do any of that, it's like he gets this… hungry look in his eyes. It's like, when he knows no one can see him do it; he looks at me like I'm prey. Like he's hunting me, and someday he's going to... I don't' know, *devour* me or something..."

"Wow, that's messed up. It reminds me of some of the dreams I've had."

"Really? That's just the way I think all the time." She shrugged, nonchalant.

"Cool, that means you're, like, the girl of my dreams." I grinned at her.

"Oh my god, you're such a dork!" she hit me over the head with her pillow, "here I am trying to be serious for once—"

"Well there's your problem." I pounced her onto her bed and tickled her until she shrieked. "Lokies is not supposteded to be all seriousness!"

She laughed until tears leaked out her eyes, and then she cried, "I give, I give!" I rolled onto the floor and there was a sharp knock at the door.

"Jess', you alright in there?" Her father's voice boomed through the thin wood and I swallowed hard as the knob turned.

"Yeah Dad, I'm good thanks..." She panted, still grinning. His gaze was intense as he looked back and forth between us. "He just tickled me, I'm fine..."

"Okay..." there was something dark in his voice and he locked eyes with me as he backed out the door. "I'll be nearby if you need me." I knew the last was more a warning for me, than reassurance for her.

"'Kay, thanks Dad."

"What was that about?" I whispered after the door latched. I was surprised there wasn't a shotgun in his hands.

She just shook her head, "I'll explain someday, just... not right now."

"Okay…" I muttered and sat next to her on the mattress, but my mood had darkened. "Loki… Do I ever make you feel like that?"

"What?" she sat up and leaned her shoulder against me, her face only a foot from mine.

"Do I ever make you feel uncomfortable?"

"Well, merciless jumper-cables are hardly the pinnacle of relaxation." She laughed until she saw the look in my eyes, then she faltered and I watched her eyes flick back and forth between mine as she bit her lip.

"You know what I mean, do I?"

"No…" she sighed and closed her eyes, then rested her cheek against my shoulder. "No Jimmy, I feel… relaxed around you. Like I don't have to hold up a façade and can just be myself." She held up a hand, "And before you go there, it's not that I think less of you. It's just— it's like I know you won't judge me like everybody else. You know how much it hurts. Sometimes I think some people forget there's more to me than baggy t-shirts and buckled pants, but when I'm with you… I can be me…"

I slid my arms loosely around her shoulders and held her, "I'm glad." I closed my eyes and smiled as she pressed her face against my chest.

"So do you know what you want to go to college for?" She turned her head and looked at me.

"No, I'm not sure I'm even going at all."

"Why not?"

"Well, first off, I don't have any idea what I want to study. Second, my GPA is shit."

"Well, why don't you try culinary school? You have a talent for cooking, and you don't need a 4.0 GPA to get into a trade school or community college."

I sighed and stared at a Marilyn Manson poster on her wall, "I've thought about it. I'm a decent cook, but I'd never make it in a real kitchen."

"Well, what about music? You're good at that too."

"Not good enough. I stand a better chance of getting sucked into an airplane engine than making it in a band, and John would never finance an audio engineering degree."

She glared at me.

"What?"

"Nothing, absolutely nothing. Forget I fucking said anything." Loki snapped and pulled away from me.

"What'd I do?" I felt so confused.

"All I was trying to do was help, and you threw it back in my face."

"I was just stating fact—"

"No," she interrupted me, "You were copping out. Like usual. You never cease to amaze me with how thoroughly you destroy yourself every chance you get; you've always got some excuse.

"You're not even eighteen years old! You have absolutely *every* possibility open to you, and people who love you and want to help; but you can't get over your own goddamned pity party! We can't even give you a compliment without you using it to degrade yourself, and I'm fucking sick of it!"

I shrank back, mollified.

"Don't you get it Jimmy? We *like* you! We see your potential; but you insult me, Fen, your parents, all of us by belittling yourself." She reached over and grabbed my face, squishing my lips like a fish. "Now tell me you're going to try not to do it anymore. *Yes Loki…*" She nodded my head up and down, "And you're going to stop throwing our compliments back in our faces. *Yes Loki…*" She nodded my head again, "Got it?"

"*Yesh Loksi...*" I lisped through squished lips and nodded.

"Good." She let go and I stretched my mouth. Despite the rough handling, I still felt her fingers on my skin, like a burned imprint. I looked at her as she looked at my mouth, and then her eyes flicked up to mine. I became hyperaware of our closeness again, and felt that strange recognition stir as something inside me pulled me to her. A soft rap at the door broke the moment, and Loki shifted to look at the clock. It was time for me to go.

"Jimmy?" she asked quietly.

"Yeah?"

"Don't tell Fen about this." Her eyes pleaded, "About these lessons. I like being able to choose who I want to be with."

"Sure thing." I said, and she returned my smile.

We gathered my things and Loki's Dad drove us back to my house. I hugged her goodbye when they dropped me off, and I slipped inside as quietly as I could. I stashed my stuff in the dungeon, and climbed back upstairs to get ready for bed. I closed the bathroom door and pulled my sweater over my head and accidentally caught a glimpse of the mirror.

At first I didn't recognize myself...

Instead of the pudgy wretch I'd seen for years, a stranger stared back at me from the glass. A stranger whose shoulders were wider than his waist. Whose stomach didn't protrude like a premature beer belly, and whose chest wasn't buried behind pads of mush. Even the eyes were different; a ring of black had surrounded my irises, and feathers of gold bled through the blue. *Almost like Fen's...*

I smiled at myself for the first time in so long, and my teeth caught my attention. I leaned closer to the mirror for a better look and poked at my teeth. My canines had grown sharp points, with the teeth behind following suit.

I leaned back and ran my eyes over shoulders that had never seemed wide before, past the dark line of hair on my stomach…

I wonder if Loki would like this…

The thought flitted through my mind before I could stop it. I shook my head as I finished undressing and stepped into the shower, but I still couldn't stop thinking about her. The thoughts slid through my imagination like red satin ribbons, and made my heart pound. Then I thought of Fen too, and everything fell back into perspective. Those fleeting thoughts were all I was allowed. Loki was not only out of my league, but also forbidden.

And what about Fen?

Yes… him too…

I felt the dragon shift inside me, making room for yet another soul-aching want, another hope denied. I turned the water off and stood dripping for a minute as I closed my eyes and leaned against the wall; feeling the ache behind my breastbone as the dragon's mass constricted my heart.

I sighed and pulled back the curtain and saw myself in the mirror again, obscured by fog. But for the first time in… longer than I could remember, I didn't see the fat, ugly, waste of life I was used to. It reflected a young man with ebony hair and tinted skin. I was not what I used to be anymore…

The dragon tried to close the door to its cavern, but it was too late; something slipped out and escaped. A little piece of self-loathing died. I felt the dragon thrash in the vacant space, but it didn't hurt… the fluttering in my stomach was quite welcome.

The weekend before Thanksgiving, Fen called me up out of the blue. "Hey Jimmy, Mom got the day off and we were going to go see my dad, did you want to come with us?" There was a thread of uncertainty in his voice, something I almost never heard from him.

"Are you sure? I don't want to intrude."

"I'd like to have you there, it shouldn't take long." Wow, how bad was this guy?

"Okay, I'll be ready when you get here."

I stepped out into the cold and hurried to their car as a dry dusting of snow blew down the street like the glitter inside a snow-globe.

They barely talked as we drove, and I could taste Fen's nerves on the back of my tongue. When Fen's mom pulled into a parking lot and shut off the engine, it all fell into place. The dried grass crackled underfoot as Fen quietly led the way across the lawn. The gray clouds and piercing wind cut through my jacket, as a loud flock of geese flew overhead and the brilliant amber leaves from mere weeks ago wove a thick mottled carpet of brown and beige for the coming winter.

Fen walked to a seemingly random spot and knelt down. He reached out with a gloved hand and gently brushed leaves and snow from a slab of black marble on the cold ground. My throat felt tight as I watched him, and his mother walked up and laid a hand on his shoulder.

Even standing back, I could read the words carved in the memorial plaque. 'Morgan James Kendle, beloved husband and father, stolen too soon'. He'd died the year I was born—the year *we* were born, the year that made us both fatherless.

It was not a similarity I'd ever wished to share with someone. At least now I knew why ghosts scared him.

I remembered the smiling man in the picture on Fen's bookcase, and tried to imagine what it would be like to know that your father had died loving you. My first impulse said it was worse to be unloved and abandoned, but then I realized it was just easier to mourn something you never really had. To know you had the sweetness of the world and had it stolen away, life would taste all the more bitter in its passing.

Fen didn't speak as he stood and walked back toward me with a weak forced smile. I wrapped my arm around his shoulder and he leaned into me. The drive back was even more silent than before, and when we parked I was struck again by how much their home looked the house where I grew up in Idaho.

Fen's mother made us mugs of hot apple cider, and the smell was warm and comforting, like something you'd curl up with in a blanket and hibernate.

"How did it happen?" I asked quietly as we sat down on Fen's bed.

"Hit and run. Police said it was probably a drunk driver, but they never found who did it. I was six months old, I... I just wish I could remember him." he said and we lapsed into silence and I fiddled with the mug in my hands.

"My father left us before I was even born. Just, vanished... Mom looked for years but couldn't find a trace of him. She finally gave up when she met John." I looked at him, "So I hope you believe me when I say I know how you feel; and I'm sorry."

He shrugged, but I couldn't tell if he really meant it. "Thanks, but it's alright. Nothing can change it, and I think it happened for a reason, just like everything that's happened to you."

"Oh?" My cynicism flared, but I was curious nonetheless to hear what he had to say.

"Our lives, and the events and choices that shaped them; haven't you ever wondered *why* everything happened the way it did? *Why* you ended up here of all places? She'd been sending me dreams of you for a long time…" It took me a moment to realize he meant Lupa. "Nothing substantial, nothing I could draw or describe, except that you would be a black wolf. 'Marked by Brother Raven,' she'd said. But as soon as I met you, I recognized your scent and your black hair. I knew you were the one."

I frowned, "I remember you saying something about that after you bit me. But… why'd she tell you I was coming? Did she do that with the others too?"

"No." At first, I thought he wasn't going to continue, "She said, 'Soon… he will come to you. He will bring strength and power into the Pack… once he overcomes himself, he will remind you all what it is to be Wolf. He will be marked by Brother Raven, and someday he—'" Fen faltered a moment, "'He will protect the Pack,'" he concluded hastily.

I wondered if that was what she'd really said, but I trusted Fen and pushed the doubt from my mind.

"Just before school started I thought I caught a whiff of you on the wind. I'd been wrong before, so I didn't get my hopes us too high; but then there you were. Right down the street from me too." He smiled wryly, "Right on Wolf Road…" I laughed with him; it really was ironic.

"What do you mean you've been wrong before?" I asked, curious about the odd reference.

"I told you, she'd warned me you were coming for a long time, years actually. When she told me you were coming 'soon', I was stupid and thought of 'soon' in human terms, not in reference to an ancient spirit." He winced, "I… made mistakes… I made assumptions, and jumped the gun. I hurt someone I cared for very much, hurt them badly because I'd tried to second-guess her. And I lost them forever…" Fen wasn't one for fidgeting, but he rubbed a hand up and down his forearm and didn't look at me.

"Why didn't you tell me? Why'd you keep it all secret?" I asked softly.

"You didn't need to know," was all he said, and something tickled at the back of my mind, clawing and scratching at the door, but I was afraid to open it. Still though, I had to know.

"Who was it?"

"It doesn't matter. It was a long time before you came here." Fen didn't continue, and I didn't press him. I saw the toll his memories took, he'd aged years before my eyes and shadows lined his face.

"The night you bit me, I'd fallen asleep in the park after fighting with John." I told him about the weird dream of the figure with the amber eyes, which had repeated a couple times in the months since.

He laughed softly and shook his head, "There are more things in Heaven and Earth, Horatio—"

"—than are dreamt of in your philosophy." I finished for him and we smiled at each other. He glanced at his clock and sighed.

"Come on, I'll walk you home." I nodded and we washed our mugs and pulled our jackets on. We stepped out the door and into the frigid night. Streetlights shut off as we passed under them, only to relight as soon as we passed; like we walked in our own pool of night.

He laughed when another one turned off.

"What's so funny?" I tilted my head in confusion.

"Our shifting energy trips out electronics. That's why the lights keep turning off."

"Really? That sounds pretty far-fetched, even for us."

He gave me a look, "Then let's let the scientific method decide, shall we?" He turned and looked behind us, one of the dark lights turned on he pointed at it. "Focus your shifting energy on that light."

It sounded ridiculous, but I tried anyway and imagined a cloud of that tingling heat stretch out like a hand. Fen's forehead was lined with concentration and I blinked when the light clicked back off again.

"Okay, stop," Fen muttered and I relaxed. As soon as we did, the light clicked back on. We did it again, and I laughed and bowed to Fen, conceding the point. I remembered the streetlights shut off the night I saw the raven too, and in the locker room, and in the bathroom, and... well damnit...

Condensation on the grass frosted into a brittle crust that crunched underfoot as we walked up to my porch.

"Thank you for coming with me today Jimmy." Fen hugged me, and I felt my face flush. I laughed it off and we said our goodnights and Fen turned to go home, but something wouldn't let me walk inside yet. Fen glanced back and noticed me standing there.

"What's wrong?"

"You know... even if I don't know this guy; I'm just curious to know his name." I muttered.

"What makes you think it was a guy?" Fen asked, suspicious.

I shrugged, "I don't know, just a feeling."

He sighed, and remained silent. He didn't suspect anything from my reaction, which was good; I already knew the name I expected to hear so it didn't surprise me. He just assumed the name meant nothing, and walked away. I whispered the name again when he was gone and felt a sliver of sadness curl inside me.

"Corwin Corbeaux..."

I soared over the ground in fluid motion and wove through trees and brush like a black wind. My heart pounded as I caught sight of

my quarry running ahead, a flash of white fur sliced through the pitch of the obsidian forest. I grinned a toothy lupine smile and put on a little more speed.

It took almost a week of calling to her as I fell asleep. I kept running into a dark wall every time I tried, shadowed and obscured, it writhed and barred my way with a terrifying dry hiss. Eventually though, I broke through and reached my destination. Lupa was always the one who drew me here, so I savored my accomplishment almost as much as the chase itself.

We broke out of the trees and raced along the shore of the lake, eruptions of sand followed our paws. I drew a deep breath and surged forward and tackled her into the sand. We rolled over each other and splashed into the water, then stood up and shook ourselves. I shifted into my human form and she followed, like her image was tied to mine.

She smiled at me, "You're growing stronger."

I smiled, "Thanks…" I forced myself to think past the warm feeling in my gut, and recall why I came here. "Um, I need to ask you a question." She nodded, "Fen told me that you'd sent him dreams of me before he met me, but not any of the others. Why just me?"

"Did Fen also tell you what I told him about you?" She lowered her head.

"He said that I would 'protect the Pack'. From what?"

"Was that all he said?" Her smile wilted, and I nodded. "I trust Fen to tell you when he feels the time is right. I am not always aware of happenings in the Middle World, and Fen has been my liaison for many years. I trust that if he has not yet told you the rest, then he has a good reason."

I sank into the water and frowned, "So you trust Fen, but not me?" I hated the childish snap in my voice as soon as I heard it. I wanted to trust her faith in Fen… but I didn't…

"Why do you sound upset?" She tilted her head, her look of confusion genuine.

"It just… it feels like you're playing favorites. And you're so cold about it, like you don't even care."

"Ah, I understand. You need to remember that even though I can look like a human woman, I am Wolf through and through. I am not human, and I don't think like one. It may seem 'cold' to you, but nature is indifferent. This—" she gestured at herself, "is nothing more than a costume…

"However, I will tell you this…" She stood from the water and walked toward me as the stars and trees faded into a black void, leaving only the two of us. "In the end you will remind them all what it means to be Wolf. You will prove to them what a true spirit of the wild is." She stopped and looked into my eyes, "Overcome yourself, my warrior wolf, and your path will make itself clear to you."

She pushed me lightly on the chest, and I was sucked back; falling, vertigo clutching at me—

My body jerked violently when I thudded back into it and I threw myself out of bed, caught in my sheets. I gasped for breath and pressed my fingers into my eyes to try and ease the pounding ache in my skull. I'd never been forcefully ejected from that place, and I *never* wanted to experience that again.

Why'd she push me out? Was she angry with me? I just wanted to know the full story. I wanted to trust Fen, wanted to believe that he just hadn't been able to remember what she'd said verbatim. But doubt nagged at the back of my mind like a bug I couldn't squash.

I looked at my clock with despair and then put on some clothes and crawled upstairs to start a pot of coffee. I tried to be quiet, but Mom shuffled downstairs a few minutes later, yawning. I poured a mug of coffee and fixed it up for her.

We sat there quietly; just the two of us, like we used to in Idaho back when I was a kid. Working at the hospital had hollowed her out almost every day, but she'd tried to make time for me every morning. We sat together and talked about anything, everything, and nothing at all, before she went to work and I went to school. But that was before John came into the picture...

The memories made me think of Fen, and his father's tombstone.

"Hey Mom," I said, hesitant, "would you mind telling me about my dad again?"

She sighed and held her head, "Really Jimmy? After everything John's done for you, you're still hung up on him? I don't know if I have the patience to deal with this so early today..."

"Please, Mom..."

She looked at me. Something in my voice must have gotten through to her. "Fine," she sighed again, "I still don't know if I can get there from here, but I'll try..." Her eyes drifted around the room while she leaned back in her chair with both hands wrapped around her coffee mug.

"Well, as you know, I met him in my junior year of high school. Taylor was kind of a bad boy. He was Coeur D'Alene Indian, artistic, and generally said 'fuck you' to the world." She shrugged, "You know I didn't really know him that well. All I really knew about him was that he fought with his dad a lot and he was dating a friend of mine at the time, Beth. One night, we were all at this party out in the woods before school started, getting totally wasted. Anyway, one thing led to another..." Her voice trailed off and she looked uncomfortable.

"Beth was devastated," she said, the guilt clear on her face, "I felt so horrible about it, so I figured that was why I felt sick all the time when school started. After a couple months though, I figured out what was really going on.

"I kept it secret as long as I could, I didn't know what to do. I was so scared. I don't really know what I expected when I told Taylor that I was pregnant. I won't tell you the things he called me before he stormed out, but I'm sure you can imagine the general theme." She cleared her throat and took a sip of coffee, "I figured giving him time was a good idea, but a couple days later his father knocked on my door. When Taylor found out that his dad came to see me, the two of them had a huge blowout and Taylor skipped town that night."

"You've never talked much about my grandfather. What was he like?"

She laughed, "I find that hard to believe Jimmy, are you sure you didn't just forget?"

"I'm pretty sure," I said and rolled my eyes, "tell me more about Taylor's dad."

"Well, the man was gruff, kind of a grizzled cynical Korean War Vet. At first impression, he was about as cuddly as sandpaper, but underneath that, he was kind of… fuzzy."

"Fuzzy?" I raised an eyebrow.

"Yeah, he was fuzzy, like a teddy bear; he always wanted me to call him Papa 'Wrench." She smiled, but it wilted fast, "as you know, I grew up alone; my parents were never there. The most attention they ever paid to me was when I got pregnant and they kicked me out. Papa 'Wrench was a loner, like me. He took me in, gave me a home, kept me fed, and made me stay in school. Even before you were born, you meant the world to him. He took care of you while I was in school."

I frowned, "That's so weird, I don't remember him at all."

She looked down at her mug, "Well, you wouldn't. He died of a heart attack a few months after you were born. Since Taylor had disappeared, when the tribe did their Memorial Giveaway, they let me have the house."

Something inside me seemed to really want me to hurt, so I finally asked a question that had been in the back of my mind for years. "Do you wish you'd had an abortion?"

She shook her head, "Jimmy, I love you so much. Please don't twist things around. I don't regret having you, but I know it wasn't a fair situation for either of us. I was still a kid, Jimmy! I wasn't ready to be a parent emotionally or financially; and at first it was hard for me to put your happiness ahead of my own. While everyone I knew was going out and having fun and being young, I had to stay home taking care of an infant. And then you had to sit in daycare all day while I worked and went to classes to get my RN. I winged it your entire childhood until John came along."

As if on cue, the floorboard creaked on the stairs, and I realized John was listening to us. I didn't know how long he'd been there. I looked at the clock, and realized it was almost time for Jake to get up. I wolfed down a bowl of cereal while I packed lunches for Jake and myself.

I walked Jake to school, and shuffled the rest of the way to the high school yawning. The late night, busy dreams, and too-early morning made me feel thoroughly zombified. It was the last day of school before Thanksgiving break, and some of the teachers seemed as excited as we were. Others were not so merciful though, and gave us assignments to complete over the break. In Myths and Legends, Mrs. Coulter drew names out of a hat to pair us up for our assignment. I didn't even try to mask my displeasure when Loki was matched up with Garrison from Yearbook, but I forgot about it when my name was drawn.

"Jimmy Walker and—Bo Tyrson!"

Shit.

I didn't want to, but I picked up my bag anyway and moved to an open desk near Bo and we turned them to face each other.

149

Mrs. Coulter wrote our pairings on the board while she explained the project.

"Your assignment is to research and present a specific Greek myth or deity. Discuss your selection with your partner and then raise your hand and I'll write you down, but every group has to pick something different."

"So, uh…" I started uncomfortably, "who would you like to do the assignment on?"

His deep voice was quiet and rather soft. "I don't care; whatever."

"Great, I have no idea either." I thought for a minute, and saw Loki raise her hand out of the corner of my eye when an idea came to me. "What about Apollo?"

"Sure, why not," he mumbled, and I turned to raise my hand. Then promptly dropped it as I watched Mrs. Coulter finish writing in 'Apollo' next to Loki and Garrison's names. She pointed at me, "Yes Jimmy, what would you like to do?"

"Never mind, we were going to take Apollo, but I guess not…" I glared playfully at Loki and her acnefied partner, and she stuck her tongue out in kind. I turned back to Bo, "I guess just look through the book and see if anything jumps out." He nodded and opened his text as I pulled mine out of my bag and flipped through, skimming over the bold section headers.

"Zeus?" he muttered so quietly I almost didn't hear him.

"Sure, okay." I nodded and Bo started to raise his hand.

He didn't even make it halfway before muttering "Dammit" and dropping his hand. I turned and saw 'Zeus' next to Lacey and Gabe's names.

Our luck held for the rest of the class, but despite the constant irritation, I noticed how—different—Bo was… He was so quiet, so *studious*… The difference was startling; he didn't act anything like Jack and Malcolm. Instead of bold and boisterous, he showed a quiet thoughtfulness that I hadn't even thought he *could* have. I'd never been close enough to realize that his eyes were a glacial blue in stark contrast to his tan face. They were quick and sharp; probably just as suited to skimming a book as observing an opponent's moves in football.

He seemed to notice me watching him, and looked up; "What?"

"Nothing, I... I just noticed how different you act when you're not around your friends."

"What do you mean?" he asked defensively and narrowed his eyes.

"Nothing bad, I swear. It's just that when you're not around Jack and them, you're all quiet and stuff."

He grunted and his eyes fell back to his book, but they didn't move. He looked back up at me after a moment, "Is it really that obvious?"

"It is to me." I shrugged, "I wouldn't worry about anyone else noticing, I just had certain expectations of you because of your friends. I sorta feel like an asshole for stereotyping you, and I'm sorry."

"Don't worry about it; I did the same thing to you," he said and cracked a brief smile.

"Oh?"

"Well, it was pretty freaky to see you lose so much weight that fast. I figured you were doing drugs or something."

"Not by a long shot. Don't feel bad though, my parents thought I was bulimic." I almost laughed and dug through my backpack. My hand touched worn creased paper, and I pulled out the werewolf book from the library. As soon I looked at it, an idea blossomed and I flipped through the pages to see if I could find... *yes!*

"Did you think of something?" Bo asked.

"You know what, I think I did… Ever heard of King Lycaon?"

"Wasn't he the king who tried to feed human flesh to Zeus, and was turned into a wolf?"

And you know this how? I struggled to keep my curiosity from showing. Surprise was unavoidable though; I hadn't expected him to actually know the legend. "Yeah, pretty much; want to do the project on him?"

"Sure, no one else has him," I was pretty sure no one else in the class even *knew* about him, except maybe Loki, "is that book yours," he held out his hand and I gave it to him.

"No, it's from the library, why?"

"I've just heard a lot about it. I never knew we had a copy here."

"I heard it sorta circulates around the state." Largely because Fen kept ordering it.

"What made you pick it up?" he asked as he scanned through a few pages then paused on one of the woodcut illustrations.

"I dunno, just sorta caught my eye I guess, I thought it looked little a little out of place." *I'd like to thank the Academy…* We were both acting; I could only hope he didn't realize it. "I really like mythology, hence this class, so I sorta ate it up. C'mon, let's go see if Mrs. Coulter's okay with it." I tried to seem nonchalant as I stood and walked over, but my mind whirred. Why did he know about King Lycaon? And how come he'd 'heard' about the book before?

The bell rang as I talked to Mrs. Coulter, and Bo stuffed a wrinkled shred of notebook paper into my hand with his phone number as he walked past. I watched his back as he walked out of the classroom, and my wolf stirred.

I made a mental note to keep an eye on him.

After the final bell, I maneuvered the chaos of the hallway and paused at the auditorium doors. I rested a hand on the ornately carved wooden doors, and an image flashed in my mind of a window, frosted and opaque, with a figure on the other side holding a hand to the glass. Only one idea left, but I wasn't so sure I wanted to know anymore. I was almost afraid, but I still had some hope that I was jumping to the wrong conclusion.

I fought the wind all the way home, and then helped Jacob out of his windbreaker and grabbed a thick worn blanket from the pile by the couch. The smell of the old cloth was familiar and roused bittersweet memories from younger days; when a single mother comforted her outcast son.

I walked into John's office and closed the door behind me. I looked at one of the sketches sprawled across his drafting table; a church taking shape, while I roused the computer from standby and minimized his CAD program. I draped the blanket over my arms so I could work the mouse and keyboard.

I fired up the web browser and went to the local newspaper's archive search, and then typed in the exact name I wanted to find. I closed my eyes and took a deep breath, then opened them and looked at the results. The first article was from this year and had absolutely no relevance, but the second was three years old and had me almost out of the chair with my face inches from the screen.

Missing Teen found Dead in School

"This morning, the search for missing teen Corwin Corbeaux (15) was called off. High school drama teacher Dana Cartwright opened the auditorium to prepare for class and discovered the boy's body. The school was closed for the day, as the investigative team processed the scene and questioned possible witnesses. Corbeaux

153

was found dead of an apparently self-inflicted gunshot wound to the head. The gun found at the scene belonged to his recently divorced father, and a suicide note was recovered from the body. The victim's mother informed police that he had been suffering from severe depression stemming from his stressful home life, and disintegrating social life at school. Counselors will be available for grieving students, and seminars will be held regarding stress management and depression. School is scheduled to reopen tomorrow morning. Funeral services for Corbeaux have yet to be announced."

My heart pounded as my mind whirled and I fell back into the chair; half remembered images bubbling to the surface.

Shadows and fog...

That dream...

A deep russet curtain, a cluttered menagerie of things lying about in dusty piles...

When the veil thinned...

A figure curled up in the shadows, weeping...

Wasn't a dream at all...

It's too hard... too damn hard for me... So much easier...

It was his memory...

No one will miss me...

It was his death...

A blinding crack of light and pain...

CHAPTER 10 – HOPE

My tears soaked into the blanket as I buried my face in it and rocked back and forth in the chair. Once the whirl of memories settled and I composed myself, I closed the browser and left the computer to the way I found it.

I fought to keep from freaking out, but the thought that I'd stood in the auditorium talking to a dead boy last month was disturbing to say the least. A dead boy who was somehow connected to my Pack... Fen looked so eroded whenever someone even neared the subject; and I couldn't forget that tang of guilt that I'd picked up from him. The nagging fly in the back of my mind buzzed a little louder, and I felt a churn in the pit of my stomach. The suspicions I'd tried to ignore crawled out again, the doubts; and that huge skeleton in his closet.

I just couldn't see how Fen could be responsible for Corwin's suicide. Maybe it was regret more than guilt; a loss like that leaves a pretty deep wound. I tried to imagine how it would feel if Loki or Geri committed suicide; someone I'd just talked to earlier that day, had pizza with, laughed with; gone forever.

Yeah, it'd take *way* more than three years to recover from that...

I wiped my face and sniffed, and then felt my expression harden. No matter what else had happened, these people were good to me and I was happy with them.

The tide of emotions left me drained and weary, so I crept downstairs and crawled into bed. It was about damn time for the day to be over.

I woke up Thanksgiving morning with a horrible knot in my neck. I shuffled upstairs to the commotion in the kitchen, and blearily considered diving into the ruckus to retrieve a much needed cup of coffee, but the chaotic flurry proved too daunting for my sleep-softened brain to process. I settled for sneaking a slice of pumpkin pie for breakfast, and then retreated to the living room.

I slid onto the couch and as soon as the first bite hit my tongue, my senses came online. The house was full-to-bursting with aroma; the sweet smoky tang of circle-cured ham, baking sweet potatoes and steamed green beans.

Mental note: holidays would be *way* more intense with the senses of a wolf...

"Jimmy, can you set the table?" Mom called from the kitchen, I didn't think she'd even seen me. I grumbled and rolled off the couch while my back groaned and popped audibly.

I wrestled the extension into the table and set out plates and silverware. When everything was ready, we passed the plates and dished up.

"So," John started as he handed me a platter, "some envelopes came in the mail this week from a few of the colleges around the state." My throat tightened and I thought I would choke. "I was thinking maybe we could go over them this weekend while you're home from school."

"Um, sure..." I felt the blood drain from my face, my stomach churned as Mrs. Ashcroft's advice spun in my head.

You want change? Take control of your life for once.

"Actually, I wanted to talk with you guys about the college thing." Mom glanced at me with expectant eyes, but John looked wary. "I've been wondering, why do you want me to go to college so badly?"

I could tell it wasn't what they'd expected to hear, and they glanced at each other as they tried to come up with a response.

"Well," John said and cleared his throat, "the key to a good career is an education, and we want to set you up for a successful life."

"Even though I haven't even *chosen* a career?" John was about to say something, but that brought him short. I seized the opening. "I don't want to waste your money, and I don't want to ruin anything, so… Would it be so bad if I didn't go to college right away?"

"What would you do instead?" Mom asked.

"Work?" I volunteered. I'd worked over the summer, but I knew that wasn't anything like a real job.

"But Jimmy… We're prepared to help you through school, why would you want to give that up?"

"Why do I *have* to give it up? Can't I just take a rain check? All I'm asking for is a year or two to get some experience and decide what I want to study. Guys I—" I struggled for a second, but finally found words for what was bothering me, "I don't even feel like I know who I am yet. Too much has changed, too fast, and I don't even know what my identity is anymore."

"Jimmy, you may never figure that out. People change over time, in drastic ways, what if you keep delaying until it's too late? I paid for my education with blood and tears and far too many years of *your* life. I missed so much of you growing up because I was trying to provide for our future, and I'll never get that back."

All this time I'd thought it was John who was pushing me, but no. John was just the financier; it was Mom's agenda.

"Mom, do you want me to go to school for me, or for you?"

I stared at her, and felt my wolf stir.

"For you, of course, I—" I fought to keep him from my eyes, but I wasn't completely successful. Her words caught in her throat, and then she shook her head like she was breaking out of a trance. "I only want what's best for you."

"I'm turning eighteen in a few months Mom." She blinked, "I'll be an adult, and I'll be responsible for my own choices. Let me choose my life." Mom looked like I'd slapped her across the face. "I promise, I will go to school. But not until I'm ready."

I felt some invisible dynamic shift. The way John looked at me, I thought I imagined a glint of respect in his eye, but Mom fell silent. She stared into space, and then stood and took some of the dishes to the sink, and then took Jake into the living room without another word to me.

John and I cleaned up the table and washed dishes. He was quiet, but I could tell he was thinking about what I said. I scrubbed the dishes and handed them to him to dry and put away.

"Are you sure about this?" he muttered at last.

"More than I am about going to college." I said, my voice firm.

"Then we'll have your back when you're ready." He pulled a hand out from under the towel and squeezed my shoulder, then went back to work. I froze; my wolf's hackles rose as forbidden emotions stirred. I quickly shoved them down and finished my job, and then I cut one of the pumpkin pies and added a flourish of whipped cream and cinnamon to each slice.

Jake squealed with delight when I came around the corner with the pie. He was propped up under Mom's arm, and she accepted a slice of pie without looking at me. I kept my thoughts to myself. John lit the kindling in the fireplace and we sat together watching the warm flicker of the flames.

I had no idea I'd nodded off until John shook me awake, and

told me to wake up so I could go to bed.

We tried to sleep in the next morning; but once Jacob came online, there was no stopping him. He'd long ago figured out that Thanksgiving made way for Christmas, which was when he got presents... amazing deductive reasoning skills were at work in that boy's head... Still, at least he wasn't as bad as the retail monstrosities that started setting up Christmas before Halloween was even out of the way.

Well, he wasn't that bad *yet*...

We had leftover ham and scrambled eggs for breakfast, and I took a chunk of ham with me into the living room and gnawed on it while we put up the tree near the big porch window. Over the years, the tree had taken on a life of its own and even the smell—dust and warm lights with just a hint of cinnamon—brought back good memories. Mom put on some of our favorite Christmas music, and I closed my eyes to drink in the sounds.

We'd adopted the habit of setting up our decorations on Black Friday as an excuse *not* to get dragged into retail hell for the day. We would eventually, oh yes... we would... but not today.

Mom distributed our most precious ornaments them one by one. Each had a story, a history, and a memory all its own. I could still remember when I was little, Mom handed them to me, just like she did now, to hang on our little desktop tree. We couldn't afford a real tree yet, but she'd found that little one at a thrift store, and I thought it looked so nice holding our ornaments on the little table in the living room.

John stood on the chair beside the tree and placed the star—which looked like a golden firecracker in mid-detonation—and a large gold bow on top. This final piece of the ceremony, and the tree seemed to wake to a life all its own as colors splashed across the room. A living, breathing symbol of our Christmas…

Jacob and I put up the remainder of the inside decorations; while John put up the lights outside and Mom very carefully set up her music boxes on the fireplace mantle. Most were almost as old as she was; her first given to her by her father when she was two; and another had followed every Christmas until she got pregnant with me and her parents kicked her out.

Because of me, she hadn't talked to her parents since then, but she still dusted them and wound them up to play as she hummed along and prepared the next. My brother and I wrapped a garland around the rail on the stairs that led up to their bedrooms, then I helped him hang up everyone's stockings at the fireplace.

When I realized I couldn't procrastinate any longer, I picked up the phone and dialed the number Bo gave me. He arrived after dinner with his backpack over his shoulder, an older gray Toyota truck parked at the curb in front of the house. I invited him inside and then led him down to the Dungeon.

I kicked my clothes from the middle of the floor to make a workspace and we spread our books out. Nothing better than doing homework over Thanksgiving Break… oh boy…

Seconds after sitting down, Bo pointed at my guitar in the corner. "Are you in a band?"

His question took me off guard. "Um, no, not really," I said. I didn't think Loki's lessons counted, but the idea had kind of wallowed in the back of my head. "Why, are you?"

"Kinda, but not really, I used to play drums for my church, but I got burnt out with that after a while. What kind of music do you play?"

"Hard rock and heavy metal, that kind of stuff. I'm not very good though." I said, embarrassed.

Bo laughed as he snagged the werewolf book out of my pile.

"I doubt I am anymore either, but I'd be down to jam sometime."

"Um, sure." Weird. Did that really just happen?

I busied myself looking through the text for more sources to cite, while Bo seemed more interested in the book than our project, his eyebrows furrowed with concentration as he pored over it word by word.

"So, why are you so curious about werewolves?" I tried to seem nonchalant as I jotted down some notes.

"Why do you ask?" he glanced up at me, his eyes defensive.

"Why do you answer questions with a question?" I snapped as my temper flared. I gestured at him with eraser of my pencil, "You know all about this obscure werewolf myth, and now you're fixated on that book. What's the deal?"

I looked him directly in the eyes. If he were like us, he would have recognized the challenge. Instead he looked at the book in his hands and sighed. Well, he wasn't a shifter, so, what then?

"If I told you, you'd think I'm crazy…"

"Honestly, I don't know what you are; but crazy isn't one of the immediate options." He didn't seem inclined to continue, so I prompted him. "How about you tell me, and let me decided how I'm going to react?"

"You promise you won't tell anyone?" he glared at me.

"Bo, you wouldn't *believe* the secrets I already keep." I rolled my eyes and sat back.

He sighed and seemed to brace himself. "I… sorta… think-that-werewolves-might-be-real…" He rushed the last part, like ripping off a Band-Aid. He winced and blurted on in a nervous rush. "I know, I know, it's stupid, and totally weird, but—"

"Whoa, Bo! Of course they're real." Whoa, Jimmy *whoa!*

"What do you mean?" *Shit, think fast…*

"Lycanthropy's a form of schizophrenia. They've been diagnosing and treating it for years."

"I know that, but that wasn't what I was talking about…" he sounded frustrated, more with himself than me though.

"Then tell me what you believe; explain it so I can understand." *And determine if you're a threat or not…*

He launched into a passionate explanation, as though it was a debate and he was trying to convince me of his point of view. I'm sure, to him, it was. He didn't know that I was just nodding along politely and feigning ignorance as he told me things I already knew. Inside, I felt a little worm of worry squirm in my gut. He actually knew a lot about us, at least our history, but that could be gathered from any number of books and websites out there, including the old paperback in his hand. What really concerned me though, wasn't the past, but the *now*.

Worry morphed into indecision. Was it good that he knew so much, or did it make him dangerous? Was he in the 'Ravening Satanic Beast' camp, or the 'Gifted/Cursed and misunderstood'? Should I correct him, or would I be empowering a threat? Tentatively, I threw out a lure, and hoped he didn't see through it.

"So, what about now, do you think they're still around today?"

"Well, yes and no…" he ruffled his short brown hair as he thought, "I don't think they exist like they used to; too many were killed during the Inquisition, so the survivors had to go underground and protect themselves with secrecy." *Interesting idea, unlikely, but interesting,* "Still, once in a while someone spots something; like the Beast of Bray road in Wisconsin, and who's to say that the occasional Bigfoot sighting might not be something else entirely."

"Wow, okay… But, why do they interest you so much?"

"Well…" he held his ankles to balance as he leaned back and

started off into space. "When I was a little kid, I used to dream that I was a wolf—that I could turn into one, I mean."

"Just a normal wolf? Not a big powerful wolf-man?"

"Yeah, just a plain, ordinary wolf. When I woke up, I felt sad that I couldn't be… *free* like that. Flying through the woods, chasing down deer and elk with a pack beside me." He chuckled, still lost in space, "The *ultimate* team sport!"

I tried to keep the surprise off my face as I filed that away for pondering. "I guess the real question is whether they're evil like the legends claim."

"I don't know… It seems hard to believe that anything that could change forms like that wouldn't be evil." I couldn't hide my disappointment.

"Why is that? Wolves aren't inherently evil or cruel; so why would anyone who could become one be any different? Just watch the news. People are perfectly capable of unspeakable evil without any outside help. At least wolves don't commit genocide, become serial killers, or sell each other into slavery. Those evils are human only; but if someone was loving, compassionate, cared for and provided for their family; wouldn't you say that was a good person?"

"Sure." He shrugged.

"Well, those are all traits that wolves share. To me, it makes more sense that if humans could become animals, that they would be no more evil in that form than as a human. No matter what your body's like, it still your soul inside it."

"You seem to know a lot for a casual hobbyist too…" He sat back on his hands and looked at me with narrowed eyes. *Shit, did I overplay my hand?* "Perhaps more than you're telling me?"

I laughed right in his face. "I'm just voicing my opinion, that's all. You said yours, and I said mine. Anyway, we've distract-ed ourselves long enough. If we really slam this thing out, I think we could totally dominate the other groups." I appealed to his competitive instinct to change the subject.

We laid out ideas for our presentation; and I guarded carefully against accidentally manifesting. It was more challenging than I thought; the more I tried to keep my wolf hidden, the more restless he became. I'd become complacent from being around my own Pack all the time.

While we worked, my brain ran a sideline query; what was it with those dreams…? Was I reading too much into it, or was there something significant there? And why was he so damn curious about us? Could he be trusted, or was he dangerous?

I hadn't realized he'd said something at first. "Huh?"

"I said; I've got a really cool idea for the presentation." He grinned.

Nobody knew quite what to expect when Bo walked into class in a toga, and it all went downhill from there.

Mrs. Coulter called our group up, and I walked to the front of the classroom with a cardboard box and laid out our notes, while Bo walked around the classroom handing people little pieces of chicken on toothpicks—since even people taste like chicken—then he walked up to the front and offered me a piece.

I pretended to get angry and started yelling at him, "How dare you! That's Jerry!" I pointed at my classmates, "You're all eating Jerry! I, the great and powerful Zeus shall punish you Lycaon!" No one had any idea what was going on as I pulled out an old latex werewolf mask and stuffed it on Bo's head. Then I turned and wrote "The Legend of King Lycaon" on the white-board behind us.

It was melodramatic and campy, but everyone loved it.

Bo wore the mask through the entire presentation. We took turns holding up visuals and explaining how the legend was believed to have been one of the first recorded werewolf myths. We returned to our seats while the class applauded and I caught a look from Loki.

I just smiled. I knew what she was thinking, but why would I risk insisting on wearing the mask when what was inside me ran *far* deeper than any costume?

Time blurred and everyone around me zoned out in anticipation of Winter Break, but I barely noticed when paper snowflakes and cardboard snowmen appeared on the walls over the lockers. I stayed late almost every day to get in that extra chunk of time in the library or the art room that might make or break graduation, and I pestered my teachers for extra credit.

On the second Friday of December, we congregated around Fen's locker and he proposed a shopping run to Colorado Springs over the weekend. Geri heaved a sigh, as he was pretty much the default chauffeur. Otherwise, everyone was excited to get out of town for a day, and I looked forward to maybe scoring a nice gift or two.

Fen arrived at my place early the next morning, and I prepped a thermos of coffee before Geri and Loki arrived to pick us up. It was still that weird pre-dawn darkness when one half of the sky was a weary shade of gray and it was cold as hell. We ran out when Geri pulled up to the curb and dove into the back seat.

"So, by some strange chance, would *any* of you like to pitch in some money for gas?" Geri asked, an edge of annoyance in his voice. "No? Yeah, I didn't think so…"

Fen shrank into his seat. "Sorry, you know I can't."

"C'mon Geri, can't you take another one for the team?" Loki teased in a saccharine voice.

"Sure, here, lemme just drive all y'all's ungrateful butt-munching hides into that ditch over there…" He grumbled like a dog licking a long festering wound.

"Somebody's feisty today!" Loki jabbed.

"Bite me…"

"Later…" she whispered with a voice that could've melted chocolate and every male in the car turned red.

I wiggled my wallet out of my pocket and handed a twenty over Geri's shoulder. "Will this cover?"

"Er—yeah." I caught his surprised gaze in the rear-view mirror for a moment, a strange expression on his face until he looked back down at the road, and Fen looked away from me.

The prairie just outside of town was dusted with a pale frosting of snow that slithered in tendrils and wisps at the winds' beckoning. The horizon blushed in orange and violet until the sun broke over the teeth of the mountains and brought blinding agony to stab at the backs of my eyes. Geri turned off the main highway and the road took us between the high rock walls of a canyon. It brought relief—though sun spots continued to dance in my eyes—as we drove through its serpentine confines, and the skeletons of yucca and scraggly bushes gave way to pinions and scrub oak.

The winter sky was the clear porcelain blue of a husky's eye as we drove into Colorado Springs. Geri negotiated the winter streets and weekend traffic, and then parked on a street that looked transplanted across time. Strings of white lights stretched between the leafless clutches of locus trees in front of renovated old-west storefronts that displayed everything from southwestern Indian art and pottery to custom t-shirts and art galleries.

I fed the meter for Geri, and then followed them as we systematically hit almost every shop along the street. Signs labeled the area 'Old Colorado City'. Werewolf metabolism could not be denied for long though, and when we couldn't ignore our gurgling stomachs any longer, we stopped at a cozy little restaurant called "The Mason Jar".

They seated us near the fireplace and I stole the seat next to Loki. My arm brushed hers when I reached for my coffee, and she teased me about touching her so much, so I poked her in the side just to watch her squirm.

"Oh!" Loki shouted as she remembered something, "Have you figured out which colleges you're going to apply to." She leaned toward Fen, who shook his head as the waitress brought the plates out.

"Not yet, there's a bunch of schools that offer my program, but I don't know for sure which ones I'll be able to afford," he grumbled, "If any…"

"Don't worry; financial aid will be a piece of cake with your grades." Loki joked, and I took a bite of my chicken fried steak as the bitter twang of jealousy snapped inside me.

When at last the beasts in our guts had been appeased, we put our money together to pay the check and the waitress picked it up while we finished off the last remnants of our meals. Loki cracked a joke about Zeus descending to earth for chicken-fried steak, so I reached over and tickled her sides until she begged me to stop. I grinned and ignored the annoyed glares of our fellow patrons while I picked up my coffee to finish it off, and caught Fen's eye over the rim.

His gaze was intense and I reacted almost instantly with a deep blush as my heart pounded. I averted my eyes and my smile faltered for a moment, but when I glanced back at him; he was still staring at me with an enigmatic smile on his lips.

That smile taunted the nether-realms of my mind as we loaded back into the car and took off to our next destination. Old-west blocks melted away into houses-turned-shops. Geri parked in front of one and everyone got out. I followed them, and saw a huge black statue of a dog guarding an iced-over fountain by the front steps. It was intriguing and sorta creepy at the same time, and I almost tripped on the steps as I followed the Pack inside.

My nose was assaulted as soon as we walked in; oils and dust, the paper of books, and several different kinds of incense smoke. The air tinkled with chimes and fountains and a Celtic version of "The Holly and the Ivy" played overhead. My eyes watered from trying not to sneeze; I wanted to whine and rub my muzzle against my paws, but settled for aggressively pinching my upper nose.

Loki flitted over to some display cases and pawed at their contents through the glass, while I stopped dead in my tracks; I was *sooo* out of my element. I'd walked into a pagan's haven, a little corner of the world where witches didn't have to worry so much about puritans and open flames.

I followed Fen down an almost hidden little staircase with colorful tapestries hanging from the walls. I looked at the pattern on one, and nailed my head on the low ceiling at the bottom of the stairs. I spilled out into a room where all manner of books lined the walls and rubbed the sore spot on my forehead while I ignored Fen's chuckling.

Fen poured over the bookcases while I sifted through a clay dish filled with amethyst. I glanced back at him as he flipped through the pages of some book, excitement plain on his face. He turned it over and checked the back for a price, and I watched disappointment wash over him. Loki thundered down the stairs grinning—though I must admit I was a little disappointed she didn't hit her head, I was apparently the only lucky winner today—and she quickly ensnared Fen with an enthusiastic "Oh my *gawd*, you have got to see this necklace they have!"

As she dragged him back up the steps, she winked at me like

she knew what I was thinking. I quickly grabbed the book Fen had hastily shoved back into the bookcase and then startled the girl behind the checkout counter. I paid and stuffed the bag into the front of my pants and let my shirt fall over it moments before their Clydesdale feet clomped down the steps.

I lifted my finger to my lips in the 'shhh' gesture as I winked at the cashier and Fen returned to the bookshelves. When he noticed that the book was missing, I walked past him with empty hands and climbed upstairs feeling quite pleased with myself. I borrowed Geri's key to pop the trunk and stashed my smuggled loot before the others came out, and Geri struck off through the holiday traffic.

I'd never spent much time in malls in Miami or Chicago, never really liked them or the people who frequented them, but as we pulled into the parking lot my packmates' excitement infected me. We circled like vultures for a while, before we finally scored a spot in my absolute farthest corner of BFE and squished through the slush. Past the bell-ringer, we entered the warm chaos of the food court.

The frenetic energy of the shoppers crashed into me like a wave, and I stumbled, though I played it off like I'd just snagged my foot on something. The Christmas Cocktail; eagerness and stress, with liberal doses of joy and rage and just a splash of desperation for spice.

We made our way in and out of a dizzying array of stores, past bath shops that oozed a suffocating blanket of chemical scents, and through the mazes of clothing racks, bloated prices, and warring states known as department stores until we ended up at the Goth Gap. I occupied myself with a stack of band tees, and glanced over when Fen walked out of the changing room in a pair of leather pants and a fishnet shirt.

Fen looked… well… like an apple in Eden. You knew you

shouldn't touch; yet you found yourself wanting to sink your teeth in anyway. Unwelcome thoughts slithered through my head and I felt sick. Fen noticed me watching, and called me over, yelling over the cacophony of loud music and ornery customers. "Well, what do you think?" *Why was he doing this? It was almost like he knew how he affected me…*

"Uh, y-you look good." I stuttered as blood tingled in my cheeks, and Loki laughed. "What's so funny?"

"It's just; Fen's all blonde and stuff, and you're all tan and dark. You two are like day and night… Ooh! I need at picture of this!" she suddenly squealed, then whipped out her cell phone.

"Well then, what a pair we make!" Fen laughed, and without warning he wrapped a leg around my waist and leaned back. I thought he was falling and panicked. I grabbed him and almost tipped over when a clicking sound came from Loki's direction and we froze. Fen looked at me, and I looked at him. He grinned, and I saw something victorious in his gaze before he leaned back up and stepped away.

My brain dissolved into chaos when I heard Loki whisper, "Oh my god this is the greatest picture *ever*, it looks like Jimmy's molesting him!"

"*What!*" I bellowed and jumped over, only to groan with disgust. The action shot on my face and odd positioning, did indeed make it look as though I was having my wicked way with him. And worse still were the images in my mind's eye as I fought the sick feeling in my stomach and pounding heart. When I looked over again, I saw Geri literally rolling on the floor with laughter clutching Loki's cell phone and wailing how "They make such a cute couple!"

"Loki, please, please delete that." I begged and tried to snatch the phone out of his hand.

"No way," Loki shouted as she pulled it out of my reach, "this is going on our Christmas card this year!"

At that moment, I glanced longingly out the front of the store and wondered if there were too many people to manage a flawless swan dive over the second floor railing...

I continued to sulk and entertain self-destructive thoughts through our hasty chicken teriyaki dinner. We hiked back to our parking spot just as the sun disappeared in a blaze of orange fire behind the mountains. As we drove home, I stared off into the starlit fields and thickets patched with snow and Fen laid down across the seat and rested his head on my thigh.

"You know," he mumbled quietly, "we did make a pretty cute couple..."

I sighed and looked out the window, and let my thoughts drift as Fen used my leg as an improvised pillow, and Geri's stereo played; "Oh the weather outside is frightful, but the fire is so delightful. And since we've no place to go, let it snow, let it snow, let it snow..."

I felt a faint smile twitch at the corners of my mouth as I indulged in the 'what if's and 'what could be's of my imagination's masochistic fancies.

CHAPTER 11 — SEEING RED

Fen and Loki stood before the dark cavern's gaping maw. Dread filled me when I looked at it, but they held out their hands to me and I stepped forward and took them both. They led me forward through a torch-lit passage and we emerged in a large chamber, where something reeked of ammonia and rot. A dry hissing like scales on sand issued from the shadows and terror seized my heart, but when I tried to run Fen and Loki held me between them like a sacrifice.

A shadow slithered toward us across the floor, and I begged them to release me, but instead they leaned in and both whispered, 'But I love you' into my ears. The shadow swelled to immense size as it drew near and finally the serpent was revealed and its broad wings spread toward the ceiling and glistened like a slick of oil against the deeper black. Its triangular head bore a red cross in the center of its forehead as my dragon opened its jaws wide; its saber-long fangs glittered like ivory in the torchlight.

As it reared back to strike, my knees gave out underneath me and a shadow flew from behind me and tore into the behemoth's throat. It hissed in rage and threw my wolf aside. It landed spread legged and ready, his teeth and eyes blazed vivid in the darkness.

Over and over they clashed, each time the dragon went for me, my wolf defended me.

The battle reached a stalemate, both wounded by the prolonged torture they inflicted on each other, and I knew, as they did, that this last round would announce the victor.

I screamed as they lunged for each other, and Fen and Loki tore me apart.

I felt my ribs separate from my sternum as my arms ripped from their sockets and I woke up covered in sweat.

I shifted in my seat for the umpteenth time since the last class began. It was the last stretch—of the last class—of the last day before winter break; and I'd *swear* that damn clock just went backwards. Today was the winter solstice, and my last best chance…

I gathered my backpack in my lap and jumped up when the bell finally toned and everybody broke for the door. However, instead of bolting for my locker and out the door, I fought the tide and slipped into the auditorium.

I wrapped myself in shadows as I snuck down the rows of burgundy-upholstered chairs, and slipped behind the bunched curtain on the far end of the stage from the drama teacher, Mrs. Cartwright's, office. I waited for her to shut down the lights and leave before I stepped out and looked around. I pulled my wolf into me and my eyes dilated; milking every last bit of green light from the emergency exit signs.

"Corwin?" I asked the green-tinted darkness, but only the room's reverb answered. "Corwin…?" I tried again. This time after a few moments delay I felt a slight shiver and a chilled tendril of air in the already cool room.

"J-Jimmy?" At first the voice was directionless, but then he coalesced from the darkness of the backstage; half-transparent in the eerie green light.

"Corwin, you're… uh…" I faltered, not wanting to commit some sort of otherworldly faux-pas.

"You can say it, I'm dead," he muttered and stuffed his hands in his pockets.

"Yeah, the Ouija board sorta gave it away; I just didn't want to believe it… So this is what you meant by 'I'm no longer a part of their world'?"

"Yeah, I'm not part of the living world. I can almost reach Loki, but either she doesn't understand, or she doesn't w-want to."

"Then how is it that you can talk to me?"

He sighed and sat down on the edge of the stage and rubbed the side of his face as he thought. I moved to sit down by him, and then froze when I noticed that I could still see the edge of the stage through his thighs—maybe I'd just stay standing… "That's just another part of the puzzle isn't it? There are so many questions surrounding you, it's impossible to know where to start."

"But why? I'm nothing special—"

"Oh, but you are Jimmy… You were destined for this, probably before you were even born. So many paths were broken and twisted to lead you here; don't you d-dare write it off as circumstance."

I snarled in frustration and paced the stage. What was the big deal; I was just another freak, nothing more than 'the Pup' to the Pack. Why was Corwin making such a big deal out of me? When no answers popped out of the ether, I asked one of the questions that bothered me instead. "Corwin, why haven't you passed on? What's keeping you here?"

At first he didn't answer, but then he sighed and hung his head. "There are things I need to say, but the people who need to hear them either ignore me or can't hear me."

"So, 'Unfinished Business" like you said?"

"Eh, s-sort of. It's not something I *have* to do—but it's something I've needed to do since that last flash of regret when it was already too late. I'm keeping myself here, in the hope that I can atone and salve the wounds I left."

"I think, somehow, Fen knows you're still here. He's afraid that you'll... 'unbecome' if you stay here too long."

He snorted, "Fen thinks it's his fault I killed myself. The truth is—well, I guess it sorta *is* his fault, but it's not his alone." *Ouch.* "I've tried to reach him in his sleep before, but the dream became a nightmare for him."

I was thinking, "So, those dreams—and that raven before Halloween—that was you?"

"Yeah, I can only manifest my animal form outside of here; I can only appear human near where my body died."

"Wait, you mean... you weren't a wolf?"

"Nope, that was where it all started to go wrong after Fen bit me." He trailed off. "I was supposed to be you..."

What the hell was that supposed to mean?

"Tell me what happened, tell me everything..." My mind reeled, but something told me that Corwin held the keys to *several* puzzles.

He looked away from me, "You m-might not like what you hear." I raised an eyebrow, and crossed my arms. He sighed and looked around the room. "Loki and I were Freshman, and I met Fen in—" He stopped and he looked quickly to the side.

I waited for him to continue, "What are—"

"Shh!" He hissed at me, his eyebrows knotted with concentration. His form faded a little as he stared off through the wall. "Jimmy, you have to go, you have to go now."

"What? Why? I finally get to squeeze some damn answers out of you—"

"I don't have time to explain, I promise I'll tell you everything later…"

"When?"

"I don't know, just… *l-later!*" He jumped up from the stage and glanced to the side again, like he heard something I didn't, "Shit, *just go*, you h-have to h-h-hurry!" His stutter got so bad he could barely speak. He pushed at me, but all I felt was a wash of cold air.

I scowled and swung my backpack onto my shoulder, then huffed up the aisle and out the door, glancing behind to see an empty stage before the door closed.

I stopped at my locker to grab my coat and growled softly as I slammed the door. I turned toward the exit, and heard Corwin's voice, faint and directionless. "N-no—l-library…" his voice faded in and out, like bad reception on a radio.

I turned on the ball of my foot and headed for the exit near the library. I grumbled and didn't even look up as I slipped my coat on under my backpack and shoved the bar on the door, the cold air rushed around me.

I heard a sound and raised my eyes, but it took me a moment to realize what I was seeing. Two sets of eyes glared at me, one pair looked with fear and hope. Jack and Malcolm dominated the small cowering form that uncovered its tear-streaked face and cried my name.

"Oh, so you know this freak, eh half-pint?" Jack grabbed Jacob by the collar of his coat and lifted him off his feet. My little brother bawled with fear, struggling and kicking.

"Put him down *now!*" I yelled and my blood pounded in my temples as I walked toward them. My wolf snarled within me as my skin crawled, every instinct screaming to protect Jacob.

"Or else what faggot? You gonna be the big man and 'beat us up'?" Jack mocked, sounding just like his father. My eyes were locked on Jacob's, and his on mine, pleading. I felt so weak, terrified that I couldn't protect my brother.

Malcolm grabbed my shoulder to keep me from getting any closer. "You put my brother down… right now… whatever issues you have with me… stay with me…" I could barely remember how to speak; my brain stopped working in words as my wolf smashed against the invisible wall inside me.

"Oh, so this is your little brother? Coulda fooled me, guess your mamma fucked the mailman huh? How sweet, is big brother gonna save you?" Then Jack head-butted Jacob's face, splitting his lip and bringing out a scream of agony that pushed my wolf and I over the edge. His little hands quickly covered in blood while Jack laughed.

Without thought, my backpack swung around and cracked Malcolm in the head with the combined mass of my textbooks. He reeled back and I tackled Jack to the ground. He dropped Jacob and I reached out for him, but Jack grabbed my leg and tripped me. I fell hard, and lost my wind when Malcolm jumped on my back. I tried to claw my way forward, but Jack pulled my arms out from under me and crushed my face into the frigid concrete.

"Jake, run home! *Run!*" I screamed.

"Jesus Jack, why'd you do that to the kid?" Malcolm grunted as he pinned me.

"Shut up Malcolm!" Jack snapped, and then leaned in close to my ear, "Does that feel good faggot? Yeah, you like that don't you… It's payback time you god-damned fudgepacker!" His knuckles collided with my cheek and bounced my skull of the concrete with a dull thunk that sent the world spinning. "You owe me big time for October! You cost me the finals, my scholarship, my girlfriend," Jack's knee rammed into my ribs and drove the air from my lungs, "you fucked *everything* up for me. But there's no teacher around to save you now; you'll be lucky if you make it out of this alive."

My wide roving eyes landed on Jacob, curled and fetal, holding his face. His tears mixed with blood as they dripped off his chin. My wolf boiled inside me, frustrated with my weakness, he raged against the wall and I felt him bleed through into me.

The growl began low in my throat, and my lips pulled back from my teeth as I tried to push myself up off the ground.

"Keep him down!"

"You ain't goin' nowhere asshole!" Malcolm growled as they shoved me back to the ground. My gaze crept from my little brother to Jack's eyes, and I felt my wolf spill into them as I pushed up again, my breath fogging in the cold air.

"What the fuck?" Jack grimaced with confusion and fear.

"I said... you ain't going... ugh!" Malcolm fought to keep me down, but my wolf was stronger. I lifted both of them with me as I pushed myself up. My growl grew louder and this time it didn't even faze me when Malcolm punched me again, and again; I was already fading out. Jack's eyes widened with fear, and a red curtain drew from the edges of my vision until all I could see was crimson, and the sound of screams seemed so very far away...

The pounding ache in my head registered even before I woke up. I cracked my eyes, and tried to pull the blurry vertical line of the ground into focus. Half my face was on fire; the other half was almost completely numb. I pushed myself up and lifted my hands to the sides of my face, but stopped when I saw they were red... and sticky... A fluttering sound drew my eyes up to the edge of the building, where a large black raven watched me. I nodded at Corwin in response to his eerily human-sounding call, and he faded from sight.

I looked back down to my hands, and swallowed down bile. *What did I do...?*

I looked around, and aside from a few splotches of blood and the pool where I was lying; there was no sign anything happened, nothing but my backpack lying about ten feet away. No bodies, no sign of Jack or Malcolm... and no sign of Jacob.

Where was... oh God! Please let him be home!

Near shock, I staggered over and grabbed my bag. My vision distorted as I stumbled the familiar route to my house on auto-pilot. I crashed through the front door and let my bag slide off my shoulder. My mind focused on only one thing.

"Jacob..." my voice broke, "*Jake!*"

"We're in the kitchen!" Mom yelled.

I almost fell, and caught myself on the door jamb as I turned toward her voice. I grabbed the doorway as I entered the kitchen to keep myself upright, and despite everything, one thing stood crystal clear. The absolute horror on Jacob's face as he looked at me and recoiled, my stomach clenched and I thought I would throw up right there on the floor.

What did I do? Please God, don't let him hate me; I could survive losing anybody but him...

The room blurred, and before I knew it, I was on the floor and my mother's face swam in my vision. Time distorted, and I felt something warm touch my face. It took me a moment to realize it was a wet washcloth in my mother's hand, scrubbing something that looked like rust off my face. She spoke in a steady stream, and I couldn't understand her words at first, but it didn't matter. Just the sound of her voice was comforting. I looked up and saw Jake, but after meeting my eyes, he jumped down from his chair and ran from the room.

Sensation slowly returned to the numb side of my face as my mother's scrubbing woke a fierce burn in my forehead. I gradually recognized her words.

"—swelling up pretty good. You'll probably have a purple cheek for Christmas, and you've got a nasty gash on your forehead here…" She prodded the area with her fingers and I winced. Once my words worked again, I managed to croak out a question.

"Is Jake all right?"

"He's pretty shook up, but he wasn't hurt too bad. He won't need stitches, but he'll have a fat lip for a while. Honestly, I've seen both of you is far worse shape than this. I'm just glad they didn't break his nose…" Her voice was calm, but the purse of her lips betrayed the seething anger and fear inside her.

"I stayed late, and when I went outside, I saw them picking on him." I rambled, my mind too scrambled to make much sense. My voice rose in volume as I grew frustrated with myself. "Why was he at the high school anyway?"

"Shh, settle down Jimmy, don't be upset with him. He wanted to surprise you. I don't think you'll need stitches either, but this cut on your forehead is a doozie. Nothing bleeds like the scalp, it's no wonder you were covered in blood." She made me follow her finger and used the little LED flashlight on her keychain to check the dilation in my eyes. I numbly performed her other tests, and finally she sighed and seemed satisfied. "I don't think you have a concussion. Come on Jimmy, let's get you to your room…"

She helped me down the stairs and I laid down on top of my sheets. Dizzying and worrisome thoughts circled in my head like sharks. I wondered what Jacob saw, how much hell Mom and John would rain upon me for letting Jake get hurt, what might have happened with Jack and Malcolm—and what did they see of my wolf?

Just after I started Middle School, I came home one day and Mom hugged me with a huge smile on her face. We lived in Corona California, a nauseatingly hot and dusty sub-city near L.A., and Mom told me she was going to have a baby. I resented them for it. I felt abandoned all over again; I wasn't good enough, so they'd given up and wanted to start over. I raged, I sulked, and I made John's life a living hell when he decided that our home in Corona was too small for a family of four.

John packed us up and shipped us down to Miami right in the middle of the school year. I prepared myself to hate this child, the spawn of John. The day finally came the next spring, and I went into the maternity ward to see this nearly hairless red potato of an infant in my mother's arms. I pretended to be happy, and she held it out for me to hold. I took the little bundle into my arms and something strange happened.

The rage and resentment I'd chosen to feel for this creature washed out of me.

I couldn't help but smile as his warm stubby little digits wrapped around my finger in his sleep. My baby brother. I swore to myself that I would protect him. I wouldn't let him live my life; I would guard him and keep him free of my darkness. In a lot of ways I helped raise him, almost like a third parent. I didn't have any friends so I spent most of my time looking after him, especially after the accident in Miami that scarred my leg.

As he grew older, he started to idolize me. I realized that if I wanted to protect him from my life; I had to force him away. It killed me to sever that bond, but I had to for his sake.

I wanted to protect him so badly; I wanted to keep pain away from him…

Something roused me, and I forced the slits of my eyes open and brought my room into focus. My right eye refused to open wider than a squint. At first the room seemed empty, but then I saw Jacob sitting on my stairs, eyeing me.

I took a deep breath and forced myself up onto my elbows. A dull ache throbbed down my forehead into my cheekbone, but I forced a crooked smile around the swelling. "Hey…"

He didn't respond except for shifting his position and averting his eyes. Acid scorched a line across my heart, and my eyes drifted down and took in the red line on his puffy lip.

I failed him; I failed him when he needed me most…

"Are you okay buddy?"

"Are you evil?"

"What?" The question took me off guard.

"He said you're a demon, and that you'll… You… You aren't, are you?"

"Oh Jake; no I'm not evil. I can't remember what happened, but whatever I did; I did it to protect you. If that makes me evil, fine. I think they're evil for what they did to you. Why, do *you* think I'm evil?" I held my breath, fearing his answer.

"No, but…"

"But?"

"You scared me really bad…"

Oh God… "I didn't hurt you, did I?"

"No, but… Your eyes weren't right." I let out a mental sigh of relief; scaring him was bad enough, I would have killed myself right then and there if I'd actually harmed him. "And that bird was scary too…"

"What bird?"

"That big black one that came out nowhere while you were fighting them, remember?"

"No buddy, I don't remember anything after they pushed me to the ground and I told you to run away. Um, would you mind telling me what happened," I asked sheepishly, "After I started to get back up?"

"That was when your eyes went all scary." He muttered and looked away again, "They sorta changed color and stuff, and it's like it wasn't you anymore. You grabbed the shorter one and threw him into the wall."

"I *what?* C'mon Jacob, that isn't funny."

"But you did!" He looked at me, his eyes earnest, "You threw him and he hit the wall, like *fwoosh!*" he mimed swinging an imaginary opponent. "And he hit the wall and didn't move, and it was really cool, but really scary too…. You're not like that, you don't throw people. You don't hurt people…"

I stayed quiet but nodded, hoping he would continue.

"Then you jumped on the one who hurt me and knocked him over. You growled like a dog and tried to bite him. That was when the bird started attacking you, flapping around your head and stuff. The guy you threw against the wall woke up and they ran off. He yelled that you were a demon, and you were evil, and that hell's going to swallow you up…" His eyes glistened and he sniffed, "I didn't know if you were really you or not, and I was afraid that you would hurt me, so I ran home... Jimmy... you... you're not going to get swallowed up by hell are you?" and he started crying.

Thank you Corwin, thank you...

"Oh Jake, come here..." I held out my arms, and for a painful second I thought he wouldn't come. But he sniffed and wiped his nose on his sleeve, and then walked over and sat down on the bed next to me. I wrapped my arms around his shoulders and flopped back on the bed, taking him with me like I used to when he was a toddler. It hurt my bruised ribs, but I needed to hold him, to know he was okay. We sighed one after the other, while my mind worked and his sniffles subsided.

"Jacob, can I tell you a secret?"

He didn't answer, but I could tell he was listening.

"But you have to promise not to tell another living soul; not Mom and Dad, none of your friends, no one, *ever*."

He looked at me, obviously thinking about it very hard, and then he nodded.

"You have to say you promise, or I won't tell you."

"I promise, I'll never tell anyone, not no one, ever!"

"Pinky swear?" He wrapped his little digit around mine and shook.

I sighed and let my eyes wander as I tried to think; how the hell was I going to explain this?

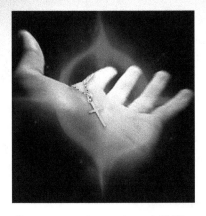

CHAPTER 12 – ALL I WANT FOR CHRISTMAS...

The lead-gray sky hovered close to earth as the first tentative flakes thickened into a light blanket on Christmas Eve. I gnawed on a summer sausage as I walked past Mom in the living room.

She looked up from her magazine as I passed, "Do you just walk around chewing on that thing?"

"Myah, sho?" I answered around a mouthful of meat.

She shook her head and looked at her magazine again, "Nothing, it's just so... canine. You've been turning into such a carnivore lately."

I snorted, and then choked. My coughing helped disguise my laughter until I was safe behind my bedroom door. Oh, if only she knew! It'd be a miracle if I could look at her tonight without laughing.

So far at least, Jacob seemed to be holding up to his promise.

I smiled as I sat down on the floor of my room and wrapped the last of the presents. Geri had been difficult to shop for, but Loki told me he liked video games, so I got him the latest "blow anything that moves into bloody chunks" game.

I wrapped Loki's gifts and set them with Geri's. And finally, with the sweetish tang of scotch-tape lacing the air, everything was done. The gifts for my family waited in a sack under my bed. I stacked the Pack's gifts in my arms and carted them upstairs where I arranged them around the tree.

I sat down in the chair by the window and admired our tree until my gaze drifted outside where little puffs of white drifted to the ground. I relaxed and smiled as I watched their lethargic one-way ballet. Christmas music played on the stereo and the aroma of cooking meat escaped from the kitchen.

The harsh tone of the phone's ringer startled me, and I growled as I snatched it and pressed the green button.

"Hello?" I grumbled.

"This is Officer Parker, is that you Jimmy?" a scratchy tenor replied over heavy background noise.

"Yeah, it's me." I replied more civilly as I sat up, he was the cop who came over after Mom called in the fight. He asked how Jacob and I were recovering, and then gave me the court date for the trial once I'd found a pen. I clicked off the receiver and heaved myself out of my comfy spot and walked into the scent-drowned kitchen to write the court date on the calendar.

"Who called?" Mom asked while shredding some smoked salmon with a fork.

"Officer Parker, he called to give us the court date." I wrote the time in on the calendar. "What are we going to do about Mr. Spritari?"

"Leave that business to me honey, I'll take care of it. Here, try this and tell me what you think?" She paused and offered me a cracker with her salmon spread on it.

"Hm, it's good. Maybe just a splash more lemon juice though."

"Thanks." A timer went off, and she reached over the stove to turn off a burner. "Dinner's almost ready; can you set the table and fetch the boys? I think your dad's in his office." I bit my tongue and got to work.

Fetch boy, fetch...

Two taper candles—red and green per tradition—lit the room along with the ambient glow from the tree in the living room. I filled wine glasses for Jake and myself with sparkling apple cider, while John poured some wine for Mom and himself. I drowned in the smell of the food, and had to close my eyes and swallow a mouthful of drool.

The food was divine, and I ate until my stomach reached the point of detonation. Though, I found just enough room to 'help' Jacob with the rest of his roast. His little belly bulged and he languished in his chair like the happiest slug alive.

"Whew, stick a fork in me, I'm done..." I muttered and slouched in my chair.

"About time," John muttered, "I thought you were going to start gnawing on the table. You shouldn't eat so much or you'll get fat again." He leaned back and sipped his merlot.

I glared at him, "So, are you the pot and I'm the kettle, or is it the other way around? I thought you used to play football? I bet the only run you could make around that gut is from the sofa to the fridge."

His mouth twisted into a scowl and he leaned forward. He opened his mouth to retort when Mom cut him off.

"John, Jimmy, stop it both of you!" Mom snapped and pointed at us with her fork, "I will *not* have you ruining Christmas for the entire family. If you don't stop picking at each other, I *swear* I will slap the both of you."

I bit my tongue and hid my smile.

We cleaned up the dishes and packed the leftovers, waddling like penguins around our swollen bellies. Then Jacob hounded John, "Dad! Dad! Can we go out and look at Dec'ies now?"

'Dec'ies' was Jacob's word for decorations. Every year we drove around after dinner looking at the lights and decorations that other people put up for the holidays.

We drove around for almost an hour before returning home and serving up Crimson Pie and eggnog for desert. John started a fire, and we took our favorite spots around the room.

Jake passed out cold, curled up in his chair. I picked him up and carried him upstairs to his room. He woke halfway up and mumbled "Don't forget to put out cookies for Santa…"

"Don't worry," I smiled at him, "I've got it covered." He was out again by the time I set him down in his bed. I pulled his shoes off and covered him, then kissed his forehead, "Sweet dreams, buddy."

I'd figured out Santa on my own when I was five, younger than Jake was now. He still believed though, and the world robs you of innocence far too early. I threw a dollop of salmon spread in the middle of a plate and surrounded it with crackers, and then set it on the mantle near Jacob's stocking. I got ready for bed and said my goodnights, then went downstairs.

I turned on the lamp beside my bed and read, while I tracked their movements upstairs with my phantom ears. Their footsteps finally tromped upstairs and went quiet. I finished my chapter and stuck the torn-off corner of one of my assignments in as a bookmark, then slid the bag of gifts out from under my bed and started up the stairs.

My ears twitched as I heard another sound over my head, coming down the stairs. I pulled the shadows over myself on reflex, and crept out to peek around the corner into the living room.

Jake crouched down by the tree and inspected the presents Mom and John set out. It broke my heart that his time was almost up. But still, I crept around the room to stand in the shadows by the cooling fireplace and covered my mouth to muffle the sound as I 'ho ho ho'd quietly. Jacob gasped and looked at the fireplace, oblivious to me, and then dropped the present he was holding and bolted upstairs.

I waited while one of the parental units opened the door to check on Jake and went back to bed before I stepped over to the tree and set my packages out; some of which were labeled, 'To: Jacob, From: Santa'.

I knew I would lose the war, but I would drag the battle out as long as I could. I took a bite of the dip on the mantle, and left a cracker with a bite mark on the plate.

The muffled thud of feet overhead woke me as I blinked drowsily and yawned without bothering to keep my tongue inside my mouth. Painfully bright light pounded through my window, and I blinked repeatedly to clear my eyes. I snuggled deeper into the soft warmth of my blankets, and smiled until Jacob barreled down the stairs and jumped on me.

"Jimmy, Jimmy, get up, get up! It's Christmas, come on, get up!"

Dear lord, give me coffee! Now!

I sent him back upstairs and groaned as I pushed my covers back, put on my slippers and shuffled up the stairs.

Mom was in the kitchen, as red-eyed as I was, standing by the coffee maker with a cup ready as the blessed black stream collected in the carafe. Well, one hurdle down.

"Merry Christmas baby," she smiled at me and yawned. The thumps of Jake herding John down the stairs drew my attention, and I watched as his eyes took in the new presents and the almost empty plate over the fireplace. He gaped for a moment, and then joined us in the kitchen while 'good morning's and 'Merry Christmas's were exchanged around the coffee pot.

"You seem to be up awfully late," Mom teased Jacob, "Usually you're awake at five, jumping all over us!"

"Yeah," John added, as he accepted a steaming mug, "Makes me wonder if maybe *somebody* stayed up later than he should have?" He gave Jake a stern look, "You're lucky Santa didn't just pass you over."

I smiled and made Jake some hot cocoa, and we took our drinks into the living room with us. Mom retrieved our stockings from the fireplace and then we opened our presents, putting special emphasis on the ones from 'Santa'.

I got a lot of—badly needed—new clothes that actually fit, and John gave me "The Wolfman", and told me again how it was the first scary movie he ever saw as a kid. I could only smile and scratch my head, knowing that somewhere under the tree was the same movie, which I'd gotten for him. He also gave me a couple of the cd's on my list, and Mom gave me one of the books I'd asked for, 'The Magic of Shapeshifting'. Fen had recommended it to me months ago, and I'd only remembered when Mom pestered me into making a list for her.

"That one was pretty hard to find," she muttered, "Getting into some weird stuff there Jimmy…"

I just smiled, "Fen told me about it, there's supposed to be some cool folklore in here. Everything else I read just sounds like the same thing over and over again." I improvised as I read the summary on the back cover.

When the oven timer went off, I started a fresh pot of coffee and set the table. Breakfast was slow; the kitchen glowed with sunlight, the ceiling washed with glare from the snow outside. After breakfast we all went our own ways, and I took the seat by the window and read while Jake played with his new toys in the living room.

I cracked open pistachios, and held the book open with my elbow when the phone rang. I scowled and held the earpiece up with my shoulder as I cracked another pistachio, "Hello?"

"Merry Christmas pup!" Loki yelled into the phone and I jumped.

"Merry Christmas, I think you just ruptured my eardrum." I muttered and switched ears so I could hear her over the ringing. Regardless, my phantom tail wagged at the sound of her voice.

"That was just your first gift, when can I bring your others by?" she chirped.

"I dunno, if they're as painful as that first one, I'm not sure I want 'em." I chided.

"Oh, don't be like that; are you trying to say there's absolute-ly *nothing* I could give you?"

Strictly platonic, I reminded myself. "I guess swing by when-ever, I'm just sitting around and eating."

"Seriously, that's all you're doing for Christmas?"

"Yup," I turned the page, "What can I say, I'm not exactly a shining example of normalcy."

"Aw, you're just fuzzy! I'm desperate to escape the extended family, so I'll be by as soon as I can talk Dad into loaning me the truck, 'kay?"

"Wait, but... what does fuzzy have to do with anything?"

"See ya later!" click, tone.

I set the phone down and almost made it to the end of the page before it rang again. Growling, I answered.

"Hey Jimmy, its Fen."

My mood brightened again, "What's up?"

"Not much, you?" His voice sounded small over the phone, even though he was just a couple blocks away.

"Reading my new book." I replied and cracked another nut, "You know, I've got something for you if you wanna swing by."

"Oh... Uh, sure, I'll be over in a minute." He hung up and I almost set down the phone, but I paused and then punched in a series of numbers.

The phone rang once, "Hello?"

"Hey Geri, its Jimmy."

"Oh hey, Merry Christmas dude. Funny, I'd just picked up the phone to call you."

Damn Pack mentality...

Fen arrived a few minutes later. The warm weather surprised me when I opened the door, and Jake begged Mom to let him play outside.

"Stay out of the puddles!" she called as he bolted past us, dinosaurs in hand.

I shook my head and led Fen into the living room. I pulled his presents out from under the tree and handed them to him, "Merry Christmas."

He stared at the present in his hands with a blank expression. When he finally looked up at me and smiled, it looked both sad and angry; but he quickly hid it all behind a mask. I wondered what he was hiding, but smiled back anyway when he thanked me.

He sat down in the chair by the window and tore the crimson paper; slowly, almost hesitantly. I swallowed hard and worried. *Did I do something wrong? What if he already has it? Is he unhappy with me, or his presents?*

He finished unwrapping and just stared at it a moment, then flipped it over to look read the back? "Where did you find this?"

I have my sources," I said, and winked. Google, mostly Google… "Open your other one." I prodded, nervous.

Like you're trying to impress him?

'Shut up!' I mentally hissed at the internal voice, which sadly wasn't wrong.

You want him to like you…

I tuned it out as he picked up the book from the new age store in the Springs and opened it. His brow creased when he recognized it, "Wait, isn't this—how'd you—?"

"You shouldn't underestimate my powers of observation, I nabbed it when Loki dragged you away."

"Wow Jimmy, this is…" he looked at me with a genuine smile this time, the corners of his eyes crinkled a little, "This is amazing, thank you!"

Whew…

"Merry Christmas Fen."

"Merry Christmas Jimmy…" he sighed and shifted in the chair so he could reach into his pocket, "Here, this is for you. I know it's not much, but—"

"Thank you," I interrupted, and was a rewarded with a small smile.

"Here, Merry Christmas." he handed me a small package with Santa's head folded over the corner on the paper.

I tore the paper off and lifted the lid on the black box inside and something glimmered at me when the sunlight fell inside. I poured the box out into my hand and a supple chain flowed through my fingers like water; a small cross pooled in the center of my palm. Awareness tingled up my arm. *Pure silver…*

"It seems Loki was playing both teams. When she dragged me upstairs, she suggested this. You're Christian like Geri, so we thought it'd suit you better." Sunlight glistened on the slightly flared ends of the cross's arms. "This one seemed to have a rather potent effect on shifting energy. I figured it'd be good for you since you're progressing so fast."

"Wow, thank you…" I spoke quietly. Considering his reaction to the price tag on the book, this must have cost him dearly. My chest felt tight, but I didn't want to show too much emotion and embarrass him. I lifted the pentagram he'd given me over my head and held it out for him. I'd grown so accustomed to its presence and weight that for a moment I felt ungrounded, disconnected. I pooled it in my hand and handed it back to its rightful owner. I was only borrowing it after all.

He looked at it for a moment, "Keep it."

"Are you sure—?" He interrupted me with a hand.

"Yes, I'm sure. But put on your new one, I want to see how it looks on you."

Blushing a little, I slipped the pentagram into my pocket and tried to pull the new necklace over my head, but the chain was too short. I looked at it puzzled.

"It's a choker Jimmy, it's supposed to be that short," Fen laughed.

I frowned and started working on the clasp. I cut myself under my fingernail as I tried to fasten it behind my neck.

"Fuck!" I hissed as it slipped again, and a fat crimson droplet formed under my nail. Fen laughed as I sucked the blood off and glared at him.

"Instead of chuckling your ass off over there, how 'bout you give me a hand instead? Jackass…" I snapped.

Still grinning, he held out his hand. I gave him the necklace and turned around. He reached around my neck to hook it when there was a knock on the door. Automatically I yelled, "Come in!"

The door opened and Loki's voice came around it before she did. "Hey Jimmy, Merry Christ—oh!" Fen's hands froze behind my neck. She stopped in her tracks, her eyes wide with surprise as an embarrassed flush spread through her cheeks. I realized how Fen and I looked together right now, and turned red as well. *Please God, don't let John come downstairs right now and see this…*

"Uh, hi Fen," she said like she'd just been busted doing something bad. Her hands toyed with the wrapped box she carried. "Merry Christmas." She said almost questioningly and flashed a nervous smile; I could almost see her ears laid back.

"Merry Christmas Loki." Fen replied with an unusually cold undertone. His hands moved again and within a couple seconds he was done. I angled my head down as far as I could to look at my new silver necklace, but could only feel it in the hollow of my throat.

"How's it look?" I knew right away that Fen was pissed about something, but his face didn't look it at all. He smiled and everything, but I could almost taste his annoyance and frustration in the air. *Weird.*

"It looks good on you, that chain's a good length, so it shouldn't get caught on anything and snap." Fen smiled, but it didn't quite reach his eyes.

"Uh, here Jimmy," Loki stepped forward and handed me her package. "But don't open it yet, I need to run out to the truck and grab Fen's gifts," she blurted and dashed back out the door.

195

I looked at Fen and shrugged, and then pulled Loki's gifts out from under the tree. She came back as I turned around, a couple packages piled in her arms. "Here Fen, I didn't expect you to be here," she said, breathless.

"Yeah, I guess not," he muttered as he accepted the packages. He looked at them with an unreadable mask, and then tore the paper.

Loki and I watched intently, and I wondered why Fen was acting so strange.

Inside the first box was a t-shirt with a werewolf on it that said "Shift Happens" underneath, and inside the second was a beautiful bust of a howling wolf, almost a foot tall.

Fen radiated dark emotions, and I couldn't even make sense of them all because his face was as benign as ever. Sadness, anger, and loss swirled off him as he thanked Loki. We stood there for an awkward moment until he muttered something about needing to go home and walked toward the door.

"You don't like them?" Loki asked as he passed her. He paused at the door, but didn't look at her.

"No, they're very nice, thank you. You know what I really want can't be bought with a credit card…" He spat the word 'bought' out like it burned his tongue, and then stepped outside and pulled the door closed.

"What was *that* all about?" I asked.

"Um, I think he's just hypersensitive about money," she muttered. "He usually hides it pretty well, but I know that he hates that we have money to spend on frivolous things, while he and his mother barely scrape by."

My intuition nagged me, "Is that all?"

She winced, "It probably torqued him that I came to see you first, since he's Alpha."

"So why did you?" I asked, almost hopeful.

"I dunno, you were on the way I guess." She flopped down in the chair and sighed as she buried her face in her hands. Rejection slithered through me but I hid it, and felt deflated. I looked down and realized I still held her gifts.

"Here, these are for you." I smiled at her, and when she smiled back my heart pounded harder.

Way to go Jimmy, just go ahead and fall for two people at once. Only you could achieve something so insurmountably asinine...

"Thanks Jimmy, you're so sweet. Oh, you haven't even opened yours yet. Open it, open it!" she insisted and pulled her hair back behind her ear. I sat down in a chair across from her and absently tore at the paper of my box while I watched her open hers.

She pulled out her hoodie and squealed with delight. "Oh my God Jimmy, I love it! It's so cute!" She scrunched it up in her hands and smashed her face into it.

I hid my envy of the hoodie's affection and pulled the paper off my own package. I opened the box and looked at the unidentifiable black fabric within. I glanced up and noticed Loki's expectant stare while she pulled her new hoodie on over her sweater. I reached inside and lifted out a black vest. It looked medieval, but with a gothic twist. And something was underneath it in the box.

I lifted out the colorful fabric and it unfolded onto the floor. I stood to open it and was startled to see a pair of wolves staring at me past the branch of a tree. One grey and one black.

"It reminded me of you and Fen," Loki whispered, and leaned forward, "I figured you could probably use a tapestry in your Dungeon. D'ya like it?"

"It's awesome!" I grinned at her.

"I'm glad," she smiled back, "Now try on your vest." she winked and sat back as though waiting for a movie to start.

"Okay, but you have to open your other one while I change."

"Deal!" she shouted and grabbed the other box. I grabbed the vest and made for the Dungeon door. "Hey, where're you going?" I turned and her face was in full pout.

"I'm not going to strip right here in the living room!"

"Aww!" she stuck her tongue out at me. I turned away and smiled as I walked downstairs. I pulled my sweater over my head and tossed it on my bed. I shrugged into the vest and pulled the snaps across to buckle it. I tried to swallow my insecurity as I went back upstairs.

You want her to like you too...

I ignored the voice and stepped into the living room. She stood when I came in, and then walked over to me and turned me around, eyeing me like a side of beef at the market. "Yeah, I'm awesome." My heart stuttered when she came close enough to kiss, and lifted her hand. Her fingers felt cool as she ran them down over my cross, framed by the vest. "I knew these would go perfect together." She smirked and looked up into my eyes.

"Did you like your gift?" my mouth was dry and my voice cut out on a couple syllables.

"I love it!" she pulled her hand away and I instantly missed her touch. "This was sort of overkill for a bumper sticker though, don'tcha think?" she held up the box full of packing peanuts.

"No," I plunged my hand into the peanuts, my fingers searching. "It's not." I withdrew my hand, a couple peanuts stuck to me as I presented the small box captured between my fingers. Her eyes flashed with surprise, and then she took the box from my hand as her mischievous smirk fell back into place. She set down the other box and held the little one between us. It was obviously a jewelry box, and she couldn't keep the curiosity from her face when she pushed the hinge open.

Her mouth fell open in surprise, "Oh Jimmy…" she whispered as she reached in, "Is this… moonstone?"

"Yeah." The ring was slender, feminine, with circle of milky-white moonstone set in the center of a three-phase-moon symbol. Celtic knot-work wound the ring's pewter band. "Do you like it?"

She nodded a tender smile on her lips. Then she looked into my eyes and her smile faltered, "But, this is awfully personal don't you think?"

"What do you mean?" Worry blossomed amid shame.

"Something that you wear on your body is one of the most personal gifts you can give…" she muttered, holding the ring but not putting it on. A tendril of anger slithered out of the dragon's pit.

"Both you and Fen gave me things to wear on my body. What's that supposed to mean?" I snapped. She sighed and closed her eyes. I felt my eyes harden as shame hollowed me out. "You're not going to wear it, are you?"

She didn't say anything, didn't even shake her head; but the tear that escaped the corner of her eye told me enough.

Angry, I brushed past her and started picking up the shreds of paper lying around the chair. "Well, keep it anyway. Maybe you'll find somebody to wear it for someday." I muttered bitterly as I stabbed my hand out after scraps. She didn't move, but I heard her breathing as she tried not to cry. When the paper was gone, I picked up Geri's gifts and held them out to her.

"You're going to see Geri later right?" I asked, my voice cold. She wiped her eyes, blurring her mascara as she nodded.

As my anger subsided, ice settled in around my heart. "Could you give these to him for me please? I don't think I'll be going out later…"

She accepted them and walked to the door. She paused with the door open and looked at me, "Jimmy, I'm—"

"Merry Christmas." I interrupted her.

She looked down, "...Merry Christmas..." she muttered, then stepped out the door and closed it.

I stood there for a moment and let my hand drift down over the silver cross and the buckles of the vest. I threw away the paper in my hand and gathered up the tapestry

I glanced out the front window and the truck was still idling there, Loki's silhouette hunched over the wheel. I wanted to comfort her, to go out and hold her, but I couldn't bring myself to move. Finally I turned away and walked toward the Dungeon.

Mom stood at the door to the kitchen, drying off a dish with a worried expression on her face. She didn't say anything, but I knew she'd heard everything. I ignored her and went downstairs.

Way to go genius. You can control your shifting energy now, but you're cursed in an entirely different way. Every piece of your existence is wrong...

I curled up on my bed and guarded the bleeding place deep inside my chest.

On New Year's Day, Fen called me a little after eleven to see if I wanted to go for a drive. His mom had been called in to work, so she said he could take the car out if he wanted to. He seemed miraculously cured of whatever rubbed him raw on Christmas, so I agreed and he picked me up a few minutes later. I desperately needed to get away; thoughts of Loki's rejection haunted me at every opportunity, I couldn't think of anything else.

The sun was bright even though it was the dead of winter, and the air a balmy sixty-two degrees. Funny how that was freezing in the summer, but t-shirt weather in the winter. I grabbed my denim jacket as I headed out the door, and asked where we were going as I belted in and he accelerated away from the curb.

"I just need to get out of the city and away from people for a while. Get my mind off some things"

We crossed over Main Street and turned onto the highway. We drove past the old prison and the road curved around a mountain as we left town. Fen exited and drove through a gate onto a narrow road that wound up the side of the mountain. I gripped the armrest as we drove further and further away from the valley floor; one wrong move and Fen could send us plummeting onto some very hungry-looking boulders.

Just as I thought my nerves were going to snap, he rounded one last corner and parked in a gravel lot just off the road. We parked on top of the mountain, the entire town sprawled below us. Fen opened his door and beckoned me to join him. We climbed onto a slanted mass of red sandstone and sat on the cold rock. The wind blew cold but the sun warmed us.

We stared out over the city and pointed out locations we recognized. Fen pointed out a long stretch of dirt at the foot of the mountain that he said was a shooting range that Geri and his dad used. A couple streets over, Fen pointed out Loki's house. I swallowed down my bitterness, and found the little splotch of brown back beyond her field-like yard where our den was. I found the high school fields, still partly frosted with snow, and then tried to find my house but all the trees made it impossible to pinpoint. I eventually just settled on a glob of houses and bare trees that seemed close enough.

"I come up here sometimes in the summer just to clear my head," Fen muttered, "It's easy to get cabin fever in a town like this; but up here I can step aside and remember how beautiful it is. In the summer… it's like an emerald. A green jewel in the middle of dead dry prairie… I've never brought anyone else up here before; don't want to give anybody any false ideas." He smiled and laid down.

"What do you mean?"

"Well, this is pretty much our town's version of make-out lane." He laughed, and I thought I saw a slight blush creep into his cheeks. I laughed too, but didn't say anything. I was busy trying to keep my imagination under control. Why would he tell me something like that?

I arranged my arms under my head in the most comfortable position I could manage on the hard rock. I watched Fen for a while, before my own eyes drifted closed and the wind's lullaby drew me to sleep.

Something cold hit my face, and jolted me awake.

I realized that the sun was dark on the other side of my eyelids and the wind had grown cold and harsh. I opened my eyes and flinched as another raindrop hit my face. Dark clouds roared over us and I saw Fen stir.

"Shit, c'mon, let's get back to the car!" I shouted as we sat up.

He and I hiked down as the clouds closed around us and the rain thickened. The frigid water hammered down, and saturated us both in seconds. We got to the car, and I heard Fen swear as he patted his pockets.

"What?"

"The keys, I don't have the fucking keys!"

Desperate, we scrambled back over the rocks as visibility dropped and we scoured them hoping to find some glint of metal against the red sandstone.

It was sheer blind luck that I stepped on the keys and felt them slide under my foot. I grabbed them and yelled at Fen as the sky started pelting us with hail. Little chunks of ice pummeled my scalp until Fen got the doors unlocked and we jumped inside, soaked and shivering. The hail hammered the ground outside in marble-sized chunks, creating a rapid-fire cacophony on the roof.

"Can you see well enough to drive?" I asked as my teeth clicked together. My denim jacket had been fine against the wind; but had soaked through and felt like cold lead on my back. Fen shook his head stiffly as he started the engine and turned the heater up, but all it did was blow cold air. Well, wasn't this freaking great?

Forget silver bullets; two werewolves were going to die of hypothermia thanks to their own stupidity. I growled in annoyance at myself as I wrenched my jacket off and pulled my shirt over my head.

"What are you doing?" Fen asked in a puzzled tone.

"My clothes are soaked; they're just pulling the heat out of me…" I wriggled out of my pants and tossed them on the soggy pile of clothing. "At least this way I can keep myself warm…" I closed my eyes and focused on the warm scent of fur and the tingling prickle as my etheric energy crawled across my skin…

A wet thud distracted me, and I looked over to see Fen stripping off his soggy clothes as well. I curled up in my seat as the warmth seeped back into my skin and the shivers subsided. I watched Fen out of the corner of my eye and then averted my gaze in shame. I shifted position and gazed out at the angry green clouds through the window. Fen leaned against me, his skin cool against mine; even just that slight touch spiked my pulse. He stopped shivering too, and we sat there for a while and waited for the storm to pass as the engine warmed up.

The car filled with his scent; some unique mix of corn chips, earth, warm fur, and vanilla. I shifted my eyes so I could look at him, the damp spikes of his golden hair, the way the muscles and bones slid under his skin whenever he moved and made the shadows slip like liquid on his skin.

I couldn't deny it anymore; I knew what I was inside. I didn't want to be this different, I didn't want to be bisexual, but God sure gave a shit about that now didn't he…

"What?" Lost in my thoughts, he'd noticed me looking at him.

"Huh? Oh, nothing…" I muttered and looked back out at the sky as my face flushed with shame.

"No really, what is it?" he asked and twisted to look at me. I kept my eyes off him, talking was difficult enough already. I had two choices about how to answer; either a cop-out or a formal request for rejection. I delayed instead.

"Why did you bring me here?" I asked.

He was quiet a moment, "It's a special place to me, and I wanted to share it with you."

"Why?" My voice sounded rough as my throat tightened. The library, his father's grave, this mountain; they were all special places he'd shared with me; so why here? Why now?

"Are you alright Jimmy?" He asked, and for once I said exactly what I intended to.

"Oh come on Fen, you know damn well that I like you."

"So…?"

"So, doesn't that bother you?" I asked, the edge in my voice from the anger and hatred I turned inward on myself.

"Not really; actually it's quite flattering. Why does it bother you so much?"

"Why *doesn't* it bother you?" I turned to meet his eyes.

"It just doesn't. I know all too well that sometimes a person has no choice, no control… they can't pick the way they are…" He shifted and looked out at the storm. "Or who their heart decides to give itself to…"

I studied his face to try and decipher just what that last comment meant. What was I willing to risk seeing if my fools hope was justified?

We sat in the car, his head resting on my lap as the winter stars spun overhead; "You know… we did make a pretty cute couple…"

Apart from my conscious will, my arm reached out and I ran my fingers lightly down the bare skin of his shoulder; the colors of our skin in contrast.

"It's just funny; Fen's all blonde and stuff, and you're all tan and dark. You two are like day and night."

My heart hammered in my throat, waiting for his reaction. For him to either embrace me or damn me. He arched his back under my fingers, as though inviting me to continue.

Damnit Fen you've made me fall for you, did you fall for me too?

I felt his heart beat beneath my fingers, and the wild part of me wanted to catch it. With each passing second my defenses gave way more and more to that dangerous little flame of hope, that he might like me too…

He put his hand back and touched my fingers on his shoulder as goose bumps spread all the way down my arm. Shaking, I lifted my hands to his face and moved to press my lips to his.

His eyes shot open and I felt his muscles tense seconds before he wrenched himself out of my hands.

"Fen…?" I asked as a cold serpent uncoiled in the pit of my soul.

"Jimmy, I'm sorry I—I just can't—" Fen crossed his arms over his chest as though holding himself as he pressed his back to the door.

Bare stupid realization washed over me, and I felt the bitter cold of the falling hail inside me. "You—" I had to swallow several times to make my voice work. "You don't feel anything for me, do you?"

A sharp jerk of his head told me 'no'. My skin crawled and I felt—numb— like when you've been seriously injured; you know you're hurt, but your mind blocks most of the actual pain...

"Jimmy, I'm so sorry..." Fen reached out but I recoiled. I felt betrayed; betrayed by him, and betrayed by myself. I curled up in the corner of the seat, and stared out at the cold and lifeless clouds, while the voice inside my head tore me apart.

Of course he doesn't love you; he never did. Neither does Loki, that's all their little games are; just games. The teasing, the smiles... But what did you expect you pathetic sack of shit? What's the matter; did you forget no one could ever love you...?

Neither of us spoke other than the most basic of parting pleasantries when he dropped me off at home. I shuffled inside in my soaked clothes, but my family had left, and I didn't even look at their note. I locked the door to the bathroom and cranked up the hot water full-blast.

I peeled off my clothes and stepped under the hot spray and stood there a moment before I grabbed the soap and started scrubbing. I could still smell him, and it sickened me. I scrubbed and scratched with my nails trying to cleanse myself of my stain, of the cold that choked my breath and squeezed my heart. I felt tainted... dirty...

Little by little, I tore through the numb as I tore through my skin until the water ran pink with blood. The cuts burned, but at least it was feeling of some kind. The pain was the only thing that didn't lie.

I collapsed to my knees in the spray of water and held my face. I dug my nails into my scalp and fought it, but something ruptured inside me, and I was glad that my family wasn't home to hear me cry.

I wanted to die.

CHAPTER 13 — TRIALS

I told no one; and neither did Fen.

We didn't speak again until winter break ended, and it was like we'd both decided to block it from our memories and continued as though nothing happened. Which was true, I supposed, since nothing actually *did* happen other than that I made a fool of myself and was rejected by both the people I loved within a week. On the outside, everything seemed the same; minus only Fen's little offhanded comments that made me feel so warm. Part of me missed them…

Part of me wanted him to burn in hell for them…

Mom got the drop on Mr. Spritari before school resumed, and took the police report into the office to make sure he didn't try to pull something shitty—like expel me. Officer Jenson didn't escort me off school grounds, nor did I catch sight of Jack or Malcolm in the halls. To keep from thinking about the painful thoughts that circled like sharks in my subconscious, I dedicated myself to wrapping up the last couple weeks of first semester without setting anything on fire.

After school, Bo caught up with me in the hall. "Hey Jimmy, um, what happened with you and Jack?"

"What do you mean?" I asked as Bo nodded at a pair of girls that said hi as they walked past.

"Jack and Malcolm were both suspended over break. No one really knows what happened, Jack's acting weird and no one's heard from Malcolm, but I tal—hi—" he responded to another duo of smiling girls that giggled past, "I talked to Jack at church on Sunday, and he flipped out on me."

"Let me guess, he called me a demon?"

Bo raised an eyebrow, "Well, after he ranted for a while... yeah."

"Oh, so he didn't happen to mention anything about assaulting my six year old little brother, head butting him in the face, splitting his lip, and then ganging up with Malcolm to bash my skull into the concrete?" I snapped.

"Uh, no, he didn't mention that..." Bo looked incredulous, so I pulled the hair back from my forehead and showed him the still-pink scar just under my hairline as a trio of giggling ladies passed us. "Holy shit dude, I can't believe he'd do something like—well, who the hell am I kidding, he's always had a mean streak, I just can't believe he did that to a little kid? No wonder his dad was so furious." He shook his head.

Bo's words made me flash back to the locker room. "Did Jack's dad beat him again?" I asked.

Bo narrowed his eyes and glanced around, "How do you know about that?"

"Jack tried to blame me for a black eye I never gave him, and I saw his dad smacking him around in the locker room after he was kicked off the football team; they didn't know I was there."

Bo heaved a sigh, "I've known Jack since third grade, and even back then he came to school with bruises and shit. Jack's managed to keep most of his shenanigans under his dad's radar but I heard this sent him overboard."

"Sucks to be him, but I'm sorry Bo—" I shook my head, whatever pity I'd felt for Jack back then had evaporated the moment he'd split Jacob's lip. "Jack's earned his punishment. The trial isn't for another couple weeks, so we'll see what happens."

"Yeah, I guess you're right. The way Jack reacted freaked me out though, he looked terrified. I dunno, you just don't seem like a bad person to me…" I smiled at him in thanks, and we turned down different hallways.

Later that week I went over to Loki's for her guitar lesson. As soon as I arrived I noticed she wasn't wearing the ring I gave her, but Fen had used up all that was left in me to grieve. I pushed it all aside and her lesson went well until we took a break to grab sodas and went back into her room.

She took a sip and leaned back on her bed, looking at me. "So, What's been bothering you lately?"

"I dunno, nothing really…" I replied and played some notes on my guitar.

"You think that someone who knows you and Fen as well as I do couldn't see the tension there? Was it because of what happened at Christmas?" I winced inside, but shook my head. "Then what is it?"

"Absolutely nothing." I replied with a dead voice as the dragon's coils shifted within me.

Loki sipped her soda and stared off into space.

"You know, a couple years ago after I broke up with my last boyfriend, Fen asked me out."

"But I thought relationships were forbidden within the pack?" I frowned.

"Ah, but he hadn't forbidden them *yet*. Fen's harbored a crush on me the size of Texas since I moved here Freshman year." My ears perked up and swiveled toward her. "But Fen's the kind of guy that I can love as my best friend in the whole world; but I wouldn't be able to love him the way he wants me to. Not to mention his timing was craptacular." She winced and her voice broke a little, "I was... *destroyed* inside. But all he could see was what *he* wanted."

Little pieces and quirks of his character clicked into place; little things that I'd ignored and polished over and excused because of my affection for him began to make sense.

She sighed and slid down onto the floor by me. "It creeps me out when I think about it, but I've known him for three years, and that entire time I don't think I've ever seen him *cry*... Never seen any sign that he feels real emotions inside." She sighed, "Jimmy, I know you have feelings for him..."

My head snapped around and my hackles rose. "What did he tell you?"

"Down boy! He didn't tell me shit! I figured it out from watching *you*. Don't you realize how often you sit there and stare at him with this moony look on your face? I didn't realize until I saw you two in school this week." Her voice softened, "Something happened over break didn't it?"

I stared at the ground and didn't answer; didn't want to acknowledge its reality.

"You don't have to tell me *what* happened; just tell me yes or no."

I swallowed and nodded.

"And I take it, it didn't go well?"

I closed my eyes against the burning, and shook my head.

"Oh Jimmy, I'm so sorry. Fen is straight, he's just… indifferent unless it helps or hinders his own agenda in some way. There's so much you don't know. Hell, Fen isn't even his real name. He picked up the nickname from Fenrir in Norse mythology—which is where I got Loki—but never mind…"

I only half listened to what she said, "Then why did he lead me on like—?"

Almost as soon as the words left my mouth, pieces flew together in my mind and I gasped as it all fell into place, "Because he still loves *you*… He saw me as a threat, and the best way to keep me away from you was to make me more interested in him…" He always knew I felt the way I did… he *knew*, and used it against me.

"Yeah, that sounds like something he'd do. Except, if he knew you liked guys, why would he see you as competition?" Loki asked and I looked at her.

"Think about it…" I said.

"Oh! It's not *just* guys, you like girls too?" I nodded at her and turned red. For a moment, it looked like she wanted to smile, but she sighed and rested her forehead on her knees instead, "Well, that explains a lot. At least now you know why I made you promise not to tell him about the guitar lessons. These were something that was just ours; special to us, which he couldn't control…" She set her hand on my knee.

I looked at her pale hand for a moment and then set mine on hers, it felt so warm. "It's been special to me too," I said softly and wrapped my fingers around her hand.

She glanced into my eyes and I felt the pull, the urge to lean over and kiss her…

Her face flushed and she looked away, "Geez, 'Weird Month' must be starting early this year."

"What are you talking about?"

"Oh, we call February 'Weird Month' because of all the crap that happens to us. Shifting energy spikes, the festival of Lupercalia; and last but not least it's our wild brethren's mating season. Hormones and tempers run haywire and lots of flat-out weird stuff happens. Woo-hoo…"

"Sounds like fun."

"Oh, oodles of fun! Or a month of hell; either way you cut it, it's always interesting!" She laughed. "February's lunar cycle just started, so things are bound to get interesting closer to the Wolf Moon."

I stared at her for a minute, then sighed; "Loki, why am I always drawn to people I can never have, or never deserve…"

"I dunno Jimmy… maybe you just *think* you don't deserve them. Fen set you up. And I feel horrible that I didn't see it in time."

Yet, you didn't hesitate to friend-zone the both of us…

"What I still don't get is why Fen went so far to lead me on if relationships are forbidden?"

Loki watched me, "Do you honestly think they'd still be forbidden if I went out with him?"

"Son of a bitch…" I whispered. *Of course!*

"Fen is a control freak. I'm surprised you haven't noticed that by now. He thinks that since he started this Pack that he's basically dictator for life, and he backs it up by the fact that he is stronger than any of us, so no one's ever won a dominance struggle with him.

"Case and point: Geri. He's no pushover, but Fen pretty much set him as permanent Omega. It's sad, but I'm not surprised he doesn't hang out with us like he used to. He's grown so withdrawn, and sometimes I feel like I don't even know him anymore. Fen expects him to drive us everywhere, and he takes out most of his aggression on him. And, he gets away with it *because* Geri's the Omega, that's his job, and since Geri can't overpower Fen, he can't escape."

"Why does Fen try to run this Pack like a school club? I would be Beta, if it weren't for his freaking politics." I stood up and turned in circles, I wanted to pace but the debris on Loki's floor would've tripped me.

"I'm sure part if it was to keep me closer to him." she muttered as she looked down and fiddled with her guitar pick.

"Bastard…" I whispered, my cold hands shaking.

"I've tried so hard to keep the peace. My god Jimmy, you have no idea *how much* I've given up, just because I wanted everyone to get along and be happy," she wiped her eyes and fought back a sob. "But no matter what I do, somebody always ends up getting hurt, and I'm tired of trying to balance everyone else's shit…" She covered her face with her hands, and I had to fight every tortured part of myself that wanted to hold her.

I went home with my head spinning, confused and angry. It wasn't fair… none of it was right! Fen was supposed to be my friend, my Alpha; he was the one I should trust without question. I should have listened to my gut months ago, first his secrecy about Lupa's prophecy and Corwin's suicide. Now this.

I really didn't know him at all, and worst of all, I couldn't trust him anymore.

Something must be done.

I hunted the black oblivion of sleep for what seemed like hours before I finally slipped away. I couldn't rest though; vivid dreams dogged me all night long. Glimpses and snippets of soon forgotten conversations with Lupa danced in my head when the too-short night ended and morning crashed into me. Night after night passed this way as Lupa consumed them, but it was like a garbled radio station and I could only recall useless splinters when I woke.

I struggled with semester finals, but kept my head above water. Before classes changed, Mrs. Ashcroft helped convince Mr. Spritari to switch my first period to Advanced Art with Fen and Loki. Three quarters of the sleep-deprived Pack stuffed into a cold art room first thing in the morning. Yeah, it was good times.

To make it tolerable, I began a passive-aggressive coup against Fen. Loki was the key, and she was pissed enough with Fen to help me. The bastard needed to learn a lesson.

I sat between them at the table, joking with her and sometimes openly flirting; daring Fen to say or do something—anything. But Loki was right, his stoicism seemed to know no bounds, and nothing I did breached his shell. His lack of emotion was disquieting to say the least. Sometimes I felt anger or jealousy from him, like a flavor on my tongue, though he showed no signs of it. I wanted to take a crowbar to that frustrating head of his, let his thoughts sift through my fingers like sand and finally know why—all of the 'why's that had plagued me since the night he bit me.

Geri became more withdrawn, and barely talked. Whenever I called him to hang out or check on him, he was always busy with some level or raid or quest or whatever in a game. Sometimes I caught an angry or jealous vibe off him, but he refused to talk to me about it. I saw what Loki was talking about; Geri seemed miles away, and that distance seemed to grow every day.

Full Moon hit in the first week of February, but Fen and Geri got into a fight that night, and none of us wanted to hang out after that. I tried to call Geri, but he didn't answer his phone. That night, my dreams plunged off the deep end; ranging from abstract nightmares to the frustrating fractured dreams of the obsidian forest and our alabaster guardian.

She tried so hard to tell me something, if only I could hear what...

I darted through the leaves and underbrush. He hunted me…
Somewhere out there, I couldn't pinpoint where.

He'd told me that if I could touch that old maple tree, he'd let
me leave alive. Most dangerous game my ass…

I smelled the sweet sap of the tree with my powerful olfactory
sense; the scent led me straight up to the house I grew up in. Except,
it wasn't any single house; it was Fen's house and all the other houses
I grew up in simultaneously.

In a burst of speed I made it through the open front door, feeling
the cross-hairs of the hunter's rifle on me the whole time. Inside,
Loki and my family were there, but no sign of Fen or Geri. They
all tried to tell me where the hunter was, tried to distract him so I
could make my final run… I could see the maple tree there, not
fifty feet from the back door.

And somewhere with a perfect vantage point of that gap was the
man with the gun. I shook as I realized I'd trapped myself. I had no
choice but to just make a break for it, and hope that my luck was
better than his aim. I launched out the back door and over the fence.
Shifting form in midair, I landed on four paws and ran. I zigzagged
and changed speed as bullets pinged around me.

Barely ten feet from the base of the tree hot agony tore through
my hind legs. I tried to drag myself those last few feet to the safety of
the tree's roots, but a shadow fell over me.

The hunter kicked me over onto my back and I stared up at him
past the barrel of his rifle, his face silhouetted by the sun.

I was so close…

My world ended with a bang as my blood sprayed across the
trunk of the tree.

I sat up and grabbed at my heart to keep it from tearing itself from my chest. I gasped for air, and looked at the clock beside my bed. Thursday morning. I shut off my alarm and got dressed. I knew I wouldn't get any more sleep.

I dressed in a nice button-down shirt and cinched my belt down to hold up a loose pair of slacks. Mom, Jake, and I drove across town to the courthouse instead of school. Officer Parker waited for us out front in a suit and tie with another man in a dark business suit. They stubbed out their cigarettes as we got out of the car and Officer Parker introduced us to Jonas Atchison, our attorney. They interviewed us inside a small counsel room while Mr. Atchison double-checked the details on his notepad. When he seemed satisfied, he gathered his papers and stood up.

"By the way, you should know Jack and Malcolm were likely offered plea bargains by the District Attorney, so if they plead guilty this should go rather smoothly. Honestly, I think they'd be idiots not to." He opened the door and led us into the courtroom.

It looked almost nothing like the movie courthouses. We walked through a very plain wooden door into an almost empty courtroom. There was no ornate banister, no dark wood benches, no jury filling the side seats—which looked like they were borrowed from my school—and no imposing deity of a judge. The room was small, benches laid out like bland and uncomfortable church pews, and the rail was just a round piece of wood.

The judge looked like one of my old grade school teachers; middle aged, her gray-streaked hair pulled back in a bun. There was nothing particularly menacing or powerful about her, and it seemed odd that she wielded so much power over people's lives and fates. Like letting old Mrs. Johnson decide whether or not someone went to jail.

Jack and his dad were already there with a lawyer talking to Malcolm and a woman I could only assume was Malcolm's mom; the curly red hair was a giveaway. Mr. Spritari sat near them in a beige suit, while Officer Jenson watched from the back of the room. Officer Parker, Officer Jenson, and the two policemen who stood near the judge's stand greeted each other silently as we entered.

There wasn't much ritual involved. We rose as the judge entered the courtroom after the bailiff called "all rise", and then sat back down and waited for Mr. Atchison to lead us through the next steps.

The judge looked from the attorneys to the District Attorney and said, "Counsel, enter your appearances." Each attorney introduced themselves, who they represented, and who was present.

The attorneys stood and made their arguments, while the court reporter typed so fast that her keyboard clicked like an angry rodent. For about twenty minutes, Mr. Atchison and the other lawyer ran through their sides of the case. It was like they used familiar words to speak a different language; things like witness statements and submitted evidence, though my favorite line of jargon was 'legal support for our relative position'.

It reminded me of the good-ol'-days with Fen, when I first learned about therians and shifting. I frowned at the twinge of pain the memory brought, and refocused on Mr. Atchison as he handed the judge Officer Parker's pictures of our injuries. Beside me, Jacob squirmed on the hard seat, and I squeezed his hand to reassure him. The judge looked over the photos, then shuffled through some other papers and called Malcolm up to the stand. If possible, even his freckles had gone pale.

"Malcolm McRae, you are charged with assault and battery on school grounds, as well as accessory to child abuse. These are misdemeanors. I am going to ask you a series of questions which I need a yes or no answer for, do you understand me?" Malcolm's voice barely worked as he rasped his replies. "Are you prepared to enter a plea today?"

"Um," he glanced over his shoulder at his mom who nodded at him, "yeah."

"Before you enter a plea, I must ask, has anyone forced you to enter into a plea?"

"No."

"Did anyone make any promises in order to ask you to make a plea?"

"Um, no?" Malcolm sounded confused and even more nervous. Even his voice shook, audible through the mic.

"How do you plea?" she asked.

Malcolm stumbled for words, "Look I—I didn't mean for any of it to happen, I thought we were just gunna scare him. Jack's the one that—"

"Dude!" Jack yelled at him and stood, "What the fuck, bro'?"

"Stop! Counsel, control your clients!" The judge shouted and cracked her gavel against the podium as Malcolm turned and yelled back at Jack, "No one's your 'bro', the only reason I'm here is because of you!" The police officers moved toward them, while Officer Parker and Officer Jenson stood.

"I said *stop!*" The judge yelled again, each word punctuated in staccato, and Malcolm snapped to attention. Jack's dad forced him bodily into his seat; his face livid with rage. *Like father like son…* The tension in the room ebbed somewhat and the cops' hands eased away from their belts.

"Please be advised that I do not tolerate outbursts in this courtroom. When I ask you to stop, you will stop talking, you will not shout, nor will you interrupt anyone who is talking. Am I understood?" The judge's hard gaze switched from Jack's nodding face to Malcolm's as she continued, "One more outburst, and I will hold you in contempt, understand Mister McRae?" Her words were sharp as razors, and her eyes just as piercing as she scowled at him, "Now, how do you plea?"

Malcolm leaned toward the small gooseneck microphone that protruded from the top of the podium, "Guilty, your honor." His voice broke like a freshman's, and I felt some small measure of sympathy for him. Everything he did was because of Jack; he was being punished for being his friend.

"Guilty," she repeated. "I have reviewed the offer and plea-bargain that was provided to me by the District Attorney and I will accept your plea agreement to a lesser charge." Malcolm's tense shoulders released a little, and it looked like he took his first breath since his outburst. "Therefore, in light of the facts that you have no prior record and are under the age of eighteen, you are sentenced to ninety hours of community service, and a $1,000 fine plus court costs. You may make payment arrangements with the clerk in the lobby. Since you are a juvenile, I will note that this record will remain with you until you are eighteen years old, at which time your file and records will be sealed. Do you have any questions?"

Malcolm's mouth moved but no sound came out, so he shook his head 'no'.

"You may be seated. Jackson Reinhart Junior, please approach the podium."

Jack and Malcolm squeezed past each other in tense silence, and Jack stepped up and clasped his hands behind his back.

"You are charged with assault and battery on school grounds, as well as child abuse; both are class one misdemeanors. I am going to ask you the same series of questions which I need a yes or no answer for, do you understand me?"

"Yes," Jack said in a hard voice, not turning away from the Judge. They ran through the same chain of questions she'd put Malcolm through. Jack handled them better though, having seen Malcolm before him.

"Furthermore, you have been advised of your situation and discussed your options with the District Attorney. Is this correct?"

"Yeah." I heard contempt in Jack's voice, despite the fear he should have felt. Didn't he realize there was no coach to vouch for him this time, no corrupt counselor to pull strings? This was the real world, and here he was nothing. Just another violent angry teen.

"I have the plea agreement that you and the District Attorney have entered into in this matter. This agreement is in exchange for your guilty plea, is that correct?"

"Yes."

"Mr. Reinhart, understand that your sentencing will be more severe than Mr. McRae's. First, you were eighteen years of age at the time of the crime, and I must sentence you as an adult. In addition, the court has also reviewed your school disciplinary records which indicate a repeated pattern of violence and anger management concerns. One of the charges that you have plead guilty to is child abuse, and this charge carries a maximum possible sentence of up to twenty-four months in jail, along with fines up to $5,000. Do you understand what I have just said?"

Jack swallowed hard, "Yes your honor." I could almost see the realization dawning in Jack's mind. I glanced at Jack's father, who stared straight ahead with a scowl carved into his features.

221

"In accordance with the plea agreement you and your lawyer made with the DA, I will grant you some leniency. You are still very young, but you must understand that you are being given one *last* chance to prove that you are not a risk to society as a whole. What is your plea at this time?"

"Guilty, your honor."

"This court hereby sentences you to seven days in the minimum security penitentiary, where you will report to at 8:00 AM tomorrow to begin your sentence. The court also imposes a $3,000 fine, court costs, and ninety hours of community service upon your release, along with one year of supervised probation."

Jack's hands shook behind his back. He looked back at his father, fear and desperation in his eyes; the eyes of a scared kid looking for his daddy to save him. Jack's father wouldn't even look at his son, he just stared straight ahead while muscles clenched in his jaw. In that moment, he reminded me a little of John.

"This court is adjourned." The judge declared and struck the gavel. Jack flinched and dropped his eyes from his father. We rose as she stood and exited a door behind her desk. I struggled to breathe around the weight of anger and fear that drowned the room, and I almost felt sorry for Jack, for both of them.

Jacob reached over and took my hand, and then looked up at me and smiled, a pink line of healing scar tissue bisected his lower lip, and I knew he wasn't sorry for them.

Then you shouldn't be either.

I smiled at him and looked back up just in time to catch Jack's glare as a uniformed officer led him out a side door.

We shook hands with Mr. Atchison and Officer Parker again, and I led us out into the lobby. Malcolm and his mom stood at the clerk's window, Jack's father near them by the door. By accident, I caught his baleful gaze as we walked past. His face was hard and mottled with rage, but I held his stare and refused to back down. His eyes flicked down to my throat and I realized he was staring at the cross Fen gave me as he said, "You are a blight in the eyes of God, and He is always watching…"

"Yeah, He's always watching," I repeated, "so remember that the next time you lay hands on your son."

He scowled at me with utter hatred, and then he turned and stormed out the door. *Hmm, no bail for Jack then…* I felt Mom's hand on my back, and it snapped me out of it. My wolf settled and I walked out into the unexpectedly warm sunlight. My eyes ached as they adjusted to the brightness.

"You shouldn't antagonize him," Mom whispered at me as we buckled into the car, "It's over, we won!" she shouted and high-fived Jake in the front seat. "Now, who's up for breakfast?"

Jake whooped and started singing "we won, we won!" I sat back in my seat and stared out the window, a slight smirk on my face. It felt nice to win for a change…

Despite my dreams to the contrary, I felt—good— which was odd enough by itself, but oh well. 'Weird Month' hit full swing; I felt strong, invulnerable even. I was a wolf in man's clothing, power drunk, and I fucking loved it. The sucky part was that Jacob got the whole day off from school, but I had to go in and finish the day's classes.

After enjoying my court victory and the short day of classes, I walked Loki down the hall to her locker after school. When she opened her locker, my arms wrapped themselves around her waist before the notion of self control even ghosted through my mind.

She twisted out of my arms and leaned back against the lockers as her eyes bore into mine. My body reacted, savoring her proximity, but I still didn't dare cross that small distance that separated us. Slowly, we grew closer and our eyes closed—

"Loki!" Fen's voice ripped through the air the moment he came around the corner, Geri wide-eyed by his side.

She looked back at me with strained eyes; "I'm sorry," and she broke past me and ran down the hallway and out the door.

I turned and looked back at Fen, who stood there glaring at me, the stink of his rage ripe in the air.

"Meet me here after sunset..." was all Fen said, and then he turned and stalked off.

"No, wait Fen—" Geri grabbed his sleeve to stop him, but Fen shoved him into the lockers with a snarl.

I ran over to help Geri up while he glared after Fen with unmasked resentment and hate, but he pushed me away. I watched Fen storm out the doors and savored the moment.

Finally Fen... your shell is starting to crack...

I smiled.

CHAPTER 14 – ENEMY

Dinner passed and dusk fell. I watched the last colors fade over the mountains from the school lawn, waiting hidden in the shadow of the football bleachers, warm within my jacket. The unusually warm day—which apparently *was* normal for Colorado—faded into a frigid night, and my breath condensed as it floated away over the brown grass while a half-moon broke the mountains. I felt Fen's arrival the moment he set foot on the lawn, even before his familiar scent laced through the breeze with a sour tang. I stepped out of the shadows and walked out to face him. His anger was plain to read and he was ready to assert his dominance. Unfortunately, so was I…

"What part of 'forbidden' did you not understand?" he snapped.

"I dunno, probably the part where it's spoken by a hypocrite! 'I can tell you what to do 'cause I'm Alpha, and I'm strongest', bullshit! We choose our own damn lives! The only reason you forbid relationships within the Pack is because *you* couldn't get the girl, so you made sure nobody else could either!"

"Liar!" he barked so hard that spit flew from his lips.

225

"Prove it!" I snapped right back and he flinched, "You seemed awfully willing to lead *me* along! All that time, you knew I liked you, but you knew I liked Loki too; so you toyed with my heart to pull me away from her! You used me Fen!"

"That's not—"

"You're a hypocrite and a liar Fen, and I'll be damned if I ever submit to you again. *You are no Alpha!*"

Our gazes locked and the contest was on… We circled each other, growling low in our throats. That amused tutoring look was gone from Fen's eyes, replaced by rage, jealousy, and territoriality. I knew mine were the same. This was no lesson, no romp…

We met in a crack of teeth, tearing and biting at each other, punching and clawing in a melee of savagery. It wasn't even a matter of thought, strategy, or timing anymore. My shifting energy swirled and surged like a cloud of electricity, crackling and itching over my skin.

When Fen realized I had the upper hand, he reached into his pocket. My gut ached as soon as he pulled out the lump of turquoise, and then he jabbed it toward me as a weapon. I jumped back on reflex and slipped into the shadows.

Fen froze, shocked as I disappeared right in front of him. I slipped around him, slapped the rock out of his hand, and then picked him up and threw him with a burst of berserker strength. Before he could even orient himself, I pounced and flattened him to the ground. With a snarl, I buried my teeth in his neck. He tried to push me off him, but I refused to relent and I squeezed until he coughed. When he realized it was over, that I had proved my dominance, he went still as death. I released him, and saw little beads of tears run down his face.

I'd never seen Fen cry before, but now his inhuman eyes looked more hurt—more *human* than I'd ever thought him capable.

He sat there with bits of dried grass all over him and glared at me. I wished I knew why he hated me so much.

"It's not fair…" His human words pulled me out of my shift, leaving only the remnant energy boiling within me. "It's not *fair!*" He screamed and surged to his feet, "Why does she love you more than me? I've been with her for years, and then *you* came along and she just discards me… It's all your fault!"

"Loki's life is her own, she chooses who she wants to and neither of us have any say in the matter!"

"Not just Loki!" He screamed, his fists balled at his sides and his face flushed crimson, "Lupa hasn't visited me for months! She's always loved you more; she just used me to get you back! You stole them *both* from me!"

He lunged at me and I tensed, but he collapsed against me. He sank to his knees, pounding his fist weakly against my chest. I knelt down with him and wrapped my arms around him as he wept out months, maybe years of pent-up anguish. Despite the pain he'd caused, I still couldn't help but feel for him…

"I don't think they left you for me," I whispered into his hair, "I think your fear and jealousy pushed them away. They'd return to you if you were honest, I have no doubt about that."

"They were all I ever had…" he sniffed, "I didn't have friends, or money, or even a fucking dad… All I ever wanted was them…"

"We've always been here with you; I think you just needed to catch sight of us again…"

A car started in the parking lot by the athletic field, and its headlights flicked on, blinding me. I held my breath a moment, wondering if it was a cop, wondering what they saw, but its engine growled as it sped out of the parking lot. I relaxed a little, but felt uneasy.

"Hey, I think we should leave, that car spooked me."

Fen nodded and we brushed ourselves off, "Let's go to Loki's, we need to resolve this completely."

We walked to her house and knocked on her front door. Loki's father answered, unhappy to see unannounced visitors so late, but he took in our disheveled and red-eyed state and then pounded on Loki's door and told her to make it quick. We needed to talk but we couldn't stay, so we quietly agreed to meet out at the den. She let me and Fen use her phone to call our parents, and we told them we were going to spend the night at Geri's.

I tried to call Geri, but there was no answer. Something about it felt strange, but I tried not to dwell too much on it.

Fen and I left and walked just far enough down the street to be hidden from her house. The neighbor's dog trotted up to the corner of the fence to greet us. She leaned against the fence and let me scratch her behind the ears as we waited.

Finally, a shadow slipped away from the house. After giving the dog one last goodbye rub, we slipped silently along the field's edge, careful not to leave footprints in the patches of snow along the fence.

Halfway back to the den the dog barked at something out on the street. I looked back, but she wasn't barking at us so Fen started moving again and I followed. At the entrance Fen slipped down first, and I looked back where the dog was still barking.

I felt watched until I heard a bird caw nearby. I forced myself to relax, reassured that it was probably just Corwin keeping up on Pack business. Paranoia appeased, I got onto my knees and crawled inside the den as a car engine started and rumbled down the street.

We lay in silence for a while, each of us spread away from the others; a stark and painful reminder of the divisions that had formed between us as friends... as Pack...

"I guess…" Fen spoke first, "I owe you an apology… Both of you and Geri too once I see him. I was greedy, and jealous; instead of holding us together like an Alpha should, I've torn us apart…

"Jimmy, I'm sorry that I misled your feelings and hurt you, believe it or not, I do love you, but not in the same way." I swallowed down the bitter ache inside me as he continued, "Loki, I can't stop loving you, I've tried, but I shouldn't have caged you either; it wasn't fair or right of me. I'm so sorry, guys…"

I sighed, hurting, "What are you supposed to say to someone when you accept their apology, but it's not 'all right'?"

"I guess you say *that*," Loki answered and fidgeted in the dark, "So… What do we do now? What comes next?"

A voice whispered in the back of my mind. *You beat Fen, you should take charge…*

As if he read my thoughts, Fen answered, "Jimmy beat me fair and square; so he's Alpha now. It's up to him." Well shit.

I cleared my throat. "I guess, we just take it one day at a time." I tried to hide the uncertainty in my voice. "Take a step back and remember the things we love about each other that we started taking for granted somewhere along the way. Right now we have to make things right with each other again."

"In the meantime, let's just stay here tonight," Fen said, "Maybe a night in the den might just help us all find ourselves again…"

We kept our coats on and snuggled together against the cold February night and eventually fell into an uneasy sleep.

It chased me, the dark being just behind me without any face or body; yet real nonetheless, and inescapable. I recognized my dream, and yet even realizing it was the same dream, I had no control over

229

it… I ran with all my might down the forest path, but this time I recognized the faces of people from school.

I ran past Fen, and tried to shake him but he merely gazed into space with vacant eyes. With a sinking powerless feeling in my gut, my body continued running against my will, and left him behind. I glanced over my shoulder and watched in horror as the onrushing wall of darkness enveloped him and tore him away from me.

I ran and ran, my chest burned and my eyes blurred with tears. This time I knew where I was heading, and eventually the path ended; and there, as before, stood the black iron gate, wreathed in fog, with the cold blue moon overhead.

I tore open the gate and dashed inside, and then stopped cold. Instead of a classroom, I'd entered the gymnasium.

I felt it at the threshold, peering in ravenously with such utter loathing that it chilled my blood. I turned to look at the door.

Loki stood there and held her hand out to me, oblivious to the hungry darkness behind her. My heart froze; I tried to scream out a warning and run to her but my legs felt like they were made of cement. With victorious hunger, the darkness reached out to consume her…

I woke with a cry and struggled, startling Loki and Fen out of their sleep. They asked me about the dream, but I told them it was some weird nightmare, while I reassured myself with their presence.

They're all right, they're okay, they're right here.

To change the topic, I asked Fen if Lupa had visited him and he grew distant. I assumed she had not until he answered, "Yeah…"

His reaction puzzled me, "What happened?"

"She told me to uh, make a choice… And that then, things she'd foretold would begin to come true." I frowned. I could tell he was editing a lot, but I let it slide for now.

Loki stretched and yawned. "Ya know, I've always been jealous of you two. It seems like you guys get to talk to her all the time, but I only ever catch so much as a glimpse once in a blue moon."

I winced has her words reminded me of the dream.

"Well, maybe that'll all change soon. Lupa made it clear that things are about to change in very big ways…" Fen looked at me in the dim light with sad eyes.

I had the strangest feeling. I didn't want to leave the den… I wanted to stay here a very long time… It was probably nothing but some subconscious panic left from my dream, but I couldn't get my heart to slow down. Fen gave me a sad smile and then started up the tunnel.

"Come on, it's time…" he said.

Fen led us out of the den and stood up outside. The sun was just teasing the sky with its earliest gray light; it hadn't even broken over the mountains yet. My coat snagged on a branch and I reached back to unhook it when I heard a dull thud as Fen grunted and staggered. Something hot and wet misted my face as Fen's knees folded and he hit the ground next to me.

The crack of a gunshot echoed from far away…

No…

Fen convulsed as he lay there in front of me, and my mind raced desperately, grasping for every conclusion besides the obvious. Fen gasped for breath with a sickening gurgle, and I crawled beside him. He turned his head and looked at me, his amber eyes faded to gray as he pressed a shaking hand to my face. The blood ran from his body and saturated his shirt while Loki struggled out of the den behind me.

No, you're still dreaming; wake up…

"Jimmy, you have to lead them…you have to protect them now, it's what Lupa meant all along…" Fen's voice was faint and blood leaked out of the corner of his mouth as he spoke. He coughed with a sick gurgle, and sprayed bloody froth as he rubbed his thumb against my cheek and smiled, "I'm so sorry Jimmy…"

This isn't happening, you're just asleep; wake up and it'll go away…

"Fen, just hold on, we'll get help for you! Just hold on—" His hand slipped from my face as the fire that lived in him drained from his dark grey eyes. His limp arm landed in the dirt, dotted with his own blood—blood that covered my face in a fine mist— and his pupils dilated as the smile went slack on his face. Though his eyes still pointed toward me, Fen no longer looked through them…

No, no this isn't real. It can't be! Wake up Jimmy… WAKE THE FUCK UP!

Cold shock froze my veins; like my heart stopped…

Beside me, Loki wept. She inched closer and touched his face, and then leaned down and touched her forehead to his tenderly, tears rolled down her cheeks and landed on his, "Fen, no… no, Fen, no…" Her whimpers grew as she gathered his head into her lap and stroked his hair while she rocked back and forth.

I wanted to reach out to her, but I couldn't move… couldn't breathe… This was too real; I wasn't dreaming this time… I gripped Fen's hand, still warm; but cooling fast. Limp and unresponsive…dead…*Fen was dead…*

I flashed back to my dream and my stomach dropped. *The darkness tore him away from me…*

Our cries tore through the cold gray sky, and echoed over the fields and streets; answered by the dogs from miles around. Together, Loki and I howled out our agony to the hungry winter cold. Tears burned down my face, cutting lines through the red mist that covered me…

Fen, no… Wake up…

…Wake up…

CHAPTER 15 – THE FUNERAL

Flashing lights and sirens cut through the cold morning. Loki's parents heard us screaming and found us out back. Her mother cried and held Loki while her dad gently tried to pull me away from Fen's body, but I wouldn't leave him. I couldn't.

The police dragged Loki and me through a maelstrom of questions. Somewhere along the way, somebody cleaned the blood from my face and Fen's corpse was discreetly bagged and removed. They wrapped us in blankets and ushered us into the back of an ambulance with Loki's parents. We bounced in unison, wearing the same blank masks of shock as we stared off into space.

I tried to remember, how long ago had Fen been alive? An hour? Thirty minutes? A lifetime? Part of me shut down, I just couldn't comprehend that he was gone, absolutely gone. We stopped and they opened the doors to let us out. We stepped down from the ambulance, and a familiar voice snapped me out of the mess of my thoughts.

"Oh, thank heaven, there you are!" I looked up and found myself in the arms of Fen's mother, wearing her hospital uniform. My God… She was working, and they were wheeling her only son's corpse into the morgue. The thought horrified me as she guided us through the ER doors.

She led us into a room and gave us some water, and then she checked us for signs of shock. I wondered how the hell she still functioned. I was about to ask when she spoke, her voice soothing but distant.

"I've already called your parents Jimmy, they're on their way," she said, and sat down beside me. Loki's mom wept quietly as her dad held them both, Loki's face a hollow mask of shock. Something was missing…

"Have you called Geri?" I asked.

"I tried, but there was no answer." *Strange…*

"What about his cell?"

Fen's mother shook her head, and I stared at the floor in front of us.

"Thank you for staying here with me," I muttered.

"Thank you for letting me," she whispered, "I can't—think about it yet, as soon as I do, it's all over…"

A few minutes later, John burst through the door, Mom right behind him. His eyes found me and he crossed the room in two strides and grabbed me by the shirt. I flopped like a rag doll as he shook me, yelling, "Jimmy Marshall Walker, what the hell is going on? You told us you were going to Geri's—"

"John, wait outside!" Mom forced her way between us while she and Fen's mother pried John's hands from my shirt. I fell back into the chair, dazed, wondering how it was possible to hurt even more inside. Mom looked tiny in front of his bulk, but she set her feet and glared up at him in defiance.

John pointed over her shoulder at me, his face livid, "That boy lied to us, and just look—"

"John, get the fuck out of this room!" His face registered

surprise as Mom shoved him out the door and slammed it in his face. She took a deep breath and walked over to me, and then knelt down and held my face so she could look in my eyes. "Jimmy, baby, are you alright, are you hurt?" I couldn't talk, so I shook my head. My body was fine, but my soul...

She put a shaking hand on the back of my head and pressed my face to her shoulder as she held me. I felt my control slip and heat rushed up into my face as I felt safe for the first time since I'd left the house last night. "Mom..." I whined into her shoulder and lost it. Her coat muffled my wails as she stroked the back of my head and rocked me back and forth.

Police questioned me again, and I had to wonder if it was my dark skin that earned this special hell as they tried to maneuver me into incriminating myself, but after a while they released us. As we left the room, I glanced back and saw Fen's mother sitting alone as the first tears slid down her cheeks. Mom walked up to her and took her hand, "If there's anything you need, any way we can help, please let us know." Fen's mother squeezed her hand and nodded.

We drove home and I retreated to the dungeon. I threw my bloody clothes on the floor and curled up naked in the sheets while I tried not to hear Mom and John rage at each other upstairs. I stared at the tapestry Loki gave me for Christmas—Fen and I as wolves—until I tore it off the wall.

I always thought it was odd when people in movies expressed disconnection from time. I thought they just lost track, I never imagined that time itself distorted. The mind and soul pull into a shell, where time and the pain of the world cannot touch them.

Slip—Fen and I laughed and ate together on his couch after school—*Slip*—Fen and I at each other's throats, snapping and snarling on the school's lawn—*Slip*—Fen's dead gray eyes staring at me—*Slip*—I stood in front of the mirror, adjusting my tie.

A fine film of condensation misted the windows of home and car alike, not quite cold enough to freeze, but I felt it in my soul as we drove to Fen's memorial service. After the autopsy, they'd sewn his body back together and dressed it in a suit for display. The mortuary cosmetician had done an unmercifully good job. So good that when I arrived, I forgot for a heart stopping moment that his soul was gone, and almost yelled at him to open his eyes.

His loss crushed me all over again. Fen's mother sat alone in the first row of rusting foldout chairs, a damp tissue crumpled in her hand. I sat down in the chair next to her and put my hand over hers. She smiled briefly at me, which only pushed more tears from her eyes while her shaking hand took mine and squeezed hard.

For a cold and barren moment I felt my own tears burning and Mom sat down in the chair beside me and rested her hand at the nape of my neck while John and Jacob sat beside her. It surprised me how much that small touch salved my wounded tattered soul. I felt another presence and glanced behind us as Loki knelt and wrapped her arms around Fen's mom and me.

Loki broke her embrace and took a seat behind us with her parents. For the first time I saw her father without his wide-brimmed cowboy hat, his salt and pepper hair parted and combed.

Not many people attended, but most of the people who came had genuinely known and cared about him. I shared hushed greetings with Mrs. Ashcroft and Mr. Decker. Mrs. Cartwright took a seat near the library and administration crews. She dabbed her eyes with a tissue, her gaze far away as if she were reliving Corwin's funeral in her mind as well. In the back near the principal, I was surprised to see Mr. Spritari's spidery frame, dressed in the same beige suit he wore to Jack's trial, but his etched grimace held no malice this time. He sat painfully straight in his seat, and his reddish eyes stared straight ahead while the woman next to him rubbed his arm and blew her nose.

Geri arrived later with his parents and sat beside Loki and her family. His mother was tall and slender with a severe expression on her sculpted face; where his father was on the shorter side and stocky like his son. A bushy mustache burst out from under his nose, accompanied by a round belly and a shiny pate of hairless skin atop his head. They were all dressed impeccably, their clothes tailored perfectly for them under black wool overcoats. I tried to catch Geri's eye, but he wouldn't look at me.

I zoned in and out through the service as a man who never knew him spoke sterile statistics of his life as though reading from a fill-in-the-blanks script. Sometimes I thought he was talking about someone else, he kept calling him James.

Only four of us knew his true nature, his true worth. Like a scab I couldn't stop picking at, my eyes returned to the spot on his chest, just under the fold of his left lapel where I had watched his heart's blood drain out of him just… what was it, minutes? Days? Years ago? Delirium knocked at my door until time slipped again and the speech was over.

One by one, we walked past the coffin and gazed at his face one last time. I didn't know if it was disrespectful to touch the dead or not, but I couldn't resist. I reached out and ran my fingers over the thin scar my teeth had left on his cheek, and then rested my hand on his chest where the bullet had entered.

I leaned over with blurry eyes and kissed the forehead of the empty shell that had once housed my best friend. I smiled and pressed my hand to his chest again, and then walked away; leaving behind his silver pentagram necklace.

Mrs. Ashcroft hugged me, and other members of the faculty offered words of consolation. Geri and his family disappeared without a word, and almost everyone else left soon after as well. Loki and I and our parents escorted Fen's mother outside where they placed a carved slab of black marble in the ground beside another one just like it.

Fen could finally be with his dad now. James Elliot Kendle was laid beside his father, Morgan James Kendle. "Fen" was carved into the stone under his real name.

Fen's mother placed flowers on both stones, and then cried desolately. The distant cries of a raven floated through the air from an old friend and I looked up across the field. The hair tingled on the back of my neck as I glimpsed the dark outline of someone watching us through the chain-link fence before cold rain swept over us and I lost sight of them.

In solitude one finds intermittent peace or torment, and sometimes simultaneous hell. In sorrow, one either seeks solitude to lick their wounds, or they crave the strength and compassion of others. In company, one vents their emotions through any means available; be it weeping on a compassionate shoulder, or screaming and attacking. The guilt that follows then drives the mourner into solitude…

I learned this cyclical ballet well as we danced to its morbid rhythm.

Loki, Geri, and I were granted a one-week reprieve from school. Geri never really told us where he'd been, just that he was out of the house, and I couldn't bring myself to care very much. If he'd been there, he would have been just as traumatized as Loki and me.

One question haunted me; who could have possibly wanted to murder Fen? Every time I tried to think of a culprit, the idea became ludicrous. He was an outcast like me, but he didn't have any enemies that I knew of; certainly nobody hated him enough to want to kill him.

The police seemed to be stuck in the same rut, so when they finally issued their official report, they labeled Fen's death as a freak accident that probably occurred from a misfire or a ricochet at the gun range in the foothills. Unless someone turned themselves in, they had no reason to suspect otherwise. As much as I craved closure, the ugly truth was that I might never find it.

I couldn't even imagine what it was like for Loki; first Corwin's suicide, and now this. Her smirk and mischievous grin had vanished; wiped from her face as she stared off into space, lost in her own torment. After Geri's initial shock wore off, he drowned us in painfully upbeat inspirational messages, trying to get us to blindly believe everything was going to be okay. I didn't want 'God's mysterious ways', I wanted my best friend back; and Geri's propaganda couldn't give me that.

It grated on my nerves instead until I finally snapped. It wasn't until I found myself standing over him, growling with clenched fists, while he cowered on the floor with the same angry betrayed look in his eyes that I'd seen before, that I realized I'd just pulled a Fen in the worst possible way. I apologized and reached to help him up, but he pushed my hand away and left. He didn't call again after that.

I coped as best I could, and tried to keep as busy as the clutching apathy would let me. Sometimes a single hour crawled by while entire days disappeared into the void. Most days I almost couldn't even muster enough initiative to get out of bed before noon for a cup of coffee.

In my better moments I tried calling Loki and Geri, but Geri usually wouldn't answer, and Loki's calls always descended into a long uncomfortable silence until one of us came up with some excuse to hang up. My inability to help my friends rotted inside me, feeding my dragon.

How could Fen expect me to lead when I couldn't even console myself? How could I? How could I find the strength to keep myself going, much less guide the others? Worthless and inadequate; Fen had wasted his dying words on an invalid. It was all so trivial now…

I needed to get out of the house, so I stepped outside and took a deep breath. Without thinking about it, I glanced down the street toward Fen's mother's house—I couldn't think of it as Fen's house anymore—and saw a moving truck parked at the curb. With a sinking feeling in my gut, I jogged down the street and knocked on the door. Fen's mom answered, wiping her forehead with her sleeve.

"Oh, Jimmy!" she said, surprised.

"What's all this?" I gestured toward the truck.

She sighed and stepped aside, "Come inside Jimmy." Brown cardboard boxes were strewn across the floor behind her.

"Why didn't you tell any of us?" I demanded, betrayal burning inside me as I looked around the half-packed living room. "What, were you just going to sneak out of town and hope none of us noticed?

"Have a seat," She waved toward the worn old thrift-store couch that Fen and I used to sit on after school. "I can't do this Jimmy, I can't live in the home I raised him in anymore, it's just too… God, 'painful' doesn't even come close. I die a little more inside every time I walk through the door and he's not here."

"Where are you going?"

"I don't know… I'm not even sure I care; it's not like there's anywhere I can get away from the fact that my son is dead. My entire family Jimmy…I've buried them all."

We sat in silence for a moment before she spoke again, her voice soft, "It's not enough that I have to process his death, but now I also have to face up to the things in his life I thought I'd have years to deal with. I feel so guilty…" She shook her head.

"What do you mean?"

"After his father died, I tried, but I just couldn't find anybody else. Fen grew up without anyone to show him how to play sports, or work on cars, or any of those things guys are supposed to know. They beat him, called him a pansy, accused him of being gay—I lost count of how many times he came home from school crying or bleeding. He never blamed me… but I did.

"I think that's why I never challenged him when he started obsessing over this wolf thing. He needed some excuse for being different, something that gave him strength. It went on longer than it should have, but I just couldn't take that away from him too." She sighed, "Even though it was all in his head, at least it made him happy."

I stared into space while her words cut deep into me. Was it all just in our heads? It was hard to imagine Fen ever not being a wolf trapped in a boy's body. Instead, he was just another fatherless victim, who allowed his obsession to transform him.

Something from his funeral came back to me and goosebumps crawled over my skin. His real name was James—Jim—Jimmy…

We were the same; two faces of the same coin, like night and day. In my mind, I looked into a mirror and saw him reflected at me.

He was what I would have been without John. I winced as I remembered John's rage at the hospital; some small part of me had still hoped that he might actually care for me. Father or not, without John, it might have been my mother mourning in that tiny little box of a house in Idaho. Which reminded me…

"What are you going to do with his ashes?"

"I don't know. The last place he belongs is a box, but I don't know where he would want to be…"

"I might have an idea."

"Oh?" She asked, and then glanced at the door. Then she laughed and lowered her eyes, "Sorry, I keep expecting to hear him drop his backpack on the deck and walk through the door…"

I glanced at the door too, and almost imagined the knob twisting… but it didn't.

The air sparkled with loose crystals of snow, caught in the wind. The sky was clear and painfully bright as the remaining Pack members stood with me and looked out over the city, bundled against the biting gusts.

Fen's mom parked and crunched through the loose powder toward us with a white ceramic box held to her chest. Loki and Geri hugged her without realizing what—or who—was in the box.

"Okay guys," I said, "we're not legally allowed to disperse human remains just anywhere. But this is important, and for all anyone knows, she's keeping him with her."

Loki and Geri looked shocked as they realized why we were there, and the precious cargo in the white box. We passed it around, and each of us closed our eyes as we held it to our hearts and whispered our last goodbyes. Geri looked uncomfortable, and passed the box to me almost immediately.

I looked at the clean porcelain lid and closed my eyes. This was all that was left of a boy who had found the soul of the wolf inside himself, and helped us do the same. My best friend, my guide and tutor, my bitter rival, my first broken love… I said goodbye, and handed the box back to his mother.

She held it a moment, and then handed it back to me and smiled. "You do it Jimmy." I felt Loki eyes on me, glistening with tears, but appreciative that I'd found a way to bring us all some small measure of closure.

"Goodbye my friend. May the winter's fangs never touch you again…" I lifted the lid and threw Fen's ashes up into a gust of wind that swept him away over the city in a sea of floating diamonds.

CHAPTER 16 — BREAKING POINT

I hugged Fen's mother one last time before she kissed my cheek and got into the moving van. I felt robbed. Like she'd packed up Fen's memory and stolen him away with her. I stood beside a couple boxes of Fen's books and movies that she'd given me, and waved as she drove down Wolf Road and turned toward the highway. The familiar worn façade of Fen's house stood hollow and empty, while a red and black 'For Rent' sign replaced the lives that Fen and his mother had lived there.

Upholding my yearly custom of flipping Valentine's Day the finger, I made a token gesture at Lupercalia instead. But even the ancient Roman werewolf festival passed cheerlessly. Everything felt like a hollow worthless ritual without Fen.

I went to sleep that night expecting a visit from Lupa since the day was associated with her favorite namesake. I hadn't seen her since before Fen and I fought and I ached to reconnect, but restless blackness clouded everything as I slept. Rather, I tried to sleep, until my useless masochistic brain woke me up by replaying Fen's death.

Over and over again.

I'd hoped to heal the rift I'd accidentally opened between Geri and I with Fen's ashes. Instead, Geri drew even further away from me, and changed the subject every time I brought it up. He told me he was fine, and then acted the opposite as a miasma of guilt swam around him. It gnawed at me, but I didn't know what to do about it.

When we returned to school, the morning was so white and frigid that the frost seemed to linger inside my bones even after I walked through the doors. In the halls, everyone pretended not to stare. A few actually had the courage to walk up to me and mutter words of condolence, though I knew few would actually mourn his loss. My stomach twisted as I neared the door to Mrs. Ashcroft's room, a room where Fen would not be waiting for me anymore with charcoal on his fingers.

I realized I'd been standing there staring at the door when Mr. Spritari cleared his throat. He delayed the inevitable and escorted me to the counseling office instead.

Fuck my life, what now?

"I'm sorry if I worried you Jimmy," he said as he closed the office door behind us, probably due to the look on my face, "but I didn't want to create more drama by calling you here through the PA system. I'm very sorry for your loss. I would like to do what I can to help you through this, the grieving process isn't easy."

"What the hell would you know about it?" I snapped at him before I could stop myself. After an awkward moment, Mr. Spritari retrieved a small framed picture from the far side of his computer monitor. He looked at it a moment, and then handed it to me.

"This was my son, Tony," he said. I looked at the school portrait in the picture frame. The boy had his father's narrow face, but a shy smile and wider cheekbones, with brown hair that dangled almost to his eyes. He looked to be either a sophomore or a freshman if I had to guess, but I didn't recognize him. The picture looked several years old.

"The day after his sixteenth birthday, he was killed in a school shooting. Much like your friend, he was just in the wrong place at the wrong time. My son," Mr. Spritari started, but his voice broke, "was a good boy, but he paid the price for someone else's rage…"

"I'm sorry," I muttered. As horrible as Fen's death felt, I couldn't even fathom what it must have been like to bury your own child. No wonder he'd been such an asshole about my record.

"No matter how much time passes, it never gets easier to talk about." He took a deep breath and composed himself while he cleaned his blurry glasses with a tissue. "So, believe me, I am *very* familiar with the grieving process."

We talked about the five stages of grief through the remainder of first period. I was already too well acquainted with denial and isolation, anger, bargaining, and depression. Mrs. Ashcroft had kindly forfeited the assignment I'd missed, but Mr. Spritari had collected a stack of make-up work for me from my other classes. Including five make up tests. Skippy.

At lunch, Bo caught up with me in the lunch line.

"Hey Jimmy, how're you holding up?" he asked with an awkward smile.

"Surviving…" I muttered, and accepted a scoop of canned pears from the lunch-lady and shuffled along, "What's up?"

"Well, not much. I was wondering if you wanted to hang out some time. Maybe jam or something?"

I raised an eyebrow at him and waited for the punch line.

"I'm serious, Jimmy. Two of my friends just got expelled—one of whom is in prison—and after I quit the football team everyone I thought were my friends stopped talking to me. They blame me and Jack for ruining their season," he scratched his head, "and they're not fond of you either. I know this sounds really weird, but you're the only authentic person I know. Everyone else is dramatic, two-faced, and sometimes downright insane. You're just... you."

"Um, thanks?" At least it *sounded* like a compliment, "Yeah, we can hang out, I don't mind. Hey, why *did* you quit the team anyway?"

Bo looked embarrassed, "I might as well tell you, it's not like it'll ruin my reputation at this point, but I wanted to focus on my grades. That's all. I haven't heard back from any of the schools I applied to yet, and I'm trying not to freak out."

"Dude, it's like, barely March, and you're worried about not getting an accepted? It'll be fine, you're a smart guy." I smiled at him to hide the twinge of pain I felt. Fen had been waiting for the same thing. Fen had wanted to go to college so badly, and he never would, while I'd walked away from it...

"I also uh, I've been thinking about what you said, about acting like Jack and Malcolm. Lately it's become painfully clear that I don't want to be anything like them. So, yeah... I'm also willing to bribe you with my Government notes if I have to."

I couldn't help but smile, "Thanks, I'm gonna need them. Mr. Spritari just gave me a mountain of make-up work."

Bo laughed as we rounded the corner of the hallway and found Loki leaning against the wall. "Oh, uh, hey Jimmy," she said as she eyed Bo.

"Hey, what are you doing out here?"

"I was waiting for you and Geri. I just couldn't... uh, the art room..." Loki's voice trailed off, "I just can't. It was hell in there without you today." I apologized and explained Mr. Spri-tari's interception while Bo hung back, uncomfortable and quiet. Loki watched Bo out of the corner of her eye with equal parts suspicion and annoyance until she snapped. "Okay, are you going to lurk there all day? Knock off that creeper shit and either say something or go away."

Woops, forgot that part. "Actually Loki, I was wondering if it'd be okay if Bo hangs out with us. At least until Geri gets here?"

"Why? Doesn't Mr. Football Hero have anyone else to bother?"

"Y'know what, she's right. I'll leave you guys alone." Bo muttered and turned to leave.

"Actually," I said as I snagged his shirt to keep him from walking away, "he doesn't. He's more like us than them, and now they know it." I knew Loki would be able to read between the lines and that she understood everything I didn't say.

"Okay, fine," Loki lifted her hands in surrender, "he can stay. We're basically the home for misfit toys anyway…" she muttered to herself and rubbed her temples. After a moment, she sighed.

"Okay Football Hero, here are the rules," Loki said as she crossed her arms and faced Bo. "First of all, no lurking and no creeping. It's fine if you don't want to talk, but if you give us the heebie-jeebies, you're out. Second, don't you dare try to pity us or think you can replace Fen. You can't, and fuck you if you try. Lastly, and most important, if you try to screw any of us over or stab Jimmy in the back, I will personally kick ten colors of shit out of you. Capisce?"

"Uh, got it." Bo muttered, he almost looked scared. I smiled at Loki's protectiveness and picked at my food while I hid dangerous thoughts.

"Good. Now, there are about five hundred topics that we are *not* going to talk about," Loki said, turning to me. Now it was my turn to read between the lines. The obvious subject was Fen, but anything having to do with Pack business was nixed as well. "When are we going to start the guitar lessons again? I really need to get my mind off things."

"Hell, we could start tonight if you want." I said, craving to have a slice of our old lives back.

Bo cleared his throat. "You know Jimmy; you've kept me waiting for months to jam. If it's cool with you, I could bring my drums over?" Bo gained brownie points for directing his question to Loki. He knew she was the one he'd really have to win over. Loki narrowed her eyes at him, but I could tell she was interested.

"I know dude, but we don't have anywhere to set up a drum set." I said.

"You guys could bring your stuff over to my house. My kit's set up in the garage, and my folks would be happy to see me play again."

I raised my eyebrow at Loki and watched her debate inside her head. "Okay, fine. But you're not allowed to make fun of us. I only started a few months ago."

"Yeah, and her teacher sucks." I muttered, which earned me a backhand to the shoulder.

"Don't worry about it. I'm probably worse than either of you right now." Bo laughed at himself while he wrote down his address for us.

Geri never showed up, so we walked aimlessly through the halls. We shared guarded small talk and barely picked at our food until the bell rang and we went our separate ways. Loki and I went over to Bo's to jam that night, and Bo's self-depreciating sense of humor gradually thawed her icy disposition. Of course, I should have expected the wash of jealousy that seeped into me. But I didn't. Way to go genius. Way to go.

After that first day, the cyclic daily routine almost fell back into groove with welcome familiarity. There was still a cold vacant seat in the art room that Loki and I were painfully aware of first period, and Geri muttered everything he said. That was, of course, *if* he said anything at all to us, or even showed up. It seemed like the more Geri was absent, the more time Bo spent with us. Though, I couldn't help but wonder if maybe it was the other way around.

Bo quickly became a bittersweet fixture at lunch and after school, which helped ease the absence of the rest of our tattered Pack. Plus, when the weather was bad, Bo drove Jacob and I home in his truck.

The world around us refused to stop, and the slow march of time seemed intent on erasing every trace that Fen had ever lived at all. After a couple weeks, a trio of twenty-something stoners moved into the house where Fen had lived.

There was a hole inside me. The love that had once been torn between Loki and Fen swelled for the raven-haired beauty that sat beside me almost every morning. Loki grew even more within my heart even as she corroded it.

I couldn't help but wonder if the jealous burn I felt around Bo was the same thing Fen felt when I came along. Following that logic, I figured that I deserved every bit of it. I remembered what Loki had said about Fen moving too fast after her last breakup, and I didn't want to repeat his mistake. I could tell that she had loved Fen, perhaps not romantically, but love nonetheless. So I waited, and wanted, and dreamed.

Of course, few of those dreams were good. I realized that my subconscious was a sadistic asshole as night after night, over and over, I watched Fen die. Every time, I watched his eyes fade to gray and stare at me, expectant. Like he was waiting for me to come to him. The worst part was that I kind of wanted to. My dragon sure as hell wanted me to. But I couldn't bear to put Loki through that again, not like Corwin did.

While I was lost inside my own head, Geri drifted further away. He'd always been a little mousy, but now he overindulged in the wholehearted pursuit of being evasive, soft-spoken, and more skittish than ever. If he showed up at all, it felt like a stranger watched Loki and me out the corner of his eye.

In the second week of March, Geri called and asked me to come over. His voice sounded strange, but we hadn't talked in so long and I felt I owed it to him. I got directions and asked John to drive me over.

Geri lived on the other side of town, in an expensive development at the base of the foothills. Geri's home tried to look like southwest adobe, though with the gravel yard decked out with yucca and cactus, all that really came to mind was an overpriced turd on a pile of rocks.

John watched like a hawk while I knocked on the door, and didn't drive off until after Geri invited me inside and closed the door. Geri asked me to take off my shoes and leave them by the door. His mom reclined on a black suede couch reading a magazine, cold sterile contrast against the immaculate white living room carpet. She seemed nice enough, even though she didn't give either of us any more attention than was absolutely necessary before returning to her article. Framed artwork and a large ornate crucifix decorated the walls, all of them mounted with almost surgical precision.

He led me back toward a hallway and my eyes lingered on the rack of rifles hanging over an unused fireplace until they disappeared behind the wall. His room was at the end of the hallway next to the bathroom. He led me in and closed the door behind us.

I took in the large, yet unremarkable, room and furnishings. The only thing that actually showed any sign of Geri's personality was the large flat-screen TV against the wall with the plethora of video game systems and computer towers tethered to it like some tentacled monster, and another cross hung on the wall over his bed. If I thought my Dungeon was barren when we'd moved in, this was almost as sterile as the living room.

"Why are your walls so bare?"

"Mom doesn't want me ruining the walls, with my 'junk'." he grumbled.

I looked around his room, "Still, for as many times as I've 'slept over' here, it's sorta cool to finally see the place."

"Yeah, no kidding. So uh… I need to talk to you about something…" Guilt swam through the room as he looked down and away from me.

Finally…

"Well, not so much as talk to but… tell you… um…" His eyes darted around, looking at everything except my eyes. In that moment, he kind of reminded me of Corwin.

"Go on, you can tell me anything." I tried to reassure him while I struggled to mask my own unease.

"Well, we're uh…" He set his jaw and took a deep breath, "my family is leaving."

"What?" I fought to keep myself calm as cold splashed down my spine. "Wait, when? Where? Talk to me Geri, what's going on?"

"Next week… Dad got a job offer out in Michigan; and after what happened to Fen…" Geri faltered and shuffled his feet, "They thought it would be best…"

"Best to uproot you in the middle of a school year? Best to take you away from your friends? Your Pack? Box you up and shuttle you away like a piece of furniture? Didn't you ask them not to go?"

I stood and paced, but he didn't answer or meet my eyes. I stopped and looked at him. Geri hunched his shoulders as though bracing for me to hit him.

"You didn't… did you?"

"I'm sick of pretending, Jimmy! Sick of trying to be something I'm not just so I wouldn't be alone. My so-called 'friends' pretended to like me just so they could have an Omega to pick on."

"What do you mean? We've never 'pretended' to be your friends, we *are* your friends!"

"Can you say that for Fen? For Loki? How can you be so sure about how they treated me when *you* weren't around?" His eyes blazed with long-bottled bitterness when he finally met my gaze and it brought me up short.

"I guess I can't. But I'm not them; and I do consider you my friend. You're not my scapegoat, you're my pack-brother…"

"We're not a Pack! Don't you get it? We're not werewolves! We don't transform under the full moon, we don't have special powers, and it sure as hell didn't take a silver bullet to kill Fen." I flinched but he kept rolling, "It's all in your fucking heads and I'm so sick of this game. I just played along so I wouldn't be alone anymore!

"When we moved here, I didn't make a single friend. Not one. I was fair game; *everybody* picked on me. So I jumped at Fen's invitation, but when he 'bit' me nothing changed. I'm sick of crawling on my belly, playing into their delusions just so they wouldn't look too close and see that I was lying to them every day."

I stared at him, silent, while he caught his breath. "I never wanted you to crawl."

Geri smiled ruefully at me, "Notice how you're the one I'm saying goodbye to." He took his head in his hands and sighed. He seemed exhausted after his outburst and we lingered in uneasy silence while he collected his thoughts.

"There's another thing too," he started, uneasy. "Um… Dad doesn't want to pay for moving my car. I know you don't have one so I'll sell it to you if you want."

I stared at him. "So basically, you called me over to tell me none of us were ever your friends, but you want me to buy your car?"

"Uh… yeah, I guess."

"Dude, that's a shitty move."

"Yeah, I guess…" he said again, uncomfortable.

I sighed and pressed my fingers into my eyes. I knew better than to think John would ever help me buy a car. Unlike Chicago, this town didn't seem to even know the meaning of 'mass transit', and I knew I'd need one. "How much?"

"How much can you afford?"

I ran some quick numbers in my head. "Not much dude, um, five-hundred bucks at best."

"That's fine," he answered quickly, "let's do four-hundred and just be done with it. I have too many memories associated with it."

I reached out and pulled him into a hug, surprising us both. I just held him while all the things I wanted to say spun through my head. In the end though, I said nothing.

He offered to let me use his phone to call for a ride, but I declined and he walked me to his front door.

"I'd like it if you'd email me when you get there. I still consider you my friend, and I don't want to lose you too."

"Sure…" He stuffed his hands in his hands in his pockets and looked down.

I sighed and zipped up my jacket. "You really don't think you're a wolf?"

"I know it."

"Well, I guess that's your thing." I stepped down a couple steps toward the sidewalk. "But I remember how you ran. I remember your eyes. Even if you don't believe in yourself, I do."

He blinked, taken aback, and I smiled sadly as I turned and walked away, catching one last glimpse of his father's rifles. He stood there a moment as if about to say something, but then he turned and closed the door.

I was a block down the street before I sat down on the curb, covered my face with my hands, and started to cry.

I miss you Fen…

Fen's Pack, his legacy; was crumbling through my fingers. I just wasn't strong enough to hold it together. Loki tried as hard as she could to convince me that it wasn't my fault, but it was all I could think of. And while spring stirred to life around me, I was dying inside.

I failed him…

What small healing I'd accomplished was ripped raw again as I watched the Mayflower truck pull away from Geri's house; a red and blue realtor's sign stuck in the gravel of the front yard and a signed title to Geri's car in my hand. My car now. It was a beautiful spring day, but no matter what anyone said, I felt like I'd betrayed Fen as I watched Geri drive away.

Was it all just in my head?

A cold numb settled into me. Sound dulled, everything slipped out of focus, and I felt… nothing…

My wolf stopped responding, and as the days passed my phantom limbs disappeared. The worst affirmation to my fears came a week later when I watched the full moon rise over the mountains and felt nothing. No shudders. No surge of energy. No reaction at all. Even my wolf had abandoned me…

But had it ever really been there to begin with?

Maybe it was just a matter of faith, and mine was spent. Doubt ate me alive, and left me broken like a discarded toy. What pathetic hubris to imagine I was anything more than I was born; so desperate to feel wanted and accepted that I'd hypnotized myself into Fen's delusion wholesale.

Was it all a lie?

Loki sensed something was wrong, I saw it in her eyes. I wanted more than anything to bare my soul to her, but Fen's memory haunted me; I hadn't survived his rejection intact. Better to well the venom inside; when you've lost everything else, you covet your last hopeful illusions above all else.

I'd reached my breaking point, and I knew I couldn't survive losing Loki too.

At home, Mom and John tiptoed around me. I came home a couple times to find them deep in some angry hushed conversation, or John would hurriedly wrap up a phone call as soon as I came near the door. Suspicion festered inside me, and I wondered if John was messing around on my mom.

I came home one day and heard Mom and John arguing in his office with the door closed. I crept close and listened from the other side of the door.

"—the hell can we believe anything he says? He *lied* to us! God only knows what he was doing over at that girl's house at six in the morning, and did you see the way he kissed that boy's face at the funeral? It made my skin crawl…"

"But those aren't what upset you John, I know you better than that. You're the one who's talked *me* back from the ledge a bunch of times with him."

John was silent. After a minute, he sighed and said. "Jimmy never saw me as a dad. He never will. He made his mind up about *that* years ago."

"Honey, you have to remember that Jimmy wasn't just an only child; I was his only parent. Emotionally, I was everything to him. When you came along Jimmy got jealous; he'd never had competition for my attention before. Besides, there's so much he doesn't know about you. There's so much you haven't *told* him."

"What am I supposed to tell him? That I have no clue how to be a father? That my old man spent his life working, golfing, and cheating on my mother; so he was never there for his own boy?"

"John, I don't know what you expected. Jimmy looks up to you, I can tell—"

"Does he? Really? 'Cause he sure as hell doesn't show it! When I married you, I swore I'd try to be the best dad I could for him," John said, and I swallowed a lump in my throat, "but he resents me for trying to teach him how to be strong; how to be a good man, how to figure shit out on his own! And god-forbid I ever try to show him that I love him… I just don't know what to do with him; I can't stand his attitude and I'm sick and tired of being his damned punching bag!"

"Look," Mom snapped, "You think *your* situation's rough? I've been dealing with Jimmy for eighteen years. *Literally* half my life John, with zero breaks! I never got to be young, I never got to go out and live! I don't resent him, it was my decision, but I'm exhausted! I can't tell if Jimmy can't see the toll he takes on us, or if he just doesn't care!"

The room went silent and I wiped my eyes. The feeling of betrayal ran even deeper that the hurt and shock.

John's sigh was audible even through the door, "So what am I supposed to do about the church? How am I supposed to teach the boys to be good men if I don't follow my own morals?"

"Look honey, I understand why you want to drop the job. But be realistic; we need that money to pay the mortgage, we can't keep living out of savings like we have." Mom muttered, insistent.

"It's bad enough that the pastor's son assaulted our boys," I blinked; I hadn't realized the church John was designing was for Jack's dad, "there's something about that pastor that reminds me of my old man. There's a serpent behind that smile, mark my words…"

I heard them move and slipped away before they opened the door. I retreated downstairs and leaned against my bookcase while I waited for the tears to stop.

With mounting desperation, I launched myself into anything I could devise to distract myself from my dissolving home life or try and rouse my wolf. The amount of time I spent alone in my Dungeon quadrupled as I devoured the small library I'd inherited from Fen, and checked out every book I could find on wolves from both libraries.

The more I read of Fen's books, the more I realized that almost all the things he'd talked about with such conviction were nothing more than adaptations of things he'd read. I'd built my entire identity around Fen's amalgamated lies. It was all there in the books; shifting energy, astral planes, turquoise… Defeated, I stared into the eyes of wolf pictures, hoping to trigger some kind of response, but all I got were dry eyes.

I turned eighteen in April, and surprised myself with how little I gave a crap. Eighteen. Woo hoo. Mom and John gave me a cell phone, which was ironic considering I could count on one hand the number of people I would actually call with it. "Oh, cool, thanks guys. Now you can track me down whenever you want."

I guess that reaction wasn't quite what they had in mind.

"Don't you like it?" Mom asked, "Was there something else you would have rather had?"

Anything I would have rather had? Bring my wolf back? Raise Fen from the dead? Bring Geri home, ruing the error of his ways? Loki's confession of eternal love? "Nope, it's great," I lied.

Clouds lingered for weeks until the slushy snow and hail finally relented to the lengthening spring days and turned to a cold punishing rain, like the weather mirrored my mood. I stared out the library window while Bo and I researched for our American Government final in the Library before Spring Break. "Still overboard about wolves?" Bo snapped me out of my reverie as he leaned over and looked at the screen of my computer.

"Huh? Oh…" I was pulling double duty; on one screen I was doing research on Teddy Roosevelt, on the other I was reading about pack hunting techniques. Like a genius, I'd left the wrong screen open when I spaced out. I was just glad it was Bo instead of Mr. Carter. I clicked back to my other window right away.

"Hey, I was reading that!" Bo pouted.

"Down boy, stop whining."

"Fuck you." he leaned back and stretched his thick arms over his head. "You know, I've always loved the idea of hunting in a pack… Everybody running together with a single purpose and flawless teamwork. I guess that's why I loved sports so much…"

My eyes closed as I remembered my first full moon; and everything from that memory that fate had stolen from me… I remembered the way the wind flowed around me as Fen and I chased Geri in a world long lost—the way Loki danced in the snow when she thought no one was watching—I'd give anything to have that back…

"Oh really?" Bo asked and my eyes snapped open as I realized I'd said that last part out loud.

"Oh, nothing, never mind…" I mumbled as I focused back on my computer.

"Damnit Jimmy, when are you going to tell me the truth?" he looked hurt and pissed. "I know you're hiding, well, *everything* from me. You can trust me—" *Could I really?* "—so when are you going to stop lying to me all the time?"

I sighed and closed my eyes. Did he deserve the leap of faith he was asking for? Did I have any right to talk anymore? My wolf was gone—if he'd ever existed in the first place—and I was just as human as Bo. And just as easy to kill as Fen...

"Bo, I'm sorry, but my best friend is dead, and I don't exactly feel like I can trust *anybody*, ya know?"

He grimaced and sighed, but I saw the anger in his eyes relent. "Yeah," he looked down, "I guess I can understand that. I'm sorry; I can't even imagine what that must have been like for you."

"I was there Bo. I was the one holding his hand when his heart stopped. Some paramedic had to scrub his blood off my face... off my hands..." I paused as my throat grew tight, and swallowed hard.

"Jesus..." I couldn't tell if Bo was more disturbed by the emotion on my face, or the gruesome details that only Loki and I knew.

"You can't imagine what it's like?" my voice broke as I struggled to keep my volume down. "The classrooms we shared, the halls we walked down together. Every second in this place is like a cheese grater carving out pieces of my soul. Not enough to kill me, but more than enough to make me wish for death. Sometimes I wake up and I've forgotten, only to relive the loss, all over again, every... single... fucking... day...

"Every time I look down the street and see those god-damned potheads living in the house he grew up in. Every time I walk into Art and see that empty seat. It all crashes over me again and—and I failed him... I fucking failed him..." I heard the cloth of Bo's shirt move as he reached out and set a hand on my shoulder.

"Geri left. As Fen died, I promised him I would look after the others, take care of them, but I failed... I couldn't lead a goddamn lemming off a cliff..."

"I don't know what it's worth, but... *I* would follow you."

"How can you say that? Bo, I don't even know who I am anymore!" I moaned, "I've lost more than I can bear, and my toes are hanging over the edge. I feel like a boat adrift at sea, lost in a storm with a broken rudder, just waiting to drown. It's like my identity—my soul—has been stripped away…"

Bo just offered me a kind smile, his dark skin creased at the corners of his bright eyes, "You're Jimmy Walker, a good guy who's had enough shit dumped on him to crush a man twice his age. This sort of thing is called 'the dark night of the soul', and like any other night, it passes. And if you were my Alpha," he nodded at my screen, "I'd follow you." He smiled again and squeezed my shoulder and then went back to work. I watched him for just a moment longer before I turned back to my own screen and went through the motions while my mind wandered…

Everything starts over…

The rain passed, though the dark clouds lingered overhead. After school, I stopped by Jacob's school and waited for a few minutes before I figured Mom must've picked him up. I got home and dropped my bag on the couch. I sighed and pressed my fingers into my eyes when I heard Mom call me into the kitchen. *God, what'd I do wrong now…?*

John wasn't there, but mom sat at the kitchen table looking terrible. It was obvious she'd been crying. I ground my teeth against the anger and suspicion that boiled up inside me as I sat down. "Mom, what's wrong?"

"This came in the mail today, must have been misdelivered." she said and slid a large manila envelope across the table to me. "I couldn't decide whether to throw it away or open it…" Her voice trailed off when she saw the look on my face.

The envelope was addressed to James E. Kendle, with the Colorado State University seal stamped on the corner. Ringing filled my ears as my shaking hands opened the letter before my brain could decide if I really wanted to see what was inside or not. It was hard to breathe as I skimmed the papers.

Fen had been admitted to the College of Natural Sciences with a full ride scholarship about month after he died.

"Jimmy? Are you alr—"

"It's not fair Mom," I interrupted her, "it's not fucking fair!" I screamed as I threw the papers across the kitchen and grabbed my head. "Why? Why did Fen have to die? He deserved to live; he had so much to live for! Why! Why him and not me, it should have been me!"

"Jimmy, don't say that! Don't you dare say that!" Mom said as she reached out for me, but I recoiled from her. Jacob came downstairs and grabbed onto Mom's leg. I didn't care about how hurt they looked, how scared. The house loomed around me, pressing in, it choked me. The world narrowed. I had to run. Had to get out...

A single thought broke through with surgical clarity.

Before I even realized it, I was running out of the house to my car. Mom ran out after me with Jacob trailing behind with wide eyes, "Jimmy! Jimmy, where are you going?"

"To see Fen." I said, and drove off.

I tried not to think as I drove into the mountains outside of town. I needed to get out. Out of my skin. Out of my mind. The nightmares that plagued me forbid me from finding a single moment's reprieve from the guilt and pain of Fen's death. Like he beckoned me even beyond the grave.

He never wanted you while he was alive…

I swallowed the bitter thought and turned off the highway. The same road Fen had taken me on that looked over the town, the same road we'd taken to spread his ashes. I hated and loved this road, this life, just as much as I hated and loved Fen himself.

The road curved through the mountain's shadow and into a stretch of snow. Before I could react, the car lurched sideways on a hidden layer of ice. The rear end flipped around the front and finally halted, tires still spinning. Shaking, I revved the engine a couple times, hoping the tires would find traction. Nothing.

"Fuck my life…" I groaned as I hit my head against the wheel.

I opened the door and slipped on the ice. I caught myself, but it torqued the muscles in my scarred calf and ignited a festering burn. Cold wind whipped around me, cutting through my clothes. I fought a wave of vertigo as I looked down the side of the mountain and realized just how close I'd come to plummeting down it. I carefully worked my way around the car and looked underneath it at the packed snow that I'd bottomed out on.

I tried everything I could think of to get the car unstuck. From pushing on it, to bouncing up and down on the trunk, to cussing the thing into obedience. No matter what I tried, it wouldn't budge.

I fished the cell phone my parents gave me out of my pocket and checked the reception; I'd forgotten I even had it. The 'No Service' icon blinked at the top of the display and I almost threw it off the side of the mountain in frustration. Fuck you Murphy's Law; fuck you so hard!

I tucked the cell phone into my pocket and admitted defeat as night grew close and I resigned myself to walking home. The jacket I wore to school was still on the passenger seat, so I layered that with one of Geri's old shirts that I found in the trunk. It hardly dulled the biting wind, but it was better than nothing.

263

Mental note, keep winter clothes in the trunk at all times.

I wrapped my arms tight around myself and limped my way up the mountain to where the road crested along the top ridge. My eyes watered as I looked out over the city for the first time since we'd scattered Fen's ashes. Street lamps just looked like little glowing dots scattered around the landscape and outlining roadways. The world felt so far away; everyone and everything I'd ever known just something off in the distance.

I'd spent plenty of time alone over the years, especially the last month. But standing on top of that mountain and looking down at the city lights like some Olympian god with nothing but the sound of the wind and my own breath to keep be company, I felt truly isolated. Trapped, stranded, and alone with memories of things I'd never wanted, or wanted and never had.

No wolf can ever be happy alone; the wolf and the pack are the same thing.

I gritted my teeth. Now was not the time to think about that. It would be so much easier if I could just forget about my wolf. About the father I'd never known. About Fen, Loki, and Corwin, like it never happened, but that didn't seem to be possible.

I resumed my descent to town and the pain in my calf grew with every step as the muscles rebelled, aching from cold and overuse. Swearing in a steady stream, I descended the mountain with a limp.

Near the halfway point, I heard something down at the base of the mountain. Water splashed nearby, but I also thought I heard voices. I stepped over to the edge of the road to look down. It almost looked like people with flashlights. Distracted, I slipped, but my foot didn't catch me in time. The ground rushed up to meet me and everything went black with a blast of pain.

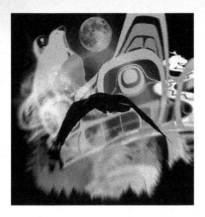

CHAPTER 17 — ANCESTORS

I didn't hurt.

I didn't feel cold anymore.

To be honest, I couldn't feel anything.

I stood up and looked down at my own body sprawled out in the dirt and slush. Logic was slow to respond as I fought the realization that nagged at me. I looked at the dark splash of red that colored the ground beneath my skull, and the jagged rock beside it.

"No… No-no-no-no-no" became a repeated mantra I chanted to myself as I fell to my knees beside my body, surprisingly weightless as I held my shoulders and rocked back and forth. Was I… was I dead?

A barely perceptible puff of steam leaked out from my face, and I froze. After what felt like an impossible eternity, I saw another one. I was still breathing, so I wasn't quite dead… yet.

A familiar fluttering sound surrounded me, and I looked for the source. Finally the fluttering stopped and a resonant 'cark' came from behind me.

"Corwin?" My stomach dropped as I turned, but the raven

that sat there watching me from the middle of the road was obviously not him. It wasn't just bigger than Corwin's raven form, *much* bigger; it also radiated a cold pulse of power. A power I recognized from buried memories, and Fen's words repeated in my mind.

"Ravens walk between the worlds of the living and the dead; they help guide souls to the beyond."

I struggled to swallow past a choked throat as I took a couple steps backward from it, and the thing spread its wings. Terrified, I turned and ran as the air churned behind me.

Powerful talons grasped my upper arm, scalding me with its touch. I cried out and flailed as the raven lifted me into the air and carried me away from the mountainside, the sound of voices and water far below.

My gut twisted as the raven dived and we plummeted sickeningly. I couldn't even scream as we reached the surface of an irrigation ditch and violet light exploded around us. Instead of smashing into the rocky bottom, the earth opened for us and we barreled deep under the ground.

A swirling marble net of blue light covered us for a moment before we exploded from the water, dry and whole on the other side. Blasting sunlight blinded me, and I clenched my eyes shut as the raven released its grip and I tumbled to the ground. I forced my eyes open and blinked as the raven's silhouette flickered through the sunlight and soared through a brilliant blue sky.

Reeling, I gazed around the massive green valley the raven had dragged me into. A towering granite cliff dominated the valley across the water from a dense forest.

"Where the hell am I?" I muttered as wonder and terror dueled inside me. If I was dead, was this… heaven? Hell? None of the above? I had no freaking clue…

The raven circled overhead and dipped toward me with a caw,

before winging toward the sprawling forest and the rows of misty blue mountains beyond. I felt a tug in my chest, just like I had the night Fen bit me, urging me toward the forest.

"He wants you to follow him," a worn and smoky voice spoke behind me and I jumped. I turned and found an old Native American man standing there, with dark skin and a strong jaw. Laugh lines creased the leathery skin around his eyes as he smiled at my reaction and stuffed his hands into the pockets of his denim overalls.

"Who the hell are you?" I asked.

"That's no way to talk to your elders boy, much less your *Qhipe*." His smile faded and I felt the pressure of some hidden power lurking behind his dark eyes.

"What is a '*keepay*'?" I asked.

"*Qhipe* means Grandfather, boy. That's who I am!" It took a second for what he said to sink in before I recognized him from my dream, and I realized how many of his features echoed my face.

"But my grandfather's dead—" after another second, the other implication sank in, "Fuck... I *am* dead!"

My grandfather waved a dismissive hand. "Relax boy, it's not your first time, and probably won't be the last. Besides, your body's not dead yet, just empty."

"Oh! Great, thanks, that's so much better!"

"Can the lip, boy, and pay attention. Raven brought you here for a reason," he said the word Raven like an old friend's name with a capital 'R', "but you need to deal with your shackle first."

"What shackle?" I said.

"That," my grandfather pointed to my calf, "needs to be dealt with before you can see *Hnt'llane*."

I looked where he pointed, and saw a dark stain on my pant leg. I lifted the fabric and almost threw up. Where my scar was in the real world, a blackened oozing pestilence ate into my body. Dark veins ran outward from the ruined tissue, through my ankle to the ground and up past my thigh.

"What is this?" I demanded as I looked up, but I was alone in the field. Over toward the forest, the raven—Raven himself apparently—cawed impatiently at me again. My grandfather wanted me to follow him, and I remembered Lupa saying that I was 'marked' by Brother Raven. In the end, I didn't feel like I had a choice really. I crossed the field and swallowed as I stepped into the eerie calm of the forest.

The woods darkened and I withdrew into my mind as I picked my way along a path. Why did he call it my 'shackle'? I frowned. Something about that scar seemed to be important, but my memories were hard to pin down. I was in Middle School when it happened, Jacob was only a couple months old. I knew I got it in Miami, and I could remember the physical therapy as I learned to walk again, but…what made it? I struggled to remember the source until—

—*A dry rattling rasp, like frying bacon—agony in my leg—sunlight flashed off too-blue water—my heart pounded in my chest as I struggled to breathe—*

—obscure memories flashed inside my head and I staggered. The disease in my leg throbbed as a steel trap slammed shut on the memories, cutting them off before I could even make sense of them. I focused on just breathing in and out until a shadow moved in the corner of my eye.

I looked up and froze. My other self stood there watching me. My wolf's black pelt and feral eyes gazed back at me. I felt the weight of his gaze as barely contained power radiated off of him. He lowered his face toward the ground and sniffed—seemed to recognize me—but tensed and bounded away toward the dark heart of the forest when I moved.

I followed as quickly as I could. The throbbing wound on my leg seemed to grow heavier and heavier as I limped along. A low mist crept between the trees and swirled around my feet as I rushed through trees ever darker and darker until—

I know this place!

I walked around a boulder and stepped into a circular clearing with a charred fire pit and looked up at the full moon, centered between the obsidian trees. Just like that dream so long ago, the first time I saw Lupa.

I smiled, hoping to see her again, but instead I heard a dry hissing sound that I recognized immediately and my throat went dry. I couldn't focus the sound though; it seemed to come from everywhere at once. I turned in circles, and then the sound focused into a single spot and my blood ran cold when I glanced down.

The rattlesnake coiled by the trunk of one of the trees, its wide mouth displayed needle-like fangs.

Past and present overlapped as long buried memories from Miami broke free and terror choked me. Time slowed, and I saw everything in obscene clarity. Even the strange red cross-shaped mark atop the snake's triangular head, like the dragon in my dream, as it struck toward my leg.

But the pain never came.

A dark blur smashed into the serpent in mid-strike and in the space of time it took me to blink the snake writhed dead, its head flopping around on a torn neck as small beads of yellowish venom gathered on the tips of its fangs. I tore my eyes away in time to watch a black lupine rump disappear into the misty trees.

I fought the choking cold that gripped me as I scrambled back from the twisting corpse. A dam ruptured inside my head, and a thousand buried memories crashed over me…

Sunlight glimmered off the water in the swimming pool in Miami, while insects droned around us. Anxious to cool off, I ran along the side of the pool ahead of Mom while she carried Jacob. I never even saw the rattlesnake; but I relived the agony that exploded in my calf. Flashing lights rushed me to a hospital, but they didn't have the right antivenin, so a helicopter flew me to a second hospital.

My heart stopped en-route. I couldn't breathe and I went into cardiac arrest. That's what they told Mom, but they couldn't see the violet light that surrounded me as Raven fought to keep my soul from leaving my body. He held me together until the paramedics could restart my heart.

I should have died. The doctors said I should have died. Days passed in torment as the venom warred with my body and Death seemed to wait at the foot of my bed. The doctors had to cut my leg open from knee to ankle so the swelling had somewhere to expand. They repaired the damage the best they could, but the scar on my calf remained.

A lingering reminder of everything I had shoved out and tried to hide from—

The memories released me, and my grandfather's voice came into focus as he whispered, "Shh, come back Jimmy. Come back to me now…" I felt his strong arm around on my shoulders, holding me tight.

"That was what broke me," I muttered as realization clicked into place, "I was terrified, not just of death, but of leaving my body at all. I forced Lupa away and then buried my wolf and the memories so deep they'd almost ceased to exist. Until Fen pulled me back…"

Another wave of sorrow, shame, and guilt washed over me. Before I could react, my grandfather jabbed the tip of a stone knife into the festering wound on my leg.

"What the fuck?" I shouted and jerked back.

Black ichor spurted out of the wound and it began to drain like a lanced abscess. All of the fear and rejected memories I had infected myself with finally released. The dark and destructive hate I had hoarded inside myself, my Dragon's very lifeblood, sizzled as its corrosion dribbled onto the ground.

"Let go of your fear Jimmy. All that rage and all that sorrow won't ever make you stronger; it's just a shackle that holds you back. In time, you will learn how to let go of the things you can never change. Things happen. Accept it, and learn what you can."

"Shit, give me a little warning next time," I snapped and stood up. My legs were already unsteady from reliving the trauma of the snake bite, and the oozing wound—which I stubbornly refused to admit already felt better—didn't want to support my weight.

My grandfather stepped next to me and lifted my arm over his shoulder with a grunt. "Boy, you've grown. The last time I saw you, I could carry you with one arm—" I looked suspiciously at his knife until he stashed it in one of his pockets. "Weapons are tools, Jimmy," he grumbled, "A hammer can build a house or crush a skull; it all depends on the person who wields it. Never confuse the two, and never forget where the accountability lies."

He helped me through the trees and along the dried up riverbed. While we walked, I glanced at my grandfather's face and tried to find myself in it. I had his jaw, though my cheekbones and eyes were definitely Mom's. The lines on either side of my mouth were his, as was the raven black hair, though his was long and threaded with gray and silver. After a moment, he noticed me watching him.

"I got something on my face boy?" he muttered and I looked away.

"So what am I supposed to call you anyway," I said, "Grandpa? Grandad? Pops?" 'Pops' earned a smile from him that looked part amused, part irritated. Actually, just about everything about him struck me as part amused, part irritated.

"If it's all the same to you, I'd rather you call me *Qhipe*. I never got to hear you say it to me while I was alive." He smiled at me, showing deep creases around his eyes that echoed a kind of weary sadness as well.

"What language is that?" I asked as we shuffled through a line of trees and the lake came into view. I could see the towers of stone on the far shore that Lupa and I had run to.

"It's *Schitsu'umsh*, the Coeur D'Alene language," he said, "the language of your ancestors. I was one of the last *t'e'kqilsh*."

I blinked at the stream of syllables, "Um, in English please?"

He groaned and said, "I suppose you'd call me a 'medicine man'."

I stopped in my tracks, nearly throwing him off balance in the sand, "I'm descended from shamans?"

"That's not what our people call us, but yes. It's in your *suumesh*, your medicine song. That's how you can walk between worlds, and do that parlor trick you love so much with the shadows," he said and pulled me along as my mind reeled. So many floating strands of confusion began to weave together into a cord tying me to the past. Corwin's words echoed through my memory, *"you were destined for this, probably even before you were born. So many paths were broken and twisted to lead you here; don't you dare write it off as circumstance"*

Qhipe continued talking, "Your father, Taylor, rejected the old ways and tried to drown out the voices of the First Peoples with drink. There was so much I'd hoped to teach you Jimmy, so much…" he sighed, "so much has been lost, and now we don't have time… You were meant for this road Jimmy; it's in your blood." As soon as he mentioned my father, I felt a familiar anger rise inside me.

"You mean it's in my stain. I'm nothing but your son's worthless mistake—"

Qhipe's hands turned rough as he whirled me around to face him and snapped. "Jimmy Marshall Walker, you are many things, but you were *never* a mistake. The man who raised you did a hell of a lot better job than my coward Coyote son would have! John raised you as his own, provided for you, fed you, clothed you, and all you've ever done is spit in his face for it."

Words deserted me. But I didn't need them. My grandfather had enough rant stored up that I didn't need to contribute. The intensity of his dark eyes seemed to bore holes to the core of my soul while his words sliced into me.

"For my part, I'm sorry I wasn't there for you Jimmy. But I've watched you your entire life, I've seen you obsess over the imaginary father you didn't have, while you ignored what was right in front of you! John is a damn good man, and it's high time you sort your shit out boy and realize he's one of the best things that ever happened to you. The only thing you *ever* needed from Taylor was my blood, and you had that all along."

I settled into stunned silence, lacerated and raw. *Qhipe's* hands and face gentled as we resumed our trek, leaving the shoreline. I let him lead me through the trees, numb and distant while my mind wandered through an abyss of memories both fond and painful.

Something he'd said flipped a switch inside me. Like he'd shoved a mirror in my face and no matter how much as I hated the ugliness it showed me, I couldn't look away. Not this time. The mirror showed me my life, my memories, for the first time outside of my own head.

Wow. You were such an asshole.

Thank you for stating the obvious, brain. John wasn't perfect, far from it, but I had made it hell for him. The realization made me queasy, uncomfortable—

Ashamed...

I couldn't escape. I'd always found a way to shirk responsibility onto someone else, but I couldn't unsee the Jimmy that I'd seen in the mirror. I'd blamed John for so many things that were my fault, while I unconsciously sabotaged my own life. Like bombing my grades every time we moved to punish him. Or, even better, constantly reminding him that I didn't accept him as my father, refusing to even call him 'dad'. I tried in every way I could to rub his face in the fact that my mother had made a child with someone else.

Guess it's finally time to put on your big boy britches and grow the fuck up.

The temperature dropped as we pushed further than ever before into the dark woods, until blowing plumes of snow broke the perfect black onyx of the trees. It grew thicker and heavier until we stepped out of the woods and were blinded by the reflective mirror of ice that sprawled out before us.

A cold land of permanent frost stretched from the blazing crimson sunset on one horizon, to the dancing colors of the aurora on the other. Above it all, the full moon reigned dead center in the sky.

Motion caught my eye under the aurora. Shadows bounded over the tundra, flinging snow behind their paws. It was a pack of five or six wolves, all led by my black wolf with his tail held high like a flag. With mounting despair I watched as they drove through the snow away from me toward the darkness of night.

I tried to follow them, mired by the thick snow, until I glanced toward the sunset. I froze as I watched the human silhouettes move against the blood red horizon; three adults of differing heights and a youth half as tall as his father. My family also walked away from me toward the calling light of day.

Lupa's voice purred behind me and I turned my head just as her wolf form emerged from the misty forest like a ghost, "The time has come…"

Agony tore through me as my arms were yanked out to the sides, throwing *Qhipe* to the ground. Fiery pain spilled down my chest, splitting my heart. I looked at my wrists and saw the cords, long shimmering strands stretched from my wrists to the diverging packs of wolves and humans. As the two groups strained for their horizons, I was drawn in agony between them.

"Lupa, what's happening?" I cried out as a fresh lance of pain tore a sharp cry from my throat.

"You have dawdled too long, and now you must choose." She said, and walked in front of me. My body convulsed as my muscles fought to hold me together and bones popped in my sternum, "Will you become a wolf, and let your body die so you can run wild and free forever? Or will you let your wolf go, once and for all?"

"Wha—what do you mean?" I strained to speak but I could barely breathe and fell to my knees. I would have fallen down but the tension between the cords held me up.

Qhipe picked himself up from the snow with pained eyes, "The bridge is burning Jimmy, and you're standing in the middle of it. Which side will you run to? It's time to choose which road you will walk…"

I finally understood. My depression had severed me from this place, so Raven forced my hand… Pulled my soul back here to decide what I would lose. But, how could they possibly ask me to give up something I could never live without?

If I chose my wolf, my human body teetering on the edge of the abyss would die. But if I returned to my human body, I would lose my soul, my identity, my entire reason for existence.

It was death either way.

A fresh flare of pain tore an anguished scream from my throat as hot tears spilled down my cheeks. How could they? My life was mine; it always had been and always would be.

It's not unnatural to die… I thought with sudden clarity. *There's nothing wrong with a natural death.*

I met Lupa's eyes with a defiant glare, "You cannot ask me to give up half of who I am. I'm dead either way. I'm not afraid to die anymore, so get it over with!" I screamed at her and she lunged. I closed my eyes and exposed my throat for release—

I never felt her fangs pierce me, but the pain vanished.

A gust of cold wind blew snow onto my face, and I frowned. Confused, I cracked my eyes open and saw the tundra field. I looked at my wrists and saw why the pain had stopped.

Lupa held the cord that bound me to my family in her jaws, her yellow eyes locked on me as she fought the tension.

On my left, *Qhipe's* arms shook from the exertion of holding the wolves' cord. "Do you realize what you are asking Jimmy?" he asked, the knife with the antler hilt in his hand. "If you choose this middle road, you will truly walk forever between worlds. You will never—*never* completely belong to either. Spirit bound to flesh, wolf bound to man, but never wholly one or the other.

This is a lonely road that only the strongest can survive. Is this really what you want, grandson?"

I closed my eyes as the enormity of my decision threatened to overwhelm me. But really, what choice did I have? I looked up at the moon overhead, and felt a determination I'd never known before settle into me, "Yes... I choose to walk between the worlds."

With a swift motion, *Qhipe* drew his knife through the cord while Lupa clenched her teeth down and they simultaneously severed both tethers.

My family disappeared into the light of the sun as it fell completely below the horizon and disappeared with them. The pack disappeared over their horizon and the aurora dispersed into a few dancing wisps of light before it died out completely, and left me under the cold light of an impartial moon.

"I'm proud of you Jimmy," *Qhipe* said as he knelt down in the snow and wrapped his arms around me, while Lupa leaned into my side and rumbled her assent. A strange sensation washed over me at his words. "You chose the hard path, but it's the path to strength and pride. You made a good choice..."

Lupa looked into my grandfather's eyes, and something unspoken passed between them. He smiled sadly at her and muttered, "Hello again old friend. I guess the time has come hasn't it *Hnt'llane*?" As he spoke, I heard Raven flew out of the woods and circled over us with an urgent 'kark'. We glanced up at Raven, as *Qhipe* swallowed and grew pale.

The entire mood shifted, and I felt nervous. *Qhipe* looked at me, his face earnest as he spoke, "Jimmy, I'm so sorry, but we're out of time." He lifted his rough warm hands to my face and pulled my head forward to touch my forehead to his. "There was so much I wanted to teach you, about your heritage, about our *suumesh* songs, about... about life. I'm sorry I wasn't there for you when you needed me, and here I am, about to leave you again."

"What are you talking about *Qhipe*, you're already dead, it's not like you can die again…" my voice sounded sure, but his silence shattered my certainty. "*Qhipe*?"

"Jimmy, you need to learn faith," he said, the resignation clear in his voice. "Sometimes the way you want things to be, isn't how they're supposed to be. You need to trust that things will work out how they need to, whether you like it or not. That includes what happens to me. This is the only way I can help you now." He stood up and pulled away from me

"No, no you can stay here." I tried to bargain with him even though my voice cracked. I tried to stand up and grab him but my wounded leg folded underneath me, "You can teach me all about our family, our tribe, shamanism, any of that crap! I'll meet you at the lake every night and we can—"

"Shh, Jimmy, it's okay. I made my choice, just like you did. *Amotqn*, the Creator, made this world with a balance that must be kept, the First Peoples like Wolf and Raven know this, and you need to learn it as well. The world cannot have life without death. Just remember that as long as you're alive, then a part of me still lives inside you…and that's worth it to me. I'm proud of you boy." I heard what the gruff words actually said.

What he really meant was 'I love you' and 'goodbye'.

My eyes burned and I felt powerless as I watched him kneel down in the snow in front of Lupa and close his eyes.

"No, *Qhipe* wait—" I forced myself to my feet despite the pain and lurched toward him. Before I could reach him, he leaned toward Lupa until their noses touched—

—and he changed right before my eyes.

His dusky human skin blurred at the edges and a wave washed back from her touch.

"*Qhipe!*" I cried as his human shape melted into a powerful black form, and he turned familiar amber eyes on me. I heard his voice in my mind, though at the same time it was my voice, the voice of my wolf. "This way, I will always be a part of you."

Part overjoyed, part shattered, I embraced him, and he lay his head down over my shoulder. I drank in the warm furry musk of his mane, the coarse tickle of his fur.

I felt like I had finally come home at last.

"It's time," Lupa said to me and touched my nose with hers, just as my wolf and I were wrenched backwards through the woods and past the lake with breathtaking speed. I held him tightly to my chest as we passed through the mist and burst back into the searing bright sun of the valley I'd arrived in.

Raven's massive shadow fell over us as he swooped down and plunged into my chest. Violet light exploded over us and I choked on my scream as we were yanked into the water. We exploded from the surface on the other side, back into the dark cold night of the physical realm.

I hugged my wolf close and the two of us merged, just like my dream with the pool, as Raven winged us up the side of the mountain to my body. I saw people below us, waving around flashlights. I realized they were probably looking for me. It felt like half a day had passed in the spirit world, but hardly any time had passed here.

As Raven winged us higher, a terrible sound rolled off the mountain. It seemed impossible that a human throat could even make a sound like that, but as we neared my body I saw the crouching figure that had made it.

Surreally, I watched John turn my body over. My lips were blue and my body moved stiffly under his hands as he pulled me up to his chest and kissed my forehead. Tears spilled down his cheeks and caught in his beard when he closed his eyes and held my head to his shaking chest, "My boy... my boy..."

Frantic, John pulled off his coat and bundled it under my head and then started CPR "Jimmy! Come back to me! Please God, give him back to me—" he sobbed as he tried to restart my heart.

After all the years I'd spent trying to hurt him, I felt tears spill down my face as I hurt for him. "I've seen enough Raven, please put me back!" I pleaded. When I turned to look back at the bird, a man stood in its place. Like Lupa, he looked Native American, but with long black hair and cobalt blue eyes just like mine. Around his neck he wore a necklace draped over his bare chest, a raven's skull and several black feathers hung from it.

"Lay down over your body, kid." Raven said, and I did as he said.

Raven cupped his hands over the top of my head and blew air through them. I felt my soul expand to fill the flesh like a balloon filling a mold; forming into place.

Nothing happened.

I looked up at Raven as his eyes went completely black and he whispered, "Never forget; you bear my mark..." Then he placed his hand over my heart and violet light washed over us as his power jolted into me.

I'd forgotten the pain of physical life until merciless sensation roared over me like electric fire and my eyes snapped open. I drew in a gasp that was part scream as I came back to life...

"Jimmy!" John cried as I coughed and struggled for air. My body convulsed as nerve endings flared back to life all over my body while the oppressive dense weight of flesh sent me into a panic.

A familiar sensation swept through me as my wolf rushed to the surface; but he smashed into the glass ceiling just as he was about to fully emerge. I closed my eyes to keep John from seeing them change color while he bundled me up in his coat and carried me down the mountain.

By the time we reached the SUV, my shifting energy was hard at work repairing my body. John cranked up the heater as high as it would go as Loki and her parents came running back from their search, relieved to see me. Loki's dad grabbed some thick wool blankets from the back of his truck to wrap me up as Loki's mom poured me a hot cup of coffee from a thermos.

Loki ran up and hugged me, before she pulled back and yelled, "What the hell were you thinking?" She stomped away from me, angrily wiping tears off her face. John thanked Loki's mom and dad for coming out to help look for me.

"Of course John, we're glad he's okay. These kids have had one hell of a year haven't they?" Loki's dad replied as he shook John's hand. Loki and her parents loaded into her dad's truck and drove off, leaving John and I alone.

"We need to go get Jake and your mom; they were looking for you at Fen's cemetery."

"Oh…" I muttered, that made sense, "how did you find me?"

"I did a GPS trace on your cell phone," he said and looked away with a distant expression.

"Are you okay?" I asked. He looked at me for a moment, and then smiled and looked off into space again while muscles worked in his jaw. When he spoke, it was barely a whisper.

"It's not easy being a dad… Nobody ever warned me about the sleepless nights, the worrying, the fights you'd have with yourself and your kid."

"What are you talking about?" My ears perked forward to catch every word.

"I'm sorry Jim…" Tears formed at the corners of his eyes and slowly traced down the lines of his face. "I'm—so sorry—that I couldn't be the dad that you wanted. That I couldn't be the father you needed me to be…" His voice broke under the weight of a decade's pent up emotion.

He embraced me as he cried and his body shook. Tears of my own slipped out as he rocked me back and forth. "And I'm so sorry that I hurt you when Fen died, I just… You can't even imagine the terror I felt, the helplessness; I didn't know what to do, that bullet came *inches* from you!"

I blinked as wheels sprang into motion in my head. I'd never thought of it that way…

"Dad," I muttered, and meant it, "I'm sorry I've been such a shit. I just never felt like I was good enough for you, I only ever wanted you to be proud of me."

He sniffed and tried to smile around his puffy bloodshot eyes. "I *am* proud of you Jimmy! I'm sorry I never told you enough, I just knew you were capable of so much more, and it frustrated me when you didn't try. Don't you ever think for a moment that I don't love you, or that I won't support you." He took a deep breath and wiped his face on his sleeve, "I should clean myself up before Jake and your mother see me. She thinks I'm the strong and silent type, I can't let that reputation break now or else I'll really be in for it!"

"Mum's the word. Oh, and dad?" I called as he turned, "Thank you… for everything you've done for me."

He smiled deeply and reached out to ruffle my hair, "It's been my pleasure. Just, *please* stop running away like that."

I laughed and said, "Sure thing." When I looked into his blue eyes, I saw what I'd been looking for all along. Genes were all that were necessary for someone to make a child, but it took way more than just DNA to be a Dad.

Somewhere deep inside me, the dragon let out an anguished shriek as more pieces of its darkness rotted and faded away. Light broke through the bleeding holes, wounding and dragging it closer to annihilation. The beast was a shade of its former self; so much of its strength had been drawn from my conflict with John—which too was fading into the past—and now the dragon was dying… it was only a matter of time…

We picked Mom and Jake up and drove home while Mom unleashed a torrent of frustration on me. I only half listened, distracted by wolf squirming inside me like a hyperactive puppy. I realized then just how much more aware I was of my wolf than ever before; he wasn't just some amorphous presence that occasionally showed itself that I referred to as 'my wolf' anymore. He was Wolf; he was me, and yet at the same time he was more truly himself, more free and unbound within me than ever before.

As happy as that made me, sadness washed through me every time I thought of *Qhipe*. Fen had been so afraid of ghosts, of Corwin's soul or his dad's unbecoming. Yet I'd been forced to watch my own grandfather sacrifice everything he ever was and could have ever been for me… I grieved over losing something I'd just found; but at the same time, I finally allowed myself to find some measure of closure where my bio-dad was concerned. It was time to let go.

The next day was sunny and warm. Melting snow ran in rivulets down the side of the mountain as John and I pulled my car free with his SUV When we got home, I called Loki and asked her to come over, but she was still upset with me.

283

"Loki, please, I *need* to talk to you. I need to tell you what really happened last night." I pleaded, and after a moment of silence, she sighed, and agreed.

I picked her up and we isolated ourselves downstairs in the Dungeon. At last, I told her everything. Well…almost everything. I came clean about Wolf's desertion and my depression, Raven, and the Lowerworld.

Finally, I told her about *Qhipe* and almost started to cry. "It felt like the first chance I got to finally connect with that side of my family, it was snatched away from me again. I know nothing about the guy, I don't even know his real name; all I know is that he was my grandfather. But… he sacrificed his *soul* to give me a second chance."

"At what?"

"At everything… Don't you see what this means?" I said, "Fen always said everything has a reason. After he died and Geri left, it was like I froze. I forgot my identity, my purpose, but now I have the chance to set things right." I leaned forward.

"What do you mean?" she asked.

"Fen…" I sighed, "When Fen died, the police wrote it off as a freak accident. But—I can't shake the thought that he was murdered… *because* he was a wolf, like us."

The idea was staggering, but I could tell that Loki shared my opinion. "Okay Jimmy, I have to admit that fits better than the police's conclusion, but… no one outside the Pack even knows what we are!"

"The night Fen and I fought for dominance; there was this car in the school parking lot. They could have seen us fighting."

"Who was in the car?"

"I don't know, their headlights blinded me. I couldn't see the driver, or what kind of car it was."

"Great," Loki snapped and held her head, "if the police couldn't find any suspects, how are we supposed to?"

"Think about it; the police can't talk to spirits. My grandfather died eighteen years ago, but in the Lowerworld he was as solid as if he'd just left his body yesterday, and he said he'd been watching me my whole life."

"So? You just said your grandfather's soul is gone for good, so it's not like we can ask him if he saw whodunit."

"No, but if I can break through the veil and reach the spirits here," *like Corwin*, "I might be able to ask their help finding the one who murdered Fen. I might even be able to find Fen himself…"

"Jimmy, you're scaring me," she whispered, "I've spent too much time under the attention of the dead. They'll drag you over if they can, please Jimmy, don't do this," she pleaded.

"But what about Fen?"

"I know—I know you loved him," uncertainty entered her voice. "But you can't throw your life away for the sake of the dead. No matter what you do, you can't bring him back."

"I know that! But I can't live with myself knowing that I had a shot at justice, and walked away from it. You said I was powerful before, well now I have a chance to use that power to actually do something."

"I know that but—wait, what is this?" she asked and pushed the sleeve of my t-shirt up. I looked down at the shiny new strips of scar tissue wrapped around my upper arm.

"That's where Raven grabbed me. Lupa said I'm marked by Brother Raven. That means more than just my hair." I sighed. "Like it or not, death is a part of my life."

Loki ran her fingers over the scars and I shuddered; I couldn't feel her touch so much as the pressure of her fingers. Her eyes glistened as she pulled her hand away and she wiped them on the back of her sleeve as I asked her what was wrong.

"Nothing, nothing… just… keep going." she said in a small voice, wary of the unknown that had become an irrevocable part of me.

"Loki… I need your help. You know that trick I do with the shadows? My grandfather said I could do it because I can walk between worlds; just like how Raven walks between the living and the dead. Now that I have my wolf back, I want to see if I can enter the Lowerworld. I need to try to find out who killed Fen."

Loki was quiet, and then wrapped her arms around me and buried her face against my chest. "You know, you scared me yesterday; I was afraid you were dead…" I sighed and lowered my cheek to the top of her head while the scarred shield over my heart ached at her touch. "You're a stubborn freak Jimmy, but I'll help you if I can. Just be careful…" she whispered as I held her in return.

For the first time since Fen died, I knew what I needed to do. I had a rudder. I could finally focus on the duty I'd let slip through the grip of my depression; and Wolf was ready to hunt.

CHAPTER 18 — THE HUNT

Loki and I made a shopping run to the new-age bookstore in Colorado Springs and bought up half their stock on shamanism and animal magick. We spent the first few days of spring break consuming the books to try and learn as much as we could.

For Loki's lesson that week, we went over and jammed with Bo. After playing for a while, Bo cracked a joke and Loki threw her pick at him. As I watched them I was hit with a wave of déjà vu. I'd learned, better than most, just how blatant fate could be when twisting her threads. My resentment and jealousy ebbed a little as different images moved through Wolf's mind; the three of us together, as wolves...

Loki gasped as her eyes changed color when Wolf moved. "God, look at me, I'm such a wreck!" She shook out her trembling hands as she tried to play off her shift. "Jimmy, would you play us one of your own songs?" She bit her lip as she forced her wolf back and the gold faded from her eyes.

I thought about it, "There's a new song I wrote over the last couple months, but I've never played it in front anyone before..."

"Please?" Loki pouted until I sighed and switched my amp over to its clean channel and started picking out the opening chords.

287

"The storm comes from the east, the wind howls like a starving beast. This shadow, moves through the storm. A dark wraith, walks alone… walks alone… In the dark night of your soul, who will find you there? In the darkness of your mind, how long until you wake up?"

I'd never sung for anyone before, but my hesitance gave way as the emotion of the song took hold of me.

"As sleep comes, so too rests pride and rage. The shield falls, the curtain falls on the stage! This shame! A lie to save yourself! The dream falls, and the black wolf runs! In the dark night of your soul, who will find you there? In the darkness of your mind, how long until you wake up? You walk alone… You walk alone!

"Come, enter the forest! Sleep, under emerald boughs! Dream, of a Pack lost! Sing… alone… to a cold sky…

"In the dark night of your soul, who will find you there? In the darkness of your mind, how long until you wake up? You walk alone… You walk alone!"

I felt tears roll down my face as I sobbed the last refrains and felt loss and isolation wash through me. I heard *Qhipe's* words in my head, "*If you choose this middle road, you will truly walk forever between the worlds. You will never*—never *completely belong to either. Spirit bound to flesh, wolf bound to man, but never one or the other.*"

I'd found a new way to be cursed.

Loki hugged me and Bo laid his hand on my shoulder, and I realized that I wasn't really alone. I never had been. I just had to be brave enough to trust them. Loki and I gathered our gear up to leave as an itch festered in the back of my mind. As we left, I gave in to the itch and said something I never thought I'd say in my life, "Hey Bo, how'd you like to learn the truth about werewolves?"

Bo's eyes grew wide and Loki dragged me outside. She forced me into the car and made me drive off before Bo could interrogate us. "Are you out of your fucking mind?" she hissed as soon as we were safe inside the car.

"Loki, do you trust my judgment?" I spoke softly.

"What? Of course I do, but I don't have to agree with everything! Why'd you do that? You didn't even ask me! You don't know him! How can you possibly trust Football Hero with that kind of information?"

"I know him better than you think; and he already knows a lot about us." I said and tried to calm her down.

"But don't you see? That's what makes him dangerous! How did he learn those things? What if he's the one who murdered Fen, once he found out the truth about him?"

I flinched, and she quieted for a moment.

"Sorry, that was low blow." She lowered her face in apology.

"Don't think I'm about to hand him everything on a silver platter; he's going to have to work for every little piece of information. But I can—see it in my mind. See him as one of us."

We drove in silence as Loki glowered out the window.

"It's spring Loki." I muttered under my breath.

"What's that supposed to mean?"

I looked into her eyes, "In the spring, everything starts over. Life grows, families—packs—grow." I tried to deliver my intention through our gaze.

"You really mean to make him…?" she asked me.

"It's like I've already seen it. Already seen him as one of us."

Loki sighed and shook her head; "You're *sooo* going to owe me for this—" she paused on the thought. "Hmm, maybe we'll start with Prom."

With that four letter word; any worries about revealing my lupine nature to a potentially deadly stranger suddenly seemed benign beside the threat of the school dance to end all school dances.

"I thought you didn't do school events?" I tried subtlety first, but I knew it would degrade to begging soon.

"Well, you only get one Prom. Well, I guess I could get two, but I want to be *taken* to prom, not be the one taking... Don't worry, I'm not expecting anything extravagant like the other kids have been tweeting about lately; but it would be nice to experience it once, ya know?"

I resisted the urge to bang my head bloody on the steering wheel. "But I don't know how to dance! You remember how much I used to weigh; I didn't exactly frequent the dance circuit!"

"Oh, don't worry about it! Everybody's gonna be off in their own little la-la land. The guys are gonna be wondering if they'll score," her words triggered images in my mind and I felt my face heat, "and the girls will be wondering if their hair is still perfect. Don't forget; you're asking for a huge exception to bring Bo into this, so you fucking owe me anything I want—*a-ny-thing!*"

"Okay." Was all I could squeeze through my constricted throat.

I had about a week and a half to prepare for an ordeal I'd foolishly assumed I would never be subjected to. I just had to hope for the best, maybe a compound fracture... or the Ebola virus?

When Loki came over for dinner, Mom and Dad were ecstatic to hear her announcement that I was taking her to prom. I figured they probably gave up on any school dance fantasies for me somewhere around tenth grade; a few years *after* I had. I wanted to crawl under the dinner table and die while my face turned beet red, but I managed to suffer through dinner in silence.

Loki and I spent the rest of spring break dodging Bo's badgering phone calls while we worked on breaking through the veil.

Loki loaded a bunch of shamanic drumming tracks onto her MP3 player, and we spent hours outside while she read and I struggled with mounting frustration to break through the wall.

On the last day of break, we sat together in the field behind Loki's house, though neither one of us could bring ourselves to go back to the den. Another day pissed away as I tried to clear my mind of the constant noise and clutter, while Loki tried to reassure me that the books said most shamans took months of training before they could achieve a spirit journey.

I couldn't help it; there was something arrogant inside me that insisted I could do better than them. Like having *Qhipe's* blood was supposed to be some kind of shamanic cheat code.

As the sun set, something moved in the brush along the irrigation ditch and Wolf stirred inside me.

Something shifted, but not like the pulling rush I'd felt when Raven dragged me over. I opened my eyes and gasped. The field was still there, but it looked vastly different. Trees stood everwhere, like imprints of long fallen trees still stood, some of them nothing more than faded outlines. Loki was surrounded by a cloud of fire in a spectrum of colors, and her house was nothing but a ghostly outline of itself.

I stood up in surprise and it all faded back to normal, like a dissolve in a movie. Loki looked up at me as I plopped back down.

"What the hell was that?" I thought out loud.

"What did you see?" Loki asked, and her eyebrows furrowed I described it to her. "I... Honestly Jimmy, I have no clue." She flipped through her book, "I've never heard of anything like what you just described—are you sure you didn't just imagine it?"

I glared at her, "Why would I imagine something that lame when I know what the Lowerworld looks like. This was different, like it wasn't as—deep?" I struggled for an analogy and it hit me, "Oh my god!"

"What?"

"I think I saw the etheric plane! The... buffer between the physical and spirit worlds. I didn't even think that was possible... Let me try again." I tried to focus and relax, but my excitement wouldn't relent. I tried unsuccessfully to slip back between, and wondered what I was doing wrong.

I remembered how Wolf stirred and it finally made sense. Wolf and *Qhipe* were one and the same now, and Wolf existed primarily on the etheric plane; like on Halloween when my mental shift in Fen's bathroom amplified the voices.

Wolf was the key that allowed me to break the veil.

Duh...

This time, I let Wolf rise and I pulled the shadows of the trees around myself. As I disappeared, I pulled deeper and the etheric overworld faded into view. The colors of Loki's aura swirled with surprised flashes of yellow when I vanished, and I could see her wolf's ears, tail, and muzzle.

Testing my control, I pushed Wolf down and everything returned to normal. Then I flexed my new muscles and Wolf and I pulled back into the shadows, but this time I pushed as hard as I could and felt my heart sync with the rhythm of the drums I listened to.

Now that the buried terror from my snakebite didn't rule me anymore, I slipped out of my flesh and down through the roots and soil. I followed the water down and came up in a lake, the sun sparkled brightly off the water as I looked up into the Lowerworld sky. I smiled at my accomplishment as possibilities formed in my mind.

Now... how do I get back?

After an 'oh-shit' moment, I felt the throb of the drums resonating through the water. I focused on it and used it as an anchor to pull myself back across the veil. I settled back into my flesh and opened my eyes as I released the shadows.

"I did it!" I grinned at Loki as I pulled her headphones off.

"Took you long enough," she laughed, "Most people take weeks or months, so your slacking is unforgivable!" Underneath the joke, I could tell she was nervous. Almost scared of me.

Inside my head, I remembered what *Qhipe* had said, "Weapons are tools, Jimmy. A hammer can build a house or crush a skull; it all depends on the person who wields it. Never confuse the two, and never forget where the accountability lies."

I'd never realized quite the arsenal I'd collected over the months. I'd never thought of them as weapons before; it just depended on how I used them. On their own, they were nothing but freakish attributes, but together... I just hoped they'd be enough. I could feel emotions, disappear into shadows, speak to the dead, enter not only the spirit world but the etheric middle plane as well, and perceive with the senses of a wolf.

My goodness Jimmy, what big teeth you have...

We went over to my house for dinner, and after we ate, Loki and I laid down outside on the front walk. We stared into the splattered stars across the deep blue heavens while the Cheshire Cat moon grinned down at us. Loki complained that the ground hurt her neck, so I offered to let her rest her head on my shoulder, and absently stroked her soft hair with one hand.

We didn't talk, but just touching her made me content and prompted foolish thoughts as I grew drunk with her presence.

"Loki?"

"Hmm?" She turned her face and looked at me.

"Would you mind telling me about your last boyfriend? …
Um, you don't have to if you don't want to…" I mumbled, as the
urge to confess gnawed at me again. My arm was tired, so I relaxed
and laid it down on her stomach.

Her smile melted away and she sighed.

"Like I said, you don't have to answer if you don't want to—"
I blurted.

"No, no… it's fine…" She sighed again and set her hand on
top of mine. "Back when I was a freshman, Fen and I took Drama
together, and there was this guy there I liked. We went out for a
couple months, but he started going through some really heavy shit
at home. I resented feeling like his life raft, and he started to lose
control of himself, and he uh… he hurt me one day—on accident—but still. That's part of why my dad's so overprotective. So,
I dumped him and he uh…" she swallowed hard as her glistening
eyes roved around the twilight sky, "He uh… he killed himself…"

Corwin?

A trap door fell out from under me. I felt lightheaded. When
she asked if I was okay, it sounded so far away.

"Yeah, that's just… holy shit Loki…" She and Corwin had
gone out? That was the rough breakup that Fen had jumped?
Corwin blamed Fen for his death though, not Loki, so what did
Fen do that pushed him over the edge? "Why didn't you tell me?"

"I was afraid…" she muttered and fidgeted with her fingers,
"It's hard for me not to feel stained by it, and I was afraid you
wouldn't like me anymore if you knew." She slipped her fingers
between mine and squeezed my hand while my pulse rocketed
despite the sick flutter in my gut.

Don't read too much into it, or you'll ruin everything…

"You're a strange one." I muttered and shook my head.

"Yeah, but you wouldn't have me any other way!" She laughed
and batted her lashes, but I felt her uncertainty.

God help me, even knowing the truth now, all I could think about was kissing her. Silence fell, not a single car or dog broke the stillness.

I love you…

The stars whirled overhead, and she looked at her watch and then yawned and stood up. My hand felt cold where her warmth had just been. "C'mon, I need to get home before my parent's curfew."

I drove her home while I suffered over my indecision, certain I was about to waste the perfect opportunity. She hugged me goodbye and started to climb out of the car. *Shit…*

"Hey Loki?"

"Yeah?" She looked back at me. I knew I was blushing, but my brain felt starved for blood regardless. I just hoped she couldn't see it in the darkness.

"Um, I uh…"

Damnit…

"You 'uh' what?"

Dammit…

"I, uh, just wanted to tell you… I…" Terror closed my throat, I felt like I was going to faint.

"Tell me what?" She asked and tilted her head.

Dammit…

"I, uh, hope you have a good day tomorrow." I wanted to bash my skull into the steering wheel, but she smiled.

"I'll try, you too. Drive home safe, okay?"

"Okay, goodnight…"

"'Night Jimmy"

She closed the door, and when I knew she couldn't hear me, I finally said the words that'd failed me. "I love you so damn much, you don't even know."

295

Despite the fear of losing her to some other suitor, I just couldn't tell her what I felt for her. Though, she *did* present me with a tempting opportunity at prom. The hopeless romantic in me liked that idea a lot, especially since it bought the coward in me more time.

CHAPTER 19 — LOSE ENDS

Time moved in a surreal rush. There wasn't enough time in the world to get ready for prom; which charged toward me like an angry linebacker. On the other hand, there were times when time couldn't move fast enough. Fen's killer was out there somewhere, and there were way too many lose ends.

I felt unnaturally exhausted by the end of the school the next day. I lucked out in World History, we just watched Monty Python and the Holy Grail, but American Government was a totally different story. Bo offered to help me study, in return for pillaging my brain about werewolves and shifters. That was fine; I'd planned on it anyway.

After the final bell I slipped into the auditorium and disappeared into the shadows. After Mrs. Cartwright turned out the lights and walked out, my eyes shifted and I walked down the grayed out aisles.

I needed answers, and the veil couldn't keep me from them anymore. I laid down on the stage and took a deep breath, and then closed my eyes and focused on the rhythm of my heart. Wolf stirred and we slipped deeper between worlds. The hum of the air vents dulled as everything shifted around me.

297

I opened my eyes and the room looked almost identical, but I felt the emotional imprint of the place. My empathy tuned in to the flowing stew of joy, sorrow, betrayal, and—*there!*

A lingering cold trace of despair wound toward the back of the stage and I slowly angled my head and looked back toward the cluttered piles of debris, stacked out of view on the stage. Corwin's faint silhouette lacked the auric glow that surrounded Loki, the fire of life. I said his name, and he looked at me.

"Jimmy, what are you…" He cocked his head to the side, "H-how'd you cross over?"

"It's a long story. Suffice to say I've learned a new trick, but if I move too much I'll screw it up."

He laughed and walked over, "Well whatever works." He sat down next to me; "Not that I m-mind the visit, but… why are you here?"

"You promised to tell me everything, and this time we won't be interrupted. I need your help. I need you to tell me what happened with the Pack, before I got here."

He sighed and ran a hand through his black hair, "You're a tenacious bastard, you know that?"

I smiled, "Let's start with what happened to you?"

Corwin sighed, and his eyes twitched around the room as he thought. "After my mom and dad divorced, I met Fen and Loki in drama club. The hazing was bad, but it was nothing compared to the other kids, and *they* didn't stop. Fen and Loki were the only ones who were nice to me.

"Fen thought I was the one 'marked by Brother Raven' in Lupa's prophesy," Corwin grabbed a handful of his hair, "He told me and Loki about shifters, and *damn* did I want to be a part of that! My mom was so focused on her own shit she d-didn't even notice me anymore; to her, I was just a weapon to use against my dad. So I virtually begged Fen to change me, I lied about dreaming I was a wolf, and eventually… he gave me what I wanted." Corwin sighed and shook his head. "When Fen bit Loki and I, we started this Pack."

"But it was all w-wrong… When I had my first dream shift, I… I was horrified! I was some stupid black bird! I was supposed to be a wolf 'marked' by Raven, not a f-freakin' raven lock shock and barrel! So, I lied to them about it. Loki and I started dating, and Fen became distant. At the time, I thought it was my fault. Like he somehow knew the truth.

"I felt so ashamed, and I tried to become the wolf Fen I thought I should have been. I pushed so hard to be something I wasn't until—something broke inside me. I thought I was losing my mind; I started shifting at the worst possible times, started having blackouts…"

"Cursed," I whispered.

"Yeah… Nobody but F-Fen or Loki wanted anything to do with me, nobody ever knew when I'd do something strange, something—inhuman— I felt this wall between me and everyone, growing higher and higher until not even Fen and Loki could stand it anymore.

"I thought Fen was disappointed in me, but I guess he was disappointed in himself. Loki tried to stick with me, but… I had a blackout one day, and when I came back to myself Loki was covered in c-cuts and bruises and she was crying." He swallowed hard and grimaced, "She told me it was over, she just couldn't take it anymore. Her dad just about killed me too. I ran over to Fen's house to ask for his help."

I winced, "Oh, that was a bad move…"

"Tell me about it, I didn't realize Fen loved her. When I told him what I'd done, Fen punched me, dragged me outside, and threw me off of his porch. Before he slammed the door in my face, the last words he ever said to me were, "I w-wish I c-could unmake you."

Corwin went quiet and covered his face with his hands. I couldn't make sense of my own anger, both at him for hurting Loki, and at Fen for hurting him. When he'd composed himself a little, he continued in a soft voice.

"I didn't understand what had really happened. At the time I only heard what I wanted to hear. I never thought he was furious at *himself* for not being able to help me. I felt lost, abandoned… And so god-damned *weary* of forcing myself to live. The depression suffocated me, blinded me, it choked the very idea of hope out of me…"

I know that feeling…

"Before she left him, Mom stole my dad's revolver, so I stole it from her. I carried it in my backpack all day, waiting for someone—God, Fen, anybody—to save me from myself. I walked around waiting for divine intervention, and then I went to the last place I felt happy, felt like I was wanted, and I hid in the Auditorium. Since I didn't want to save myself—couldn't think about anyone *but* myself—I put my father's gun into my mouth and pulled the trigger…" We both shuddered as he remembered the sensation, and I felt the memory through him.

"No light opened for me. The anger still burned in me, the rage; I wanted them all to see what they'd made me do. It wasn't until I watched them discover my body the next day that I realized what I'd done. My mother collapsed screaming when she identified my body. Loki wailed herself to sleep while her father spent every night awake on the couch wishing he could help her. And Fen… Fen almost followed me.

"What do you mean?" I asked.

"Fen put on a strong front for everyone, but when his mom worked late he would stare into his reflection in the bathroom and debate with himself which way he should cut his wrist, or his throat, or what kinds of pills his mom had and if it'd be enough to t-take him out."

"Why did Fen want to kill himself?" I asked, and remembered the scar on his arm.

"Fen thought he'd stolen my life, and didn't deserve his own anymore. When I tried to reach him in his sleep I scared him so bad that he almost went through with it, but as soon as the blade broke his skin he freaked. He realized just how close he came and panicked. He tried to find something to hold on to, an anchor to keep him here."

"That was when he asked Loki out, wasn't it?" I asked.

"Yeah, the v-very next day. She had no idea, of course, and shot him down." Corwin continued, "Fen never told Loki the truth; he just let her hate him. He thought he deserved to live in misery because of what he did to me.

"I was terrified Fen would repeat my mistake, but a new kid transferred in, an outcast like I was. Since Loki refused to anchor him, Fen turned him."

"Geri?"

"Yeah, the poor guy never had a chance; he walked into an emotional shitstorm. Fen took all his anger and hurt out on him. But it still wasn't enough and time after time I watched Fen tear at his hair and scream in silence until I thought his heart would rupture. You asked me before if it was unfinished business. Well, there it is. I *have* to apologize to them. I have to let Fen know that I don't blame him."

"Then what are you going to do now?" I asked quietly.

"How do you mean?"

"With Fen—*gone*—are you still bound here? Or are you free to go?"

He sighed again and lowered his head, "I don't know. Truthfully, I haven't tried to leave yet. I won't until I know you and Loki are safe."

"Safe from what? Do you know who killed Fen?"

"I'm sorry Jimmy, I don't know who did it. When I helped you protect your brother, it exhausted me. I haven't been able to leave this stage since then."

"Wait, then that wasn't you I heard at Fen's funeral?"

Corwin shook his head. "No, I've been trapped in here since then. But, I've caught scattered thoughts through the veil. Whoever killed Fen is still out for blood, and more fixated on you than ever."

"Wait—me?" I blurted.

"Yes, you. Your face was f-fixed in his mind." My mind reeled; I couldn't think of anyone who wanted to kill *me* either. Jack, maybe, but he'd been in prison when Fen was killed. "Whoever it was, they seemed familiar for some reason, but I haven't felt anything for a while now, so I don't know if they've given up, or just moved away." Geri had moved away...

"I d-don't know, it's not like there's anything I can do," Corwin continued, "but I can't just s-st-stand by. You're a strange creature Jimmy Walker, at first I resented you for being what I should have been, but now I want to protect you like you were my own brother." He shook his head and laughed humorlessly.

"We were both born to the same Pack weren't we? Just 'cause you're a bird—and dead—doesn't mean you're not my Pack-brother."

Corwin's smile was bittersweet. "I wish Fen had seen like that," he stood and nodded at me, "you don't have much time before the janitor makes his rounds. I'll see you around Jimmy, be careful."

"Thanks, see ya Corwin." He dissolved from view as I stood, and I rubbed the sore muscles in my back. I wished I could do more to help him, and then I turned and walked away as I stitched the pieces together.

I'd hoped Corwin would have answers, not more questions.

Bo and I studied after school the next day, or rather, he pumped my brain about werewolves while I ganked his notes. My brain was not happy with me for switching back and forth so many times between American Government and Shifting 101.

"Hey, what's this word?"

He leaned over to check where my finger pointed, "Corruption."

"Your 'R's look mutated…"

"Just keep talkin'…"

I rolled my eyes. "Finally, there are the supposed physical shifts. Some exhibit almost superhuman, berserker-like strength and speed; and then there is also the famous full physical shift where your flesh actually transforms into the body of a wolf."

"But that's just myth right? You don't really believe that's possible do you?"

"I don't know," I said, and frowned, "you decide what you believe. Any physical shifter who expected to survive wouldn't advertise their ability, not even to others of their own kind. I wouldn't even expect them to socialize with others if they held a secret like that."

"Wow, so where do you fit into all that?"

"My Pack was—is—something of an oddity. Judging from what I've learned from books and the Internet; we sorta skirt the line of what's 'normal' for other shifters. Most therianthropes don't have as many psychic quirks as we do, and they don't feather the lines between phenomena as much.

"Fen's eyes were amber twenty-four-seven. That wasn't their natural color, but he wasn't always shifted either, he and his inner wolf were just very integrated with each other. We've all tapped into some of that berserker strength and speed, sometimes with a light mental shift. Also… No other pack has ever mentioned anything about a patron spirit, much less a territory in the spirit world. Yet we do."

"So what if I asked to join your pack?"

I laughed. "I'd say 'Wait your turn, pup'. You need to prove yourself before I'll even *consider* changing you." Which wasn't entirely true, but he didn't need to know that.

"So how does the change work? Is a bite like in the movies? Or is it more of a ritual, like in the old legends?"

I shook my head smiling, "Sorry, that's all for today!"

"Bastard…" He glowered at me and snatched his notes back, even though I'd already memorized them, "Who the fuck would I tell? You and Loki are the only people who still talk to me anymore. I don't even have anyone to tell about this." He picked up a manila mailer envelope and tossed it at me. I slid a stack of papers out and glanced at the first page.

Letter of Acceptance; University of Colorado College of Arts and Sciences.

"Oh my God Bo, you got in!" I shouted and tackled him with a huge bear hug while he laughed. "Congratulations! What are you gonna study?"

"I'm thinking cultural anthropology."

"Sounds right up your alley." I grinned with him, and tried to ignore the small worm of envy that squirmed inside me.

You chose your road, now you have to follow it. It's too late to change your mind, just be happy for him.

Bo helped me study through the week. School reached a meltdown point of stupidity. The halls were filled with bragging gossiping half-wits obsessed with dresses and limos and who was taking so-and-so. Of course, my exhaustion didn't help my foul mood at all.

Every night, instead of sleeping, I practiced phasing into the Lowerworld. I looked everywhere I could, exhausting myself night after night in the hunt for Fen's spirit. Desperate to find him, I journeyed to our Pack's lake and howled.

Fen never answered, but Lupa did, and she met me on the lake shore.

"Lupa, please, do you know where Fen is? Have you seen him?"

"No Jimmy," she answered and my ears drooped, "but I'm not the one you should be asking either…"

A shadow crossed the moon as Raven flew over the water and plopped down on the shore beside us with a dignified 'klok'.

I sat down on my haunches and looked at him, "Um, Brother Raven, can you help me fi—"

"Your friend never came to this place," he cut me off in mid-question. "So, sorry kid, I can't help you find him."

"Well, where else could he go?" The thought of Fen's soul dissolving into nothing, trapped in some nowhere land filled me with dread.

Raven answered with an indignant fluff of his feathers, "Jimmy, every afterlife ever imagined exists within this world. From Heaven and Hell, to Valhalla and Hades. Believe me, if your friend were in *any* of them, I would know. So use your head kid, where do *you* think he is?"

Raven hopped up and pecked me hard in the center of my forehead, slamming me back into my body. "*Oww!* You've got to be kidding me…" I moaned as I held my pounding head. At least now I knew where Fen wasn't.

Fen never crossed the veil. He was still here somewhere…

After school, I drove Loki home. As she let me inside, she seemed to remember something, "Hey, did you get an email from Geri?"

"No, why?"

"He wrote me a couple days ago. He said he was going to try and make it back down this weekend; right around Prom! I heard a few other ex-students are going to be there, I wonder if we could find a way to smuggle him into the dance. Didn't Geri write you too?"

Doubts and suspicions stirred in the back of my mind as I shook my head.

"He didn't? Weird."

I stayed quiet until we were safe in Loki's bedroom, "Hey Loki, can I talk to you about Geri? I feel weird even thinking this, but before he left I went over to Geri's house. When he told me he was leaving, he also told me about how Fen used to treat him…"

Loki dropped her eyes as she sat down on her bed, "It was pretty bad… Whenever Fen lashed out, Geri was always in the line of fire. That was his 'job' in the Pack but…I wasn't able to do much to help."

"Loki, I know about Corwin…" I whispered.

She flinched as though I'd slapped her. "What? Did Fen tell you?"

I shook my head and rubbed my temples. Even with her this was going to sound crazy, "Corwin and I have been uh… chatting since just before Halloween. He made me promise not to tell any of you about him though. He was trying to reach Fen through me—"

"He tried to use you to get his revenge on Fen?" she squawked, and I winced.

"What? No! No, that's just the thing, he doesn't blame Fen; he wanted to apologize to him!" she blinked in surprise, "He tried for years, but you know Fen was a psychic brick. Plus, you blocked him out, so he was pretty much screwed until I came along! Unlike you two, I wasn't blocked by memories of him." She seemed to calm down just a little, though she still had this scared gloss on her eyes like an animal about to run. "I swear Loki, he just wants to apologize for the pain he put you two through."

"That'll be difficult now, won't it?" she whispered.

"Well, I've got a couple ideas; but I got off track. Back to Geri. Geri resented Fen a lot and only stayed because the Pack was all he had in this town. Anyway, you know better than I do what it was like for him, do you think Geri could have been angry enough to… murder Fen?"

Loki was speechless for a moment, "Jimmy, how could you say such a thing? Your own Pack-brother!"

I held up a hand to ward her off, "He'd already stopped considering himself part of the Pack long before he left, and re-member, he never told us where he was that night. Just answer me; do you think he could have hated Fen enough to kill him?"

"I—I don't…" The fact that she couldn't immediately say 'no' said it for her. She realized it as well and lifted a hand to her mouth.

"When I was leaving his house, I saw hunting rifles hanging over the fireplace in their living room, within easy reach. Also, you said yourself; no one outside the Pack knows what we are, and who else knew where the den was?"

"What about the car you told me about at the school when you fought Fen for Alpha?" Loki said.

"Geri had a car didn't he? Also, you didn't see what happened after you ran off that day in the hall. You didn't see the look on Geri's face after Fen shoved him into the wall."

"Oh my god… Jimmy, oh my *god!*" she whispered and wrapped her arms around herself. "Maybe that's why they were in such a rush to move afterwards too…"

I wanted to be merciful and leave it there, but there was one more thing I needed to ask. "Loki, did Geri have a crush on you?"

"What? Why?" she stuttered.

"Please, it's important!" I urged her.

"I… I don't know, it's possible I guess… He never said anything about it—"

"Do you really think Fen would have let him?"

Loki's jaw dropped open, "Goddamnit! As if high school drama wasn't bad enough; we have freaking 'Days of our Teenage Werewolf Lives' going on here…"

"We don't know anything for sure yet, but when we see him this weekend we'll just have to get him alone somewhere and get our answers from him. I'm probably wrong." I hoped I was wrong…

"And if you're not?" I didn't want to answer her, I wasn't sure if I'd be able to hand him over to the authorities. *Intact* anyway… And then there was the other problem; if Geri didn't email me, only Loki, what if he was coming down this weekend to finish what he started with Fen…?

"We'll deal with that when the time comes…" I said to both her question and my own thoughts, and a picture on her dresser caught my eye, "Hey, when was this taken?" I picked up the picture and frowned. A much younger version of Loki smiled out of the frame with chocolate brown hair, with a couple other girls her age under a bright blue sky.

"Oh, that was seventh grade. Those were my friends in Montana, they promised to keep in touch when I left, but they never did. Not a big loss…"

"Your hair's not black?" I asked, feeling stupid.

She just laughed though, "No, that's my real hair color there. I've been very diligent about maintaining my color since we moved here, so I'm not surprised you didn't know. I don't think anybody here even remembers me with brown hair…" she quirked an eyebrow thoughtfully. "Nope, doubtful…"

"That's strange; you look so familiar from somewhere…"

That night I tossed and turned, restless, as I plunged in and out of nightmares. Some felt more like memories than dreams, and others I wasn't even sure were mine.

The bullet tore through my leg as I ran for the tree. I tried to drag myself the last few feet to safety, until the hunter's shadow fell over me and he kicked me onto my back and pinned me with his foot. I stared up past the barrel of his gun at the obscured silhouette of his face, and then the muzzle flashed and I watched my blood spray over the trunk of the tree as the bullet punched through my skull—

The familiar girl with the soft brown hair wrapped her arms around me. I promised to protect her, even as my own birthmark doomed me to sacrifice her. I loved her, and she would die because of it—

My breath steamed in the cold winter air, the early morning pall felt all the colder as icy light edged toward the horizon.

—"Cleansed by any means necessary…"—"Bless me father for I have sinned"— I didn't recognize the voices, but the world dissolved into images of violence, helplessness, and a seething sea of buried resentment and blood.

I shook my head to clear it and returned my gaze to the eyepiece of my rifle's scope, a seemingly haphazard pile of bracken and fallen wood centered beyond the drifting crosshairs.

—All his fault—All his fault—

Despite the distance, I watched Fen and I crawl out of the den while the rifle scope's reticle danced over us and my finger tightened.

—He ruined everything—"Bless me father for I have sinned"—

Fen looked up directly at me through the scope, seemed to pierce my soul with his unnatural eyes from so far away, and panic nudged my finger back that last fraction.

—What have I done?—No, it's not my fault—Not my fault—"Bless me father…"—

I scrambled back to my car while the world spun out of control, the new ache from the recoil added to the myriad of bruises my body already bore from his retribution. Again, images of pain and helplessness consumed me, too fractured to make sense of.

—What have I done?—"Bless me father…"—"Thy will be done…"

The scenario replayed over and over again without remorse; fracturing more each time as the relentless agony of images ate away at my mind like grinding teeth and tore me open only to remake and devour me again. A broken mind of muttered voices, hateful repetitive images, and behind it all an unending scream heard at all times and places, simultaneously myself and a terrified child contorted by rage, but through the madness, my own face appeared over and over until it became the only thing I could focus on.

—Jimmy Walker—"Bless me father for I have sinned"—What have I done?—Jimmy Walker—All his fault—He ruined everything—Jimmy Walker—All his fault—"Thy will be done…"—

He must be punished…

—"Thy will be done…"—

It chased me, the dark being just behind me without any face or body; yet real nonetheless, and inescapable. Yet again the same dream tortured me, and I was powerless to resist. I ran with all my might down the forest path, past the familiar faces, past Fen's staring eyes. His loss crashed over me again as the darkness consumed them all and I ran and ran, my chest burned and my eyes blurred with tears.

I tore open the black iron gate and the room shifted before my eyes. I looked one way and it was my English classroom, but I turned again and it was Mrs. Ashcroft's Art room. I turned around completely and stood in the middle of a dark cavern; the girl with the brown hair and emerald eyes from my other dream stood in front of me. I screamed as I ran for her and the darkness crawled into the room behind her. She held out her hand and smiled at me as my words of warning fell on deaf ears, my legs were bound in cement and no matter how hard I fought, I just couldn't reach her!

—"Thy will be done…"—

With victorious hunger, the ravenous darkness reached out to consume her…

Shrieking, I thrashed free of unfamiliar blankets in a sinister room, until I fell completely out of my bed onto the floor, hyperventilating. That was how John found me when he came downstairs to check on me. Shaking and disoriented, I whispered over and over…

"Loki… Loki… No, not Loki…"

I opened my eyes, and then clamped them shut again when I remembered what day it was. Tonight was prom, may God have mercy on my soul…

The dreams haunted me through breakfast, and put me in a foul mood. Corwin had said the killer was fixated on me, but my dreams told me Loki was in danger too; she was in danger because of me. I was only too aware that the clock was ticking. I still had too much to do, and I didn't even know where to start. I only had one hope left to try and find any answers.

Mom argued with Jacob in the living room, and I tuned in when I heard my name.

"—solutely not Jacob, your brother has a big day ahead of him. He's really nervous about the dance tonight, and he doesn't have time."

"But Mom," Jake whined her name out for a full three seconds, "Jimmy never spends any time with me anymore! I just want to go out and look at clouds like we used to!"

I was hit with a pang of nostalgia, we hadn't laid on the ground and cloud-watched since we were in Chicago. To be honest, I also welcomed the distraction from prom and homicidal were-wolf hunters. I grabbed our jackets and walked down to Jacob's school with him. We sprawled out on the grass; head to shoulder with each other.

"Why don't you want to go to your dance?" he asked while we watched the clouds move and morph above us.

"Because I don't know how to dance. Turtle." I said, pointing up at one of the shapes.

"You're going with Loki right? She's nice. Maybe she'll teach you how?"

"Maybe… Ooh, good one!" I said as he pointed out a man's face.

"You like her don't you?" he teased me.

"Maybe, a little bit. But don't tell her, okay?" I whispered conspiratorially and he giggled.

"Jimmy and Loki, sittin' in a tree, K-I-S-S-I-N-G!" Jacob sang and I smiled, "How's your wolf doing?" he asked with the same easy tone someone would comment on the weather.

I almost laughed, "Rabbit. We had a rough time, but we're doing better now."

"I'm glad, I don't like it when you're sad…"

"Thanks buddy."

"I know you miss Fen, I miss him too…"

I sighed, "Yeah…"

We were quiet for a moment, watching.

"Daddy knows you like boys."

"What!" I snapped and looked at him.

"It's okay Jimmy, I heard him talking to Mommy about it. He's not mad, he's just sad. He said he's waiting for you to say it."

"Well…okay." I muttered, completely knocked off balance. I winced as one of the last hooks my dragon had in me tore free, and it went silent inside me. My heart pounded, it terrified me just thinking that John knew. I rubbed my face and tried to change the subject, "So, do *you* have a gir—"

"Flower!" Jake shouted, cutting me off as he pointed up at a particular puff of cloud. My blood chilled when I saw Jacob's cloud; I didn't see a flower…

I saw a skull, hanging there in the sky leering at us. A cool gust of wind blew across the field, throwing leaves and dirt around. "Come on Jake, let's go home…" I said as I stood up, and pulled him onto his feet.

"But Jimmy, we just got here!" Jacobs's bright blue eyes grew wide, his feet already prepared to dig in.

"Jacob, enough!" I snapped, "I'm sorry buddy, I'm not feeling good, can we please go home? Please buddy?" I pleaded with him.

He hung his head and sniffed, "Jacob, stop, you know that doesn't work on me. I'm not mad, I just don't feel well; I'll take you out again in a couple days, ok bud?"

"Ok," he muttered, sullen, and then hugged me, "I just miss you Jimmy…"

"I'm not going anywhere Jake. You know I love you."

"I love you too Jimmy…" his mood improved somewhat. Excellent. "I wonder what we'll see when we go out next time?"

"Who knows? Next time's gonna be awesome!" Jacob took my hand and I felt his disappointment evaporate with his distraction. A low blow, but effective nonetheless. "C'mon, let's go home; I have a lot of things I need to get done."

And somebody I need to talk to…

I drove down to the flower shop and picked up Loki's corsage, and then drove around to every place I associated with Fen. The library, the cemetery, the wooded copse by the school; I even tried scoping out his old house, which just pissed me off worse when I saw what a mess the stoners had made out of it.

My stress grew as I visited each place. What if he wasn't just hanging around as a ghost somewhere waiting for me?

When I ran out of ideas, I just drove on impulse while wondering *Fen, where are you?*

I worried about Loki's safety and Geri's visit. It felt surreal to even consider the thought, but Corwin said that whoever it was had been distant for a while, and Geri had moved months ago. Plus, all the church-speak in my dream reminded me of Geri's weirdness after Fen's death. He'd never pushed his faith on us before then. Hell, he owned a Ouija board. I trusted Loki not to meet him alone, but I felt sick to my stomach thinking about it.

I realized where I was headed as I drove out of town, and felt stupid for not thinking of it sooner. I put my car in low gear and climbed the side of the now snow-free mountain and then parked and looked out over the town. I got out and hiked along the ridge of sandstone while the wind buffeted me. I sat down and closed my eyes and listened to the wind whistle through the shrubs until I felt a tingle on the back of my neck that had nothing to do with the wind.

He's here...

I pulled Wolf up and slipped through the veil between the planes. When I opened my eyes, the town looked different, and someone sat beside me.

"Hello Fen." I carefully turned my head to look at him.

"Hey Jimmy..." He laughed and shook his head, "You never cease to amaze me. Only you would be stubborn enough to even *think* of this, much less pull it off. Not to mention, those were some amazing gymnastics on the ice a few weeks ago."

"Har-har. Would you rather I leave?"

"No, no, I'm just teasing you. I haven't been able to do that for a while, sorry."

"It's good to see you again."

"Same to you Jimmy..." He made that familiar guarded smile again, and my heart burned.

"Fen, I need you to tell me everything. About how you died, do you remember anything; do you know who did it?"

"That's sort of an uncomfortable topic, ya know..." He winced and absently rubbed his chest.

"Please, Fen, I think Loki's in danger." That got his attention.

"Aren't you forgetting yourself?" he narrowed his eyes.

"I don't care about that; I just want to keep her safe."

He sighed, "I don't know who did it. I just remember dreaming that night… Lupa warned me that no matter what words I'd said; in the morning I would choose honor or greed once and for all. When we climbed out of the den I looked up and something flashed up here in these rocks," he gestured around us. "I don't know how, but I knew it was a gun."

"Did you see who was behind it?"

"Of course not! I only knew I could either dive out of the way and let you die… Or I could die protecting my Pack—my family—I've been enough of a bastard, I just wanted do one chivalrous thing after ruining someone's life and making misery of so many others."

"You didn't ruin Corwin's life." I said, and he looked at me surprised. I was happy to see that Fen retained his golden eyes.

"How do you know about Corwin?" I briefly explained and Fen moaned as he dropped his face into his hands.

"Look, you need to let Corwin apologize."

"Let *him* apologize?" Fen looked at me like I'd lost my mind.

I nodded. "He regrets what he did, what he put you through; he was watching you the whole time. You're what's keeping him here, and he's bound to earth until you forgive yourself."

"Easier said than done." He muttered.

"Actually, I think it's a cruel irony that the two of you can actually talk face to face now. He could never reach you before."

"Yeah, I know, I've always been dense as a brick when it comes to that psychic stuff."

I laughed at his metaphor, and earned a small smile from him. "I miss you Fen." I whispered through a bittersweet smile.

"You too Jimmy, I'm so sorry… for everything…"

"It's okay, I'm healing." I smiled, and knew it was the truth. I sighed and my smile faded, "I'm sorry I can't stay longer, I have a ton of shit to get done."

"Then get going. Keep your eyes open, and take care of the woman we love…"

"I will… And, I think you should go visit an old friend in the auditorium." I winked at him and stood. His image evaporated before my eyes and the wind almost knocked me off my feet. The clouds began to clear out and I made my way back to my car and paused before I got in.

I pulled Wolf into my eyes and looked down over the town, and found the large pasture behind Loki's house, with a clear shot of the brown pile of bracken in the back where the Den lay hidden and unused.

—I gazed through the eyepiece of the rifle's scope at the seemingly haphazard pile of fallen wood centered beyond the drifting crosshairs, and watched as Fen and I crawled out of the Den. Fen's gaze pierced my soul and panic nudged my finger back on the trigger.—

My eyes narrowed in a glare. "When I find you, may God have mercy on your soul…" *…because I sure as hell won't…*

CHAPTER 20 — NEMESIS

"I'm sorry Mom, what?"

"I said," she repeated irritably as she fixed my tie, "that you look very handsome and that you'd better remember to get those pictures we asked for. Why are you so distant? I know you're nervous, but this is… it's like you're not even on the same planet right now."

"Sorry, I'm just… more scared than nervous…" *Somebody wants to hang my hide on his wall, and I'm going to do the YMCA.*

"Oh, relax honey; it'll be fine. It's hardly life or death." I rolled my eyes. Mom turned me to face the mirror while she adjusted the strap in the back of my vest. I regarded my reflection, and rather liked the way I looked. I stood a little straighter, held my shoulders broader; I looked good, respectable—and rather human.

Mom peeked around me to look at my reflection, I hadn't realized just how much taller than her I'd become. She set her hand on my shoulder and I watched tears slide down around her smile.

"I guess you're really not my little boy anymore are you?" I turned to hug her, but she held me away, "No, I don't want to cry all over you, I'll be fine, just give me a second…" She blew her nose, and then took a deep breath and composed herself.

"What's the matter?" I asked.

She was quiet a moment, and when she spoke her voice was soft, "I miss you. I hardly ever get to see you or talk to you anymore. I know you're an adult now and I'm *trying* to let go, but—for the longest time you were my entire life. And now I just can't shake the feeling that I don't even know you anymore."

If they could harness the power of mother's intuition, we'd never fear terrorists again. I frowned as I debated with myself.

"I'm still your little boy, yet at the same time I'm really not…" She didn't reply, but I knew she was listening. "For a while now, things have been changing—I've been changing. I'm not who I was before, but trust me, that's a good thing. I've only just figured out who I really am in this last year, and sorted out some personal demons."

"Can I ask you something?"

"Sure."

"I noticed you haven't been calling John 'John' anymore."

I smiled, "I love how observant you are, it makes things easier for me."

"Don't be a smart ass."

"Sorry, it was meant as a compliment!" I laughed. "After my accident, Dad and I had a talk and I think we finally understand each other now."

"I'm glad you got that sorted out. I was about to shoot the both of you." she muttered, and then looked down. "Jimmy, it's okay to tell us if you're gay."

"Woah, that was unexpected. Um, I'm not gay, not exactly…" I muttered as I turned red, "I'm not entirely straight either though; I kind of walk the middle road."

"Thank you, for telling me the truth. You know, we're not as dumb as you think we are. Real parents love their kids, no matter what, and we'll always have your back."

"Thanks Mom," I smiled, both embarrassed and relieved.

When she couldn't find anything else to fuss over, and I hugged her and Dad goodbye, and reassured them that I would be careful. I sat in my car a moment with the windows rolled down and took a deep breath of the cool night air. I went to rake my hand through my hair, only to be thwarted by the gel that glued it into messy spikes. In compromise I turned the volume on my stereo up a little more and sang along half-heartedly as I tried to force the stiff muscles in my shoulders to relax.

I knew the cops were already scoping out teen drivers tonight, so I set my cruise control at the speed limit and it felt like an eternity before I finally pulled into Loki's driveway.

I grabbed her corsage and then walked up to the door and knocked. I heard voices and movement behind it, and Wolf gnawed at the periphery of my mind, summoned by my unease.

When Loki opened the door my heart stopped dead.

She looked like an angel sculpted out of ebony and ivory. Her black gown flowed like ink from beneath her velvet corset, and her skin sparkled with a dusting of glitter while a silver necklace disappeared down the front of her dress. It was her eyes that crushed me though, shining like emeralds when she smiled with crimson lips. She looked elegant, delicate, powerful, and romantic all in one break of my heart.

A brilliant flash tore me out of my stupor, and I blinked and shook my head as spots danced in my eyes.

"Oh dear lord, the look on his face was priceless! Look!" Loki's mother crowed as she showed the camera to her dad, familiar cowboy hat in place, which only made him laugh louder as I turned even redder. Like mother like daughter.

"Jimmy? You uh… dropped something." Loki pointed down at the box that had slipped unnoticed out of my hands. I crouched to pick it up and wondered when this train wreck would end… My hands shook as I took the corsage out of its box and slid it onto her wrist; its rose matched the crimson of her lips and I caught myself staring. She stole my breath with another smile as she leaned in to whisper; "Thank you Jimmy…" and I knew she wasn't just talking about the corsage.

Her mom snapped some more pictures of us and then she hugged her parents and I shook her dad's hand. She grabbed her lace parasol and we left.

Safe in the car, Loki took my shaking hand, "Why are you so nervous?"

"Because I wanted to impress you?" She heard the 'duh' in my voice even if I didn't say the word out loud. It was funny, I was only nervous about her seeing me, but I couldn't care less about what my classmates thought.

We parked and joined the coalescing tide of taffeta, pastels, and sequins. We climbed the steps and waited by the cordoned off area where dancers were already trying to cool off. I thought I felt someone watching me, and looked over the crowd for Geri's face. There was no sign of him, and I shook off the feeling as I opened the lobby door for Loki.

Whispers and cruel jabs followed us as we headed for the ticket booth, but beneath it I felt their jealousy. They were all so deathly afraid of standing out from the brainless flock, and yet at the same time yearned to feel as free as we were; unbound by the structured lies of High School social life.

I whispered as much to Loki, and she laughed. Tabby got in the line behind us and loudly chided that it looked like we were attending a funeral, not a dance.

We laughed at her and I didn't hide my scorn as I ran my eyes over her blue silk dress, that couldn't even be qualified as a 'gown'. "I'd be jealous too if I looked like a Smurf threw up all over me." I shook my head and turned my back on them.

A shift of air warned me before a firm hand grasped my shoulder and tried to turn me around, but I'd become immovable. I turned my head and met the eyes of Tabby's latest Biff-du-jour boyfriend. My aura reached out and surrounded him, while I thought the command, *let go*. His ego crumbled under the force of an Alpha's will and he complied with a dazed look, and I turned back and guided Loki to the cafeteria while Tabby tore into him.

Filing that new trick away for future use…

Already, the thud of the bass echoed out of the gym. We stepped into the seemingly infinite line that led up to the photographer. With hushed voices, we discussed Geri's potential whereabouts, until a familiar booming baritone cut through the din. Bo's dense form parted the sea of people, while a brunette I recognized from the hallway trailed in his wake clutched to his arm.

Loki gasped and waved excitedly when she saw her, "Kat! Oh my God, I didn't expect to see you here!"

Kat blushed and smiled, "Hey Loki, I didn't expect to *be* here! Bo didn't ask me until the day before yesterday!"

"Way to go, waiting 'till the last minute!" I teased him, "You're lucky no one else snatched her up."

"And just look at you!" he gestured at me, "Who'da thought you could clean up so well?"

"Gee, thanks buddy." I thumped him on the shoulder as Kat complimented Loki's dress. I felt for her mood, but there was no deceit or jealousy from this girl. I grinned and muttered so only Bo—and perhaps Loki's supernaturally gifted ears—could hear, "Congratulations; I think you might have found the last genuine girl in this school."

"Yeah, we have Calculus together. I wasn't planning on going to Prom, but hey, somebody needs to keep you out of trouble."

"Oh? And for some reason you feel you're up to this task?" I raised my eyebrow at him.

"Well, it gave me an excuse to ask her out..." He grinned.

"Hey, whatever works."

I skimmed over the photo options and chose one for Loki and me, and then blurted, "Hey, we should do a group photo. My treat."

They all agreed, and after we took our photos, Bo and Kat took theirs, and then Loki and I stepped back into frame. We allowed one serious picture, but for the final shot, we struck goofy poses and Bo and I held our dates in the air while they threw their arms and legs out like some roaring twenties jazz act.

I took Loki's gloved hand and we threaded our way into the darkness of the decorated gymnasium. Vast swaths of fabric swayed overhead and glowed when the lights from the DJ booth swept over them, as a horde of kids jumped and moved in time with some hip-hop song I'd never heard before. We claimed a spot on the edge of the floor, where Loki and I stashed our things, hidden under my jacket.

I already felt overheated and claustrophobic from the body heat pressed into the room. That was another reason school dances never really appealed to me. The loud music hurt Wolf's ears, so he kept well away from the surface. Loki and I watched for a little while, and I tried to memorize how everyone else moved, but then she dragged me out into the crowd and held me to her as the music changed and the DJ played 'Angel'. I tried to swallow my nerves and shuffled like Frankenstein's monster at first, but eventually I remembered to unlock my knees and move. As the beat sank in I let myself sway with it and Loki laid her face on my chest.

I loosened my cast-iron grip on my self-control as we lost ourselves in the faceless mass of bodies. Eventually we bumped into Bo and Kat, and formed a little circle with them and a couple of Kat's friends. We laughed and danced until both of us were covered with sweat and panted from the heat. As the first notes of "Jump Around" started up, I pulled Loki into the shadows with me and we slipped away.

We pushed our way outside into the cordoned area and I gasped at the intense brush of the cold night air. Down from the parking lot, I recognized Tabby's incoherent ranting drifting over the cars as she screeched about something. My eyes started to scan for Geri until Loki distracted me.

"You know, you're not half bad for someone who's never danced before!" Loki laughed, breathless and beautiful, while Tabby fell silent in the background.

"Yeah well; just 'cause I haven't done it, doesn't mean I haven't imagined it very hard!"

Loki laughed again and looked at me with that heart-stopping smile of hers, and then her eyes drifted over my shoulder and widened.

"*Get down!*" Fen and Corwin's screams tore through the dimensional fabric and I threw Loki to the ground just before the window behind us blew out with a crack of thunder. Silver daggers rained down around us as people screamed and ran. They tripped over the cordon as they panicked and rushed blindly in every direction.

I pulled Loki up and met the fierce glare in her eyes as my own shifted. My hackles rose as I looked down the school's front steps. My stomach dropped out when I recognized the face of Fen's murderer.

Jack flowed up the steps with unnatural grace, his face haggard and haunted with sunken too-wide eyes as he chambered another round into his hunting rifle.

My eyes hardened and I pulled Loki through the ruined window and dead-on into the sea of people. Somebody in the crowd screamed that he had a gun, and everyone broke into a panicked frenzy; all of them reduced to fight or flight.

I swam against the stampeding tide as I gritted my teeth and grunted with every blow I took, elbowed, kneed, and punched by the onrushing mass of students. I glanced behind and saw that my plan seemed to be working, as our hunter fell back from the onslaught of humanity as well. I lowered my center of gravity and heaved harder through the mob, the muscles of my arm burned from their lock on Loki's hand.

Loki pulled me toward the wall, and I watched her reach out for the fire alarm as shots cracked through the air, impossibly loud in the enclosed space, and a fresh wave of screams swept over the crowd. Upbeat dance music still blasted in the gym, oblivious to the events unfolding in the lobby. Something warm sprayed onto my hand as someone screamed and fell onto Loki. I lost my grip as they knocked her over, but she surged up from underneath them and yanked the red fire alert switch down, setting off an ungodly loud alarm.

My ears rang but I heard a familiar voice yell and I glanced over my shoulder. Bo struggled with Jack for control of the gun, the back of Bo's suit jacket stretched taut as he fought to over-power his old friend.

Loki seized the opening and pulled me out of the lobby. As we rounded the corner we found Kat cowering there as Officer Jenson ran past. I lifted her over my shoulder as Wolf rose within me and lent me his strength. Despite the painful alarm, my ears flicked back as Jack let out laugh that sent chills down my spine. Jenson yelled over the chaos, his handgun drawn and aimed, but Jack kept Bo between them as a human shield.

My eyes latched onto a door handle, which thankfully opened when I turned it. I pulled Loki and Kat inside and locked the door as soon as it was closed. Even with my eyes fully shifted, it was difficult to make out the interior other than it was a janitorial closet, and I felt over the walls for the light switch. Loki panted as she gripped me, and I clenched my eyes shut to flip the light switch.

"Jimmy… It hurts…" her voice was so faint, and a wave of fear staggered me as I flipped the switch. Hot pain seared my eyes as I opened them too soon and turned around. She looked fine, aside from a few places where sweat had soaked through her dress and her unusual pallor.

"What—" Her knees gave out and I kept her from falling. My hand fell on one of the wet spots, but it was hot to the touch and a thin film of crimson colored my fingers. That stain wasn't sweat, and it was getting bigger…

"Oh no, Loki no!" I yelled, and fumbled with her corset. Kat stared, frozen and useless, watching with wide deer eyes.

"Jimmy…" Loki moaned as she hyperventilated. I tore my vest off and wadded it up, and then shoved it into her corset to try to stanch the bleeding. She cried out as I pulled the laces of her corset tight again. *'Stop the bleeding, make her safe, stop the bleeding, make her safe'* recycled over and over again through my head.

"Okay Loki? Listen to me, here's what we're gonna do, okay? We need to get you to the hospital. Do you think you can walk?"

"I'm fine, I'll fucking crawl if I have to…" She growled as amber faded in and out of her pain-filled eyes. She gritted her teeth and struggled to stand, tenacity written on every part of her body, and I loved her more than ever. She lost the fight against gravity with a pained gasp, and I lowered her back to the floor.

"Yes, Loki, you are obviously the definition of 'fine'." One thing was clear; she'd never make it out fast enough. Jack could just take us out one-by-one at his leisure. "Okay, plan B. You need help, so we can't stay here. I'll draw him away. Wait a minute or two, and then get outside, okay?"

Terror overpowered the pain in her eyes, "No... No, Jimmy, don't go out there, he'll kill you! Please, I can't lose you too!" Her slender hands fluttered, clenched onto mine, then reached for my collar; the pain was too much for her to hold still.

I forced a smile and tried not to flinch as I heard more gunshots through the heavy door, "Don't worry, there's no way I'll lose." I said with forced cockiness, and my smile slipped as I realized it was truly now or never. "Loki, please forgive me, but I love you. I love you so damn much, you have no idea—"

"Shut up Jimmy."

Her words stabbed deep into my chest.

"I think I know... *exactly* how much..." She gasped as she slid her fingers under her necklace and lifted out the moonstone ring that hung from it. The scarred shield over my heart cracked like porcelain, and then she slid her shaking hands up to cup my face and pulled me down into a kiss. Our wolves stirred and a cloud of energy burst around us as our auras entwined each other like lovers' legs and goosebumps erupted all over my body.

I wanted to scream; all this time, if I hadn't been so afraid of losing her, I could have been with her!

"Kat? Kat!" I shouted, and finally shook her out of her shocked reverie. I dug my cell phone out of my pocket and forced it into her hands, "Kat, I need you to call 911. If the coast is clear, I'll come and get you. If I don't, then wait for me to draw him away, and get her out of here. Do you understand?" She nodded shakily, and I made her repeat my directions back to me before I turned back to Loki.

"Loki, you simply do not have the option of dying on me, got that? I'll come find you when I lose him." I grabbed her face and stole another kiss, because I didn't know if there would ever be another. My fingers smudged her own blood on her chin. "I love you!"

Her choked cry broke my heart as I ducked back out the door and engaged the lock behind me. I surveyed the hall with a quick sweep of my eyes. People screamed in the gym, so not everybody was out yet, at least they'd killed the damn music. My ears shifted, and identified a few trampling victims nearby mewling with pain. I eased around the corner and looked back out into the lobby.

A grinding squeak shot through my jaw as I clenched my teeth. Bo lay face down in a dark pool that soaked through the short carpet. *Another one...* One after another this fucker was trying to destroy everyone that I held dear. Not far away, Officer Jenson lay crumpled in his own bloodstain.

Click.

My muscles screamed in protest as I pushed them to their extreme. Jack was still raising his rifle as I blurred backward smashed my fist into his face.

Too close to Loki... Jack stood directly in front of the closet, so I dashed past him and around the corner that led to the mostly dark hallways. For the briefest of moments, I'd actually entertained the notion that I would do just as I'd told Loki I would; lead him away and double back for her. But in my heart I knew I would end this fight tonight, either with my life or his.

At least now I had something to live for.

"Fuck!" I rounded the corner and nearly ran right into the security fence they'd pulled across the hallway to keep students out. I prayed my skull was thin enough to make it between the vertical poles as I shoved myself into the gap. It felt like one of

328

my ears almost ripped off, and I popped buttons off my shirt as I fought through.

Jack came around the corner and emptied Officer Jenson's handgun at me as I tried to pull my other foot through. My free foot slipped and I fell down out of aim. Sparks showered over me as they ricocheted off the steel fence, but I wrenched my foot through and ran.

That oughta slow him down...

Another shot flashed with a metallic clang as he blew out the lock.

Maybe not.

My body screamed in protest and my legs almost buckled. My chest heaved as my lungs struggled to feed enough oxygen to my starving cells. When a shadow detached itself at the end of the hallway, I lurched to my feet and ran.

Our footsteps echoed in the hall, and I tracked him with the sound. I heard him enter into the hall behind me.

"Fuck!" He screamed as he tried to shoot, but didn't have any bullets left in the magazine. I threw myself into the hallway toward the library. Wolf liked that; the library gave cover, and deep shadows to hide in. Finally, a chance to turn the hunt on the hunter...

I slammed against the bars on the library doors with enough force to bruise my shoulder, but it forced the doors open. I dove under the computer desks and crawled under the tables until I was out of view from the windows, then I loped into the heart of the Library and the concealing forest of eight-foot tall bookcases.

Half of the overhead lights were still on, so I reached out with my shifting energy and pushed as hard as I could at them. I ground my teeth and strained until the flickering fluorescent tubes popped one by one and went dark. Only the flashing strobe of the fire alarm system survived.

Dark at last, I wrapped the shadows around myself and slipped in between the tall shelves, just as I heard the door open. Jack crouched down and swept his gun under the computer desks, searching. He popped the magazine and loaded four more rounds into it. How many shots did he think it'd take to kill me?

"Come out, come out, wherever you are…" he sang as he checked behind the checkout counter and then sidestepped toward the bookcases with his rifle ready. "It's time to send you back to Hell."

"You think *I'm* a monster? You're a murderer Jack!" I blurted before I could stop myself. Lucky for me, the bookcases diffused my voice and he glanced around for its source. Wolf growled low in my throat, and my ears laid back as my temper rose and I fought to keep my head clear. "Why did you kill him? Why did you kill Fen if you were after me?"

"I saw you and that freak fighting at the school, so I followed you." *That car!* "No one else saw you for what you were; only I knew the truth! Only I knew my duty. I waited all night for you to come out, but he got in the way, he… He looked straight at me, and I—" Jack's voice broke, and I realized that was where the rot had taken hold; the panic that pulled the trigger back, the cold-hearted murder of an innocent. I felt so stupid, I'd assumed he was in jail, it never occurred to me Jack's father might have come back to bail him after we left.

"Only, now I understand." Jack continued his fanatical rant, "It was God's will. Every night I saw his eyes, until I realized he carried the same demon you did." Jack laughed and it made my skin crawl, "It wasn't a mistake! God found me in that cage you put me in, and showed me my mission. God charged me to destroy the devil by any means necessary!" He said it like it was his shield and sword all in one, and I thought I'd be sick with disgust. I flashed back to my dream, and realized that it was Jack's voice I'd heard, his obsessive nightmare I'd tuned in to.

Bless me father for I have sinned...

Jack entered the rows of bookshelves and I muffled the sound of my voice with my hand. I needed to remove the advantage his weapon gave him... "Is that how you've justified the blood on your hands? That it was God's will? That you murdered in his name? Somehow, I don't think that'll endear you to him at your judgment."

"Shut up! I've lost everything because of you!"

"Oh, you poor blameless soul. None of it was your fault; attacking a six-year-old boy, or treating your so-called 'friends' like peasantry. I bet you even think that I made you pull that trigger." He passed the end of my aisle, rifle ready at his shoulder, and I held my breath. When he'd passed I slipped out of my shadows and crept down the aisle. "'God's will' is just a pathetic excuse, and you fucking know it. You're just twisting faith to justify your sins."

"Shut up! Shut-up-shut-up-shut-up!" he screamed. "You're a freak! An abomination!"

"No wonder your daddy beat you," I growled, "You're the reason some mothers eat their young." A plan formed in my head, simple, but it was the best I had.

I looked down at my hands. Loki's blood had dried into a crust that cracked in the creases of my fingers as I made fists. I had to stop him. Hatred devoured my urge to run. My rage waited for the moment I'd need it most. For Fen, Loki, Bo... For my family...

I swallowed hard and reached out toward a book propped up on the shelf. I nudged it with a finger so it fell over and slipped off the shelf with a soft thud. I whispered, "Shit!" and then silently slid to the end of the aisle and eclipsed myself in the shadows. The sound of Jack's shoes tapped over to my aisle. He double-checked the aisles next to it, and then stepped toward the book I'd knocked over. I'm sure he thought he was silent, but I heard him breathing like he was right next to me. I slipped down the next aisle and laid down on my stomach where I watched for his shoes through the gap under the bookcase until he stepped into position.

I stood and said a silent prayer, and then braced myself and slammed all my weight into the bookshelf between us.

Several hundred pounds of paper and wood crashed down, the sound of his panicked cry almost lost in the cacophony of splintering wood and falling books. I went down with it, carried by my own inertia.

My fall stunned me, and I shook my head as the cloud of dust started to settle, and then froze when I heard a metallic click to my left. Cold fear congealed in my belly and I forced my head to turn.

Jack stood just outside the rubble with his rifle aimed at my head. He smirked, and the gold cross on the chain around his neck glinted red in the darkness. In a sinking moment of horror, I realized I'd waited just a moment too long and missed him. Now it was his turn…

And my last…

This close, there was no way he'd miss. Wolf's rage flared in me and my hand seized one of the books underneath me in a defiant last reflex and I threw it at his face as a crack of thunder flashed out of the gun's muzzle.

The sickening sensation of tearing flesh and cracking bone flooded my brain.

Chapter 21 – Absolution

I felt every inch of the bullet's path with agonizing detail as it tore through my chest just under my collarbone, and out the other side in a wet explosion that drenched the back of my shirt.

The book hit him dead in the face and knocked him back, just enough to foil his kill shot. I fell as my nervous system shorted out and I writhed in agony.

He stepped on my chest and pinned me down as he chambered another round. The spent shell pinged on the round beside me and Jack sniffed at the blood that leaked out of his broken nose while he took aim at my head.

Like the moment when Fen's teeth sank into my hand and changed my life; time stood still. An instant stretched into a lifetime…

This agony was the last thing Fen ever felt in this world. The last Loki would feel too, unless I stopped him here. *Now!*

Wolf surged inside me, and I snarled as I grabbed the scalding hot barrel of the rifle and tore it out of his hand. I threw it into the darkness of the library where it clattered to a halt somewhere in the shadows.

333

Shocked and disarmed, Jack took a reflexive step back. With a half human roar, I threw myself at him and tackled him to the floor. He twisted underneath me as he screamed and blubbered. He punched and clawed at my face, and I caught one of his hands in my jaws and clamped down until I tasted blood and felt a bone crack.

He screamed and dislodged me with a hook from his other arm. The pain of his punch barely registered, but it knocked the cross Fen gave me out of my shirt and it snagged on his flailing hand.

The silver chain broke with a snap, and that crystalline wall that held wolf caged within me ruptured.

As the wall fell away, Wolf's fire engulfed me and filled me until I thought I'd burst at the seams. For a moment, the feeling of wholeness eclipsed the agony from my shoulder. Sensations overwhelmed me; blood roared in my ears, sounds amplified to almost painful levels, and colors bled out of my sight. Scents bombarded my brain with an intoxicating cocktail of blood, my own and his, and the thick musk of his terrified sweat.

My hand captured his neck. I felt his pulse beneath my fingers, and clenched. Jack killed my Alpha, my friend, my family, and dreadfully wounded the woman I loved—I couldn't let myself think she wouldn't survive.

I'd become the true horror of a werewolf; all the ferocity of a force of nature, with a human's wrath and rage.

I couldn't even think in words anymore, images flooded in a stream through my mind in Wolf's simpler and purer form of awareness. It was clear; by taking innocent life, Jack had forfeited his own.

Convulsions racked my body while my lips pulled back from lengthening teeth and a bestial roar tore from my throat. My breath choked by in shuddering gasps as my diaphragm clenched and contorted. Beneath me, the hand that gripped his neck and the wounded half-limp one spasmed as the sweat that covered by body evaporated in wisps of steam. The tendons in the back of my hands stood taught under the skin as the nails grew long, dark, and curved.

Holy shit it's happening, it's really happening!

My bones elongated and shifted while my innards churned and changed to match. My stomach purged itself all over him, laced with blood.

His screams reached fever pitch as what little sanity might have remained in him was annihilated by the sight of a teenage boy transforming into a wolf—right on top of him. A spasm shot down my arm and cut off the sound as the change consumed me.

I let go of myself, and let Wolf and I become one…

The thick gray pelt sprouted first, joined soon after by coarse black hairs. My legs shrank as my arms lengthened, and my hands and toes grew more paw-like until I couldn't hold him down anymore.

He scrambled out from underneath me, making hiccupping gasping sounds. I tried to pursue him, but could barely move. The cloying stink of fear trailed behind him and left an easy trail to track.

My tail-bone popped as the bones elongated and developed into the physical counterpart of the phantom tail I'd experienced for so long. The bones of my face elongated and reconfigured themselves. The inferno of shifting energy boiling off of me shredded my clothing, and it slithered off me in tatters.

My ears lengthened and moved up the sides of my head while my nose and mouth projected into a muzzle. With audible pops, the bones of my chest deepened and narrowed, while the muscles of my neck thickened to hold my head in front of me instead of over my neck. With a final satisfying shake, I rid myself of any remaining scraps of clothing.

I panted with my long wet tongue, and stretched my newly reformed muscles. My left shoulder burned, but the blood had slowed and it was somewhat functional.

Limping, I followed the ridiculously traceable scent trail he'd left behind. His blood and fear curdled in the air like a trial of incense smoke. I wedged the library door open with my muzzle, and quickly adjusted to walking on four legs as my claws clicked on the hallway floors.

His head start was no match for my sense of smell and relentless pace. My padded feet loped in a steady rhythm down the hall as his stench grew stronger. I slowed to a stop, his pungent smell was strong and I heard him gasping for breath around the corner by the auditorium. He jumped at every shadow, caught in the throes of ancient fear.

I lifted my head and let out a full-throated howl. A primeval warning and promise of his fate—he got the message—

With a choked cry he threw himself through the door and staggered outside. I waited in the shadows until I was sure no one would see me, and then I gave chase.

He was an athlete though, and I was wounded, and he drew further from me as he ran across the athletic field. I panted hard from the pain that radiated from my shoulder and worried that even on four legs I wouldn't catch him.

As he passed through the trees on the far side of the field, he stopped dead. My hackles crawled with a familiar sensation and my eyes widened as a gray wolf evanesced in the air before him.

"You murdered me..." Fen's voice whispered from the semi-transparent wolf, which laid its ears back and snarled.

"No... NO!" Jack whimpered and backed away from the specter.

A raven appeared nearby, see-through like the wolf, and together Corwin and Fen chanted the word '*murderer*' in a mocking whisper while Jack cried and remembered one last weapon. He unfolded a three-inch pocketknife and brandished it at the ghosts as I reached the trees and disappeared into their darkness. I growled softly, and his head snapped toward me, but I'd already moved. Fen's ghost growled too and Jack looked back at him as I moved closer. Together, he and Corwin herded him closer to me.

Jack backed up against a big elm, unaware that I crouched behind it. I inhaled a snout-full of scents; sweat and blood, the tang of juniper bushes, and the rich tannin of moist soil and rotting leaves. As the sirens approached I knew that my time was up. I gathered myself and lifted my voice into another howl, right behind him.

He screamed and ran. Instinct kicked in and I pursued as he bolted in the only direction that wasn't blocked by Fen or Corwin. I drew alongside him as he neared the irrigation ditch.

I snapped out and severed his Achilles tendon with a quick flash of my teeth. He fell and urinated into his pants, and then lifted himself into a desperate crawl toward the earthen bank of the ditch while dirt and grass clumped around his bleeding ankle.

I followed, a shadow with burning amber eyes. At the edge, I knocked him over and pinned him down with one of my massive forepaws, like he'd done to me in the Library, like the faceless hunter that'd haunted my dreams for months.

I stared down at him while the water rushed by, flickering silver in the night, and saw that any shred that was left in him that was human had shriveled up and died. I lowered my face and took his throat between my teeth, but at that moment we met eyes. His eyes were empty, his madness eclipsed everything, but through my rage a thought broke through and pity swept over me.

I made him this way…

He'd done the deeds, but I'd pushed him down the path to insanity. I was the one who'd driven him over the breaking point. I wanted to blame him, but I couldn't; it wasn't all his fault…

He seized my moment of hesitation and plunged his knife up and into my side—

Behind my eyes I relived the moment he split Jake's lip—when the amber light faded from Fen's eyes—when Loki collapsed in the closet—when I saw the crimson pool around Bo's crumpled form—

—An agonized snarl tore from my throat as my jaws convulsed and drove my fangs together through the soft tissue of his neck.

Blood washed over my muzzle. Too late to stop myself, I jerked away from him and vomited. He rolled over and tried to escape into the ditch until he weakened and went still. The slow pull of the water dragged him in and carried his body away.

Shock took me, and I stumbled dazed through the shadows on autopilot while I bled, until the world twisted out from underneath me and pitched me into the black abyss.

"My poor child, my sweet warrior, you have fought so hard…"

That voice seemed so familiar. "Mom?"

Out of the dark, I saw a body, so familiar, yet strange and alien… A huge black wolf lay on its side in a puddle of blood while its tongue lolled out; its furred sides unmoving.

Lupa appeared and walked up to my body.

"Your sacrifice was not forgotten…"

Lupa looked up from my body and pierced me with her stare. Then she touched it with her nose and my body started turning human again.

I floated so free, weightless in the light, until I felt the tug. An urgent pull drew me back down, but I felt so weary, I couldn't bear it anymore, all I wanted was to end the pain…

I felt Fen and Corwin beside me and I opened my eyes. They laid their hands on my shoulders and pushed me back down as they smiled.

"This is what it means to be Wolf", Fen whispered, "To be Wolf, is to survive… No matter what; you face pain, you face trials, you face all the adversity of the world, and with pride—you survive…"

"Your road doesn't end here…" Corwin added.

I heard ravens in the darkness as the features of my body melted back to human form. I reached out desperately to Fen and Corwin as I was pulled back toward the pain.

They shifted into their animal forms before my eyes, and I watched as the wolf and the raven faded into the light. The birds grew louder, and the rustle of feathers surrounded me with streaks of violet. I heard Raven's voice as I was drawn in and devoured by my material shell, and the suffocating weight of flesh and agony, "Oh, no you don't kid, you're not done yet…"

Plastic objects clacked amid a sporadic beeping sound while a siren howled over a roaring truck engine…

A strange man's voice broke the darkness—"We have a pulse! Inform the hospital that we'll be coming in, Code Three…"

CHAPTER 22 – WAKE

Beeping woke me.

That, and the dry ache deep in my throat.

When I finally persuaded my eyes to open, I blinked the bleariness out and tried to look around but the tracheal tube resisted the movement in a nauseatingly internal way. A bank of monitors blinked next to my IV drip, and I let my eyes sweep over the blue blanket that covered my body, the brace that held my left arm close to my chest, and the little white clip on my index finger. In the uncomfortable-looking chairs on the other side of the room, Mom was asleep in Dad's lap, his head slumped and he breathed loudly as he slept, just shy of an actual snore.

I couldn't speak with the tube down my throat, so I tried to sit up and a hot bolt of pain liquefied my muscles.

Ooh, SO not gonna try that one again…

I located the 'call nurse' button and reached for it with my good hand, trailing the tether that tied my finger to one of the machines. A minute or so later, a man with lightly graying hair and a goatee came in, a woman in lavender scrubs with a thick brown braid followed.

340

"Welcome back to the land of the living Jimmy. Good to see you awake," he said in a gruff rumbly voice and used a penlight to check my pupils while the woman picked up a clipboard from beside my bed and wrote down stats from the various machines attached to me. I pointed over toward my parents with my meter-encumbered finger. He followed my gesture then nodded and stepped over to John and shook his shoulder gently.

John startled awake and looked around the room, before he noticed me looking at him. I raised my eyebrows and saluted him with my tethered fingers. He whispered my name as emotions I'd never seen in him before crashed through his wide blue eyes. He shook Mom awake and they rushed over to me.

"Jimmy!" Mom cried out as tears burst from her eyes and she threw her arms around me in a huge mom-hug. My eyes bulged as my wounds flared like hot pokers and I flailed my arm. My reflexive gasp fought with the machine breathing for me and rewarded me with a hurried beeping from the EKG.

Thankfully, Mom got the picture, and stepped back into John's arms. "I'm sorry baby, I got carried away…" and she laughed while tears dripped down her cheeks. John held her shoulders and she put her hands over his.

I looked at the doctor and pointed at my breathing apparatus, and then threw my thumb over my shoulder. Universal sign language for 'This. Out. Now.'

"You want that tube out?" he clarified, and I nodded with pleading eyes. "That should be fine. Nurse, could you please help me sit him forward…" They sat me up, and I clenched my eyes around the pain from my shoulder and side. "You okay son?" he asked, and I nodded despite the perspiration that filmed my skin.

He unhooked the machine from my mouthpiece and I got my first lungful of unfiltered hospital air, "Okay, we're going to count to three, on two I want you to take a deep breath, and push out on three, understand?" I nodded again, and he grasped the end of the tube. "Here we go now, one… Two…" I sucked in a deep breath through the open tube, "And three…" and as I pushed out the air in my longs, he pulled the tube out of my throat. I felt the end of the tube climb up from impossibly deep inside my chest.

As soon as my throat was clear I coughed violently which pissed off the wound in my shoulder again. I reached up to hold my throat as I shivered from the pain. I really wanted to vomit, but thankfully I was able to hold my stomach in check as the nurse gave me some water. I took the little plastic cup with shaky hands and drank greedily. It didn't quite cool the fire in my throat but dear lord it felt good!

"I was afraid we'd lost you…" I didn't recognize the soft voice at first. I'd never heard John speak like that before.

I looked up at him and grinned, "C'mon, you're not rid of me that easily…" I croaked in a horrifying parody of my voice, which sent me into another coughing fit.

John looked at me while the muscles in his jaw worked, it looked like he was chewing on words, and trying to find the ones he wanted to say. Finally, his blue eyes shimmered as he put his hand on my good shoulder and squeezed, "I'm proud of you son…"

I wanted to say something witty and sarcastic back at him, but I couldn't make my voice work, so I just smiled at him instead and put my hand on his. "Gee Dad, if I'd'a known all it would take to make you proud of me was to pass PE, and face a murderous zealot, I'd have done it sooner."

He laughed. "You little shit…"

"Admit it; you wouldn't want me any other way," I teased as the nurse ran a loop of clear plastic tubing around my head and situated a piece in my nostrils to feed me oxygen.

He sighed, "Yeah, you're probably right…"

I reached out and took Mom's hand and squeezed it as John released me. "Where's Loki, is she alright?"

"Loki's here, she's doing fine," Mom said softly, "In far better shape than you I daresay. She's been here with us as often as she could while we were waiting for you to wake up. The bullet broke one of her ribs, but they removed it fine and she's recovering."

My brain tried to restore order to my memories and gain some sense of time. I swallowed hard and winced. I remembered everything perfectly—*everything*.

I noticed the light coming in under the drawn curtains of the window. "How long was I out?" I asked suspiciously.

Mom sighed and her smile slipped. "The three and a half longest days of my life…"

"Then where's Jacob?"

"He's staying with his friend Adam, telling everybody about his brother the hero." She smiled at me and distinct discomfort bloomed inside me. I didn't feel like a hero…

I changed the topic, "When can I see Loki?"

"Nurse Catlynn, would you mind getting Jessica for us?" Mom smiled at the nurse, who nodded and left the room. A couple minutes later, Geri pushed Loki through the door in a wheelchair.

My breath caught as I saw those familiar emerald eyes. Eyes I thought I'd said goodbye to forever in that dirty school closet. I strained my arm out for her as far as the pain would let me, and at the first touch of her skin, joy flooded me. Her hands shook but she leaned forward in her chair to rub her cheek into my hand as the hot water of her tears fell through my fingers. I closed my eyes and heaved a deep breath, my chest tight and yet liberated at the same time. She turned her face to kiss my palm, and looked up at me with glistening eyes and ruddy cheeks.

"You son of a bitch, don't you ever do that again!" she cried.

"I'm sorry—" I started.

"I thought I'd lost you!" she screamed at me and clenched my hand so hard it would have hurt if I didn't already have bullet and knife wounds, not to mention morphine.

I looked away, "You almost did. They… sent me back, they wouldn't let me go."

"Who?"

"Corwin… and Fen…" my mouth stretched tight in a grimace as I clenched my eyes against the tears. My sobs pissed off my wounds but I couldn't stop them, and Loki cried too. Inside, I silently mourned for *Qhipe* too. Geri looked away, and shrank into himself.

"I thought you were just down for the weekend?" I asked him.

"Well, I figured I'd stay a little longer since my friends just got shot." He shrugged, and held himself low.

"Oh, you and I *so* have a score to settle," I growled, and a look of panic spurted through his eyes, "Suffice to say: it's not all in our heads." He frowned, puzzled, and everybody looked at me like I was speaking in tongues.

"Okay, enough, the suspense is killing me. Now that everyone's here, will somebody please tell me what the hell happened?"

They took turns telling different parts of the story.

"That was such a bullshit move Jimmy, telling me you love me right before going on a suicide mission!" Loki griped. "I had no idea if you were even alive until your parents came to see me after my surgery. The police interviewed us all, but until they find Jack, you're the only one that knows what happened in the Library. They found you shot, stabbed, knife still in your side, bleeding and unconscious on a pile of your own shredded clothes."

So they hadn't found his body. Well, yet anyway.

"The police are baffled, nothing makes sense." Mom muttered, "They found three different blood samples on the school floor, yours, his, and a third that tested as canine. One of the neighbors said they saw a black dog follow him from the school, someone else said they heard howling, and now the tabloids are having a field day claiming there was a hell-hound or some other super-natural nonsense." Loki and Geri's jaws dropped open and they looked at me. I looked back at them and nodded ever so slightly while Wolf flashed in my eyes.

"Okay, so what's the final tally? Damage report please?" I steered the conversation away from carnivorous lunar activities.

"The newspaper said Jack's first victim was his dad; he shot him in his own living room." Loki said, "Tracy Walsh, Patricia Summers, Randy Price, and Officer Jenson are all dead. That fucker used Bo as a shield and shot Jenson through him…"

"What about Bo?" I asked. *Please, not him too…*

"Bo's—" Loki started, and the doctor picked up when she faltered.

"He's in a coma, like you were. He's still hanging on for now, but he's unresponsive. He suffered a serious blow to the head, and the lung he was shot through collapsed. A machine is breathing for him right now. He made it through surgery, but some of us are afraid he might be locked in a vegetative state."

His body's alive, but no one's home? It might just be possible…

No one seemed to notice that my eyes had focused just a little beyond the room as Loki continued, "I think the paper said that there were about sixty injuries, some just from panic or broken glass, ten were serious though. Four fatalities… So far anyway." She sighed and pressed her face into my hand again.

I twisted my hand and pulled her head into my shoulder while I looked at the doctor. "Hey Doc, is there any chance I could see Bo?"

He crossed his arms as a stern crease formed on his forehead. "Not right now, we still have to finish checking you out." I focused and pushed at him with my shifting energy, "Well, maybe later, if his parents are alright with it." Handy.

"Well then, let's get this show on the road. Time's wasting, and Bo can't afford it." I smiled, free for the first time of any overshadowing fear.

The shadow from my dream, the shapeless darkness that pursued me, was finally gone. While hope remained, there was one more soul that I wouldn't let that madman tear from me.

The doctor seemed surprised, "Are you sure you're ready? You've been through a terrible ordeal—"

"And I've had sixty-plus hours of beauty sleep." I cut him off, "I've had plenty of rest, but I would like some food, please."

He shook his head bemused and left as Officer Parker stepped in with another officer I'd never met. They chased everyone out, and took my statement. It took all of my skill to blend the line between truth and lie. It seemed to work though. I didn't try to explain more than I needed to, so they accepted my version without too much cross examination. I didn't even try to explain why my clothes were shredded; I just said I'd already passed out. I didn't know why he left either, but he was obviously unhinged and muttered something about dogs as I blacked out.

As they got up to leave, Officer Parker hesitated. "Jimmy, you can't tell anyone, but I think you deserve to know. We ran forensics on Jack's rifle, and the barrel markings matched the bullet that killed your friend."

"I figured it would," I muttered, "Jack said he was aiming at me."

After they left, Loki and I finally had a moment alone. There was so much I wanted to say, so much I wanted to ask, I couldn't even think where to begin. Just rubbing her hand with my thumb was a blessing. "So, how long have you uh… liked me, like this?" God, I sounded so awkward…

"How long have I had a crush on you?"

"Uh-huh."

"Well, pretty much all along. I don't know, it was weird. I mean, at first you drove me nuts with your pity-parties, and you don't exactly fit my usual type. But it was like, right away, there was something about you that just… fit. Almost like I knew you, and knew I loved you, long before I ever met you. Your face was so familiar, and before and after you lost all that weight, nothing changed to me. I hid it to try and keep Fen off your tail, but yeah… what about you?"

"Look, you don't honestly think I had girls fawning all over me did you? You were the first girl I'd ever met who was both beautiful, *and* would give me the time of day. You pretty much hook-line-and-sinkered me the day you tackled me…"

"Ugh, you would remember that wouldn't you!" she whined.

"Damn right! And I'll tease you about it 'till the day I die."

"Which is *not* going to be any time soon got it? I took a freakin' bullet for your ass, and now your soul is mine." she said and clenched my hand to her chest. "All mine!"

Several hours, a multitude of tests, and most of my patience later, the doctor walked back into the room and flipped through some papers. "I just don't get it," he muttered, "The way you and Jessica have bounced back from your injuries and surgeries is nothing short of miraculous. I just can't figure out why…"

"Good metabolism?" *And May's Full Moon…*

He sighed, and they loaded me into a wheelchair and rolled me down the hall. Movement led to the sensational discovery of my catheter, which was delightful in a permanently-kicked-in-the-balls, deep-in-your-gut, why-god-why-do-I-have-nerve-endings-there kind of way.

Mom pushed Loki's chair and they loaded us into the wide elevator. We went up a couple floors to the intensive care unit, and I looked at Bo as they wheeled us in. Finger in clamp, blue blanket, trach' tube, intravenous drip, cluster of machines either metering or assisting his body. He looked just like I had that morning.

One of his eyes was swollen purple blue, and a large bandage wrapped around his head. His parents looked at me with sunken eyes, their vitality sucked out by the endless hell of not knowing if their child would wake up or not. Forced to observe a wake for their son, whose body wasn't even dead. I'd only met them briefly a couple times we'd gone over to Bo's house.

"If it's all right with you, I'd like to try something. I don't know for sure if it'll help or not, I just know it won't hurt to try."

Eyes too afraid to hope looked at me, and Bo's father agreed. Bo had his father's glacial blue eyes and build, but his mother's dark olive skin. "What makes you think it could help?"

I smiled at him, "It brought me back…"

He closed his eyes a moment, his face long and somber, and took my hand between both of his. He nodded as he released my hand and took his wife's back. "At this point, we're willing to try anything."

"Just promise me you won't make a sound, and no matter what, you won't try to interrupt."

They nodded and Mom wheeled me over next to Bo so I could take his hand, mindful of the IV taped to his wrist. Since Wolf and I weren't separate anymore, it was almost too easy to slip out of myself and down through the soil into the earth.

A great roar grew until I rose to the surface of the water and opened my eyes. A tall waterfall tapered into the distance through the mist, and I closed my eyes and smiled as the water beaded and rolled off my face.

So good to be back...

I rolled over onto my stomach and shifted smoothly into Wolf, and then paddled over to the side of the pool and shook myself dry. I put my muzzle into the air as a breeze hissed through the canopy of trees and with it—there!

I took off down the river and then climbed the hillside. There was something here that stank of human, and I sought it with all my will. My tongue lolled out of my mouth as I flew uphill. The massive trees of the waterline thinned into sagebrush and the scent grew stronger. I came upon a path of worn dirt that curled around a large rock on the side of the hill and I shifted back into human form.

Bo sat on a rock and looked out over the breathtaking valley while one hand absently rubbed the ears of a russet brindled wolf with bold black markings and a dark gray back and mane. I sat down beside him and looked out over the forest. An eagle soared in slow circles over the treetops while the sun bathed us in a warm golden aura.

"You know, I always thought that greeting card heaven with clouds and little harp playing angels was crap. It never made sense with the way God made his creations, the way he made the world. When the light brought me here, I never imagined heaven could be this... perfect..."

"When'd you find him?" I nodded at his wolf, who grinned with half-cocked ears as Bo scratched a good spot.

"That's the funny part. I didn't find him anywhere, he was already with me."

"He's you, Bo. He's part of your soul."

"You've got so much explaining to do, it's not even funny." He laughed.

"Well, I was getting around to it. Not my fault we were shot before I could tell you more."

"But you never really trusted me, not enough to tell me the whole truth."

"I'm sorry Bo, but I couldn't trust anybody. Hell, I even suspected Geri…" *Woops…*

"It was Jack, wasn't it?" he asked softly, sympathy in his eyes.

"Yeah…" I took a deep breath, "But the real bitch is that he was trying to kill me the whole time. Fen just got in the way, like you did, trying to save my life."

"God, I should have known. Jack started acting weird after your fight, and I saw him at church just a couple days before the trial, when his dad gave this big sermon about the war on evil. He made this big hoo-rah about destroying Satan 'by any means necessary.'" Bo fell silent for a moment, "Is Jack gone now?"

"Yes."

Bo sighed and looked down at his feet. "Did you do it?"

"Yes." I braced for his anger.

"Good. Mad dogs need to be put down." Bo's wolf sensed his agitation and looked up at him, then whined and rubbed his head against Bo's side as he sighed and closed his eyes, "So, I guess we're dead then?"

"Not quite. Your body is still alive, I can try to take you back if you'd like."

"You can do that?" as he turned and looked at me, his wolf did as well.

"I think so…" I answered, slightly less than certain.

Bo sighed and looked at me "I want to go back… But I don't want to leave him." He resumed rubbing his wolf's ears and smiled.

"So bring him with you."

"Can I do that?" he asked surprised.

"Yes, but there are consequences. You've always been fascinated by wolves, because you had one deep inside you. If you fully embrace it, you'll become like me, and then there's no going back."

"God yes!" Bo laughed, "I don't even have to think about it, it's what I've wanted my whole life!"

"Good, let's go. Oh, and just a warning, it's going to hurt like a bitch and I'm not even capable of expressing the joys of catheters and tracheal tubes."

He moaned, "Maybe I'll just stay here after all."

"Oh, shut up. It's not going to be easy, but I'll be with you and so will Loki. We're a Pack now right?"

"Right." He smiled and held out his fist. I hit my knuckles to his and turned to guide him back to the pool. His wolf whimpered as a shadow moved on the silhouette of the boulder.

Lupa's pure white coat shimmered gold in the sunshine like a fiery halo. She hopped down from the rock and approached Bo's wolf. She sniffed noses with him and rubbed her flank along his, and then turned toward the path and looked back over her shoulder at him.

"Bo, you like to run right?"

"Yeah, why?"

"Because you'll need to soon…" I shifted into my wolf form and Bo's eyes grew wide. I greeted Bo's wolf, who stood taller than me in the shoulder, but he lowered himself in deference to me. I nudged his muzzle, and then jumped back in an invitation to play. His tail wagged as he stood.

Lupa changed into her human form and whispered something to Bo, who smiled at her and nodded, and then ran down the hill. His wolf and I chased him and Lupa caught up with us. I led them to the waterfall and then shifted back to my human form and smiled at Lupa, "Thank you, for saving my life."

Her muzzle stretched into a wide lupine grin. "My warrior wolf, this battle is over, but the war still remains ahead of you. At least now you have a good Beta, a strong knight by your side, and I'll always be with you, in my way."

Bo paled as he neared the edge of the water. "Hey Jimmy, I guess this would be a bad time to mention I have aquaphobia…"

I looked at him and raised an eyebrow, "Seriously? You charged in to wrestle a sociopath with a rifle without a second thought, but you're afraid of water?"

"Um…" Bo flexed his hands open and closed, "Yep."

"Bo, you literally *can not* drown here. Please come with me… I don't want to lose you too." I held out my hand to him.

Bo swallowed and edged his way into the water, but his wolf stayed on shore and whined. Lupa nudged him, but the unknown still terrified him. He sensed that something was about to change in a very big way, but he didn't know how.

"Bo, lead him into the water and hold him to you."

Bo walked toward him and held out his shaking hands for him to come. They stood still a moment, and then Bo turned to me. "He wants me to put my hand in his mouth."

"Then do it, he needs reassurance."

"But what if he bites me?"

"Bo, he *is* you." I laughed.

Reluctantly, Bo held out his hand and his wolf wrapped his jaws around Bo's wrist. Together they walked into the water until his wolf could no longer touch bottom and had to doggy paddle.

"Now, hold him close and don't let go, got it?" He nodded and I wrapped my arms around them. We sank below the surface while the sunlight on the water's surface cast rippled shadows over my eyelids. I reached deep inside and felt Raven's cool violet light within me as we flew back up through the soil, the pipes, and back into my aching, heavy body.

I felt them inside me, not as two forms, but like an egg of vapor lodged in my chest. I summoned my shifting energy and focused it as I lifted Bo's hand, careful not to let his parents see my eyes. I placed his hand in my mouth and bit down into the yielding flesh of his palm. My teeth sharpened just enough to break the skin and when I tasted the copper of his blood, I shoved my shifting energy into Bo's inert body and pushed his spirit in with Raven's power. The weight lifted from my chest and I fell back into my wheelchair, exhausted for the first time since I woke.

The room exploded. Everyone was yelling, Mom stood between me and Bo's father as he gestured wildly, enraged. It all sounded muffled and far away, and I clenched my eyes shut while I willed the pain down.

Blip. Blip. Blip…

Everyone froze as Bo's heart monitor sped up. Bo's unbruised eyelid twitched and then opened. For a moment, the only sound in the room as the clicking, wheezing, and beeping of machines, and then Bo's mother let out a wail and lurched for his hand.

I slumped in my chair, exhausted and drained. Loki wheeled over to me, and I took her hand while we watched a family ground down by despair be lifted completely by joy. After his parents settled down, Bo reached for me. I let go of Loki for a moment and took his hand.

A familiar tingle teased the nerve endings of my fingers as he squeezed, a silent 'thank you' in his eye as the image of his russet and black brindled fur flashed in my mind' eye. He let go of me and reached out for Loki, and at his touch Loki gasped and then looked over at me and I smiled. She smiled too and let him take his hand back.

I whispered low enough that only she could hear. "In the spring everything starts over. I'd like you to meet our new Beta…"

We smiled at each other and then she kissed me, long and deep. Her lips felt like satin, smooth against the raw edges of my soul.

Like Lupa said, the battle was over, but the war was just beginning. There would be more challenges and pitfalls, new joys and anguishes, but we would survive all of them. Loki and I had each other now. Our Pack would endure.

To be Wolf, is to survive...

The Wolf Road Chronicles will continue in Book 2:

BEARING RAVEN'S MARK

ABOUT THE AUTHOR:

Brandon M. Herbert is an author, graphic designer, musician, entrepreneur and voracious biblioholic. He was born a third generation Colorado native, but his heart and soul belong to the Pacific Northwest.

Brandon wrote his first short story in fifth grade, and hasn't stopped since. He enjoys writing Urban Fantasy, both for Young Adults (*Walking Wolf Road* and *Tertiary*) and Horror fans (*World of Shadows* and *Tales of the Underground*). He is a passionate wolf supporter, and has spent most his life researching the history, mythology, and reality of werewolves, shapeshifters, and therianthropes. Brandon has a degree in graphic design and plays guitar when he's not kayaking Puget Sound or quaffing inhuman quantities of coffee.

Brandon is a member of the Pacific Northwest Writers Association, Whidbey Island Writers Association, and the EPIC Writing Group. He currently resides in the Seattle area with his wife, and welcomes contact at:

WWW.BRANDONMHERBERT.COM

FACEBOOK.COM/BRANDONMHERBERT

TWITTER.COM/BRANDONMHERBERT

GOODREADS.COM/BRANDONMHERBERT

WALKING WOLF ROAD:
THE (UNOFFICIAL & ABBREVIATED) ALBUM

- 10 Years – Seasons to Cycles, Shoot It Out, Luna
- Angeli Milli – Requiem, Sarah, The Field, Surgery
- Apocalyptica – S.O.S. (Anything but Love), Sacra
- Breaking Benjamin – Fade Away, Dear Agony, Anthem of the Angels, So Cold, Breath, Hopeless
- Chevelle –To Return, The Red, Panic Prone, The Clincher, To Return, Bend the Bracket, Breach Birth
- Cold – Wasted Years, Black Sunday
- Dianna Krall – Autumn Leaves
- Disturbed – Darkness, Dehumanized, Devour, Awaken
- Evanescence – Before the Dawn, Anything for You
- Gurdjieff/Tsabropoulos – In Memory, Gift of Dreams, Bayati, Trois Morceaux Apres de Hymnes Byzantins (Three Pieces After Byzantine Hymns)
- Howie Day – Numbness for Sound
- James Newton Howard – Rituals, Noah Visits, The Gravel Road
- Leona Lewis – Run
- Linkin Park – My December, Leave Out All The Rest
- Loreena McKennitt – Dante's Prayer, Full Circle, The Mystic's Dream, All Souls Night, The Highwayman
- Michael Andrews & Gary Jules – Mad World
- Nine Inch Nails – Hurt
- Placebo – Running up that Hill
- Ra – Walking and Thinking, Sky
- REM – The Sweetness Follows
- Sacred Spirits – Ly-O-Lay Ale Loya
- Sarah McLachlan – Angel
- Slipknot – Circle, Snuff
- Stabbingback – The Enemy Within, Graveyard Hill
- Staind – Lost Along the Way, Take a Breath, Something to Remind You, Devil
- VAST – Lady of Dreams
- Vertical Horizon – Footprints in the Snow
- VolkoV – You Walk Alone, Memories in Snow, Requiem
- Within Temptation – The Howling
- Wolf's Rain OST – Leaving on Red Hill